"It's a riot."
—Joe Muggs, *The Word*

"Rock novels often shy away from the music, but this one comes alive every time someone strums a chord or opens their mouth to sing... Fans of the music will enjoy Murray's spirited homage."
—Jonathan Gibbs, *The Independent*

"Here are characters that live and breathe, propelled into situations that invariably enthral, as events leap off the printed page at a pace that's positively cinematic. Can't wait to see the film... And hear the soundtrack."
—Ian Fortnam, *Classic Rock*

"A heavily hip tale of bluesmen, rockers, rappers and gangsters, sprawled over decades and continents, with some supernatural suspense thrown into the mix... Charles Shaar Murray has drawn on four decades of music journalism to create a memorable debut novel."
—Olaf Tyaransen, *Hot Press*

"One of the best music novels ever written."
—John May, *The Generalist*

"Absolutely rivetting."
—Rich Deakin, *Shindig Quarterly*

"Charles Shaar Murray has given us a phenomenal story, with a handful of characters so completely drawn, you think they're jamming in the next room. From a barbershop in the Delta in the 1930s to the bustle and movement that was rock's birth in early 1960s UK to the sun-baked canyons of LA in the present day, Murray takes us on a journey of family, passion, culpability, and talent. It's all here: The ties that bind, the price you pay for the choices you make, and oh, man, the music! There's not a note, a harmonic, a single chord progression, that doesn't ring out like the voice of Robert Johnson's devil-haunted guitar.
The Hellhound Sample is staggering. It achieves something rare in fiction: it makes you feel and it makes you wonder."
—Deborah Grabien, creator of the *JP Kinkaid* series of books

ALSO BY CHARLES SHAAR MURRAY

Crosstown Traffic:
Jimi Hendrix And Post-war Pop

Boogie Man:
The Adventures of John Lee Hooker in the American Twentieth Century

Shots from the Hip

THE HELLHOUND SAMPLE

by

Charles Shaar Murray

www.WorldHeadpress.com

To all the blues and soul men and women
To all the rockers and rappers
To the restless spirit of Robert Johnson
And most of all to
ANNA CHEN
... my big gold dream ...
This book is lovingly and respectfully dedicated

PROLOGUE

CLARKSDALE, MISSISSIPPI, 1932

Ten-year-old James Moon didn't know how much longer he could wait for his daddy to finish up his business in the store. The sun was almost directly overhead, and he was hot and thirsty. He'd only been wearing his brand-new overalls, starched stiff as cardboard, for half an hour, but they were already beginning to chafe his thighs raw. And, worst of all, he was busting for a pee, shifting uncomfortably from foot to foot like that was somehow going to help.

Through the plate-glass window, he could see his daddy arguing with the man he called 'the Jew' over the price of the sacks of feed and seed he was buying for the farm. Judging by all the arm-waving that was going on, neither Mr Birnbaum nor Reverend Solomon Moon looked like they were planning to budge any time soon.

Gazing down the block, he saw a small slender man in an immaculate grey suit and snap-brim hat stroll onto the corner. He had a guitar slung behind him. As James watched, the man stooped to place the hat, crown downwards, on the sidewalk beside him, and scrabble in his pants pocket for a few coins to toss into it. He pulled a metal flask from inside his jacket and raised it to his lips, taking two or three long swallows before stowing it again. Then he swung the guitar forward and produced something from his jacket pocket which he carefully fitted onto the pinky of his left hand. Then he started to play.

The sound James heard almost made him wet his pants. Even at almost midday on a busy bustling street, with folks going about their business and mules and automobiles passing by, the quivering sliding moan the man was conjuring from his guitar strings cast a chill shadow over James, like the sun was still shining for everybody else but some spooky old cloud was blocking it off just for him. It was like the sound was a cold hand reaching right deep down inside him and gently squeezing his heart.

The man raised his head, looked around him. For a second he seemed to be staring straight at James, his eyes flashing as his gaze met the boy's. James felt like those eyes – one wide open, one oddly

1

hooded – were drilling right inside him, every part of him laid bare. He was actually shivering now, his rubbed-raw thighs and bursting bladder forgotten. Now the man was dropping the glass cylinder back into his jacket pocket, swiftly retuning his guitar, was starting to play a different song. He began to sing, in an eerie high moan which sounded just like his guitar. "*Got to keep moving, got to keep moving,*" he sang, "*blues falling down like hail. Got to keep moving, got to keep moving, hellhound on my trail.*"

Then his daddy was wrenching at his arm, shoving him so he nearly lost his footing and fell. "What you doin', boy?" his daddy thundered. "I *told* you be ready to he'p me move these sacks to the car." He dragged James into the store and set him to moving a sack of cattle-feed near as big as he was to his daddy's rusted Model T Ford. "I'm sorry, sir," James said when their cargo was loaded, "I was listening to the man singing."

Solomon Moon didn't say a word as he drove them to the barbershop. "I need to pee," James murmured into the humming void of his father's grim silence. "You can go at the barbershop," his father said after a while. He parked the car outside Sam's Barber Shop, and gripped James by the arm.

"Do you know what that man was doin'?" he rumbled. "He was doin' the devil's work. He was tryin' to drag your soul down to hell."

"But he was just singin' and playin' git-tar," James protested. "An' I was just listenin'."

"The *devil* live in the git-tar," growled Solomon Moon. "And the worst music you can play on the git-tar is the *blues*. That's what that man was playin'. The *blues*. The devil's own music. Every blues singer work for the devil. An' out of all the blues singers around here, that man is the evillest of 'em all. I spent ten years tryin' to bring you up right and raise you in the ways of the Lord, and now I find you on the street..."

"But, sir, you done *told* me to wait there!"

"*Quiet*, boy! I find you on the street listening to the man who *sold* his *soul* to the *devil*, just standin' there not even sayin' a prayer to save yourself while he try to take *your* soul too! Boy, when we get home, we gonna have ourselves a *talk*."

James knew what that signified. It would be years before he realised that 'having a talk' didn't always mean getting a whuppin'.

In the barbershop, the guys were talking shit and playing the dozens. The air was thick with smoke and a couple of them were taking discreet nips from hip-flasks or brown-bagged bottles. Everything went quiet when the Reverend stalked in with James, his bladder troubling him again, waddling painfully at his daddy's heels.

"Mornin', Reverend," Sam said, "and what can I do for you this fine day?"

"Let the boy use your bathroom an' then you cut his hair good'n short," Solomon Moon told him. "I be back for him in an hour, get my own hair cut. And I don't want him hearin' nuthin' that he shouldn' be hearin.'" He wagged a warning finger at James, turned on his heel and walked out. "Whoah!" said one of the customers. "There surely goes a real, true man of the Lord." James wasn't sure why the other men laughed at that.

In the bathroom, he scrabbled frantically at the stiff new denim, splitting a thumbnail attempting to wrest the metal buttons through the unyielding fabric, spotting his fresh overalls before threading his stubbornly retracted li'l thang through the fly, like pulling a marshmallow through a slot machine and, just in time to avoid embarrassing himself by soaking his clothing and puddling the floor, unleashing a gusher so powerful that the sense of relief almost made him pass out. But soon Sam had him safely sat up in the big chair, napkin tied around his throat as the clippers buzzed around his ears and neck. "And what you been doin' today, young man?" Sam asked him.

"We been in town shoppin'." James told him. "I got me new overalls and my daddy bought feed and seed from Mr Birnbaum. An' I saw a man singin' and playin' git-tar on the corner, but my daddy got angry."

Sam laughed. "The man you saw, did he have a real good suit on him? Nice hat? Have kind of a high shaky voice?" James nodded. The men chuckled quietly and gave each other meaningful looks. "That be Little Robert. Just got back to town. He had him a lot of names, ol' Robert. Been Robert Dodds, Robert Willis, Robert Spencer, but he going by his natural father's name now."

"My daddy said Robert is a real bad man. Said he work for the devil."

"Oh, Robert had him some troubles, that's for sure. Few years back his wife died givin' birth, and she weren't but sixteen years old. Robert wasn't even there, he somewhere out in the country playin' his git-tar. He play good, don't he? Well, he didn't always. Ol' Sonny House told me Little Robert used to be the worst git-tar player he ever heard, but since he come back he been playin' like a different man.

"Now I heard tell..." Sam lowered his voice into a deep hoarse whisper, "… that Little Robert wanted to play the blues so bad that one night when the moon didn't shine he took himself down to the crossroads way out down where forty-nine meet sixty-one. And dead on midnight, he met the devil there. And the devil took Robert's guitar and tuned it, and played a song and then give it back to him. And after that Robert could play just about anything he wanted to. But the devil…" Sam bugged his eyes and waved his hands, lowering his voice even further, "the *devil* got his *soul*."

"Aw man," one of the guys interjected, "That's just bull. You talkin' like an ol' woman now. Little Robert just been practicin' and learnin' is all. An' you don't want to be feedin' the boy up with all that old time conjure sh… nonsense. You just gonna get him in trouble with his daddy."

As Sam's busy scissors fluttered and snipped around his scalp, James could still hear Little Robert's whining, desolate voice and guitar reverberating in his head. Get to be able to sing and play like that and all you got to do is sell your soul to the devil? Sounded like a pretty good deal to him. After all, he'd never seen the devil, didn't even know if there really *was* a devil. But he'd seen Little Robert, all dressed up sharp: even standing on that dusty ol' stinkin' muleshit-spattered corner, he looked like a million dollars. One day I'm'a do that, he told himself. Be dressed up slick. Gonna play git-tar. And when I sing and play, my music gonna make folks *feel* stuff deep down inside. But I ain't gonna be workin' for no devil, I ain't gonna take no souls down to burn. Just steal a little fire to warm 'em up a little on cold nights, cook up some soul food, make 'em feel *good*.

"So what name Little Robert go by now?" he asked.

"I tole you, now he done took his natural father's name. Go by Robert Johnson."

Robert Johnson. James Moon filed that one away. He was going to remember that name his whole life. In his head, once again, he was hearing the song the man had been singing. He could hear every word, every note, even every breath.

"Got to keep moving, got to keep moving, hellhound on my trail…"

4

TEN YEARS LATER

Got to keep moving. *Got* to keep moving.

He was tiring badly now, lurching on through the darkness, but every flash of lightning found him closer and closer to the highway. He knew why they called the Delta 'the low land': it was flatter'n a field hand's wallet the night before payday and there was nowhere to hide, not like North Mississippi where they had hills and woods and a man on the run could lose himself unless the dogs already had his scent.

His mind was a jumble, everything just rammed in any old how and spilling out every which way, seemed like everything that had ever happened to him in his whole life had happened in the last few hours. If he could sit, rest awhile, think things through, he might be able to make some damn sense out of everything, but all he knew right now was that he just had to keep on moving, reach the highway. Just what he was gonna do when he got to the highway he didn't rightly know, but...

He could feel each breath knifing into his lungs, hear it rattling in his chest. He could feel the guitar on its cord banging into the small of his back with each step, hear it exhaling a ghostly chord with each bump. He could feel the rag stuffed into his left shoe to pad out where his missing toes used to be starting to chafe his sore foot as he staggered onwards, and the weight of the Browning automatic pistol his daddy'd brought home from the Great War in his right-side jacket pocket thumping against his hip like it didn't want him to forget it was there. His left hand still clutched the cardboard suitcase of clothes and his right the shotgun with one last shell in the chamber. He wanted to ditch 'em, but that'd just make him easier to track...

Damn. He swore he could hear hound dogs begin to howl way back there in the distance, even over the faraway rumble of thunder. Heckuva storm was gathering, and if it started to rain before he reached the road and the field got all muddied up he'd be leaving tracks a blind man could follow.

How could the world do you like this? How could your whole life be one way all the way back to when you were just a little baby, and then one thing happen, or a bunch of things all hooked together, and then wham, nothing ever be the same again?

Got to keep moving...

5

The inside of his head was like a movie where someone had cut the reels apart and put 'em back together all wrong. Each lightning flash calling up a scene. FLASH: there he was, sneaking out to the old barn to get his guitar, all those years he'd practiced and finally he'd grown enough of a pair to head out to ol' Johnny B's jookjoint and try to play some songs. And there was his daddy blocking his path, saying something about a meeting down at the church house, a special meeting to talk about what was happening to their people in this white man's hell, and what they were gonna start to doin' about it. Him gettin' a red mist and sayin' he wasn't goin' to no church on no Saturday night. His daddy getting' swole with rage, grabbing an old broom to beat his ass all over again.

His mama holding on to his daddy's arm, pulling him back, sayin' we ain't got *time* for this. His daddy sayin' either you come to the meeting or you ain't got no home here no more, this is about *our people*, boy. Him sayin' well, *fuck* it then, turning on his heel, walking away.

FLASH: he's walking into the jook, heads turning, folks sayin' ain't that Reverend Moon's boy, showin' up with a git-tar? Drinking a beer, then another, an unfamiliar warmth spreading from his belly, room turning kinda soft round the edges. Then FLASH: he's standing up there with his guitar, everybody looking at him, room gone quiet. Guitar feel strange in his hands, his throat all dry and his hands all sweat-slick and his voice comes out a squeak and the strings won't do what he tell them to. People start to murmur now, turning to each other, sayin' well, *he* ain't *shit*.

Then FLASH: something weird and beautiful happens to him. Suddenly, every song he's ever heard, every chord and lick he ever learned, are all laid out in front of him, clear as day, like they're on a map, and he can see how they all join together, and the world starts to make sense in a way it never done before, his hands are dry, the guitar strings obedient and his throat feels loose and easy. He starts to sing and play a song he once heard Big Joe Williams do on a record and he can only remember two verses but that don't matter: he fills in with a few lines from something by Big Bill Broonzy and he caps it all with a guitar lick by Scrapper Blackwell he'd always loved but never quite learned, and it rolls off his fingers like butter and honey, and suddenly it's over and a bright shower of applause is taking his breath away and there's money falling at his feet and they're calling him to play some more and he does...

FLASH: a big fine woman in a shiny dress with a flower in her hair, smelling of whiskey and cigarettes and perfume and, well, *funk*, is saying walk with me, daddy, and she takes him outside and leans against the wall and pulls him to her. Her dress goes up, his pants come down, there's slickness and heat and a pressure which tenses and relaxes and tenses and relaxes over and over again and red balloons pop behind his eyes. Then they go back inside and by now someone else is playing and folks slap him on the back and say, hey, son you *good* and better not let your daddy know what you doin' here, your daddy say folks come here gon' *burn* and he buys a bottle of whiskey and he's *still* got twenty-six dollars and change in his pocket...

And FLASH: he's walking towards home, guitar over his back, a stickiness at his groin, a slight unsteadiness in his step, a tightness in his soul he'd never even known was there gloriously released and something inside him silently singing the way his outside voice was singing back at the jook. He figured he was gonna go home: daddy still be mad but mama gonna talk him round, one way or another. Something must've been guiding his path because after a while he realised, almost incuriously, that he'd taken the left, rather than the right, fork in the road, and that he was heading towards the church. Didn't know why, 'cause everybody be long home and in bed after the meeting. FLASH: he turns the corner and there's an orange light in the sky that no way should be there.

The old woodframe building is a glowing hulk and the air smells like burnt meat. There's white-robed figures standing all round the carcass of the church, and he hears laughter and he knows the voices, those robes and hoods don't hide nuthin' from nobody knows the voices of the sheriff and his deputies.

FLASH: he's back at the house now, slamming his way in. It's dark and silent as... he calls for his mama and his daddy and his brother, and no-one answers, it's like one of those nightmares where you scream at the top of your voice 'til your throat shreds and you *still* ain't making no sound...

FLASH: he's sobbing and cursing as he throws clothes into an old cardboard suitcase and without any conscious thought he grabs his daddy's twelve-gauge shotgun, slaps the only two shells he can find into the breech. A part of his mind that's walled off from everything else is saying ain't it strange, daddy always said the jook folks were gonna burn, but the way it come down, it was the church folk burned and the jook folk who lived... but of course most of those Saturday night jook folk was gonna be in church Sunday mornin', 'cept there ain't no church no more...

FLASH: and he's outside again and his feet seem to be taking him back towards the church... and Sheriff John Brown is in his path like a one-man roadblock, out of his robes, all stubble and gut, gunbelt slung low under his belly, hat tipped back on his head. The shotgun is in his hands and the sheriff takes a step back, sayin' don't be doin' nuthin' stupid now, nigger, my deputies just over the way. And there's nuthin' but a red mist in his head and the sheriff in his path and the shotgun in his hands and CRR-ACK he cranks it once and hears his own voice, like from a long way away, sayin' now *you* burn, mutha*fuck*a...

FLASH: and he pulls the trigger. FLASH: and Sheriff John Brown flies back and crashes to the ground and FLASH: he runs...

... and FLASH: now the thunder rolls and rain starts to patter around him just as he reaches the highway. Way, way behind him, dogs begin to bark and hounds begin to howl, but he's just a few yards back from where forty-nine crosses sixty-one and he sees an old 1936 Hudson Terraplane parked right on the crossroads, pointing towards Clarksdale. The front passenger door swings open and someone calls out to him, "Young man! Young man! Get your ass in here!"

And he stumbles towards the car, tosses his guitar and the case and the shotgun into the back and falls into the front seat. Car smells of cigarettes and whiskey and it's dark as the devil's asshole.

"What'choo waitin' for, young man? Close the muthafuckin' door!"

And he slams the door, settling back in his seat as the old Terraplane rattles into life and takes off down the highway as the skies finally open and rain machineguns the roof of the car. A bottle of whiskey is pushed into his hand and he takes a grateful glug.

"Man... who *are* you?"

Young man hears a quiet chuckle from next to him. Still can't see a damn thing.

"I hear you done killed yourself a deputy," the driver says.

Young man's still catching his breath. "I shot the sheriff," he says, finally, "but I did not shoot no deputy."

The driver lights himself a cigarette, the match's flame reflecting red from his eyes before he blows it out. He chuckles again.

"You ain't gonna remember sayin' that," he says, "but if you do, you be findin' it funny 'round thirty years from now. Some'a this you gonna remember, some'a this you won't. Your head in a tangle right now, like anybody's would be."

Young man takes another drink. He's in a small bubble of dry warmth, barrelling down the highway with everything he ever knew in smoking ruins behind him, and his mind is echoing chaos. He can't think straight. He knows he can't think straight. And he also knows that when he *can* think straight, he still won't be able to make any sense out of what's just happened to him.

The driver's talking again. "Train be leaving Clarksdale in forty minutes, goin' to Memphis. When you get to Memphis, get you another train to Chicago. By the time them crackers figure out which way is up, you be long gone like a turkey through the straw. Reckon you got enough money to get your ass to Chicago?"

Young man fumbles in his pocket, counts through the bills and change. "Yeah, reckon. But..."

They were in Clarksdale now, speeding through the rain as the sun began to rise in the east. The Terraplane pulled up outside the station. Young man reaches for his guitar and the case and his daddy's shotgun. Driver clamps an iron grip around his wrist, takes the shotgun from him.

"Nuh-uh. Won't be needing that where you're goin'. Leave that here with me. All you gonna need when you get to Chicago is that guitar. You take care of the git-tar, git-tar gon' take care'a you. Now git. 'N don't look back."

Young man has his jacket off, shielding his guitar from the rain. "I owe you, man. Owe you big time." In the feeble morning light, he can just about see the driver's face. Driver chuckles.

"Forget it, young man. Forget it."

Young man says, "I won't forget it."

Driver says, "Hell yes you will." Chuckles one last time, slams the passenger door, drives off into the rain as young man trudges into the station.

Driver heads off back towards the forty-nine highway. "Yeah, you forget it, young man," he says, as if to himself. "But you owe me just the same."

And, even with the sun on his face, his eyes flash red.

ONE

There's an old photo of Mick Hudson and James 'Blue' Moon, taken sometime during the late sixties at The Scene Club or Café Au Go Go or some other superhip after-hours Manhattan bar. Or maybe it was backstage at the Fillmore East. No-one's quite sure, including the photographer, who stumbled across it on an old undeveloped roll while unpacking his stuff after moving studios in 1998.

They're sitting side by side on a pair of Fender Twin Reverb amplifiers with guitars in their hands, playing. In the background, barely in focus, you can just about see a drummer. They're not looking at each other: it's almost like they were strangers who ended up in the last pair of vacant seats on a crowded bus. Hudson is pale and haggard, unshaven, great black rings under half-closed eyes almost obscured by a swathe of long lank hair, playing a battered old cream Telecaster decorated with peace-symbol and pot-leaf stickers and floral splodges that look like they were painted by someone who was tripping at the time. He's wearing a paisley kaftan, pink trousers, fringed buckskin knee-boots and way too many scarves.

Moon, by contrast, is dapper-duded up in a slick grey sharkskin suit with a slim-jim tie and a white tab-collar shirt. His black loafers are polished to a blinding sheen. He's sporting a black fedora with a grey band which exactly matches his suit, and he's staring abstractedly ahead and up, head tilted slightly to one side, listening out. In his hands is a brand new sunburst Jazzmaster with the tags still hanging off the tuning pegs. It's probably around three in the morning, but Moon seems freshly showered, shaved and dressed. Hudson looks like he hasn't been to bed for a week.

Moon has a microphone in front of him on a boom stand. Hudson doesn't, but then he was mainly just a guitar player in those days. He didn't start singing until a few years later, after his band had broken up for the final time and the singer who was supposed to be fronting the new group walked out during the second week of rehearsals. Hudson had decided to take the microphone until they found someone else, and he'd never let it go.

There's only one other frame from that evening. In the foreground is

Hudson, lips tight, eyes hooded, wrenching a high bent note from the top end of his fretboard. Just behind him is Moon, ostentatiously filing his nails with an emery board.

What the photographer does remember about that night is that Moon and Hudson didn't seem to be talking, but their guitars were. The only thing he remembers Moon saying to Hudson was something like, "Heard you on my daughter's record, playin' my shit. Maybe I'm'a buy some'a your records, see if you got any shit of your own." And he also remembers one of the songs they played. The lyric went, "Dogs begin to bark, hounds begin to howl."

When James 'Blue' Moon's first European tour in seven years was abruptly cancelled, hardly anyone was surprised. In fact, it had been rather more surprising that his management had booked him a fifteen-date overseas tour in the first place. Moon was, after all, at least eighty years old and, depending on which reference book or album liner note you happened to consult, possibly considerably more than that. The previous year, he'd undergone hip-replacement surgery.

His management company had been gradually trimming back his performing schedule to a few major summer festivals, the occasional prestige TV showcase and the odd local club gig: a far cry from the gruelling slog of 300-some shows he'd played each year for most of a career now in its sixth decade. Over the past fifteen years his once-lean frame had gained considerable weight and, sometime in the mid-nineties, he'd actually started sitting down on stage, only rising to his feet for the last couple of tunes of each show. There were bands in the charts now whose members' parents weren't even born the last time Blue Moon did the splits on stage with his guitar behind his head like in the iconic picture — the cover shot from the legendary 1950s *Once In A Blue Moon* album — which still appeared on his concert posters.

The promoters issued a curt statement to the effect that the old master's doctors had advised him to withdraw from the tour for health reasons. The other performers in the touring package would still play, and a replacement headliner was being sought. In the meantime, they were offering a full refund on the tickets they'd already sold. Moon's manager Simon Wolfe was quoted as saying, "James 'Blue' Moon is sorry to disappoint his many friends and fans in Europe, but his recovery from his surgery last year has proved slower than we'd hoped, and he is also suffering from a lingering case of flu he caught in the spring. His doctors have advised him to take things easy until he is restored to full health. Mr Moon is currently resting comfortably at his home in Venice Beach, California, and looking forward to getting back on the road as soon as possible. He has written several new songs and we may well record a few of them while we're waiting for him to be able to return to live performance."

A further press release direct from Wolfe's office at Macro Management led with the same quotation before going on to plug the release of an expanded fortieth Anniversary CD edition of *Once In A Blue Moon*, fully remastered and pumped up with a few uncollected singles and live recordings from the same period; Moon's appearance, recorded four years earlier, in an all-star *Mick Hudson And Friends Live!* DVD; the recent award of platinum status to a heavy metal album which had included a cover version of his 1950s hit Smile When You Say That, and the donation of the original hand-built prototype of his signature Fender Blue Moon Jazzmaster to an AIDS research charity auction to be held the following month at the House Of Blues on Sunset Strip. It also reminded readers of Moon's seven Grammy Awards, his dozens of classic compositions, his scene-stealing cameos in a couple of Hollywood comedies and his starring role in a series of cult beer commercials. It ended with one-line testimonials to Moon's genius, influence and all-round importance from BB King, Buddy Guy, Keith Richards, Eric Clapton, Bonnie Raitt, Billy Gibbons, Robert Cray, JP Kinkaid and Mick Hudson.

Quite a few of the press release's recipients opined that it read very much like the first draft of James 'Blue' Moon's obituary.

Adrienne Moon could hear the phone ringing as soon as she slammed the door of her Mercedes 360SL and started up the path to the front door. Normally, coming home after a workout, she'd pause for a moment to admire the panoramic view of the canals just behind the Venice Beach coastline, but she knew that if she didn't answer the phone, nobody else would. At first it was just her husband who preferred to have her or the answering machine screen his calls, but now it seemed like everybody else around the house had somehow acquired the same damn phobia. They'd chitchat for hours on their mobiles, let the landline ring all day long.

She dropped her gym bag in the hall, and reached the phone just as the answering machine cut in. She heard a snatch of Blue humming in unison with his guitar followed by her own voice reeling off the standard spiel — "Hello, we're not able to take your call right now, please leave your name and number and someone will get back to you" — and then the beep. A second's silence and then an English voice, crisp and articulate but with a residual hint of dry-drunk slur.

"Hi there daddy, it's young Mick here. Heard you were a bit poorly and thought I'd give you a tinkle and send me best. I'm in town for a week or two and I fancied dropping by for a chat if you're feeling up to it. Dunno what the number is here so I can't leave it for you but I'll call again tonight or tomorrow. Hope you're feeling better. Love to the sprog and the missis. Ta-ra."

Poorly? Tinkle? Sprog? Ta-ra? Brits said the weirdest stuff, and then looked at you like there was something wrong with you if you didn't understand.

The house was unusually quiet for mid-afternoon, the only audible sound a TV murmuring from the master bedroom down the hall. The only living creature in sight was one of the dogs, sunk deep in canine dreams on the sofa. Normally, even when Blue was doing nothing more than holing up in his bedroom or the music room sipping a beer and watching the ball game on TV, he liked having a lot of people around him, just the other side of the wall, in case he felt like chatting or jamming or sending someone out for Chinese or barbecue. Blue's band generally used the place like a clubhouse, but most of them were working other gigs while he was off the road. Charlene, Blue's daughter from his previous marriage, who lived in Compton with her mother, often dropped in so that she and her latest crackhead boyfriend could eat up just about everything in the fridge before asking Blue for a 'loan' but, thank the Lord, she didn't seem to be around today, unless she'd overdosed in the bathroom. Their own daughter, fourteen-year-old Donna, was off somewhere, probably at the mall with her friends. Josh, her own son from her previous marriage, had left home to start college, but he was back for a few days: he still liked to hang once in a while. Since he was out too, she hoped he was looking after the girls — or, more likely being driven crazy by them, like any cute nineteen-year-old guy road-managing a bunch of thirteen- and fourteen-year-old girls with their own credit cards.

Typical, she thought: all those times she'd wished she and Blue could be alone in the house together, without kids or musicians or hangers-on, and now, just when Blue ought to have someone around at all times in case he needed anything, everybody was out. She tapped on his bedroom door and walked in.

"Hey, sugar." Blue turned the TV sound down with his remote and spun his wheelchair around to face her. Over the past few months, a decade and a half of weight gain had reversed itself, and now he was once again as lanky as he'd been in his prime. A short silver beard covered his mahogany cheeks and chin. He wore loose blue jeans, a dull brick-red sweatshirt and a baseball cap emblazoned with the logo of the Ground Zero Blues Club in Clarksdale, Mississippi. His feet were bare. Three of the toes on his left foot were missing, the result of the childhood farm accident which had kept him out of the forces during the Second World War.

"Hey yourself. How you feelin'?"

He grimaced. "Like an eighty-year-old guy with cancer. But —" he raised his eyebrows and held one finger up in the air " — like an eighty-year-old guy with cancer who got a ve-e-e-ery beautiful young wife."

"Tchah. An eighty-three-year-old guy with cancer, you mean."

"Like I said. Havin' a good day, don't feel a minute over eighty."

Still, she couldn't deny she was pleased by the compliment. Three afternoons a week, she left her little Santa Monica jewellery store in the capable hands of her manager and gave herself a hard two-hour workout at Golds Gym before heading home, and she knew it paid off. Adrienne was tall, lean and elegant in her pink sweats, long braided hair still raven with only a little bottled assistance, coffee-coloured skin almost completely unlined. She might be forty-six next birthday, but Donna was always telling Adrienne that the guys in her class at school had voted her 'hottest mom' after she'd brought a few of them home one afternoon and they'd seen her sunbathing out back by the hot tub.

"Who that on the phone?"

"Mick Hudson. He's in town and wants to drop by." A beat. "You gonna tell him?"

Blue shrugged. "I ain't made up my mind. Simon say less people know the better."

"Huh. Simon says a lot of things."

"Simple Simon says/put your hands in the air," they sang quietly together. It was a ritual which had begun as a joke: the ritual still remained long after the joke had stopped being funny. Adrienne had never gotten on with Blue's English manager. She freely accepted that he was fiercely devoted to her husband and scrupulously honest in all matters financial, but she just didn't like the guy. Couldn't help it. She found him cold, stiff and crushingly literal-minded, and his arctic grey stare gave her the creeps. "Simon's a man got his own way about him," Blue had told her back in the early days. "He ain't the first guy I'd call to go out and have a beer, but he ain't scared'a hard work and he done made me rich." It was true. Through sheer tenacity and attention to detail, Simon Wolfe had steered Blue back from the wasteland of the club circuit and the occasional one-day-in-the-studio album for tiny French and German record labels to the forefront of the roots music revival. He'd assigned staff at his Macro Management company to trace and chase the back royalties which had seeped away from Blue through several decades' worth of what Simon called 'dodgy' recording and publishing deals, and invested the fruits of these raiding missions into real estate, blue-chip stocks and gallery art. By the time he was seventy years old, James 'Blue' Moon had become a millionaire. Now he was worth considerably more than that.

Simon was one of only two other people who knew that Blue had been diagnosed six weeks earlier with liver cancer. Adrienne had told her son Josh, whom she'd sworn to strict secrecy, but neither of them had felt ready to break the news to Donna. "Hell," Blue had said. "She don't even know any old people other'n me, probably thinks we all in wheelchairs when we get up in age. She gonna know soon enough."

It had started out as a routine medical exam, a formality necessary to get the insurance policy to cover Blue's planned European tour. Usually, all that happened was that Doc Strong would check him out, caution him about his raised cholesterol level and — since he'd put on weight — warn him not to work too hard on stage. This time, it had been rather different. Instead of sending the certificates over to Simon's office to forward to the promoter, the doc had asked him and Adrienne to come in and see him. Then he'd sat them down and said the word that reverberated in Adrienne's head like God's own echo chamber. He'd said that unless they did something about it right now, Blue had maybe a year, tops. He'd talked about surgery and chemo, and each time Blue had clamped his lips tight and decisively shaken his head.

"Let me just get this straight in my mind," he'd said finally. "If I have surgery, they gonna cut away half my insides and we don't know if it gonna make a difference. If I take the chemo, my hair gonna fall out and I'm gonna feel like shit every day, and we don't know if *that* gonna make a difference. You say I got a year." The doctor nodded. "Well, I'm eighty-three years old. Didn't hardly think I was gonna make it this far in the first place. If I got one more year, I'm gonna live it in one piece. I'm gonna spend a lotta time with my kids, play my git-tar every chance I get..."

He looked up at Adrienne, who'd risen from her chair. She just stood there shaking, fists at her mouth, eyes staring wide down at him. "... and long as I still can, make love to my wife. Thank you, doctor." He climbed to his feet, back straight, face closed like a fist, nothing but a slight tremble in his hands to betray what he'd just heard.

On the way home, he'd told Adrienne to stop at the store. He came out a few minutes later, clutching two bottles of Jack Daniel's and a carton of Marlboro Light. Adrienne's eyes widened: he hadn't smoked a cigarette since the day she'd found out she was pregnant with Donna. "What they gonna do?" he'd asked. "Give me cancer?"

That night at his club gig, he called a tune he'd never played before with his current band: a slow blues by St Louis Jimmy Oden called Going Down Slow. The first line went, "I've had my fun/if I never get well no mo'." Then he played a solo which, as one awestruck audience member was heard telling a friend on the phone after the set, "went from melancholy jazz to really mean, slashing blues in twenty-four bars." They played it again in the studio two days later and this time, according to the band, Blue's solo was even better. His new album was finished and ready for mastering, but Blue had called Simon and insisted that the new track be added to it. He also demanded that the title, *Moon Landing*, be changed to *Goin' Down Slow*, but Simon had won that particular argument. The title stayed, complete with artwork depicting Moon in a NASA space suit against a glittering starfield, still clutching his sparkly blue Jazzmaster.

A muffled whine announced the big German Shepherd, awake now and ambling through the open door, tail wagging. "Attack!" snapped Blue, and the dog, hearing his name, curled up contentedly at his master's feet to have his ears and neck scratched.

"Get Mick on the phone," Blue said, "and tell him come by tomorrow afternoon."

"He didn't leave a number. Said he didn't have the number where he was at."

"He gonna call back? Tell him then."

"You gonna talk to him?"

"I'll talk to him when he come by." Moon wheeled over to the window and scooped up the guitar propped in the corner of the room. Most of his instruments lived in the music room, but he was never far from a guitar. This one was his oldest Jazzmaster, the finish rubbed away to bare wood, and long retired from the road. He cradled it in his lap and meditatively thumbed the opening riff to an old Miles Davis tune. It was called So What.

TWO

CHICAGO 1974

"MICK! MICK! MICK!"

From his tiny dressing-room somewhere in the bowels of Chicago's International Auditorium, Blue could hear what sounded like most of a 20,000-strong crowd chanting the headliner's name. Around him, his band were warming up and getting changed. Back in the late fifties, in his prime, he'd carried twelve pieces with him on that old converted Greyhound: three saxes, two trumpets, trombone, piano, rhythm guitar, bass, drums, a girl singer and an MC to warm up the crowd, valet his clothes for him and take a turn behind the wheel. Now he was down to five: tenor sax, trumpet, organ, bass and drums. Elias the tenor player handled the announcements, said, "Ladies and gentlemen, it's star time, put your hands together for the lean mean blues machine, the governor of the state of blues..."

Right now Elias was standing in the corner of the room barechested, running scales on his horn. Sonny the drummer was beating his sticks on the arm of the worn-out overstuffed arm-chair: *klookety-mop, ba-ba-re-bop, klookety-mop, ba-ba-re-bop.* Billy the trumpet player, an old-time jazz guy ten years up in age on anybody else in the band, even Blue, was deep into the sports pages. Eddie the organist was down the hall hustling some chick on the pay-phone. The baby of the band, bassist Hakim, was already in his stage suit, working out jazz runs on his unplugged Fender, first two right-hand fingers a blur as he speed-plucked the strings.

Right now, Mick Hudson was pretty much at the top of his game. Any time Blue went past a corner news stand, if they sold rock magazines he'd see Mick's face staring back at him. When he and Blue first met back in England ten years back, Mick'd been almost too shy to talk to him, even after Blue'd helped him acquire his first good guitar. For the first few gigs of that '64 British tour when Bluebottle had backed him up, Mick Hudson had just been a hank of hair and a Telecaster. He hadn't even sung back-up vocals then, just concentrating on his guitar. When Blue told him he played good he'd just smile weakly, shove his hair out of his eyes like it wasn't going to fall back a second later, and say, "Th-th-thanks, Mister Moon."

Then Blue came back to England a year later and asked for Bluebottle to be his band this time, too. The agency told him that since he'd been gone the band had had three British hit singles, the second of which had been Moon's own song Smile When You Say That pumped up with a hot new guitar riff, and a big album. Now Bluebottle weren't backing nobody up no more, weren't even opening shows for anyone less than The Beatles and the Stones theirselves. Then Bluebottle broke up and Mick had himself another band named Cabal and this band got real big in the US: three Top Five albums, five Number One hit singles and tours like you wouldn't believe. Then *that* band broke up and now Mick was solo and bigger than ever.

Mick already had an opening act for his tour, some band named Bloodwork who sounded like a slaughterhouse, all meatgrind and pig-squeal, but for the Chicago date he wanted Blue and his band to open up the show as 'special guests.' He told the local papers Blue had been his idol when he was a kid and now he wanted his fans to hear the guy who'd first made him want to play blues guitar. Blue had said yes: hell yeah, of course he had. His manager told him he was gonna be seen by 20,000 white kids never seen him before, and at the least he was gonna sell a few hundred extra albums, pick up a few new fans. What the hell else was he gonna do that time of day, sit home and read the paper, watch TV 'til it was time to head out to the south side and play his club gig for the night.

Now his dressing-room door was swinging open and Mick was practically falling into the room. A bottle of Jack was clamped in his left hand and his right was reaching out for Blue. "Daddy Blue!" he cried, steadying himself against the table. One of his roadies hovered solicitously at his side.

"How you doin', young man," Blue replied, courtly as ever. He clocked the grains of white powder in the stubble on Hudson's upper lip. When the Brit pulled him into a bear hug, he could smell the bourbon, not just on the younger man's breath but seeping through his pores, feel the coke revving Hudson's engine even though the chassis was up on the blocks.

"Great to see ya, man. My guys looking after you all right?" He didn't wait for an answer, even though Blue would like to have told him that more than two minutes to sound check would've been nice. He waved the bottle at Blue. "Have a drink with me, man!"

"I'll be happy to drink your whisky when you and me done both played our shows," Blue told him. "I likes a drink as much as any man, but I don't have me nothin' but a beer or two 'til I done my work."

"You got to get up with us at the end, man," Hudson told him. "We'll save Smile When You Say That 'til last so you can jam with us."

"I'm sorry, I can't do that," Blue replied. "We workin' a club tonight and soon's we done here we got to go make our own gig. I tell you what, though. You got anything left after those young folks out there get through wearin' your ass out, come by Duke's around one o'clock and play the last set with us."

Mick's face lit up. "Wow, man, that'll be fantastic. 'Course I'll be ready!" Swaying slightly, he clasped Blue's arm. " You know, I get bored playing rock and roll in arenas all the time," he confided. "Blues is where it's really at, always will be. You really want me to come and play with your band? Be great to go somewhere after all this..." he waved his free hand "... and play some proper blues for a change." He pushed his roadie forward. "Tell Simon where the club is and he'll make sure he gets me there."

Blue smiled. "All right then, young man. Just one thing — don't bring all them big amps you got out there tonight. This club got a small stage, you bring all that stuff, won't be no room for me and the band."

As it turned out, Blue's proposed half-hour set ran only slightly more than twenty minutes. The crowd were out of their heads on downers, weed and cheap wine. Despite an introduction which stressed that Blue was Mick's favourite bluesman and that the band were 'Mick's personal guests,' all they did was howl for 'rock and roll!', 'boogie!' and 'Mick! Mick! Mick!' Some of them even booed and threw shit at the stage. Watching from the wings through splayed fingers, Hudson saw a wine bottle arc, impossibly slowly, from the crowd towards the musicians until it smashed on one of the spurs of Sonny's bass drum, showering Blue and Hakim with splinters of glass. God, no, he thought, not on my stage, shouldn't have let those fucking little animals anywhere near him. He stumbled towards the stage howling, "Fucking little bastards!" but Simon the roadie wrenched him back before he could get to where the audience could see him. As soon as Blue had played long enough to ensure that he and the band were going to get paid, he cut the set short and led his guys off.

Hudson was waiting for him in the wings, ashen-faced but for a spot of bright red in the centre of each cheek. "I'm so sorry, man! These kids are fucking pigs! I'm gonna go out and tell 'em just what I..." he lurched towards the stage, but Simon held him back again.

"Ain't no big deal," Blue said evenly. "Dealt with worse in my time."

The band turned back to the stage to rescue their instruments, but Simon stopped them. "Don't worry about your gear, man, " he said. "My guys'll deal with that."

Hudson was on the verge of tears. "Look, Blue, I'm sorry. I thought this was gonna be good for you, and I thought it would be good for them to see you, 'cause your music means so much to me ... this is all my fault, man!"

He was practically crying now. Booze and drugs carrying this young man every which way, Blue thought, and he don't know where to turn.

Bloodwork's crew were already swarming over the stage, Hudson's band's amplifiers looming over everything else. Three Marshall stacks dominated Mick's side of the stage: six huge cabinets each containing four twelve-inch speakers, topped by three separate 100-watt amplifiers, the whole thing over six feet high, matched by a similar set-up on the other side for his bass player. The drum kit, with two bass drums and a dense forest of cymbals, sat atop a five-foot riser. By comparision, Blue's band's set-up looked like a bunch of toys. Blue and Hakim had already wiped down their guitars and put them back into their roadworn cases, but Mick's guys were stripping down Sonny's drum kit, humping Eddie's big Hammond B3 organ, hauling their little Fender amps off to the battered station wagon out back of the arena. "Don't you pay it no mind, young man," Blue said, laying a consoling hand on Hudson's trembling shoulder, thinking *damn,* he's gotten even skinnier since he got real rich and famous. "You just remember you got your own show to do. Then come see us at the club. Yeah?" He clapped Hudson on the back, gave him a tricky power shake and ended up by tapping his fist gently against Hudson's own. The younger man followed his moves one beat behind. "*All* right." He raised his fist briefly to shoulder height. "Later, y'all."

Blue was right: Duke's *did* have a small stage. Forget Mick Hudson's onstage setup: even his dressing-room amp — a single Marshall cabinet and a 50-watt head — took up almost a quarter of the bandstand at Duke's. When Simon and his assistant Pete had hauled it in shortly before 1am, there'd been an outbreak of raised eyebrows and the occasional muffled comment from the mostly middle-aged, blue-collar clientele sparsely scattered around the dingy bar, all of them black apart from a couple of white kids who looked like college students, thirty or forty people in a club which could legally hold about a hundred and on a good night packed in twice that number. Simon and Pete had had to help Sonny and Eddie, both cussing under their breath, to shift the organ and drums a few feet over towards the side of the stage to make room, and Blue was practically sitting on his amp. Now Hudson's amp, ringed with a half-circle of effects pedals, squatted stage left, looming over everything around it like a skyscraper surrounded by a shantytown, its single red eye gleaming balefully over all it surveyed. Leaning up against it was Hudson's extravagantly decorated old Telecaster.

Hudson and Blue were conferring in a corner at the band's table. Hudson was flying, still up from his slam-dunk show at the auditorium, and bouncing around like a pinball on a potent combo-platter of natural and artificial energy, fingertips drumming the tabletop. He had changed out of his stage clothes into a pair of patched blue jeans and a fringed cowboy shirt already stained with beer. His hair was plastered to his forehead with sweat. Can't wait to get started, get on that stage, blow away the bad aftertaste, make it up to Blue for what just happened.

"So what we gonna play then?" he asked Blue. "We gonna do some of the old songs, then?"

Blue gave him a slow, crooked grin. "We certainly are, young man," he said. "We gonna play some *real* old songs."

Then he got up from his seat and led his musicians onto the stage. "Welcome back, ladies and gentlemen," he told the audience. "We got a special treat for you here tonight. It's my very great honour and privilege to introduce you to a young man who's come down here just to play for you with us tonight. Now this is a very *special* young man, one of the greatest rock and roll stars in the world. Matter of fact, when I first went to England back in 1964, his band was my back-up. Yeah!" Blue chuckled to himself, seemingly adrift in memory. "He's just got through doing his own show at the International Auditorium and he's here with us tonight, so I want a very special Duke's welcome for Mister! Mick! Hudson!"

Hudson followed Blue onto the stage to a polite smattering of applause, the college kids clapping the loudest. Simon flicked the Marshall amp from standby to on, handed Hudson his guitar and pointed to the bottle of beer next to the amp before scuttling back to the table he and Pete were sharing towards the rear of the club. Then Blue counted in a slow four and the band were playing, not a rocking shuffle, a Memphis soul stomp or an anguished slow blues, but a slinky, silky version of Hoagy Carmichael's The Nearness Of You, with Blue crooning the lyrics in a buttery, caressing baritone. Hudson had heard the song, and songs like it, the whole time he was growing up. This was the music his parents liked. This was what they told him he ought to be listening to. He'd always hated those songs, too, as much he'd always loved the rock and roll and blues he'd discovered for himself. He'd certainly never learned to play any of them. The band had already reached the middle-eight by the time he'd figured out the key: B-flat. Perfect for pianists and horn players, a nightmare for guitarists who liked the open-string keys like E, A, D and G. He just about managed a brief but muted arpeggio on the song's final chord.

Hudson fared no better on The Shadow Of Your Smile, which followed, or The Very Thought Of You and Fly Me To The Moon. The songs were all full of 'jazz chords': augmenteds and diminisheds and flat-nine minor sevenths, changing with every beat of every bar, chords he'd sort of learned when he was first exploring the guitar but had never had any call to use in Bluebottle's music or Cabal's or, latterly, his own. He was utterly out of his depth. Somewhere in the back of his mind he heard his mother saying, "I wish you'd play some *nice* music, darling, but I suppose those old songs are a little *difficult* for a lazy boy like you. They need a little more *work* than you're prepared to do, don't they, dear?"

Sweat turned the comfortable, familiar rosewood fingerwood of his guitar tricky and treacherous, dripped from his fumbling fingers and his burning forehead onto his untouched foot-pedals. He could feel blood rushing to his face, turning bright and hot under the dim red and blue lights. Three hours ago, he had been rocking 20,000 kids right out of their minds, his band keyed to follow his slightest cue, master of his music, emperor of his stage. His house, his band, his audience. He owned them. Now here he was, dying on his ass like a stumblefingered bumfluffed amateur. He could see the audience whispering amongst themselves, imagine he heard each muffled snort of laughter. He couldn't even raise his eyes to meet the rhythm section's gaze. "Jive-ass can't-play white-boy muthafucka." They might not be saying it, but he knew damn well what they were thinking. It was exactly what he'd be thinking if he was them.

Between songs, he hissed, "I'm lost, man!" but Blue just turned around and smiled seraphically at him. What was the old bastard playing at? Why was he doing this to him? Kippered, he thought. Absolutely fucking kippered. He caught Blue's eye and gave him a twisted grin: half grimace, half smirk. Then he resorted to the ultimate bluffer's trick: turning his guitar volume right down and strumming inaudibly at muted strings, nodding time to the music with his eyes closed, smiling like he was really, really into it.

Duke Ellington's Do Nothing 'Til You Hear From Me, which was sort of almost a blues shuffle, provided some respite, and he actually managed to pull off a semi-respectable solo which didn't veer too far away from the underlying chords. But then Blue called another Ellington tune at a rattlingly fast clip, the complex harmonies of Take The A Train sailing into the distance, each chord long gone by the time Hudson had even figured out the one before it. He waited the song out, then switched his amp off, unplugged his guitar and stumbled towards Simon and Pete. Their table at the back of the tiny club seemed miles away, a lot further than the distance from stage centre at the International Auditorium to the back row.

"Mis-ter! Mick! Hudson!" came Blue's mocking voice from the stage as Simon handed Hudson a cold beer. "Let's give him a nice round of applause for coming all the way down here to play for you!" Blue turned round, nodded at Sonny and kicked the band straight into Smile When You Say That — played his way, the original way, not the way Hudson had played it with Bluebottle in 1965, or even the way he'd played it to his 20,000 fans earlier tonight. Hudson drained his beer in one swallow and lurched to his feet, rocking the table and spilling the drinks. His face was burning, the floor shifting beneath his booted feet. He grabbed his guitar, not even bothering to look for the case, and trudged towards that impossibly distant exit.

"C'mon, we're going," he told Simon and Pete.

"What about your amp?" asked Pete.

"Leave it."

Behind him, Blue brought the song to a crunching finale. The next time Mick Hudson saw that Marshall amp, it was occupying pride of place in Blue's music room.

LOS ANGELES, SUMMER 2004

Mick Hudson emerged from the shower, vigorously towelling his hair. At least he still had some hair to towel, he thought, grabbing the dryer and ruffling up his mop into the trademark spiky sixties-style rooster 'do he'd worn since his early twenties. Three weeks after his tour had climaxed at Madison Square Gardens on his sixtieth birthday, his hair was returning to its natural grey. When he was touring he usually dyed it either jet black or that richly unnatural shade of chestnut favoured by the likes of Paul McCartney and Tony Blair, but dyeing his hair and having to remember to do his roots was basically a drag. If he could ever be arsed to go out on the road again he was seriously considering leaving it the way it was. Everybody knew he was sixty, and if a sixty-year-old guy wasn't allowed to appear in public with grey hair, then who could?

Another thing that pissed him off about getting old, he thought as he shaved, is that if you're a dark-haired guy, the greyer you get the harder it becomes to spot every last bit of stubble. It's less of a problem for blonds, he'd decided, because the transition from blond to white is a less dramatic change — your old photos don't look as spectacularly different — and you've always been used to chasing pale bristles. Now his beard was mostly white, he found himself missing bits and not realising it until he saw a close-up photo of himself somewhere with a clearly visible patch of white stubble. It worked the other way for black guys, he guessed: the older they got and the whiter their beards became, the less chance there was for errant bristles to escape the razor.

One thing he was absolutely certain about: he was a firm believer in shirts for the over-fifties... over-sixties, he corrected himself. Unlike some of his contemporaries, he had decided to keep his sagging pecs, weedy arms and grey chest hair to himself, and assembled an enviable wardrobe of slick suits and fancy shirts for stage and formal wear. Just like Blue and the real blues guys, he thought. You'd never catch them onstage in tight jeans and sleeveless T-shirts. The only way you're gonna see BB King's belly is if you sleep with him.

It always came back down to the Real Guys. BB, Muddy, John Lee

Hooker and Blue. Hudson was proud of his rock and roll success. He'd not only made it — "to the Toppermost of the Poppermost!" his inner DeeJay Voice trumpeted — but he'd managed to stay there, a front-bench member of the rock and roll House of Lords. It might take him longer to sell three or four million albums than it used to, but they always sold, and he always made the best record he possibly could.

But no matter how big you get in rock, he thought, you're still only top of the Second Division. The blues was the First Division. That was where the Real Guys did the Real Stuff. He'd never stopped playing blues, on his albums and in his his shows, and once in a while he cut something — or came up with a new lick during an improvised solo — which was somewhere close to where he wanted to be. I'm sixty fucking years old, he thought, rinsing his razor, and I'm still playing kids' music for people who were kids twenty, thirty or forty years ago. Fuck my lost youth, and fuck theirs.

Time to make that Real Record. Not cranked-up, fuzzed-up ageing-white-boy blues, but a Real Record. See if I can do something which feels real. See if I can meet one of the Real Guys on a level playing field, finally make it all the way. Leave something behind that's more than just a bunch of heavy chords and flash solos and sentimental singer-songwriter bullshit. Muddy and John Lee had passed away. BB had just made an album with Eric Clapton. Soon there'd be none of the Real Guys left. Did that mean that overgrown kids like him would be the next generation of Real Guys? Or simply that there'd be no Real Guys left at all?

Fuck, this is depressing. He needed to derail this train of thought pronto. He laid a giant boulder across its track, and headed into the bedroom to pick out some clothes.

One long-standing sartorial habit he'd found it hard to kick was his penchant for leather trousers. In his sixtieth birthday interview with *Rolling Stone*, he'd delighted in explaining why leather trousers were absolutely ideal for the elderly, especially in winter. "They keep your legs and groin area nice and warm," he'd explained. "They're pretty much rain- and snow-proof, and when you get indoors you just wipe 'em off. Same if your hands start to shake and you find yourself spilling beer on them. Or even hot stuff like soup or tea. You won't get scalded, and a nice damp cloth sorts it out in a second. I'm thinking of setting up a foundation to buy leather trousers for every pensioner in Britain."

Fortunately, he'd kept his figure as well as his hair, though he freely conceded that he looked a lot better with clothes on. He'd briefly employed a personal trainer to get him in shape for the tour, and she'd told him he was 'skinny-fat,' which meant that he looked adequately lean and trim when fully dressed, but flabby and untoned when he wasn't. She'd managed to whip him into good enough shape for eight months' worth of two-hour shows, but the truth was that he much preferred watching her demonstrating the exercises to doing them himself.

The period right after a tour was always weird, and it sometimes took him a few weeks to chill out enough to go back home and settle into the cosy domestic groove of the English countryside. This time, he had a live album from the tour to prepare, so there was a ready-made excuse to rent a little place in the Hollywood Hills for a month while he and his producer went through the tapes they'd recorded on the road. They'd have to listen to the twenty shows they'd recorded, pick the best performances and then go into a studio to do some editing and mixing and — if any of his own guitars or vocals hadn't quite cut the old mustard — do some discreet overdubbing and re-recording. The girls would understand: if he made good progress on the album he could fly them out for a week. Had their school holidays started yet? It was so easy to lose track of these things when you'd been out on the road. Plus there were old friends to catch up with in LA. People you really wanted to sit down with properly, not just chitchat with for five minutes in a dressing-room just before a show, when you were all cranked up to play, or after, when you were totally shagged and just wanted to curl up with the drink and spliff he no longer allowed himself until after the gig.

The day before he'd caught up with his old roadie Simon, now doing very well for himself in management over here. That Real Record on his mind, he'd asked after Blue, and Simon had said not to bother him, the old guy wasn't feeling too good. Fuck *that*, thought Hudson, if Blue's under the weather he could probably do with some cheering up, a new project to get how ever many teeth he's got left into. So he'd called anyway, but he couldn't leave the number because, bloody typical, the office had forgotten to tell him what it was. Or maybe they'd written it down somewhere and he couldn't find it. It'd been at least four hours since he'd called Blue's house to leave a message. Someone had to be in by now. Giving his hair a final fluff-up and shrugging into his Armani leather jacket, he pulled the phone towards him and, from memory, punched in the number.

THREE

Even if Adrienne and Blue hadn't been expecting Mick Hudson, they'd've known it was him at the door. He always announced himself the same way. Didn't matter whether he was pressing a bellpush or knocking, it was always Da-DA-dada-DA, two-and-three, like the riff from Muddy Waters's Hoochie Coochie Man.

Dogs at her heels, their claws clacking on the polished hardwood floor, Adrienne opened the door to Hudson's seamed, smiling face. "'Allo Missis Blue!" he yelled, dropping his bag and spreading his arms. Every man I get to hug these days is skinny, she thought as she embraced him, feeling his ribs through the thin leather. "Hey, young man," she said. *Young man? This guy is sixty years old, nearly fifteen years older than me.* Still, that was what Blue called him, and she'd always called him that too.

Something was making urgent whining noises and nudging at their knees. Hudson stepped back to greet the huge brown German Shepherd gazing imploringly up at them. "Attack!" he said, dropping to his knees as the dog obediently lay down to be petted. Adrienne was looking down at him, something small and furry in her arms. "You ain't met this one, have you?"

Hudson did a double-take. "What on earth is *that*?" Adrienne held the little bundle out to him: a tiny dog, skinny and hairless but for a spectacular platinum mop cascading from the crown of its head. If any dog could pout, it would be this one. Hudson was reminded of his ex-wife. "She's a Chinese crested something-or-other. Her name's Wu Li. You think her hairstyle could catch on in England?"

"It's already been and gone, love. Rod Stewart got there first. Anyway, how's himself? Si says he's a little under the weather at the minute."

The smile on Adrienne's face didn't flicker, but the one in her eyes disappeared like somebody just flipped a switch. She took the little dog back from Hudson and dropped her gently to the floor. "You go ahead on into the music room. He's waiting for you. You want a beer?"

"Yeah, why not? I ain't driving today."

"I'll bring it in. You go in and say hi."

Hudson sauntered down the hall and tapped out his signature knock on the heavy wooden door, just below the sign that said 'If you don't rock, don't knock.'

"C'mon in."

Blue's music room was just the way Hudson remembered it. A few microphones on stands in the corner. A display case taking up half of one wall held the awards and trophies which Blue didn't have room for in the living room. Out front he kept the obvious items: Grammys, WC Handys, photos of himself at the White House with Jimmy Carter in the seventies and Bill Clinton in the nineties, the onstage shots with BB King and John Lee Hooker and Eric Clapton and Stevie Ray Vaughan and Mick Hudson and Buddy Guy and Robert Cray and the Stones. In here was the more obscure stuff: British Blues Awards, plaques from European cultural institutes, honorary-doctorate-in-music certificates from universities all over the world. Pictures of Blue with lesser-known bluesmen familiar only to hardcore buffs and people who'd actually been there when they were in their prime. Along the facing wall, a counter with a Korg MIDI keyboard and two computers, one for email and the other running music software. A line of amplifiers: beat-up old Fender combos, two Twins and a Deluxe, their tweed coverings stained with ancient beer spills and abraded by countless exhausted late-night loadings in back alleys after last sets in forgotten clubs; a spotless hand-built Matchless valve combo cased in french-polished pine, and a battered old Marshall four-by-twelve cabinet topped with a 50-watt head.

And guitars. A *lot* of guitars, lined up on stands like they were on parade awaiting inspection by the commanding officer. Unlike some of his peers and contemporaries, who kept their instruments in closets and only pulled them out when they had a gig or a session, Blue's guitars were all polished, freshly strung and ready to work. There was his old rubbed-raw 1959 Jazzmaster, his first one; the '68 sunburst he'd bought to replace it on the road, and two of the special blue-sparkle ones Fender's Custom Shop had made for him. There were a couple of big old hollow-body Gibson jazz guitars, a pair of ornate Martin D-45 acoustics, a six-string and a twelve, an ancient Stella acoustic, and a steel-bodied 1930s National Resonator. Finally an Eric Clapton Stratocaster which Blue had received from Clapton's own fair hands, and right at the end, two prototype Mick Hudson signature Telecasters, one plain cream and the other complete with carefully reproduced peace and pot-leaf stickers and blobby psychedelic flowers. It was a serious collectors' item: anti-drug campaigners had demanded the removal of the pot sticker from the versions sold in stores.

The only thing different about the room was the motorised wheelchair parked in front of the keyboard. That, and his host. The last time Hudson had seen his mentor, four years ago, Blue had been lively and energetic, an incipient belly stretching his slick suit; his only slightly thinning hair dyed an improbable reddish-brown and his trademark pencil moustache immaculately trimmed. The man walking slowly and carefully towards him, right hand extended, was white-bearded and painfully thin, wearing baggy jeans and an old LA Raiders sweatshirt, nappy white hair visible below his Delta Blues Museum baseball cap. For the first time in all the years they'd known each other, Hudson thought, Blue looked old. Like *really* old. Old as he actually was.

"How you doin', young man," said James 'Blue' Moon. Numbly, Hudson took his hand. It felt like a bundle of dry sticks.

They embraced gingerly, nothing like the back-slapping old-time bear-hugs, Hudson clasping Blue's newly frail body as gently as he could before releasing him. Adrienne brought in a couple of frosty beer glasses on a tray, dogs inquisitively following close behind. She set the tray down on the counter and steered Blue to his wheelchair. She cocked her head towards Hudson.

"There has," she said, "been something of a *change*."

"Yep," said Blue, "they liable to start callin' me 'the lean mean blues machine' all over again."

Hudson was shaking his head like he was punchdrunk, opening his mouth to speak and then closing it again. Finally he said, "I talked to Simon just last night, and he said you had a bad flu."

"Simon says a lot of things." Blue and Adrienne sang softly, "*Simple Simon says put your hands in the air...*" He shrugged. "I seen better days, but right now I'm puttin' up with these."

"Blue has cancer," Adrienne said flatly.

"What kind of cancer?"

"You know the kind of cancer you get better from?" Blue asked. "Well, this is the *other* kind."

"Liver cancer," Adrienne said. "Kind of unfair considering that he ain't done any serious drinking for a long, long time."

"'Til now, that is," Blue said. He wheeled his chair over to the far end of the counter and produced an unopened bottle of bourbon and two highball glasses. "How 'bout you? You still drinkin'?"

"Now and then," Hudson admitted, "but not usually this early in the day."

"Well, this is kind of a special occasion," Blue said, twisting the bottle open and pouring a healthy splash into each glass. He handed one to Hudson and hefted the other. "Here's to you, young man. Long life." He raised the glass to his lips. When he lowered it, it was half empty.

"The doc gives me about a year," he said. "Hey, young man, you ain't touched your drink." Absently, Hudson raised his glass, took a sip and put the glass down on the counter. "But there's stuff you can do about it," he said. "You can have surgery, or chemo, or else there are some alternative treatments..."

"No," Blue said. "Nuh-*uh*. No cuttin' my ass up, no radiation to make my hair fall out and have me feelin' like shit for my last year on this earth. And none'a that coffee-up-your-ass whale-cartilage crap in no ten-grand-a-week clinic in Mexico, neither. I told the doc: I'm goin' out the way I come in. I'm gonna drink a little whiskey, spend some time with the people I love, play a whole lot of git-tar..." he reached out and pulled Adrienne to him. "... and make love to my beautiful young wife." He laughed and clapped his hands. "I'm sick'a talkin' about this shit. What about you? You just come off tour, done pretty good, I hear. You been home to see your kids yet?"

"Not yet," Hudson said. "Got to get this live album done and dusted before I go home."

Blue shook his head and wagged an admonitory finger at Hudson. "You never could fool me none, young man, and you ain't foolin' me now. You got some fine studios back in England. I been to your big old house out in the country, you got a studio right there as good as anything we got here in LA. If you still out here, you got to tell me a better reason than that."

Hudson smiled. He lifted Blue's big Gibson L-5 from its stand and began gently chording his way through The Nearness Of You. Blue smiled back. He plugged his sunburst Jazzmaster into the old Fender Deluxe, flipped what he called 'the jazz switch' above the pickups and joined in, simply and eloquently stating the melody before starting to improvise, graceful arabesques floating lazily around the chords.

Adrienne ushered the dogs out and quietly closed the door behind her.

"Now," Adrienne said, "see if you can recognise this young lady here."

Hudson went theatrically down on one knee on the living-room floor, arms spread wide. *"Oh-h Don-na, oh-oh Don-na,"* he sang in an exaggerated doo-wop cadence. Donna giggled. She only vaguely remembered Uncle Mick, one of those weird old guys who always came around to see her daddy. Mom and Dad had told her she was only ten when she'd seen him last, and that was a real long time ago. Josh came forward to shake hands. Much to Hudson's surprise, Little Josh, who he remembered as a dumpy adolescent from his last time here, was now a broad-shouldered, rangy basketball god well over six feet tall. Four years wasn't much time as far as Hudson was concerned: not much more time than it took to write an album, record it, tour it and take a little time off to rest up before doing the whole thing all over again. For kids, four years was a huge chunk of their lives. He remembered, guiltily, that he hadn't seen his own daughters for nearly three months, when he'd flown them out to Florida during a week's break from the tour. Damn, and it'd be too late to call them tonight.

Dinner was a prime example of what Hudson thought of as 'designer downhome': blackened catfish over spicy rice with collard greens and seemingly endless platters of deliciously moist cornbread. Adrienne produced a bottle of champagne but Blue and Hudson opted to stay on beer. Blue's portion was less than half the size of everybody else's, but Hudson noted that he barely picked at it. The conversation was a blizzard of anecdotes: Blue reminiscing about legendary bluesmen in their prime when Hudson was still a war baby in Berkshire, throwing his rattle out of his playpen to the sound of the BBC Home Service; Hudson delivering semi-scabrous anecdotes (suitably toned down for the kids) about some of the stuff his peer group used to get up to on tour; Adrienne telling Hudson about how her business was going and some of the more bizarre items of personal jewellery (descriptions equally toned down) commissioned by a few of her better-known clients. Donna was a little fidgety: after all, this was old folks talking about people she'd never heard of, but she quizzed Hudson eagerly about his daughters: what kind of clothes did they wear, what music did they listen to, did kids in England like *Charmed* or *The OC* better than *Buffy*. Josh contributed a few monosyllables about how he was settling in at college — he was going for an MBA and playing a lot of basketball — but mostly he sat back and took it all in.

Around nine o'clock a couple of Josh's new college friends, both white, drove by to pick him up. Their eyes widened fractionally when they spotted Hudson: keen classic rock fans, they recognised him immediately from his old videos and their parents' album covers, though one of them later told Josh that they didn't realise Hudson was so old. An hour later Donna retired to her room to commune with her TV set and phone round her friends to catch up on the last of the day's gossip. The grownups reconvened in the music room.

"All right, young man," Blue said. "What's on your mind?"

Hudson swallowed a gulp of bourbon and took a deep breath. "I want you and me to make an album together," he said. "I had the idea before you told me about..." he gestured towards Blue's wheelchair, "... but now I *really* want to do it."

Blue's face was impassive. He rolled his wheelchair back a couple of feet. "If you want to talk *bidness*," he said flatly, "you need to call Simon."

Hudson spread his hands. "Before I know whether you want to play," he said, "there's no business to talk *about*." He pulled his chair a few inches closer to Blue. "Look... we've known each other for forty years. That's two-thirds of my life and damn near half of yours. You know you've always been my... I backed you up when I was just a kid. We've done gigs together. We've made TV shows together. I've played on a couple of your records, you've played on a couple of mine. But we've never made a *whole record* together from the ground up. I want us to plan the whole thing together. We'll produce it together. We pick the songs together, we write some new ones together, we both sing, we both play lead. We can use my band, or your band, or the best guys from both of 'em. We'll record in any studio you want... hell, we can get a mobile in and cut it right here, if you like. And you take top billing. Sixty per cent of the money, anything. Let's just *do* it."

Blue didn't say anything. He spun his wheelchair away and rolled himself to the counter, started tapping keys on one of his computers. A screen sprang to life, showing a MIDI file. He slipped on a pair of headphones, tapped a couple more keys and listened intently. Hudson glanced over at Adrienne. Her face was expressionless.

The track came to an end. Blue tapped another key and put the headphones down next to the keyboard. He rolled himself back to face Hudson.

"The way I figure it," he said, "I got just one more album left in me. There's a few songs left on the shelf from the last few records, but none'a that's gonna be put out 'til after I'm gone. I been thinking about making that one more record, too. And I figured that what I want to do is sing with my family."

Hudson kept his face as straight as he could, but his shoulders slumped fractionally. "Right," he said. "Venetia."

Blue said, "Yeah. Venetia. She and I ain't seen eye to eye for a long time. But she's my daughter, she's a musician, and before I go I want to make some music with her." He gazed down into his lap, contemplating his hands. "See, the religious folk say that when you know you goin' to die, it's time to get right with God. Now, you know how I feel. I don't mess with that stuff. I figure that if God made me, He made me the way I am, and if He wanted me to be different than I am, He would'a *made* me different. But what I *do* know..." he raised his head, looking Hudson straight in the eyes "... is that I got to get right with the people closest to me. Now my family ain't been close to me for a long time."

"You got a family," Adrienne said quietly. "You got a wife and a daughter and Josh, too. Right here in this house."

"I know, sugar," Blue said. He wheeled over to her and put his arm around her shoulders. "But Venetia's my family too. Her and her boy. He come see me once in a while, and he don't always get on with his mother, neither. He make records, too. Hip-hop kinda thing. Had himself some hits." Blue chuckled. "Hits run in the family."

"Yeah, I know," Hudson said. "Hell, what with him and Venetia, that's three generations of your family got Grammys."

"So I want to make music with her, and with him too. That way, some of the younger folks might get to hear me while I'm still here."

Hudson drained his glass and stood up. "Okay," he said. "I can understand that." Blue rolled himself forward until the wheels of his chair were almost touching Hudson's boots. "Sit your ass down, young man," he said. Hudson sat down. Blue reached out, patted Hudson's knee.

"Young man, young man," he said. "You right. We been knowin' each other a long time. We been makin' music together a long time. You like my *son*. When I say I'm gonna play with my family, that mean you, too."

Hudson brightened. "So we're gonna do it."

"Yeah. *We're* gonna do it. *All* of us. You, me, Venetia and young Calvin. The four of us gonna make the record."

Hudson asked, "When's the last time you talked to Venetia?" Blue turned to Adrienne.

"When was that last time?"

Adrienne's face was stony. "About fifteen years ago."

"I gather it didn't go well," Hudson said.

Adrienne, giving nothing away. "No, it did not."

Blue asked, "And when did *you* last talk to Venetia?"

Hudson shrugged. "1973."

"Didn't you and she get close for a little while? Round about 1971, '72?"

Hudson, giving nothing away. "For a little while."

"You played on one'a her records, didn't you?"

"Back in '68 or something. That's how we met. We were recording down the hall from her and her producer called me in for a solo." He accepted a fresh glass of bourbon from Adrienne. "You want to call her or have Simon call her people? Or my office can..."

"Oh, I ain't gonna call her. And Simon ain't gonna be callin' her, and I don't want none'a *your* people callin' her people, neither. I want *you* to talk to her, your own self."

Hudson put his glass down. He said, "You're kidding."

"No, I ain't kiddin'. No way, young man. You recollect what I just said about gettin' straight with people close to you? Now you ain't dyin', not that I know of, but you sure ain't gettin' no younger. What are you now, sixty years old? You may still be jumpin' 'round that stage like a crazy man every night, but back when I was growin' up, sixty was an old man. And it's never too early — or too late — to start getting your stuff straight. Now, I don't know nuthin' 'bout nuthin', but I reckon you and Venetia might just have some catchin' up to do."

Blue hauled himself up out of his chair and held out his hand for Hudson to shake. "This album is gonna happen, young man," he said. "But you the one gonna have to make it happen. Now I'm gonna say good night, 'cause all this talkin' done tired me out." He sat back down in his chair. "You got a ride?"

"Yeah, sure." Hudson pulled a mobile phone from his pocket.

"Now you sure you can *remember* your number?" Adrienne asked, grinning.

Hudson grimaced. "One of the guys in the office programmed it for me." He called up a menu and speed-dialed. "Sam? You can pick me up

35

any time you like... yeah, same place. Okay, see you in ten."

"Now remember what I said, young man. You call Venetia yourself. No managers, no go-betweens, no flunkies. *You* are gonna talk to *her*."

"Yes, daddy. I'll have somebody track down her number in the morning."

"Oh, you don't need to do none of that. I got her number right here." He rolled over to the counter, leafed through a battered leather Filofax and jotted something down on a yellow Post-It. He handed Hudson the slip of paper. "Course I got her number. I got *all* her numbers. I can reach any of my family any place, day or night."

Hudson blinked. "You got all her numbers and you never call her?"

Blue smiled. "Good night, young man." He raised one fist in salutation and rolled himself out of the room.

FOUR

"Okay... let's go for it. Take one."

Venetia Moon heard the backing track start up in her headphones, four sharp electronic clicks and then a rich deep piano and organ chord unfolding before her like a lush red carpet for her to stroll on, easy as you please. She took a breath and let her diaphragm swell full of the spirit until her belly pushed against the waistband of her skirt, hard as a rock. She could feel her voice building up within her, as natural and unstoppable as a tidal wave or a hurricane. Venetia focussed on the microphone a foot away from her and closed her eyes. She'd already forgotten the young fool engineer, used to working with kids who hadn't been raised in church and never learned to sing for real and couldn't even make a squeak without half swallowing the mic, who'd set it up just an inch or two away, and how when he asked for a test she'd given him one low note straight from her gut, and he'd had to jump up from behind the board and fuss on into the studio to move her mic far enough away to be able to handle her voice without overloading the machines.

She heard her cue coming four beats away, and let her voice just roll out of her and into the world.

"*Some-tiiimes I feel so worried...*" she got four notes out of 'feel' and eight out of 'worried.' The bass and drums kicked in on two and four.

"*Some-ah times I fee-eel so-o bluuuue...*" . On 'blue,' she hit a note so deep and vibrant that she bet she'd made their speakers buzz.

"*Some-tii-iimes I get so-hoo ti-ii-ired, yeh...*" On the second syllable of 'so,' she made an effortless octave leap and by the time the note died away she'd floated it almost all the way to the top of her range.

"*That's when I-I-I reach out for you...*" On the opening r-sound of 'reach' she put a gritty rasp into her voice, a gutty sensual inflection that took the mood right out of the Lord's house and into a flash of funky sweat-soaked sheets and the muscle-memory of how it feels to make love just one more time than you felt you had in you.

"*So-oo-oul Co-ho-ho-luhhhhhhh...*"

She gave the last low note one more shake, like she couldn't bear to let go of it, and opened her eyes, saw the ad execs high-fiving each other behind the glass. The engineer hit the talkback button. "That was amazing, Venetia. I think we got it right there. Wanna come in and hear it?" What she wanted to say was, "You pay me enough to sing this shit, but you sure as hell don't pay me enough to make me wanna listen to it." What she said was, "Be glad to." She slid her headphones off, put them on the stool behind her and marched into the control room. Ad execs, corporate suits, assistant engineers and assorted flunkies respectfully scattered to clear her path. Gratefully, she lowered her bulk into the producer's chair next to the engineer.

Venetia knew her demographic, and she knew her value as a corporate spokesperson. She was the perfect choice to front for Soul Cola, the soft-drink giant's new product. She polled consistently high among just about everybody over the age of forty-five, with her greatest strength amongst black consumers of fifty-five and up, who remembered her as one of the greatest gospel singers of her generation, right up there with Aretha Franklin and Mavis Staples, from way before her late-sixties pop-soul breakthrough. She knew her worth, and she made sure everybody else knew it too. That was why whenever it was time to cut a commercial, she demanded a substantial bonus on top of her already substantial corporate retainer for singing; half as much again as her producer's fee; a private jet to ferry her and her entourage — personal assistant, personal trainer (even though no-one at the company could see any evidence that her personal trainer was actually giving her any training), hairdresser, make-up artist, publicist, musical director and two bodyguards — from her home outside Chicago to LA or wherever else they were cutting or shooting. Plus, of course, penthouse-suite accomodation, twenty-four-hour limo service and $5,000 pocket-money *per diem*. Why? Like the saying goes, "Because I'm worth it." Venetia Moon was fifty-seven years old. Long as she lived, long as she could draw breath, Venetia Moon was never going to settle for anything less than exactly what she she was worth. How about more than she was worth? No such thing.

"Roll it," she told the engineer. She listened critically as the track played back. Sounding good, but not as good as she knew she could sound. If this had been a session on one of her own songs for one of her own albums, she'd already be back on the studio floor to do it again. She'd sing it over and over again, all night if she had to, tirelessly pushing through whatever inner barriers remained between her and the song, until the walls cracked and the spirit moved on the face of the water and the earth sang back to her. But for this? This was a fucking soft-drink commercial, and she'd already given them, in just one take, a lot more than they deserved.

Anyway, now they had the track completed, all she had left to do was shoot the visuals, which was supposed to happen in four days' time. They'd pretty much finished building the set, and the director was explaining to her, as if she couldn't tell from the storyboards, that what they wanted to do was kind of *suggest* that she was in church without actually saying so or showing a church, which might offend folks of a religious disposition, and then the camera'd pull back and she'd be standing on a divinely glowing stained-glass-style Soul Cola logo floor which the CGI guys'd put in later. There would also be a second version of the commercial which wouldn't be screened in the US or Europe: a 'duet' with a guest star — to be decided upon later — who would be shot and recorded separately and blended in by computer, but she, the execs assured her, would unquestionably remain the star.

Venetia said her goodbyes, left her PA to sort out the details and had to wait several seconds too long for someone to open the door and walk her to her limo. As contractually specified, it was a white Cadillac Brougham and not a Lincoln Town Car. It said, right there in her contract, that provision of a Lincoln Town Car or anything else not on her list of approved limos would be taken as an indication that the company wished to terminate its agreement with Ms Moon, thereby activating a series of extremely expensive penalty clauses.

She was only a few blocks away from the Beverly Hills Hotel when her mobile went off. The ringtone was the first two bars of What A Friend We have In Jesus, which was a bad sign: it meant she was receiving a call from an unfamiliar number. Normally if that happened, she would hand the phone to her PA so he could answer it for her, but Ramon was still back at the studio finalising the details of the commercial shoot. Hey, live dangerously, she told herself. Go 'head, girlfriend, answer your own phone.

"Hello?"

"Venetia? Long time." Limey accent. Who...? "This is Mick. Mick Hudson. We have to..."

What it felt like was a giant hand slamming her back into the soft leather seating. She dropped the phone. Her heart was pounding in her chest like it wanted to get out. She could hear a tinny little voice still twittering away from the phone at her feet. She fumbled it back into her hand, hit the disconnect button and dropped it back to the floor. Immediately, What A Friend We Have In Jesus restarted. A part of her looked on in disbelief as she picked it up and answered.

"Venetia, listen." Him again. "This is important. It's about..."

She wound the window down and threw the phone, as hard as she could, out onto the asphalt. Two seconds later it was crushed into splinters of plastic and circuitry under the wheels of a Humvee.

"... and the third time I called didn't go so great, either," Hudson said. "This time I got diverted to someone called Ramon, said he was her assistant. Told me if I ring her again she'd consider it harassment and sue me for seven million dollars."

Blue chuckled, but the smile didn't get within a light-year of his eyes. "Oh my lord," he said softly. "Oh... my ... lord. Looks like you got your work cut out for you there, young man."

Hudson rolled the volume control on his Telecaster all the way down and leaned the guitar up against the nearest amp. "Look, pardon me if I'm being a trifle thick here," he said, "but even if you've fallen out with her, Venetia's still your daughter, and she needs to know what the situation is. I'll talk to her about making the record, assuming I ever get the chance to talk to her, but someone ought to tell her about... all this." He gestured towards Blue's wheelchair. Three large bottles of pills sat on the counter next to the computer keyboard, alongside a pitcher of ice water and a couple of glasses. They hadn't been there on Hudson's first visit. "So why does it have to be me? I mean, the way this is going, if she won't talk to me, she ain't even gonna know you're... not well until she reads your bleedin' obituary in the paper."

Blue didn't seem to be listening. He just kept sliding the glass bottleneck on his third finger up to the octave fret on the resonator in his lap, applying a slightly different vibrato to the note each time. Hudson persisted. "Why doesn't Adrienne call her?"

Blue chuckled again. "Adrienne wouldn't piss on Venetia if she was on fire. Well, maybe she would, but not enough to put the fire out." He played another slow, meditative riff. "Only time they met was a long time back when Adrienne was pregnant with Donna. Venetia came round to visit, told Adrienne she wasn't nuthin' but a ho tryin' to get her hands on my money. Huh! Didn't *have* no money then, least not like I got now. Told me if I wasn't a senile old fool I'd see that there'd be no other reason a fine young gal like that'd be with some dried-up old man.

"So we got us a little problem right there. Adrienne said she ain't never gonna be in this house if Venetia's here. The next time Venetia walks in, Adrienne walks out. I had to choose, right there and right then, between my wife and my daughter. Ever since I been knowin' her, Adrienne been nuthin' but good to me. And my daughter been even more of a bitch than her mama was. She done me like that with every woman I was ever with after her mama'n me broke up." He looked Hudson in the eye. "You shocked to hear me talkin' like this, young man? I ain't got enough time left to talk anything but straight. My wife or my daughter? When it came to it, wasn't no choice at all."

Hudson shifted in his chair, picked up his guitar again. "Look... why don't you have Simon call her people, just to let her know you're sick. It's her choice what she does after that. If she calls you, then we can meet up and I'll take it from there, tell her about the record. If she doesn't, then..."

"Then we ain't *got* a record," Blue said, without heat. "The reason we ain't got a record, young man, is that you holdin' out on me 'bout stuff that concern my family. I done told you why I can't be calling Venetia. I know she don't want to talk to you, but you ain't told me *why*. I'm gonna be making my last record here. Either it get made in a spirit of trust and truthfulness..." he returned the resonator to its stand and stood up, to Hudson's eyes a little more painfully than he had before "... and *love*... or it don't get made at all." He made a show of looking at his watch, though Hudson was fairly sure Blue already knew exactly what time it was. "Right now, I ain't feelin' too good and it's time for my nap. Next few days, they want me back at the hospital for more tests, though I don't know what they can say that they ain't already told me. And the next time we meet, young man, I hope you're gonna have some better news for me than what I'm gonna get from them." He held out his hand for Hudson to shake, but didn't offer an embrace. Lowering himself back into his wheelchair, he rolled out into the hall.

Very slowly, Hudson packed up his guitar and let himself out.

They'd shot the commercial on a sound stage on the Paramount lot. Apart from some minor technical problems with the lights and a brief dispute with Mario the director, resolved in Venetia's favour, about the outfit she was going to wear, the whole thing went smooth as butter.

She lip-synched her studio vocal perfectly each time and there was a dutiful spatter of applause on the final take, when she raised arms and eyes to heaven on that last soulful note.

Jeff Ansell, the senior account exec, was waiting for her when she returned to her dressing room. "I've got some *wonderful* news!" he announced, waving a CD at her. "We've got the guest star for the second commercial! We recorded him this morning! It's a real coup for us because he hardly ever does commercials and he's never done one for a soft drink before, and the best part of it is... oh, let me just play it to you."

Venetia's contract specified a state-of-the-art sound system in each and every dressing-room, location trailer or hotel suite she occupied. Ansell inserted his CD and pressed play. There were those churchy piano and organ chords, sounding almost as lush and rich as they had over the studio's giant speakers. Then she came in, singing the first line and sounding *good*, girlfriend. And then, responding to her call, an electric guitar sounded three quick notes, the last one sustained, only dying out as her voice returned to sing the second line.

Her first thought was *that's my daddy*, and his face flashed up before her, images of Daddy Blue in that crummy little apartment in Chicago, cussing at her and Mama as they tried to get him out of bed for church on Sunday morning, shouting "Goddammit, woman, I just got in from playin' two hours ago!" as he pulled the covers back over his head. Then she heard herself singing the second line, answered this time by a long sustained high note that matched her low one, and a rapid flurry, DEEEEEE-DADELAAA. No, she thought, that's not my daddy. Daddy always play smoother than that. This sound too sharp and dirty to be my daddy.

Then came her third line, ending on that ethereal high note. The guitar came back at her with a low-string snarl slowly bending up a full tone and then hitting the midrange note — BAAAA-OOO — on which she started the fourth line. Two high, ringing notes from the guitar and then the pay-off, but now there was another voice harmonising with hers, male, nowhere near as rich and full in tone as hers, but snaking around her melody line, starting out above and ending below, matching her phrasing perfectly.

"Sounds pretty good to me," she said absently, her mind whirring. She suddenly had a very bad feeling about this 'guest star.' "Who is it?" she demanded. Ansell was acting all skittish and teasing. If he had a tail, she thought disgustedly, it'd be wagging right now. "Let this be a surprise," he said, and ushered back towards the sound stage. "We're just setting up some lights," he told her. "*Jeff*-rey," she said menacingly, but he just kept hurrying her along. Why hadn't she been told any of this? Where the hell was Ramon?

The set hadn't changed, but now there was a circular three-foot riser off to the side and about ten feet back of where she'd been standing. On it was a tall skinny white guy in a drop-dead black Paul Smith suit. His grey hair was rooster-spiked, and hanging from his narrow shoulders on a slim black leather strap was a Fender Telecaster guitar emblazoned with a peace-symbol sticker and blobby painted flowers.

Thoughts were colliding in her head like a multi-car pile-up. Simultaneous inner voices were yammering *that fucking bastard, what's he doing here, how the hell did he pull this one off, what does he want from me after all these years.* She wanted to yell, "Security! That man's been harassing me! Get him out of here!" But her mouth refused to work. Jeff Ansell saw the confusion and horror on Venetia's face.

"I know what you're thinking," he said. "You're absolutely right. Some of our stockholders aren't going to like that peace symbol, especially not in an election year." He pulled a walkie-talkie from his pocket. "Mario? That peace symbol's got to go. Can you get him to use the plain white guitar instead? It looks so much better with his suit."

FIVE

NEW YORK CITY, 1968

The first surprise Venetia got when she signed to Boulevard Records was realising just how many of their funky stomping R&B hits had been produced by a couple of old Jewish guys with hoarse Brooklyn voices and greying beards. Nate Adler wasn't a musician or an engineer, but he had ears. He'd been recording jazz, jump and R&B for almost two decades. He knew how to pick a happening song and match it to exactly the right singer, and how to recognise real vocal talent and marry it to exactly the right song. He also knew when to send out for barbecue, which beats and grooves would get kids a third his age dancing, and how to cajole musicians into playing exactly what he wanted to hear. Even more important than that, at least to Venetia, was that he could recognise when they'd played it. Nate Adler could always tell which take was the one to keep. When he said, "Okay, we got it," no-one doubted that it had been got. You could take that to the bank. Which was exactly what Boulevard had been doing since 1949.

Venetia hit the final chord on the piano. She waited to let its rumble and ring die down, fading along with the last sizzle of the drummer's ride cymbal. Behind the studio glass, communing with whatever spirits told him whether he had a take or not, Nate Adler scratched his beard and stubbed out his cigarette in the oveflowing ashtray at his elbow. Then he leaned forward and pushed the talkback switch. "Okay," he said, "we got it." He jumped to his feet and bustled out onto the studio floor to join Venetia at the piano. "That was great, darlin'," he told her. "Cert for the album. Might even make a single if the horn section don't fuck up."

They crowded into the control room while the engineer played back what they'd just cut. "Yep, that's the one," Adler said. No-one disagreed. Venetia and Adler went into a brief huddle to discuss the backing vocal and horn section overdubs they'd be laying down once the basic tracks had been completed. Then Adler checked the clock on the studio wall. "We got almost an hour left in here before anyone's due for the next session. You got anything else you want to do?" Venetia struck a few chords on the piano, winding up with a bluesy run down to the bass end of the keyboard. "Got a blues I'd like to try."

Adler raised his eyebrows. When she'd come to the label Venetia had been insistent that no matter how secular her material got, she was never going to sing the blues. Still, people change over time and despite her initial resistance, she'd gotten fonder and fonder of the funkier stuff the longer she spent recording with Boulevard. Maybe the fact that she'd left her preacher stepdad's name behind and signed as Venetia Moon rather than Venetia Holland meant more than he'd thought, or more than even she'd realised. "How many verses you got?"

"Four." She rummaged in her bag and propped a scribbled lyric sheet on the piano.

"What's it called?"

"Right now it's called Sweet Man."

"Hm. Lotta songs called Sweet Man. Aretha got one out right now called Sweet Sweet Man..."

"We can change the title later. Just call it Blues for now."

"Okay... what key?"

"C."

He turned to the musicians. Her second Boulevard surprise had been finding out that most of the studio guys who made up the house band weren't downhome Southern funksters straight out of some barroom in Memphis or Atlanta, but Juilliard-trained jazz players who didn't arrive until after midnight, when they'd finished their regular gigs in cabarets or jazz clubs or TV and radio studio orchestras or Broadway musical pit bands. Like these guys. Five pieces: bass, drums, a keyboard player to handle organ and electric piano parts while Venetia was at the baby grand, and two guitarists. Richard Carter was a jazz player who'd never, in Adler's experience, been confronted by a chord or scale he didn't have right under his fingertips. Purvis Watson was the exception to the Boulevard rule: a young gospel-trained songwriter who'd sold a few songs but was still chasing his own record deal. Meanwhile, he paid the bills by bringing his unique style — gospel piano licks transplanted to the guitar — into the studios. She loved those soulful trills and hammered-on major arpeggios Purvis fed her. Between them he and Richard worked most of Boulevard's New York R&B dates, Richard's crisp chording blending perfectly with Purvis's lilting fills.

"Okay, guys," Adler told them. "Slow blues in C. One chorus instrumental, two verses, guitar solo — Richard, you take lead — third verse stop-time, last verse straight, and take the ending however you feel it. Just follow Venetia. Okay, let's hit it."

The red light went on. Venetia gave them a slow count of three, hit her first chords on four and the drummer brought the band in on one. She leaned into the mic to croon the first lines; she'd rear back before really letting her voice loose on the second verse. Richard took his solo: smooth, cool, deft lines flowing effortlessly from his fingers. The red light went out. Adler walked back out onto the studio floor.

"Sounding good," he told them, "but that solo ain't making it. Richard, you got it happening like Wes Montgomery or Kenny Burrell, but this needs to be... less jazz, more *blues*. Dirtier, more downhome. Like Albert King or BB or..."

He didn't want to say "like Venetia's daddy," but James 'Blue' Moon's name hung unspoken in the air. "Try it again. Purvis, you take the lead. Everybody else, do it just like you been doin' it."

They took it again: this time with Richard laying some sophisticated substitute chord inversions over the basic blues changes and Purvis dropping sweet melodic fills around Venetia's vocal before launching into the solo. Five bars in the red light went out again. "Take ten, folks," Adler told them. "I just had an idea. I'll be right back." He dived back into the control room, out of the studio and down the hall.

Seven minutes later he was back. Following him was a tall skinny white kid with long messy hair sticking up all round his head, wearing bright red jeans, green cowboy boots, a fringed buckskin vest and an awful lot of scarves. He was carrying a beat-up Fender Telecaster covered in stickers and paint, and he smelled of pot smoke and stale sweat. "This is Mick," Adler said. "He's from England." The kid smiled and muttered greetings in the general direction of everyone's knees. "He used to be in a very successful band called Bluebottle, and we got his new band Cabal cutting their first album down the hall. He's got about fifteen minutes while they fix the bass amp, so we're just gonna try something here." He turned to the band, sitting there on their folding chairs casting a sceptical eye over the newcomer. "Purvis, sit this one out and let Mick use your amp. Richard, stay with rhythm."

Purvis stood up, unplugged his guitar and offered Mick his cord. Mick nodded thanks, and plugged in a round grey metal box between his guitar and Purvis's Fender Twin. Venetia was wondering what in the name of Jesus this funny-looking white boy from England was gonna do that Richard and Purvis, two of New York's premier studio guys, couldn't. Eight bars in, she understood. The kid was playing the blues, and he sounded a lot like her daddy. Not *exactly* like her daddy — no-one could be that — but his playing had some of the same flavour, screamy and fuzzy and kind of too frantic as it was. It made her want to put a little more growl, a little more gut, into her voice.

Halfway through the second verse, Adler stopped the take and sent Purvis back in to replace Richard on rhythm guitar. His chords and fills locked in tight with her piano on this tune, just as Mick's solo lines, crackling and sputtering like a bare wire shooting off blue sparks, played tag with her voice. Mick was halfway through his solo when Adler stopped them again. "Mick? Turn the fuzzbox off and go straight into the amp. And don't try so hard. Relax a little. Just play every other note. Okay?"

And the third time was the charm. Everything fell right into place. Venetia felt Purvis practically climb inside her piano, they were so tight on the rhythms. And now he'd turned that fuzz-box off and stopped crowding too many notes into each lick, Mick was talking to her with his guitar, talking to her like her best girlfriend, *mm-hm, yeah I heard that, no shit?, you tell 'im girl...* She found herself changing the lyrics as she went, dropping the third verse, singing the fourth verse where the third one used to be, improvising a whole new last part.

"*I don't know what's happenin,*" she sang, "*but I'm'a figure it out somehow,*

"*Ye-ess, I don't know what's happenin' people, but I'm'a figure it out somehow,*

"*I don't know what's buggin' me, but you can call it the blues for now.*"

She and Mick hit the ending together, his guitar line climbing as her piano chords descended. On the last chord, he detuned his bottom E string by four semi-tones, the note diving down to a bowel-shaking low C which he vibratoed by pressing and releasing the string between the nut and tuners. Big Tee the drummer stomped on his kick-drum pedal for the last downbeat, simultaneously smashing out at his top cymbal one last time and then clamping it between his fingers to cut off the ring. There was a moment's silence. Then everybody said *yeah* and all *right*. Adler emerged from the control room grinning all over his beard. "I think we're about done here tonight, ladies and gentlemen," he said. "Y'all wanna hear that back?" Behind him, an amiable potato face fringed with blond hair poked around the door.

"Please mister," it said in a broad Liverpool accent. "Can Mick come out to play? We're just about ready next door."

Mick blinked a couple of times. "Coming, Si," he said. He gathered up his guitar and pedal, shook hands all round and scuttled out. Big Tee turned to Richard and Purvis, grinning evilly. "Hell of a thing when some white boy from England got to come in to show two niggaz how to play the blues," he said. "You muthafuckaz ain't *never* gonna live this down."

The engineer hit the playback button. The new song rolled out of the speakers. "We're gonna call that one Blues For Now," Adler announced. Venetia barely nodded. She seemed drained, miles away.

"Kid played good, didn't he?" Adler asked her.

"Yeah," she said absently. "He played good." She reached out for the last remaining barbecue rib.

And promptly forgot all about Mick Hudson for the next three years.

MIAMI POP FESTIVAL, 1971

When it rains in Miami it's like having a bottomless bucket of warm sweat perpetually dumping itself on your head. Venetia's limo finally bogged down a couple of hundred yards from the backstage area, forcing Venetia to squelch her way to her trailer, wrecking her shoes and depositing an inch or two of mud on the hems of her flared red pantsuit. It was the final day of the festival, and she was booked for a mid-afternoon 'special guest artist' slot. Her band had gotten in first thing that morning, and they were tuning up and shooting the breeze in the trailer next to hers. Her backup singers had a third one to themselves.

It was a good band, too. She'd even managed to get Big Tee to take a break from the studios to come out on the road with her, and she hoped the other guys never found out exactly how much more she was paying him than the rest of them were getting. He was worth it, though: he kicked so much ass that everybody in the band played their very best each night, and that raised her game as well. Right now Tee was leaning on the trailer smoking a joint with one hand and twirling his sticks in the air with the other.

"Hey, Princess," he said. "ready to get these soaking-wet muthafuck-az up off their asses?"

"Long as you ready to get me up off mine." He offered her the joint. She waved him no: the Princess of Soul wasn't going to smoke any pot in front of a bunch of raggedy hippies.

"Say," he said, pointing with his sticks. "Look'a there. See who that is?" He was pointing at a bunch of rock and roll looking guys chatting a few feet away. "The tall one. In the leather pants." She looked closer. Tall skinny guy, leather pants right enough, lacy white shirt, hair sticking up like a black pineapple on top and hanging down past his shoulders at the back. "That's Mick Hudson."

The name seemed familiar. "Mick Hudson?"

"Yeah. Got him a group called Cabal, headlined last night, tore this place *up*. Three gold albums. Not as big as Led Zeppelin or the Stones or The Who, but gettin' there."

"Yeah? So?"

Tee looked exasperated. "You *got* to remember him, Princess. That time in the studio in New York? We was making your second album? English kid, came in to play on Blues For Now when Richard and Purvis wasn't getting it? That was him."

Of course it was. Venetia recollected him now: stoned and shy and a little intimidated by Boulevard's studio A-team, but playing his ass off once he'd gotten over his nerves. "I got an idea," Tee said. "We gonna play Blues For Now today?" She hadn't considered it. They played it occasionally, and Venetia had insisted that every guitarist she hired for the road band, like this kid Jerry she had now, learn the solo off the record, but somehow it never came out quite the way she wanted it. "Here's the thing. I'm'a go say hi to the man, ask him if he feel like stepping up and playing the song with us today. If he say yeah, put it on the list. He gotta lotta fans here, give the show an extra kick."

"Go do it." She climbed into her trailer, watched from the window as Tee sauntered up to Hudson and his friends. She couldn't hear the conversation, but she could fill in all the *hey man, how you doin', remember me?, listen, how'd you like to...* jive for herself. She saw Hudson nodding enthusiastically and him and Tee giving each other a power shake. Her assistant Paulette had made sure that her sparkly stage dress was already neatly laid out for her, and she settled back on her chair so that Paulette could apply a last-minute touch-up to her hair and make-up.

The band hit the stage cooking with gas, stomping out a revved-up showtime intro before the backup girls shimmied out in their fringed red minidresses, shaking their tailfeathers and cooing truncated versions of a couple of current soul hits. Then Mack the tenor sax man intoned her intro, exhorting the crowd to put their hands together for the Princess of Soul. She stepped out and, give thanks and praise, before she'd even sung a note a few of the rain-soaked hippies were already up on their feet trying to dance in the mud. She grabbed her mic off its stand and belted out Givin' You Up For Lent, the lead single off her second album. Some of them were even shouting back the second line: *you can't even pay your rent.* Now there were more of them standing up, twitching like epileptics as the groove hit them. She had 'em. Settling back behind the piano as the bright shower of applause washed over her, she got down to work.

Half an hour later, she looked over into the wings. Her road manager was giving her a big okay sign, and she could see Hudson next to him, guitar in hand.

"All right!" she announced. "Ladies and gentlemen, we gonna do something a little bit special here for you today. We gonna bring on a very good friend of ours for this next song. Anybody here today ever hear of Mick... Hudson?" Huge affirmative roar. Looked like damn near everybody was standing up now. "A few years back, in New York City, we were cutting our second album, an album called *Ain't That A Good Thing,* which turned out very, very good for us. And we brought our friend in to play some git-tar..." — she pronounced it the old Southern way — "... on a song called Blues For Now. He's gonna come out and join us on that song right now, so please let me hear you give a warm Miami welcome for Mister! Mick! Hudson!"

Bedlam. Hudson strode purposefully to the borrowed amp set up next to the piano and plugged in his Telecaster. For the first time, he raised his eyes and stared directly at her, a faint smile on his pale stubbled face. He don't seem shy no more, thought Venetia as she counted the song in. She hadn't even reached 'three' when Hudson laid into his guitar, a mean snaky line reaching out to meet her piano intro. He wandered forward as he played, not upstaging her but coming close enough to share her spotlight. The song was catching fire under her and

Hudson's guitar was stoking the flames. His playing had changed since they'd originally cut the tune: now he sounded more like her daddy and at the same time more different, more like himself. His solo reached its climax but instead of heading into the stop-time third verse like on the record and like they usually did, she signalled to Tee to keep the groove in the pocket and she played a piano solo she'd never played before, low rumbling runs on the left of the keyboard like she was reaching right through the keys and messing with the piano's insides, high tinkling slurs up on the right.

She looked up at him. His eyes were squeezed tight shut, and his mouth was wide open in an ecstatic grin. Big Tee slammed the band into the stop-time sequence, but instead of her voice singing the third verse, Hudson was there with an impossibly high-bent note. He didn't resolve it, just kept worrying away at that same note, giving it more and more quiver each time until the tension stretched to busting point. She'd never heard Tee play like that, and the whole band was with him. She was standing up at the piano now, longing to grab the mic from its stand, walk out from behind the piano and *move*, but the song needed the piano, so she had to just stand there and shake it in one spot. She was singing the last verse now, and Hudson was kneeling down in front of her, rearing back and forth, grinning all up in her face and lashing at his guitar. He scrambled to his feet for the ending, detuning the guitar way past low C until the string was too slack to sound. He tossed his guitar in the air, caught it deftly, waved it at the crowd and ambled off back into the wings.

Venetia wanted to follow him right there and then, but she had five songs left to play. She beckoned her road manager, mouthed *tell him not to leave* and then suddenly remembered that she was in the middle of playing a show to the second-biggest crowd she'd ever faced in her life. Sometime during the set the rain had stopped and the sunshine was already starting to dry the crowd out. Waterproofs and ponchos were discarded. The kids stayed on their feet. By the time she took it home they were shouting *nee-sha nee-sha nee-sha*, and it took three encores before they'd let her out of there. There was a guy from Boulevard waiting in the wings to tell her how she'd got herself a whole new market now and did she realise how many albums she was gonna sell to white kids who'd never bought her records before, but she practically trampled him trying to get back to the trailers and see if Mick was still there.

He wasn't. But he'd left a scribbled note with her road manager to say what a gas it was to play with her again, how he was a huge fan of her music, how her daddy was his favourite musician and how he'd played with Blue back in England when he was starting out. And how he'd be in the bar at their hotel around seven-thirty and he'd love to meet up with her for a drink with her when she got back.

Eight o'clock she was showered and dressed and strolling into the bar. Sure enough, there he was, chitchatting over beers with a couple of guys from his band and a few fans and a big blond guy called Simon. Soon as he saw her, he made his excuses and came over to her. Next thing she knew, she was rubbing a pinch of the material of his shirt between her forefinger and thumb. Next thing she knew after that, they'd disappeared into his suite with a bag of weed, a wrap of coke and three bottles of Jack Daniel's. Soon as they got in there they closed all the curtains. Nobody who didn't work for room service saw hide nor hair of either them for the next day and a half.

They talked some too, just chitchat about record companies and people in the business they both knew. He wanted to talk about her daddy, but she steered the conversation away whenever he tried to go there, and he wasn't difficult to distract. He said he had a girlfriend back in England, but that things weren't too good between them. Later, what she remembered best was rocking above him, listening to him holler her name, as she gazed down at his half-closed eyes and that pale heaving skinny-rib chest, irregularly tufted with black hair. And he remembered her nipples, thick purple thimbles on her brown chest, the way she wordlessly sang and hummed deep down low as she straddled him, her knotted navel popping in and out and what looked like a bowling ball rolling up and down her broad gleaming stomach, and every time it rolled all the way down to where their bodies joined, her inner muscles sucked at him hungrily and red balloons burst behind his eyes.

SIX

"So she's like, 'he did *not* say that!, and I'm all, 'you *wish!*' and..."

Donna was on the phone, with the TV on. Adrienne couldn't figure it out. She sees her friends all day at school, then she gets home and spends the whole evening talking to them some more. She called Donna again, louder this time.

"Hold on... I'm on the phone!"

"Your father and I need to talk to you."

"I'm talking to Debbie!"

"Donna, it's important."

"So's this!"

"*Now!*"

"Gaaaaaaaaaad... Debbie, listen, I got to go." She mooched out into the hall in her tight little top and big droopy jeans, saw her mama waiting for her. Adrienne led her into the music room. Blue was sitting there in his wheelchair. "C'mere, honey," he said, spreading his arms. She went to him, and he enfolded her in a warm hug, kissing her forehead and the top of her head.

"Listen up," he said. "We're gonna have to talk some serious grown-up shit now, sweetie-pie. You ready for that?"

He didn't sound like he was mad at her, and his voice was soft and reassuring. But just the same she had such a not-good feeling. Her mama had this tight look on her face, not like she was angry, but like she was very sad, more sad than she could handle, and she was trying not to let it show. This was scary, like in the movies, but this wasn't the movies. She nodded silently. "Sit down here by me," he said. She curled up on the floor next to his wheelchair, holding tightly onto his thin dry hand. Adrienne moved closer, sat down on Donna's other side, her arm curled protectively around Donna's shoulders. Donna rested her head on her father's knees, closed her eyes, hoping that if she could go to sleep here she'd be safe, and whatever was making Mama and Daddy so sad and worried would be gone when she woke up.

"Nuh-uh. Open up those sweet brown eyes and look at me, pun'kin." Donna raised her head and stared at him, but now there was anger on her face.

"I'm not a baby," she said evenly. "I'm fourteen years old, and I want you to stop treating me like I'm still a child!" She started to pull away but Blue and Adrienne held onto her.

"Okay, Donna," Blue said. "I'm'a give it you straight. You know I'm pretty old, right? Pretty well up in years. Most of your friends at school, I'm old enough to be grandaddy to their *parents*. And you know I ain't been too well these past months. Here's the thing, sweetie. The doctors tell me I got cancer, and it ain't gonna go away. I'm gonna try to be around for your fifteenth birthday but..." he bent down and kissed her gently once again on the top of her head "... I can't guarantee that."

This time Donna did manage to haul herself free. She scrambled to her feet. "You're *dying*?" Blue grimaced.

"Yes, honey. I'm dyin'." Donna had gone pale beneath her milky-coffee skin.

"How long have you known?"

"Coupl'a months."

"Does Josh know?"

"Yeah, Josh knows."

"You told Josh and you didn't tell me?"

"Josh is older, honey."

Donna turned on her heel and ran for the door. She slammed it behind her. "I hate you! I hate you both!" she screamed, and then they heard the door to her room slam as well.

"That went well," Adrienne said. Even through two closed doors, they could hear Donna crying, huge deep wracking sobs that sounded like someone being torn apart. Adrienne rose to follow her, but Blue raised his hand to forestall her. They sat and waited. Within five minutes Donna had quietened. Within another two they heard her bedroom door open. Then she was back in the room, holding on to them both with all her strength, her tearstained face buried in Blue's shoulder. "I don't want you to die, Daddy," she snuffled.

"I don't want me to die either, pun'kin," Blue murmured into her neck, "but I don't know that I got a whole lot'a choice in the matter." He clasped her closer, rubbed her back in slow circles. "When you were born, honey, I was just a young kid of sixty-nine. Some folks said your mama and me didn't have no business havin' a baby when there weren't no guarantee I'd be around long enough to see you grow up. Said it was *selfish*. Said we'd be puttin' our needs ahead'a yours. And, I got to admit, your mama and me, we *talked* about all'a that. Thought about it long and *hard*. But we wanted you more than anything, and we was so happy when you arrived.

"I always knew I wasn't gonna have as much time with you as I wanted. But I was glad of all the time I've had with you bein' my daughter, and however much time we got now I know I'm gonna be glad of that too. Just like I been glad of every moment I've had with your mama, even when she been mad wit' me, and how I'm gonna be glad of all of the rest of the time I'm gonna have with her. I'm a very *lucky* old man, and I love the both of you very, very much.

"Wherever I'm'a go when I die, I'm gonna miss both y'all *so much...*"

His voice caught on the last few words. His eyes were brimming. Adrienne let out a long shaky breath and allowed her face to crumple. She shifted closer to Donna so she could reach up and put her other arm around Blue. As the sun sank in the sky and the room darkened, the three of them clung onto each other and cried themselves dry.

"... it's a real thrill and a great honour to be working with both of you," Jeff Ansell announced, beaming, "because I've been a huge, huge fan of both your work since I was just a little kid. Venetia, this is Mick Hudson. Mick, this is..."

"This is Ms Moon," Venetia said icily, in the guttiest and most resonant tone she could muster. Christ, thought Hudson, she sounds like *The Exorcist*. No, that wasn't quite fair. Maybe Darth Vader. He'd seen photos over the years and occasionally caught her on TV, but he wasn't ready for just how big she'd got. Not blimpy, though. More like a tank.

"It's a pleasure," he said, extending his hand, then dropping it after Venetia's expression made it clear she was prepared to carry on ignoring it for as long as she was forced to remain in his presence. Ansell beckoned to a hovering photographer. "Now we just need a couple of pictures..."

A couple of pictures was all the photographer got. One showed Venetia staring straight ahead, a fixed smile stitched to the lower half of her face and her eyes boiling. Hudson is also smiling at the camera, but his eyes are flicked over towards Venetia. The other was much the same except that, in between them, one arm flung over Hudson's narrow shoulders and the other curled around Venetia's substantial waist, was Jeff Ansell, grinning like an ape.

As soon as Ansell and the photographer were a few paces away, Hudson swallowed hard and mentally crossed his fingers. He said, "Nee-sha..."

She turned her back on him.

"I need to talk to you."

Still with her back turned, she said stonily, "You got nothing to say I want to hear."

"That's probably true... but this is something you *need* to hear." A pause. "It's Blue. He's got cancer. He's dying." He waited for a reaction, but she didn't reply, or turn to face him.

But at least she hadn't walked away. "He's got less than a year, the docs say. He's making one more record, and he wants you to sing with him."

Venetia stiffened. She turned around, and looked him in the eyes. "If you or my father have a business proposition for me, you should approach me via the appropriate channels. Have your representatives or my father's contact my office." Then she marched away, moving across the studio floor like a galleon in full sail, straight towards Jeff Ansell. Yeah, right, Hudson thought, *that went well.*

BERKSHIRE, ENGLAND, 1973

In England, back in the sixties, they used to call it 'the rockbroker belt,' a swathe of the southern counties, like Surrey, Berkshire and Kent, within an hour or so's drive of Central London where the prosperous stockbrokers who lived there were joined by rock stars desirous of sinking some of their loot into bricks, mortar and gracious living. Mick Hudson had joined the influx in 1970 when his manager, Henry Mac-Shane, had finally prised a royalty cheque out of Boulevard Records after Cabal had their first real success. He'd bought a generously-acred Victorian pile in the Berkshire countryside, less than twenty miles and almost three-quarters of a million pounds from the dowdy suburban street where he'd grown up.

Jocasta had been back from the hospital for six days. In that time she had spoken maybe six words. The baby had arrived seven weeks early. It had been a long and difficult birth culminating in a caesarian, and Laurence Oliver Hudson had survived outside his mother's womb for precisely two hours and seventeen minutes before being declared legally dead. Now they sat in semi-darkness on opposite sides of the huge living room, amidst the overflowing ashtrays, empty bottles and stacks of crusted crockery. Outside the sun was blazing, but the curtains were drawn and only occasional table-lamps, covered with Indian shawls, provided lonely islands of light. Since they'd moved in, the room, like much of the rest of the house, had been occupied but never decorated. It was still furnished in the overstuffed, faded, ancient plush stuff inherited from the equally faded minor aristos whose grip on their family pile had steadily weakened for generations until they'd finally been forced to sell to this nouveau-riche oik.

One end of the room was dominated by artefacts of Hudson's success: gold and silver discs, concert posters and framed press clippings hung on the oak-panelled walls, huddling for warmth around a poster of Hudson, framed against an implausibly blue sky behind the mic at some open-air festival or other, black hair whipping around his face and the shoulders of his tie-dyed shirt, brandishing a white Gibson Flying V instead of his usual Telecaster. The other was a shrine to Jocasta's now-defunct modelling career: spreads and covers from *Vogue* and *Harpers* and *Elle*, dominated by the famous poster from the swimsuit campaign, a staple of male teenage bedroom walls, Jocasta Meadowes on a Bahamian beach in a bikini with a sarong knotted carelessly around her hips, all streaky blonde hair and big turquoise eyes and flashing teeth, the focus so crisp you could see the dusting of golden down glinting on her tanned belly and arms.

The two iconic images faced each other through stale, dusty air. Clouds of smoke hung suspended and unmoving like unanswered questions. The real-life present-day Hudson and Jocasta weren't facing each other: they were both lost in private worlds of fogged-in hurt. Hudson was slouched in his armchair, hugging his beloved Martin D-28 acoustic guitar. On the coffee table beside him was a spiral-bound notebook, a biro and a small Philips cassette recorder, microphone stretching invitingly towards him on the end of its cord, ready to capture any riff or melody he might want to commit to tape. Also on the table were a tumbler of Jack Daniel's, a thick joint of Jamaican grass precariously balanced atop a mountain of butts in an ashtray, a pack of Marlboros, a plastic lighter, a rolled-up £10 note and a smeared mirror. Resting on the mirror was what might have looked from a distance like an untipped cigarette, but was actually a substantial line of cocaine.

Jocasta was curled up on her own chair, her back to Hudson. On her table was a brandy snifter, a bottle of Courvoisier, a plastic bottle of painkillers, a pack of mentholated Peter Stuyvesant. She was staring at the mirror in her hand. Her reflection stared back at her from between two lines of heroin, running from the top of the mirror to the bottom like prison bars.

By their own wish, they were alone in the mansion. They'd had lots of offers of company. Jocasta's sister and her old pals from the fashion scene, Mick's bandmates, Henry MacShane and his tour manager Simon Wolfe, even their parents, had all offered to stay and look after them, but they'd been monosyllabically rebuffed. The housekeeper and gardener had been told to stay home on full pay. The silence was absolute. Occasionally Hudson would pick absently at his guitar, but fall quiet again after a few tentative notes or chords.

Far away, at the outer fringes of Hudson's consciousness, a telephone started to ring. It was all the way across the room by the window. Answer it? Not answer it? Did it fucking matter whether he answered it or not? Jocasta hadn't budged, but then she hadn't moved for hours. Maybe it was Jo's sister, or Henry or Simon or one of the lads. He'd better answer or someone'd think they were both passed out in a coma or dead, and be round kicking the bloody doors down. Setting the guitar down, he hauled himself to his feet and stumbled off on the long trek to the ringing phone.

"Hello?"

The humming of a transatlantic line. Then...

"Mick?"

"Who's that?"

"Mick, it's Neesha."

Hudson wished he was still back in his chair, listening to the phone ring until it eventually stopped. All in all, he'd've been better off with Simon and a bunch of sweaty roadies battering at the doors. At least he could have given them a drink and a smoke, told 'em he and Jo were okay and sent 'em off home again.

"Neesha," he said tiredly. "Hold on a sec, I'm gonna move to the upstairs phone." He set the receiver down on the table. "Just taking this one in the bedroom," he called to Jocasta. She showed no signs of having heard him. He crossed the room to her, kissed her gently on top of her unresponsive head, and climbed the winding staircase to their bedroom. Settling down on the four-poster where Laurence Oliver Hudson had been conceived, he bawled down the stairs, "Okay, you can hang up now," but there was no response from downstairs and no reassuring click on the line.

His affair with Venetia had petered out almost as soon as it had begun. For a start, they were both almost always in the studio or on tour. Sometimes he'd be in Chicago to play, but then she'd be touring in Japan. She'd be working in Europe, but he'd be recording in LA. Once they'd found themselves on the same bill again and he'd gotten up on stage to recreate their Miami jam on Blues For Now, but the music hadn't caught fire and, in their hotel afterwards, neither had the sex. A chance encounter at Chicago's O'Hare airport had led to a frantic coupling in the restroom of the first-class lounge, but that had been pretty much the final spark of the conflagration which had engulfed them in Miami. They'd had no contact for almost six months. During that time, he thought of her sometimes while he and Jocasta were making love, sometimes while he was improvising blues on his guitar, and most often while he was singing. After playing with Venetia in Miami, standing just a few feet away from her and watching her sing, he'd started wanting to do that himself, to sing with his own body and his own voice instead of just through his instrument. And after Jack Ferris, the singer he'd picked for the new band he formed after Cabal broke up, had stormed out halfway through the second week of rehearsals because he was uncomfortable with some of Hudson's new songs, it had seemed only natural that he should take the mic himself.

But he hadn't thought about her, not really, for months. And now she was on the phone, calling not just from another country but from another universe. Hudson's world had shrunk to a clenched core of himself and Jocasta and the inescapable presence of the absence of Laurence Oliver Hudson, whose entire life had been shorter than some of his father's concerts.

"I'm here," he said into the phone, wondering if he really was. He heard her take a breath.

"Mick, how you been?"

How'd he been? He could think of a dozen ways to answer that question, and none. How'd he been? How'd he been what? He didn't even know if the person Neesha thought she was talking to still existed.

"Neesha, I..."

"Mick, are you all right? You high?"

"Neesha, I..." What was the next word? What could he say to her? What could he say to anyone? "I really can't talk right now."

"Baby, we *got* to talk. I've got something wonderful to tell you."

"I really can't talk right now," he repeated mechanically. He'd learned how to say that. He could keep saying it until she went away.

"Mick. Listen. This is important. This is real."

If he took what she was saying and broke it down, he could understand each individual word. But when he tried to put them together and make sense of the whole thing, he was unable to translate it into anything he could comprehend. What could be 'important' or 'real' to him now?

"Neesha..."

"I'm pregnant," she interrupted him. "We're having a baby."

All he could think of was that he'd left his cigarettes downstairs, reflexively fumbling for Marlboros and lighter in the pocket of a jacket he wasn't even wearing. 'Pregnant' and 'baby' seemed like words from a foreign language. They were similar to words in his own language, but they couldn't possibly mean the same things. 'Pregnant' was the haggard, bony, near-mute woman downstairs, rolled up on a chair in unconscious mimicry of the foetus she no longer carried. And 'baby' could only mean Laurence Oliver Hudson, born at 11:05am on September 15, 1973; died at 13:23pm on the same day.

She was still talking. "I need you over here. With me. Now."

He forced himself to form words. "Neesha... I can't."

"Is it because of what's-her-name? I thought you were breaking up."

"We... were. But she was pregnant." The word felt weird in his mouth. "We lost the baby last week."

"Honey, you've got a baby. Or you will have in four months. I need you. *We're* gonna need you."

Hudson's mouth was dry. His head ached. Icy steel fingers were squeezing his heart. He could hardly breathe. There was a glass of water on his bedside table. How long had it been there? Long enough for a coating of dust to have formed on its surface. Gratefully, he gulped it down anyway.

"Neesha, I've got to stay with Jocasta," he said eventually, feeling his way one word at a time. "At least for now. She's in really, really bad shape. If I walk now it'll finish her. I've got to stay and take care of her...

at least until she's strong enough to leave me."

When Venetia spoke again her voice was low and dangerous. "You mean you don't want to be havin' no baby with no *nigga*. Is that *it*?"

"Of course that isn't it!" The sting of her accusation was cutting through his numb torpor. "It's Jo... some things you can't just turn around walk away from."

"You can walk away from me though, can't you, you limp-dick racist limey shit!"

"Neesha... listen to me," he whispered into the phone. "Are you... absolutely sure you want to have this baby?"

She was yelling now. Even with the phone held a foot from his ear he could still hear every razor-edged word. "So all you can say is that you want to send your nigga whore away to have an abortion so you can stay in your fuckin' castle in England. That's how little I matter to you? That's how little this *black* child I'm carryin' matters to your skinny white rock-star ass!"

"Neesha..."

"I'm a Christian! I believe abortion is murder, and murder is a sin. And you want me to commit a sin and murder our baby so you can stay nice'n safe with your skinny blonde bitch!"

"Neesha... please listen to me. I'm not..."

"Okay, I'm going to give you exactly what you want. Never speak to me again. Never come anywhere near me or my child. And, in case you're worried, I don't want any goddam money from you. I got plenty money of my own. And you know what? My child is gonna be better off with no father at all than with a treacherous, gutless, racist bastard like you."

Hudson was crying now, the first tears he'd shed since he said his farewells to Laurence Oliver Hudson. "Neesha, *please*...!"

"That child is never gonna know who its father is if I can help it. I ain't gonna tell *no*body, *never*. I won't even tell my daddy, so you and him can carry on being big fuckin' pals. And if you ever grow enough balls to tell him — *which! I! doubt!* — then you an' him'll have something to bond over. He know a thing or two his own self about leavin' a woman and child don't suit his plans."

In Chicago, the phone slammed down onto the hook. In his silent mansion, Hudson wiped his eyes, blew his nose. He'd lost two babies inside little more than a week, and one of them hadn't even been born yet. He wandered numbly back downstairs to the living-room, replaced the telephone receiver still lying on the table, relit his joint. Had Jocasta been listening? She still didn't look like she'd moved an inch since he went upstairs, but one of the lines of heroin on her mirror had disappeared. She showed not even a flicker of reaction when he bent down, put his arm around her hunched shoulders and kissed her gently on the cheek.

Mick Hudson and Jocasta Meadowes's relationship didn't survive the death of Laurence Oliver Hudson by much more than a year. They broke up in late 1974. Much later Jocasta married Mick's former roadie, Simon Wolfe, and helped him establish his fledgling management business in Los Angeles. Hudson's roadies noted that, as the seventies wore on, the groupies he chose after the show were, more often than not, black. And on the groupie circuit where the girls themselves compared notes on their conquests, it was observed that what Mick Hudson most liked to do in bed was lie back and look up at his chosen girl while she straddled him and flexed her stomach muscles until he came.

And when, in the early nineties, Calvin Holland got into the music business and started making records, Hudson collected them all.

Donna and Blue had both gone to bed. Adrienne was dozing on the sofa, the TV murmuring reassuringly out on the furthest fringes of her consciousness, when the phone rang. She picked it up.

A small voice said, "This is Neesha. Can I talk to my daddy?"

SEVEN

The morning after the climax of Lock N Load Productions Inc's celebration of the tenth anniversary of its relocation from Chicago to LA, its CEO, Calvin Holland, awoke to an overwhelming sense of absence. Specifically, a sense of the loss of a dream. Some nights Calvin experienced rich and complex dreams and returned to the waking world with a clear recollection of his dream or, at the very least, retaining from it one powerful clear-cut piece of imagery to guide him through his day. Other nights his sleep was entirely dreamless, and after such nights he generally awoke rested and refreshed.

But sometimes, once awake and back in his body, he would know, with absolute certainty, that he had been dreaming, but find himself unable to recall even the smallest detail of where his spirit had been and what it had experienced. On such mornings it would sometimes take him most of the day to shake the nagging sensation of disquiet and unease that these missing dreams invariably left behind. This was one of those mornings.

Located specifically in time and space, Calvin found himself, at 7:27am on a Friday morning, in bed in his home in Bel Air, purchased eight months earlier for five million dollars to celebrate the stock-market flotation of the Fully Loaded clothing line he'd spun off from Lock N Load Productions. He'd been making crazy green for years, first from rapping and then from production, but it was the clothes which had put him over the top. He was the third generation of his family to make it in the music business, but neither his mother nor his grandfather had gone over big like he had. James 'Blue' Moon was comfortable, though he'd already been an old man by the time he'd gotten there and he'd needed a white guy to step in and run his business before he got his payday. Venetia Moon was a legend who'd sold millions of records and played just about every major concert hall in the world, including Russia and China, but she'd never made the mainstream rich lists. Her sometime husband, Swiss banker Dieter Mannheim, had, however, occasionally showed up in the lower rungs of some European tallies. Venetia's company, formed to deal exclusively with her own career, did little more than tick over while it picked up and invested her royalties, touring money and endorsement fees.

But Calvin, now... with his thirty-fifth birthday still almost a year away, Calvin had gotten all the way over. After a few quick hits rapping as Ice Blue, he'd realised that his true gift didn't lie in performing, like his moms and grandaddy, but in the studio. Which was why he'd set up Lock N Load, producing and remixing for rappers and R&B singers alike. He'd also discovered that he could spot talent, read markets and cut deals. Soon Lock N Load had become a record label and a management operation as well as a production company, and it was a rare week when the charts didn't contain at least half a dozen artists produced, remixed or managed by Calvin Holland. Calvin even had a rock subsidiary, called Rock N Road, with five white guitar bands on its books, one of 'em well on the way to its first platinum album. He hadn't bothered cutting a record on himself for five years now. Hadn't needed to. Or even wanted to.

Right now, lying in soft darkness behind his heavy white curtains, Calvin had to deal with two major problems. The first was a recent Lock N Load signing, a Jamaican ragga duo called Screwdriver and Omega Man. Calvin was convinced that they were the ragga act to go pop nationwide and break the music out of its local strongholds like Miami and New York. Their first album was ready to go: Calvin had cut seven new tracks on them and remixed his choice of their biggest Jamaican hits. So far, cool runnin's.

But then they'd cut a new Jamaican single, Battyman 9/11, which gleefully fantasised that the World Trade Center had been exclusively populated by gay men and lesbians when it was destroyed. The record was a smash in Jamaica, all over the clubs in London, busting out in Miami and New York and showing up heavy in the download charts. Screwdriver and Omega Man were insisting that Calvin add the track to the US release of their album. Gay activists in London were already protesting, demanding — and getting — the withdrawal of the duo's nominations for an important music biz awards ceremony. Some other ragga guys who'd cut songs celebrating anti-gay violence were getting important shows and tours pulled out from underneath them. Calvin needed to break these guys mainstream, which meant he couldn't risk anything like that coming down down around Screwdriver and Omega Man. Wal-Mart and the other major retail chains had to stock the album if it was going to stand a chance of selling like he needed it to sell. And there was no way in hell that was going to happen with Battyman

9/11 on the album. Not that the retailers gave a fuck about gays or their rights or their feelings, but shit, dog, no-one was gonna make light of 9/11 on any record sold in their stores.

So Calvin was gonna have to tell Screwdriver and Omega Man that the track wasn't gonna be on their album. That meant getting called a sell-out and accused of censorship, plus risking the Jamaicans telling everyone that he must be a battyman himself. Which he seriously didn't want. In the hip-hop world which was still his home base despite all his pop success, 'faggot' and 'cocksucker' were such common insults that their use barely qualified for comment anymore. A long time ago, Ice-T may have rapped, *"I'm straight, you're gay/muthafucka, have it your way"*, but the community still wasn't noted for its openmindedness on what his therapist called gender issues.

Another reason Calvin didn't need no weedhead Jamaicans calling him a battyman was because he was one. Some of the time, anyway. He was genuinely attracted to women, and the stunning semi-famous whatever-girls on his arm whenever he attended some industry function or other were genuine girlfriends, albeit highly temporary. But he was turned on by boys, too, and once in a while some big-eyed gym rat who could sing or rhyme gave him an itch that needed scratching. And scratching that itch was something he did very discreetly indeed and never with one of his artists, though he'd come dangerously close more than a couple of times. As far as the world was concerned, Calvin Holland was a high-living babe magnet, and as far as the world was concerned, that was how it was gonna stay.

Which brought him to his second problem of the day: someone was snoring lightly next to him in bed. He reached over and explored. His questing hand fell on a firm round shoulder, and his heart skipped a beat. Wandering further, his fingers found an equally firm and equally round breast topped with a thick, erect nipple. He let out an explosive sigh of relief, threw back the covers and clambered out of bed to make some coffee.

Hudson could hear the piano music even before he knocked on the door of Blue's music room. Something classical he didn't recognise. Blue was in his wheelchair, watching the score to the music unreel on the computer monitor on the counter in front of him. He was wearing his glasses, which he did but rarely. He heard Hudson enter and swivelled round to face him. "Mozart," he said. "Fantasia in D Minor." He held up a finger for silence. Hudson dropped into an armchair, closed his eyes until the piece finished and the last elegant notes faded away. Blue tapped a key and the score disappeared from his monitor.

"I didn't know you read music," Hudson said

"Only a little bit," Blue said, "not enough to hurt my playin'." It was a jazzman's joke so old its whiskers were white, but Hudson chuckled anyway.

"Should've guessed, though. After that night at Duke's."

"See, the thing with Mozart," Blue said, like he hadn't heard, "was that he was like a jazz cat, liked to improvise. What I heard, he used to throw dice, and he assigned musical values to the numbers on the dice, so he'd roll 'em a few times and start playin' somethin' based on the sequence he'd thrown. Then if he liked what he'd come up with, he'd maybe write it down and start composin' on it. Did a bunch'a these, but that one's my favourite."

"The thing I could never handle about classical music," Hudson said, "was that all the great composers were simply cranking out what aristocrats and kings and rich guys in wigs wanted to hear, stuff they were willing to pay for. Like if every musician working now needed to please George W. Bush or the ghost of fucking Nixon or someone. I've never worked for the Man, and I never wanted to listen to anyone who did."

"Young man, I can't believe you got to the age you done got to and still be foolin' yourself that way. We *all* workin' for the Man, one way or 'nother, and don't you be kiddin' yourself that don't include you. You spent your whole life recordin' for big companies affiliated with multinational organisations that make bombs, that build chemical plants kill poor people in India, drive up the debts in Africa... all musicians like you and me can do is to do the best work we can, get it out to the people, hope we usin' the companies more than they usin' us.

"An' you wrong about Mozart. He didn't always do what the ol'massas in the wigs told him to. One time he got physically thrown outdoors 'cause he wouldn't play what the Archbishop of Salzburg wanted.

"Salzburg," he added. "That's in Austria."

"I know," Hudson told him. "Played there." He wandered down the line of amplifiers until he came to his old Marshall. He pressed the clunky old power switch, watched it turn red, leaving the amp on 'standby,' to let the ancient valves warm up. A faint acrid smell seeped into the room as the thin coating of dust on the valves began to burn off. Blue grinned. "Ain't ever used that big boy there. Never even switched it on. Too loud for this house. And the house before this one."

"So why'd'you keep it?"

"Souvenir."

"Souvenir of what?"

"That night at Duke's."

"Oh, man," Hudson said. "You taught me a load of real Zen lessons that night. After that I realised how much music I still didn't know. Got some lessons, bought some theory books, brushed up on my jazz chords. Plus I made up my mind never to get seriously fucked up before playing, though it took me a while to start putting that into practice. " He picked up his guitar, noodled a few chords, put it down again. "Yeah, you taught me a lot that night. The old Zen whack on the head from the master." He stood up and executed an elaborate kung fu bow, fist in palm.

Blue's grin got even broader. "Young man, I wasn't tryin' to teach you no Zen nuthin'. I was just fuckin' witcha 'cause I was pissed off about the way things'd gone down at the International Auditorium."

A pause, almost imperceptible, unless you were looking. And Blue was.

"Ahhh... *Master*. Your immaculate wisdom continues to enlighten this humble grasshopper." Hudson bowed again, then sat down. "Okay... so. Any word from the hospital about the results from your tests?"

Blue shrugged. "Still got cancer. Still dyin'. They say it's still spreadin' on me, though the spreadin's slowed down some. Meanin' I ain't gettin' any better, but I'm gettin' worse a little slower than they expected. Meantime, every day I'm in a little more pain, every day it gets harder and harder to hold food down, every day I feel more and more tired and every day I spend more time asleep." He looked up at Hudson, took his glasses off to polish them on his sweatshirt. "And they don't think it's a good idea for me to be on my own in the house. So Adrienne and Simon done fixed me up with a nurse gonna be comin' in daytimes while Donna's in school and Adrienne's at work. She wanted to close the business or let her manager take care a'things, but I reckon it's good for her to keep goin'. Just like I'm tryin' to keep goin.'" He put his glasses back on. "How you been doin' with your live album?"

"Not bad. We've gone through all the tapes and chosen the best ones.

Now we got to mix 'em and start patching things up."

"You got a lot of that to do?"

"Surprisingly little, actually. Some of those shows were a lot better than I remember. Didn't fall over, didn't drop the guitar, only forgot one lyric... forgot the third verse, sang the second one again. Broke a string once, coupla solos could've been better, but..."

"See, you done learned some stuff over all those years you been doin' it. Way I see it, I still make as many mistakes as I ever did, but the older you get the better you get at coverin' 'em up. How about your girls? You gonna fly 'em in?"

Hudson shifted uncomfortably in his chair. "Spoke to 'em night before last. Their mum's taking them to the Bahamas next week."

"So you ain't gonna see 'em for a while?" Hudson busied himself unlatching his guitar case and fixing a strap onto his Telecaster. "Doesn't look like it," he replied. Blue shook his head disapprovingly. "There is gonna come a day, young man, when you gonna wish you'd spent a lot more time with those girls. The time you losin' now is time you ain't gonna get back.

"See, since ol' Mister Cancer put me under house arrest, I been doin' a lot of thinkin'." He raised one hand, let it fall back onto his skinny thigh. "Ain't had the strength to do much else. Been thinkin' about a lotta things, putting a few two an' twos together..." He seemed lost in thought for a moment, then came back to himself. He slapped his palms down onto his thighs.

"Neesha called me last night," he said.

Hudson, giving nothing away. "What'd she say?"

"Not much. But she's comin' to see me tomorrow night. Now... she don't want to see *you*, an' Adrienne don't wanna see *her*, so tomorrow night I'm stayin' in with Donna and the nurse, and you two kids are goin' out to dinner. The Mirabelle, on my tab.

"By the way... that was a hell of a stunt you pulled, doin' that commercial with her. How'd you get that one together?"

Hudson grinned. "That was all down to Henry. First he got someone in the office to check out what Venetia was doing in LA and found out she was working on this commercial. Seems we'd already been approached by the cola people and Henry was just about to turn 'em down the way he usually does. Surprised the hell out of him when I told him to say yes this time. 'Oh, by the way, who's already signed up?' 'Venetia

Moon.' 'Oh, *really?*'" Both men burst out laughing, Blue clutching his ribs in not entirely feigned pain. His laugh turned into a splutter and a brief fit of coughing. Hudson ripped a kleenex from the box on the counter, handed it to Blue and put his arm around the old man's shoulders until the coughing subsided. Blue wiped his mouth and sipped at a glass of water.

"Got to say though, young man... a cola commercial? Your fans might not like that too much."

Hudson shrugged. "I'll live it down. One of the nice things about getting older is that some days you just don't *give* a fuck. Most of 'em won't see it, anyway. It's only going out in Asia. Plus I'm not keeping the money. It's going to charity. Half to cancer research. And the other half towards setting up a James Blue Moon Foundation for blues education in schools." Blue didn't move. He seemed lost in thought. Finally he looked up. It may just have been a trick of the light, but it looked like his eyes were watering behind his spectacles.

"That's nice," he said at length. "I thank you for that, young man." Hudson plugged his guitar into the tiny old Fender Deluxe amp and checked his tuning. "You feel up to doing some work?" he asked Blue.

Blue rolled over to his guitars, selected his rubbed-raw Jazzmaster. "You got anything particular in mind?" Hudson plugged Blue into the amp next to his, adjusted the controls. "Play something," he said. Blue played a couple of runs on his low strings. "Too loud," he said, "Turn me down a touch. Little more high end." Hudson fiddled with the amp some more, sat back down once Blue was satisfied with his sound.

"Okay," he said. "I remember you telling me about seeing Robert Johnson playing on the street in Clarksdale when you were just a kid. You said you remember him playing Hellhound On My Trail and I thought maybe we could..." He broke off as he saw the expression on Blue's face.

"Oh, *man!*" Blue sounded really irritated. "That what you want to do?" He put his guitar back in its stand. "Robert, Robert, Robert, always Robert. I got to tell you, young man. Most of us blues singers who're still around get sick and tired'a *talkin'* about Robert Johnson or even *hearin'* 'bout Robert Johnson. Seems like lots of folks believe Robert was the onliest blues singer ever lived. Man been dead since 1938 and we all still hearin' about him." He took another sip of water. "'Mr Moon, Mr Moon,'" he said in a high-pitched voice. "'Mr Moon, is it true you saw Robert when you was a kid?' Sometimes I wish I'd never told no-one about that, because it's the first goddam thing any reporter ever ask me." He sighed. "I don't wanna do none'a Robert's songs. And I most specially ain't gonna do no Hellhound On My Trail. That's a bad song."

Hudson looked surprised. "It's a *great* song."

"Yeah, you right, it's a great song. But bad things go with it. You notice a lotta singers do a lotta Robert's songs. Now most of 'em you *can* play. But a few of them songs'a Robert's got badness around 'em, and the guys who know don't go nowhere near 'em.

"You had this one young man a few years back in England. Great musician, very talented boy. You probably know him. Peter Green, started up Fleetwood Mac. Now *he* cut that song, and look what happened to him. Whole mess'a troubles came down on him, went into the wilderness like one'a them old prophets in my daddy's Bible. Didn't play hardly none for twenty-some years. *That's* what I'm talkin' about."

"Yeah, but... what happened to Greeny had more to do with some fucker spiking him with bad acid backstage at a gig in Germany or somewhere. You don't know that it was anything to do with the song.

"But you know something, Daddy Blue? First time I heard Robert Johnson, I damn near wet meself."

Blue shrugged, shot him a sidelong glance. "Yeah, me too, young man.

"You know what you know, an' I know what I know. And I know two things I'm'a tell you right now." Blue raised a fist, two fingers pointing ceilingward. "One: ain't a damn thing that can possibly happen to ya in this world wouldn't be twice as bad if you was bustin' for a pee at the time." He folded one finger back down into his fist. "Two: I ain't havin' that song on my record. *Final word.*"

"Got a nice groove for it, though." Hudson started to play. Instead of the slow, threatening lope of the Johnson original, he was plucking out a hip-twitching funk-blues riff. Softly, he began to sing. "*Got to keep movin', got to keep movin', blues falling down like hail. Got to keep movin', got to keep movin', hellhound on my trail...*"

Blue wasn't listening any more. He was drifting back in time. Robert Johnson had re-entered his life one last time, and he'd never told anyone about it. Especially not Mick Hudson.

EIGHT

CLARKSDALE, MISSISSIPPI, 1938

James Moon was sixteen years old, and he'd never had $25 in his over-alls before. The money burned a hole in his pocket all the way through the twelve-mile drive along Highway 49 to Clarksdale. He had to get himself a new church suit, the old one being so far outgrown that folks would laugh at him behind their hands every Sunday morning. He had to go by old man Birnbaum's store for fresh supplies of flour, sugar, feed and seed. And he needed a haircut.

So he went round by Sam's Barber Shop first, parked the battered V-8 Ford which had replaced the old Model-T that died on them two years back. Seemed like nothing ever changed in Sam's. Guys were still sitting around with bottles of white lightnin' in brown bags long after they'd had their hair cut, or even if they weren't getting haircuts at all. Prohibition might've ended years ago and Coahoma County might no longer be officially dry, but Sam hadn't quit earning himself a little bit extra each week, keeping his customers topped up with the moonshine he made with a fifty-gallon still he had way out in the country some-where.

There was some guy there James had never seen before, long and tall and skinny in a suit that was probably real slick once upon a time. Now it was threadbare and stained, like the hat he wore pulled down over his eyes. He had an old gunny sack with him, the neck of a guitar poking out where the bag was tied up with string.

"... and he was down on his knees, barkin' like a dog," the man was saying in a deep creaky voice. "Took him five days to die." Sam looked up from the head he was cutting as James entered the shop, the bell ringing merrily to welcome him. "How you doin', young man?" he said. "How's the Reverend? He don't seem to be comin' to town much these days."

"Daddy's fine," James said. "His back don't pain him so much now he has me drivin' the car and doin' the chores."

"Hey, Willie," Sam said. "Tell this young man what you just been tel-lin' us. You remember," he said to James, "when you was just little and your daddy bring you in here and you'd just seen Little Robert — Robert Johnson — playin' on the street?"

"Sure I remember," James said. He could still see Robert, clear and sharp in every detail, and hear his music exactly as he'd played it. His friend Snooky at school even had one of Robert's big old ten-inch Vocalion records, Terraplane Blues, which he let James listen to on the family's hand-crank phonograph when he came over to visit sometimes. But he couldn't go over by Snooky's house very often, 'cause Snooky's folks didn't go to church. And Reverend Moon didn't know that Snooky's daddy had an old beat-up guitar, and once or twice when he'd had his 'shine he'd shown James one or two things on it. Didn't play no bottleneck, though, and James bet he wasn't nowhere near good enough of a musicianer to play Robert's song. Couple more sessions and James bet he'd be able to play everything Snooky's dad could.

"Well, Robert done passed last week," said Sam. "Willie just been tellin' us."

"Yeah, man," Willie growled. "I was there. Saw the whole thing. Can't talk about it no more, though."

"Why not?"

"'Cause my throat's awful parched. Can't be talkin' when I'm dry." He drained the last few drops from one of Sam's moonshine bottles and waggled the empty meaningfully at Sam. The barber put down his scissors and bustled into the back, returning a moment later with a fresh half-pint. Willie put it to his mouth and tilted his head back, adam's-apple yoyoing up and down his scrawny throat.

"Ahhhhhh...." He smacked his lips a couple of times, shook his head rapidly from side to side. "That's better." He took another grateful swig. "Was down in Greenwood, just eight days back. Robert was playin' that jook up by Three Forks, an' he took awful sick to his stomach. Had to put his git-tar down, throw up. Kept on throwin' up. Then he started throwin' up blood. They took him away someplace, put him to bed, but couldn't no doctor do him no good. Like I said, took him five days to die. Five days before the devil came'n got his bought'n-paid-for soul and took it all the way down to hell."

Sam's customer extracted his hand from under the barber's cloth draped over him, and took his unlit cigar out of his mouth. "C'mon, Willie, that's horsehit," he said. "Wasn't no devil come'n took him. Way Robert carried on, most likely some woman's husband done poisoned him."

Willie hefted the gunny sack. "Tell you what, though. Got Robert's git-tar right here. Figure on chargin' folks five cents to see it." There was a moment's silence. "All right, Willie, I'll bite," the customer said. "Let's see Robert's git-tar."

With a flourish, Willie untied the string at the bag's neck and pulled out the guitar. "Let me have a look at that thing," said Sam's customer. Willie handed the guitar to James, who accepted it with a mixture of eagerness and trepidation. Was this the same guitar Little Robert had been playing that day outside old man Birnbaum's? Sure *looked* the same, but...

James carried the guitar over to the man in the barber's chair, who looked it over for a second. "Willie," he said, "you a jive muthafucka, an' you should be 'shamed'a yourself lyin' to these folks like that. This ain't Robert's guitar. Robert had him a nice brown Gibson, an' this be nuthin' but an old Stella like you get from Sears, Roebuck."

"Never said it was Robert's *last* git-tar," Willie retorted. "This be his *old* git-tar, his original one."

"How'd you get it, then?"

"Robert done pawned it one time in Memphis. He needed money to pay some ho, so he pawned his git-tar. I got there 'fore he got back with the money to get it out." Willie cackled. "*Ooooohh*, he was mad!"

"I don't believe *none* of it," Sam said contemptuously. "First of all, most'a the musicianers round these parts got them same Stellas just like this one. Could be anybody's. Could be nobody's. An' second of all, everybody know Willie a lyin' so-an'-so, never tells the truth 'less he got no choice. Was talkin' 'bout his seven kids last time he was here, an'everybody know Willie ain't the father'a nuthin' 'cept a whole bunch'a lies. So listen here, O Father Of Lies, you ain't gonna get no five cents showin' that beat-up ol' git-tar to nobody."

James handed the guitar back to Willie, who started to put it back in its sack, then changed his mind and rested it on his lap. "I tell you what," he said after a moment. "Any'a you gents want to buy this git-tar?"

James heard himself say, "How much you want for it?"

Willie said, "Fifteen dollars."

James heard Sam snort derisively. "*Fif*-teen dollars? Fifteen *whole* dollars? Son, you could send away to Sears, Roebuck, get yourself a brand new one for a whole lot less than that. Second-handed git-tar oughtta run you maybe two-fifty, three dollars."

Willie said, "Sears, Roebuck can't sell you Robert Johnson's git-tar for *no* amount'a money."

"An' the onliest thing sayin' it's Robert's git-tar is the say-so'a the biggest goddam liar in the whole damn county."

James said, "Let me try it." Willie said, "Just a minute," and began to tune the guitar, turning the stiff rusty pegs this way and that. He took his time, changing the pitch of each string by a miniscule amount and then playing a little run to make sure it was harmonising perfectly with all the other strings. He played one final riff, a strange ragtimy picking thing with notes that jangled in places that seemed both right and wrong at the same time, and then offered the guitar to James. As Willie looked up at the boy, James fancied that his eyes seemed to flash beneath the shade of his hat-brim.

James took the guitar. It felt warm and comfortable, almost snuggling into his arms. He sank down on one knee, propped the guitar on his thigh and cautiously tried to remember a simple progression he'd learned off Snooky's daddy. The customer in Sam's chair said, "Well, you got to admit it's a good sounding git-tar."

Sam said, "Hey, young man, I didn't know you could play." A thought struck him. "Do your daddy know you been playin' git-tar? You know how he feels about the devil's music an' all that kinda stuff. An' if he think you got a git-tar here he gonna kill *me*, send *my* soul right down to hell." He laughed. "Prob'ly book me a place right next to Robert."

James did indeed know. His father made it all too clear, every day, close enough. If his daddy had his druthers, James would be in church every second he wasn't devoting to his school homework or his chores on the farm. And the onliest thing James liked about church was the singing. He was in the choir and the mens' quartet, and sometimes he got to sing solos.

"I like me the git-tar, sure 'nuff," he told Willie, "but I can't spend no fifteen dollars."

"The git-tar seem to like you, too," Willie said. "I'll take ten."

James didn't know which way to jump. He'd wanted a guitar ever since the day he saw Robert on the street. Sam was right, you could get a messed-up second-hand guitar for two-three bucks if you knew where to look. And he'd always been too scared of his daddy to bring one home even on those few occasions when he'd managed to save up enough of his nickels and dimes. But this guitar *was* special: special to him, anyway. He didn't even care whether it had really been Robert's or not. All he cared about was that he wanted the guitar, and the guitar seemed to want to be his.

But how was he gonna pay for it? He had $25 of the family's hard-earned money, and every cent of it spoken for. There was exactly enough, counted out right down to the last penny, for his suit, for the supplies from Birnbaum's and for his haircut. If he came home without anything he was supposed to have, he was going to get as big a whuppin' as his still-powerful father was capable of handing out. Which was con-siderable: James was lanky and uncoordinated and shy, and Solomon Moon was built like a barrel with tree-trunk arms and the most terrible temper James had ever seen on anyone, like he'd been put on this earth simply to serve as a channel for the Wrath of God. And if James came home with a guitar — "the *devil* live in a git-tar!" — it'd be smashed right over his head the second his daddy saw it.

He just couldn't take the chance. Reluctantly, he stood up and held the guitar out towards Willie. "I'm sorry," he said. "I just don't have the money."

"Tell you what," Sam's customer said. "I think you got yourself a tal-ent, boy. A *gift*. And I believe talent should be encouraged." Under the barber's cloth, he rummaged in his pants pocket and fished out some crumpled bills and a fistful of coins. He selected a five-dollar bill. "Now, if Willie here is gonna take ten for that git-tar, I'll pay half. You reckon you can come up with five of your own?"

Even as he was saying, "You sure?" and stammering his thanks, James was calculating wildly in his head. If Sam would let him pay for the haircut next week, and if old man Birnbaum would either give him a little credit or let him pay off the difference by working a few hours in back at the store, he could just about do it. Hands shaking, he counted out five dollars, two dollar bills and the rest in change, and gave the money to Willie. And when he got home he could always keep the guitar in his secret place in the barn, practice out in the fields when no-one was around.

"I reckon you got yourself a bargain, boy," Willie told him. "That git-tar be *special*. Gonna make a real difference to your life." He took the five from the customer, folded it around James's dollar bills and put the money somewhere inside his jacket. The coins he dropped into the side pocket of his pants. "Yeah... a *real* difference." He mock-saluted James, smiled and sauntered towards the door. His eyes seemed to flash once again as he paused for a second on the threshold before disappearing onto the sidewalk.

"I reckon you a natural-born sucker, young man," Sam said, brushing his customer's shoulders. "Could've got yourself a git-tar way better'n that for a lot less money."

"Maybe," James said, settling into the chair, still clutching the guitar, "but this one's the *right* git-tar. For me, anyway." The customer paused at the door, flashed him a gold-toothed grin. "Good luck, son," he said. "Maybe one day I'm'a hear y'all on the radio. Make me proud, now."

Sam said to James, "You feel like puttin' that thing down long enough for me to cut your hair?"

Blue emerged from his reverie, his spirit still attuned to the strength and flexibility of a sixteen-year-old body, now finding itself suddenly in a frame so frail he could feel his bones grinding together as he drew in a long shaky breath. Mick Hudson was still sitting beside him. He'd put down his Telecaster, switched off the amp. He was picking an old Muddy Waters riff on the low frets of the old Stella. "You know what?" he said, beaming. "This is the cheapest acoustic you've got, but I reckon it's the nicest. I really like this one..."

Adrienne jogging on Venice Beach, Attack galumphing at her heels, narrowly avoiding getting knocked off her feet by a pram pushed at a truly insane velocity by a girl on roller skates in a bikini top and denim shorts, thinking God help us all when that baby gets to be old enough to drive. It was an uncommonly cool grey day by SoCal summer standards, Adrienne taking longer than usual to work up her customary sweat. There were comparatively few tourists around. Turbo Pram Girl and the occasional dogwalker aside, the footpath unwinding ahead of her was relatively clear. She pounded past the souvenir shops and tack stalls, past the tattooed weightlifters grunting over heavy iron in their boxing-ring-sized enclosure, past the beachfront houses with the comedy architecture which most days made her smile as she ran.

When she'd married Blue seventeen years ago, she'd known that their relationship would seem weird to some: after all, he'd been six-ty-seven, ten years older than her father would have been if he was still alive, and she not quite thirty, eleven years younger than his oldest child. What could they possibly have in common? He was a career bluesman, born in a shack in the Mississippi Delta; she'd come out of a fiercely aspirational California middle-class home — her father taught high school physics, her mother was a civilian employee of the LAPD — where blues was never heard. Yet they'd clicked, and all these years later they were still clicking.

She'd also known that her time with Blue would be limited, that even managing to stay together 'til death did them part was going to leave her a comparatively youthful widow, bringing up whatever kids they ended up with in the shadow of a lost father. Practically the whole time they'd been together, she'd been preparing herself for the inevitable loss of her husband: bracing herself emotionally and psychologically and spiritually, thinking it would be like the old days when he'd be out on tour most of the time, except that he wouldn't call and there'd be no fixed date for his return, printed right there in the tour itinerary she'd keep pinned up on the notice-board in the kitchen, with another copy by her bedside. Yet now that the moment she'd always dreaded was finally upon her, she didn't feel prepared at all. The cornerstone of her life was crumbling. Every day, there seemed to be a little less of him; every day he seemed to be drifting further away.

The last couple of weeks, a new routine had developed. Mick would spend the mornings holed up with his co-producer and engineer in a studio in Hollywood, working on his live album. Most days, he'd show up at the house after lunch and he and Blue would go to ground in the music room, jamming a little but mostly talking. Sometimes he'd stay for dinner, but he'd generally split shortly after Donna got back from school.

Adrienne was starting to get worried about this album Mick and Blue were supposed to be making. Here he was, his strength visibly ebbing away, getting ready to cut an album with a bunch of people who had decades'-worth of serious problems with each other. For an old man weak as Blue was getting, even recording with musicians alongside whom he felt totally comfortable and who were completely cool with each other would be an ordeal. This, on the other hand, was just nuts.

She'd said as much to him just that morning. "What the hell you playin' at, Blue?" she'd said. "First of all, you're gonna make a record now when you can hardly stand up. Plus you want to make it with a bunch of people who hate each other."

"Mick don't hate no-one," he'd responded mildly.

"No-one 'cept himself." Blue didn't answer straight away, drifting off into another of his reveries. A few moments later, his eyes snapped open.

"Not many men have the privilege to know when it is they're gonna go," he said eventually. "I don't believe I done too much wrong in my life, but I know I left a lotta right things undone. This is my last chance to take care'a my unfinished bidness. Me'n Mick'Neesha'n young Calvin got unfinished bidness with each other. Makin' music is what I know how to do, an' it's what they know how to do. So we gonna do it together. 'Sides," he grinned, "if I'm'a go out, I'm'a go out in style."

"Bullshit," she said. "Your last album was fine. If *Moon Landing* was the last record you ever did, no-one could say you didn't still have it all going on." He shrugged.

"That was just another album," he said. "Better'n the one before, not as good as the one before that. I been making records since nineteen-and-fifty-one. Started out playin' behind other people, then cuttin' on myself. There's guys in Europe, doin' all this research, makin' lists of all the records I cut, all the sessions I done. Simon showed it to me: runs thirty-forty pages. You know there's more'n a hundred albums out there? Some of them real good, some not so good. Some I get paid for, some I don't.

"It's been a long road, sugar. A long *hard* road. When you start out, you don't know where you goin'. You just walkin', tryin' to get *some-where*, tryin' to figure out which way to go. Then you get somewhere, an' if you been lucky maybe where you at ain't too far from where you thought you was goin'." He took her hand, started to stroking it, enjoying the feel of her smooth skin and strong fingers, honouring the calluses and tiny scars she'd earned in her workshop. "Now where I got to is a way better place than I ever thought I'd get to when I started out. I got a ve-e-e-e-ry beautful wife..." he smiled and kissed her cheek "... got a beautiful home, got a lovely daughter. I got plenty'a money, nice cars, good friends, a guy I can trust lookin' after my bidness. I got git-tars like I never imagined back in Mississippi. People all over the world love me, love my music. An' I had my health a lot longer than most guys my age.

"So I'm a lucky, lucky man. Most folks jus' go when they go. Every-thing stay where it were when they pass. I can see the end of my road right up ahead, baby, but I don't wanna be leavin' no mess behind me. An' that mean getting' everything straight 'fore I check out. This record gonna be my way'a doin' that. It's my last chance to say who I was as a musician, an' who I am as a man."

The slapping of her Niked feet on the pathway and the pounding of blood in her veins brought Adrienne back into the here and now. She checked her watch: Blue's new nurse was due to arrive at the house in less than twenty minutes. Gratefully, she slowed her pace and came to a halt, bending over, hands on her knees, until her breathing returned to normal. She took a sip of water from the bottle in her backpack, whistled up Attack and headed for home.

NINE

Calvin Holland had his game face on when he arrived on Sunset Strip for his meeting with Screwdriver and Omega Man's people. Fully Loaded shades clamped across his eyes and dressed from head to toe in box-fresh gleaming white Fully Loaded sportswear, he waited outside the Mondrian with BLT while KanD sorted out valet parking for the white Humvee. Skinny little BLT might look like the LAPD's idea of a gangsta with too much money to be legit, but he was a highly-trained CPA, the keeper of Calvin's briefcase and, in just about everything to do with Lock N Load's daily runnings, his right-hand man. KanD was a former WWF wrestler, six feet tall with shoulders a yard wide, all blonde hair extensions and gold-studded piercings. She was Calvin's chauffeur and body-guard. A blinding vision in their snowy-white outfits, the three of them strode stony-faced across the wooden-floored beige and cream lobby to the poolside restaurant/bar, where a table was booked for high noon.

Calvin was glad that Screwdriver and Omega Man themselves were still back in Jamaica. He wasn't in any mood to listen politely to any interminable weed-drawled platitudes about stayin' in touch wid da yout'-dem in da ghetto or keepin' faith wid da street; he'd be getting enough of that crap from their managers. He'd cleared out Cecilia, the girl in his bed this morning, just about as quick as he could force some coffee down her and steer her into the shower. She wouldn't be coming back. If they couldn't figure out that he wanted 'em gone by the time he woke up, they didn't get to come back. Now, mind and body humming with finely-tuned energy after his regular morning workout and a quick draw on a blunt while playing the Screwdriver and Omega Man album during the ride over, he was pumped and ready to tell everybody exactly what time it was.

Jethro and Julian sounded like a double-act. Trouble was, they weren't a very good one. Jethro was a stocky little yardie tough guy flex-ing way out of his league; Julian was a flabby limey lawyer dressed for autumn in London rather than an admittedly cool and overcast sum-mer's day in LA. They were both drinking beers. Calvin ordered Perrier for himself and his sidekicks and got down to business.

"We just been listenin' to the album again while we was comin' here," he began, without preamble. "It's kickin', mabrutha, it's happenin' just the way it is. It's tough enough to sound down, but it's got pop written all over it. This album gonna sell four-five million copies, put your boys way over the top. They got a career ready and waitin', all they got to do is step up and take it. You really sure you wanna fuck it all up?"

"Mi bredren-dem love the album," Jethro said, smiling broadly to show off his gold caps. Terrible work, Calvin thought, any LA dentist did work like that be lucky to keep his own teeth in his mouth. "The album fine, mon. All we wan' do is add dis-ya one song to it. It's already a big song, mon, it na harm the album."

"It does specify in the contract," Julian interposed, shuffling papers, "that nothing can be released by Lock N Load without the approval of the artists and their representatives..."

"You right," conceded Calvin. "That's exactly what it says. It says it in every Lock N Load contract. Which is why I took time out of my day to come here and meet with y'all so you can approve putting out the album I want to put out.

"And you can bet your ass that song is gonna harm the album. You ain't gonna find an album with a song like Battyman 9/11 on it in Wal-Mart. Or an album with a song like that gettin' any tracks whatsoever played on any Clear Channel stations. Those suckers sell an awful lotta records, control a lotta radio stations. We ain't doin' 'underground' here. If y'all wanna stay underground, you already know how to do that. Y'all don't need me if you wanna stay in the market y'all already got."

"But this tune, mon..." Jethro started to protest, but Calvin just rolled right over him.

"You already got the tune out," Calvin told them. "It's a hit in Jamaica, it's a hot import here and in London, it's a top download. Just leave it where it is. Y'all wanna go pop, we got an album right here's the one gonna do it. You don't wanna go pop, we ain't got no more deal. I got a dozen artists can sing or rap over those backgrounds I made for your boys and, Mister Lawyer, you check your contract one more time. You'll see that Lock N Load owns those beats and those tracks. Keep listenin' to your radio. Keep checkin' out the clubs. You gonna be hearin' those tracks real soon. Only thing you got to decide is whether it's gonna be your boys on top of 'em, or some'a my people. Hell, I ain't cut nuthin' on myself in five years, but I could drop some rhymes on a couple'a those tracks myself.

"You got about forty-five seconds to make up your minds." BLT snapped Calvin's briefcase shut. KanD pressed a button on her wrist-watch and stared at it with fierce concentration. All three of them stood up from the table.

A minute and a half later they were heading back across the lobby: mission accomplished. Screwdriver and Omega Man's album was coming out exactly the way Calvin had sequenced it, without Battyman 9/11. Bad enough they cut the dumb thing at all, Calvin thought as KanD opened the Humvee door for him, we gonna have to do some advanced spin control to stop it rebounding onto the album, but at least the album itself is safe.

Within a year they'd be thanking him. And you could take that to the bank. He certainly intended to.

The entire meeting had taken just under eighteen minutes.

The nurse was a plump, kindly-looking Filipino-Chinese woman in chainstore sweats. Her name was Maudie Lam. Middle-aged, Adrienne thought, then instantly amended that to 'my age.' Maudie exuded reassuring, motherly warmth, and Adrienne felt instantly safe and comfortable with her. Blue seemed to like her, too, even struggling to his feet to shake hands. And she wasn't likely to be star-struck, either: Blue's name clearly meant nothing to her, and she reacted not at all to the far more famous names of Mick Hudson and Venetia Moon. All he was going to be to Maudie was a terminally ill old man who needed caring for.

She wasn't just comforting, she was also majorly efficient. Within an hour Maudie knew everything she needed to about Blue's medication schedule, what time he tended to go to sleep and wake up, what his panic button sounded like, his diet and his favourite diet-breakers, where everything was in the kitchen. She had brought her massage table, currently folded against a wall in Blue's music room, and after examining him for a few minutes, informed them that she'd have the details of his physiotherapy programme worked out for him by tomorrow. The only thing that had seemed to shock or surprise her was Blue telling her that he would be having no surgery or chemotherapy, and that her task was basically to keep him as comfortable as possible for as long as possible.

"I can do that," Maudie told them. Adrienne believed her. "The massage can keep your muscles loose and relaxed so that you can move a little more and not tire so quickly. Also, if you wish, I can treat you with a little acupuncture. Focus your *chi*, give you more energy, ease pain, help you sleep a little better."

"That sound good," Blue said. "You got a mobile?" Maudie nodded yes. "You get all your calls on that?" She nodded again. "We let the machine pick up the calls in this house, so if no-one be calling you on our number you don't need to worry about it. Just let the damn thing ring."

The giant German Shepherd padded into the music room to claim a formal introduction ("Attack!"), closely followed by the tiny, snuffling Wu Li. To Adrienne and Blue's relief, both dogs seemed to form an instant liking for Maudie, sniffing her eagerly and competing to get their ears scratched. The dog acceptance test triumphantly accomplished, Maudie had another major diplomatic mission on her hands, but the less she knew about the significance of Venetia coming here tonight the better.

"Our daughter is staying over at a friend's house," Adrienne told Maudie, "so Mr Moon is gonna be home by himself. Whenever there's no-one with him, check him out every half-hour or so, see he's comfortable and got whatever he needs. If he wants something he'll buzz, but if he's feeling okay he's liable to roll into the kitchen and get it for himself. He's due for his medication around 8:00, and he's expecting a visitor around 8:30. Let her in and check that Mr Moon is awake before bringing her in here. I should be back around eleven."

"I wait till you get home," Maudie agreed. "Mr Moon, he be fine." She began setting up the massage table. Adrienne headed for the shower, wondering what to wear tonight. She hadn't eaten out at a fancy restaurant for months, and she hadn't been to one with anyone other than Blue for more years than she cared to think about right now. Besides, she and Mick would be going out for dinner together partly because Blue wanted them out of the way while Venetia was at the house, and partly as a way of fulfilling his hospitable hostly duties when he couldn't join them in person. And Mick was an old friend, an integral part of Blue's extended family. When those two guys had first met, she'd have been about six.

So nothing too fancy, then. Nothing too formal. But it was the Mirabelle, after all, so nothing too casual, either. By the time she'd stepped out of the shower and wrapped herself up in a towelling burqa, she'd more or less decided on a loose cream linen Nicole Farhi suit and an emerald silk sleeveless top, plus a full selection — necklace, earrings, bracelets, rings — from the 'Africa' range of silver jewellery she made in her own workshop. Through the open door of the music room she could hear some half-familiar sounds.

"Ohh, that's gettin' good to me," Blue was murmuring. "Yeaahhhhh... right there, just like that. Don't stop..."

She grinned, and put her head round the door. Blue was stretched out prone on the massage table, a towel across his butt, smiling seraphically as Maudie worked on his back.

"Y'all havin' a good time?"

"Hell, don't know why I was dumb enough to wait 'til I got sick before gettin' me some'a this."

"Very stiff," Maudie said disapprovingly. "Muscles too tight. Get Mr Moon loosened up, he feel much better."

"Hey, I already do," Blue said. He looked up at Adrienne. "Don't worry about drivin' tonight. I got a car booked for you, case you wanted a few drinks. Car be here seven-thirty, Mick be waitin' for you at the restaurant 'bout eight."

Eight o'clock and Sunset Boulevard was bumper-to-bumper. The sidewalks were crammed, strollers wandering in and out of restaurants, bars and boutiques. The doorman at the Mondrian Hotel's Sky Bar was only just arriving on duty, but the queue was already stretching down the heaving sidewalk.

True to Blue's word, Hudson was there, waiting for her behind an empty martini glass at a corner table. The last traces of dye had gone from his immaculately spiked grey hair. He was wearing a slick black Paul Smith suit, a white cowboy shirt and a string tie caught in a silver bolo from, she noted with a flash of annoyance, one of her principal competitors.

"Missis Blue!" he greeted her. "Dwahling, you look faaaaabulous! Mwah mwah!" He planted a couple of fashion kisses an inch or two outboard of each cheek, raised her hand to his lips, beckoned a waiter. "Small tipple?"

Tipple? Oh... a drink. She nodded yes, and Hudson ordered a couple more martinis. She slipped off her jacket and hung it over the back of her chair. "Where'd you get that bolo?" she asked.

"Oh, this old thing? Can't remember the name. Some place on Rodeo Drive."

Good call. She was right: she knew exactly where he'd gotten it. "I think you can do a lot better than that," she said. "If you like, I can arrange for one of our representatives to display a few items from our own range for your approval. We also have some earrings I'm sure you'll find to your liking."

"Sorry, lady," he said. "When a man gets to my position in life he only deals with the boss." She smiled. "I'm sure the boss will be more than happy to make you one of her personal customers." Their martinis arrived with a couple of menus. He raised his glass. "Here's to the lean mean blues machine," he said softly. "Here's to him," she replied. They clinked glasses. Both of them were thinking that they'd never been alone with each other before, but then neither of them really felt like they were alone at the table.

"God, I love this town," Hudson said. "Not that I'd want to live here or anything, but... I saw some motorcycle cops while I was stuck in traffic on the way here, and they were posing for a bunch of tourists taking pictures. Campest thing I've seen in public for years. Those uniforms! Like they were on the way to an audition for *Village People: The Next Generation.*"

Their waiter was hovering just outside their range of vision, so they flipped through their menus before summoning him. "Hi-there-good-evening-folks-my-name's-Todd-and-I'm-your-waitperson-this-evening," he machinegunned. "We-have-some-wonderful-specials-tonight-including..." Hudson waved him into silence. "I'll have the filet steak with bernaise sauce, rare," he announced, "and the lady will have...?"

"Grilled sea bass," she said. "Vegetables of the day."

"Make that twice."

"Excellent choices," Todd commended them. "The sea bass is especially good today. And something to drink...?"

"They've got a pretty good Merlot here," Hudson told her, "which I'm having with the steak. You want a nice dry white to go with the fish?"

"Merlot's fine for me."

"I should have known," he lisped in a passable Sean Connery voice. "Red wine with fish..."

"I was really tempted when you ordered the steak bernaise," she confessed, "but I've got to watch what I eat."

Hudson did an exaggerated double-take. "You've got to be kidding," he said. "You look fit as a fiddle. Make that fit as an entire triple-scale string section."

"That's because I watch what I eat. Plus I run, and I work out, and I do yoga. And even the occasional belly-dancing class."

"Well, you're obviously an excellent advertisement for healthy living."

She raised a bent arm, clenched her fist, popped up a craggy asymmetric little bicep, smiled at the startled expression on his face. "It was basically forced on me. Four months after Donna was born, people were still asking me when the baby was due, so I thought I'd better do something about that. After all, I don't spend months on end running around a stage under hot lights the way you do, or Blue did..." Her voice tailed off. "Anyway, I started enjoying it. Partly because it was so boring and uncomfortable that it gave me a lot of time to think. Started coming up with a lot more new designs. Don't you take any exercise?"

"Only when I have to. Just before a tour, usually. Do some guitar practice, vocal exercises, and get some babe in to put me through some basic limbering-up and stamina training. It's a bit ridiculous, actually. When I was a kid at school I used to bunk off gym and games to go and play guitar with me mates. Now I've got to do all that gym stuff just to be fit enough to play the guitar. Otherwise me hands seize up or me throat goes half-way through a show, or I get an hour into it and feel like going off and having a nice lie-down for half an hour. It's a drag." He shrugged. "But when you're twenty you've got all this energy and you just figure that's normal and that it's always gonna be like that. I mean, I never worried about what things were gonna be like when I was sixty. Huh! I never thought I'd still be *alive* at sixty."

"Yeah, Blue said you used to be a wild one. I bet he never thought you'd make sixty either."

"Well, I used to drink a bit." Adrienne looked pointedly at Hudson's martini glass. His second one was almost gone. "Okay, I still drink a bit. But I used to drink a *lot*. Bourbon for breakfast, all that kind of thing. Plenty of beer to wash it down. Few bottles of wine a day when I felt like taking it easy and being a bit sophisticated. Plus the old white powders. You name it, I did it."

"Don't you regret it?"

"Wish I did. No, I don't regret it. I don't do that stuff now because I know I can't handle it and still have anything even faintly resembling a life, but I have to say I enjoyed it at the time. And the bits I didn't enjoy were when the drink and the drugs were protecting me from some basic life stuff that I wouldn't have been able to handle straight. I'm afraid I wouldn't be much of a poster boy for any 'just say no' campaigns. I didn't start saying no until I'd spent most of me life saying yes... yes, please! Got any more?

"It's like... you didn't order the steak tonight, right? You could have had it, but you chose not to. It's not because all of a sudden you stopped liking steak, or decided that there was something evil and immoral about steak and turned veg-o. You still like steak, but you decided that not screwing up your diet is more important to you tonight than enjoying...."

Todd was at their table, sliding the sea bass in front of Adrienne and the filet in front of Hudson. He carved off a chunk, slathered it in the sauce and waved his fork at Adrienne. "... a lovely... delicious... juicy... dripping with aromatic bernaise sauce... bleeding... *steak*!" Todd poured a few drops of wine into Hudson's glass. He tasted it, nodded approval. Todd filled their glasses and shimmered off.

"Okay, you talked me into it," Adrienne said. "I don't normally do red meat these days, but I'll have a forkful." She raised a finger. "Just the one." Hudson held the fork out towards her. She leaned forward, ate the piece of steak off his fork. Her eyes closed in theatrical delight. "Mmmmmmm... that's wonderful. But I'm not having any more."

"See? Just like me and drugs," Hudson said. "Still like 'em, but choose not to do 'em. Maybe one little taste once in a while."

Adrienne was shocked. "You still do heroin?"

"No, no, no. Not smack. That's right off the menu. Haven't touched any of that in more than twenty years. And I've never done crack cocaine. Or any of those designer pills. I'm too old for new drugs. Too old for most of the old ones, quite frankly. In real life, I still like to smoke weed, and once in a very great while, when I'm not working, I'll have a line of coke. That's about it, really." He raised his wine glass. "Shall we drink another toast?"

She picked up her glass, absently playing with the stem. "What shall we drink to? The future? The future scares the hell out of me, Mick. Good health? I've got mine, you've sort-of-semi got yours, but..." She fell silent, looking down at her half-eaten fish.

"How about drinking to friendship?"

She looked up at him. "Yeah, I like that." Hudson reached out and gently clinked his glass against hers. "To friendship."

A car door slams in Venice Beach. Venetia walks up Blue's driveway. As she rings the doorbell, a dog barks and a light goes on inside.

TEN

CHICAGO, ILLINOIS, 1953

Blue was sitting at the foot of Venetia's bed in his trousers and under-shirt, fingerpicking his old Stella guitar. In a few minutes he'd have to set off for his Saturday night gig at Esmerelda's Lounge leading the backup band for Big Daddy Gilmore, but even when he was running late, like tonight, he never left the apartment without singing a couple of bedtime songs for Venetia.

This one was something he'd made up to the tune of The Best Book To Read Is The Bible, a song Venetia had been taught at Sunday School. Blue's version went,

> *Down South the hog is man's best friend*
> *Down South the hog is man's best friend*
> *The hog is man's best friend*
> *Cuz you can eat him end to end*
> *Down South the hog is man's best friend*

Venetia clapped and giggled, looking very much unlike a little girl who's ready to curl up and go to sleep. "Sing 'nother one, daddy," she commanded. Blue put the guitar down and gave her a hug.

"Sorry, sug', I can't," he said. "Daddy's got to go to work."

"But you just got *home* from work, daddy."

"This is my other job, sweets," he told her. "I only drive the meat truck in the day. Night-times I play music. Got to keep that money comin' in so you'n me'n your momma got a place to sleep an' food on the table."

"Are you gonna come to church with us tomorrow, daddy?"

"We'll see," he said, thinking *all I wanna do tomorrow is sleep*. He picked up his guitar, blew her a kiss and headed for the bedroom door. As his hand touched the doorknob she sang out again.

"Daddy... tell me again why you've got a funny foot." She kicked back her covers, raised her left leg, wiggled her toes in the air. "Why do I have lots of toes on this foot and you've just got two?"

Blue sighed, sneaked a quick look at his watch and sat down again.

He pulled the covers back over Venetia and tucked them in. "It was a very long time ago," he began. He'd told her the story so often that she practically knew it by heart: tonight he'd have to give her the very shortest version if he was going to make his gig on time.

"This was down on the farm where I grew up down South in Miss'ssippi. I was just six years old, same age you are now. Now you know I came along very late, quite a surprise for your grandpappy and grandmom, since they thought they was done havin' kids twelve year before I was born. All my brothers an' sisters were way older'n me, done left home an' gotten married an' stuff, so the onliest one left was my big brother Joseph, an' he couldn't do too much on the farm 'cuz he was blind.

"But he always wanted to help. Now you know blind people can really surprise you sometimes, doin' things you don't think they gonna be able to do. They hear better than sighted folks and they learn to tap things with a stick, figure out where stuff is, even listen to the wind blowin' around things and tell there's somethin' there. Now Joseph, he'd been figurin' out how to chop wood when he couldn't see nuthin'. He'd feel around the woodpile for a log, put it up on its end, 'member exactly where it was an' chop it plumb in half with a big ol' axe. Folks round where we were'd take bets on him doin' it right, an' he always did. Never told daddy 'bout none'a that, cuz daddy was a preacher and didn't hold with no sinfulness like gamblin'.

"So he's choppin' wood an' I'm right next to him and suddenly I think, if I move the log, will he know? So I start to givin' the log just a little nudge..." he prodded her gently with his finger, such an essential part of the story that she'd complain if he didn't "...with my foot." He patted his maimed left foot.

"An' right then BAM! Joseph swings the axe, an' he swings it so fast'n so hard that a little ol' fly just buzzin' by... " he swept his hand through the air just in front of her eyes and made a little *bzzz-bzzz* noise "... got cut clean in half. An' the axe comes down..." He paused. This was Venetia's cue to squeal and put her hands over her eyes. "... and it come down right where the middle of the log used to be. But what your daddy forgot to do was to pull his foot back out of the way of the axe. So the axe came right down on my poor little foot..." he fondled her foot through the covers "... and took these three toes..." in turn, he gently squeezed her three smallest toes, raised his foot from the floor so she could see it, peeking through her fingers "right... *off*."

"Did it hurt, daddy?" The ritual question: she always asked that.

"Only for a second, cuz I fainted dead away." He mimed unconsciousness, let out a little snore. "When I woke up, doctor was there, had me all bandaged up. He an' my daddy drove me to the hospital. But I got to say some good come out of it. If I hadn't hurt my foot, I'd'a had to go overseas, fight in the war, all them Germans and Japanese be tryin' to kill me. 'Stead'a that, I got to stay home in the USA, meet your mommy an' have you." He kissed her again, tucked her in one more time. "Okay now, sug', got to go. See you tomorrow."

He picked up his guitar and made his escape. Or part of it. Mary was waiting for him in their bedroom, wearing that frowzy old housedress, wig on its stand, thick arms akimbo and a scowl stitched firmly across her face. "Why you sing that song to her?" she demanded. "That was a Bible song she learned in Sunday school, now you put them silly words 'bout a hog on it an' she gonna go back to school, teach that to all her friends, get us in trouble with Reverend Holland."

Reverend Holland. Blue was sick of hearing about the Reverend Cleotis Holland and his wonderful sermons and his shining holiness and all the different things he said were sinful. These things included drinking, gambling, listening to (or, even worse, playing) worldly music, making love to anyone you weren't married to and most especially not going to church every Sunday and giving Rev Holland every penny you had that you didn't need for food and rent. Blue was out playing music four-five nights a week 'til four in the morning, and that was after working a full day driving the truck, and all he wanted to do on Sunday mornings was get him some sleep. Plus he was going to night school, working on earning himself the high school diploma he'd never gotten in Mississippi. Day job, night school, playin' music and still trying to spend some time with Venetia, be a good daddy to her. That didn't leave much time for church. And he couldn't set foot in any church without a flood of unwelcome memories of Reverend Solomon Moon, earthly repository of the Wrath of God, his grating voice and ever-ready cane.

He shrugged into his white shirt, knotted his silk tie in the mirror. "An' how come when you say good night to her you never pray with her? I got to go in now, say her prayers with her, an' she always want to know why daddy don't pray with her. What you want me to tell her? That you goin' out to play that music in them bars full'a drunks an' gamblers, come home stinkin'a whiskey an' cheap perfume? When you gettin' ready to go out to them houses'a sin, the Lord's name would turn to ashes in your mouth!"

He'd shined his shoes the night before. They were waiting for him now, gleaming like streetlamps reflected in a rainy sidewalk. "I recall back when we met. Them bars didn't seem like such bad places to you then. Had to carry you home more'n once, get in fights with guys thought you were gonna give 'em somethin'." The big Gibson he'd saved three years for was in its case, next to his little tweed Fender amp. He picked them up like suitcases, headed towards the door, looked back. "All I see in them bars are workin' people lookin' to forget their troubles after a hard week in a hard ol' town. Everything they see an' feel, all week long, be designed to put them in they place, keep 'em down, make 'em feel like they ain't nuthin' and they ain't worth nuthin'. When they go out, they want to feel good, feel like they matter, like they deserve some fun. They want to put on they nice clothes, have a few drinks, dance a little, maybe play some cards. I don't see no sin there. Reverend Holland, he see sin most everywhere. Feel almost sorry for the man, got to spend his whole life surrounded by wickedness.

"An' most'a them be in church Sunday mornings, lookin' like butter wouldn't melt in they mouth. Who knows, maybe one night I'll see Reverend Holland in there his own self, leanin' up against Esmerelda's bar drinkin' beer an' tellin' jokes." He winked at her, closed the door and headed for the stairs. If he didn't hit too many red lights, he'd just about be there on time.

Venetia scurried from behind the bedroom door, made a dive for her room, almost made it back into bed before her mother came in. "I told you before 'bout listenin' at the door when big people are talkin'," Mary scolded. "You ready to say your prayers before goin' to sleep?" Venetia's little forehead was rumpled with thought.

"Mama," she said, "is daddy a bad man?"

"Your daddy's a good man inside himself," Mary told her, "but he move in a bad world without the power of the Lord and the Lord's word to protect him."

"Did you really used to go to bars when you were young?"

"Yes I did, sweetie. But then my friend Ida took me to hear Reverend Holland preach, and I found Jesus, got saved, learned about what's right and what's wrong. And the way I was livin' in my old life was wrong."

"But is daddy still living his old life?" There was a long silence.

"Yes he is," Mary said at length. "He heard the word of the Lord from *his* daddy when he was growin' up, but he never found Jesus. Now your daddy is a very, very good musician on the git-tar, but he play nuthin' but worldly music when what he should be doin' is playin' the sacred songs, makin' a joyful noise for the Lord."

"Does that mean daddy isn't saved? Is he going to hell?"

"'less he can find somebody go in his place."

"When I grow up," Venetia decided, "I'm going to save daddy. I'm gonna make sure my daddy goes to heaven so we can be together for even'n ever."

Mary laughed and stroked Venetia's head. "You do that, sweetie. Right now, it's time for your prayers. Say 'em with me, now. 'Now I lay me down to sleep....'"

"'Now I lay me down to sleep,'" Venetia repeated obediently, but in her head she was singing, *down South the hog is man's best friend.*

Esmerelda's Lounge was packed. Esmerelda herself and One Eye the cigar-chomping barman were practically rushed off their feet. Seemed like everybody was there. Everybody, that is, except Big Daddy Gilmore. Ever since he'd had him those two hit records, he'd taken to getting to shows later and later, like he was some big star now. Even when he was there he hardly ever played the first set, which was mostly instrumentals and a few current hits by folks like Muddy Waters and this new guy out of Memphis, BB King. Blue usually sang those, and Pete the piano player would sing him a couple of those slick jazzy ballads full of Chinese chords Blue'd had to sit up half the night learning. They'd played that one the way they always did, the only difference being that Big Daddy wasn't holding court at his sidestage table, talking trash with the guys and buying drinks for the pretty ladies.

But now it was time for the second set. Big Daddy usually took the stage three numbers in, but there was nary hide nor hair of him. Man that big, Blue thought caustically, if he was here you'd know it, couldn't hide him under a table or nuthin'. Big Daddy's microphone was here, ready and waiting on its stand centre-stage. So was his amplifier and even his leather case full of harmonicas. But he wasn't. The jukebox was still blasting out Lowell Fulson and Big Joe Turner and John Lee Hooker, but Esmerelda was starting to cast meaningful glances at the clock on the wall.

Blue rounded up the band. "I swear, next time that fat muthafucka don't show up I'm'a kill him," growled Curtis the drummer. "How you gon' kill him if he ain't there?" asked Little Joe the bass player, who thought he was a comedian or something. "Lookit," Pete said. "We better get up there and play somethin', keep everybody busy 'til Big Daddy show up."

"What if he don't show up?" asked Curtis.

"Then we keep playin'," Blue decided, and led the way onto the stage. They played two jump instrumentals back-to-back, the way they usually did but where Blue usually introduced Big Daddy, he gave them a brief apology for the leader's absence. "We're goin' to do our best to entertain you tonight, ladies'n gentlemen," he said, "so have yourselves another drink an' let us know how we're doin'." They played most of Big Daddy's repertoire, with Blue's guitar filling in the solos usually taken by the bossman's mouth harp. Blue and Pete were calling just about every song they knew, and a few they didn't. They played some of their slow songs fast and their fast songs slow, with Blue making up new lyrics off the top of his head and throwing in verses and phrases from just about every song he'd ever heard, either down South when he was growing up, or on jukeboxes and radios here in Chicago. Folks were dancing and calling stuff out, and their thirst kept One Eye so busy he didn't even have time to relight his cigar. Only two or three customers demanded their money back.

Coming off stage mopping his brow, lighting a cigarette and gratefully slurping on a cold beer, Blue spotted a white guy at the bar. Face it: any time a white guy showed up at Esmerelda's he'd be pretty goddam hard to miss. He recognised him: Isaac Silverstone was one of the brothers who ran Elite Records, the company who'd cut Big Daddy's hits. The first one had been recorded with studio musicians, but the second and more successful, My Heart Needs For You, had featured Big Daddy's own band. It hadn't been Blue's first recording session, but very few of the records he'd made before had been released, and none of those had been hits. He was still getting used to hearing his own guitar on jukeboxes, but the few dollars he'd gotten paid for the session were long ago spent.

"Hey, Blue."

"Hey yourself, Mr Silverstone. How you doin'?"

"Fine, fine... you were sounding good up there. Didn't know you could sing."

Blue spread his hands. "We-e-e-ell... just a little bit. I try, y'know?"

"How you feel about tryin' in the studio?"

"You mean like... my own session?"

"That's exactly what I mean. You got any songs?"

Blue hadn't. But there was no way he was letting Silverstone know that. "I got a few things I been foolin' with," he lied.

"Why don't you come by the office 'round eleven Thursday morning and play me some stuff? If you got the material, we can set up a date." Blue was speechless. Silverstone was looking at him curiously.

"Did you hear me? I said, if you got the material..." Blue found his voice.

"Yeah, that's great, Mr Silverstone, I'll be there. Got some songs I know you're gonna love."

"Okay, then... I'll see you Thursday." They shook hands. Silverstone put his empty glass down on the bar and headed for the exit, nearly colliding with Big Daddy Gilmore, bustling in looking like he'd just got dressed in the dark.

"Oh... Mr Silverstone. How you doin'?"

"Got to run, Daddy. Sorry to have missed you." Silverstone looked back over his shoulder, waved goodbye to Blue and disappeared out onto the street, one of the few white guys Blue had ever met comfortable enough around black folks to walk their streets after dark with a smile on his face and no fear in his eyes. Esmerelda was storming up to Big Daddy with an expression made her face look like forty miles of bad road. Blue, Curtis and Pete looked at each other, nodded, headed out the back way into the alley to blow a little reefer before playing the last set. You had to hand it to Big Daddy, though: once he actually hauled his fat ass onto the stage, muthafucka knew he was ready to *work*.

It was close to 4am by the time Blue lugged his guitar, his amp and his weary self up the stairs to the apartment. Quiet as he could so's not to wake Mary, he hung up his sweat-soaked suit and slipped into bed. "Wha'time izit?" she murmured sleepily.

"Don't you worry none," he whispered back. "Go back to sleep." He snuggled up to her warm bulk and closed his eyes. "'Neesha say when she grow up she gonna save you so you can go to heaven," she mumbled.

"Amen to that," Blue said, kissing the back of her neck.

Charles Shaar Murray

Next thing he knew, the morning sun was blazing into his gummy eyes. Neesha and Mary were standing over him in their church clothes. He shouted something at them and pulled the covers back over his head. The door slammed so hard that a framed portrait of Jesus fell off the wall.

ELEVEN

READING, BERKSHIRE, ENGLAND 1958

"*Dar*-ling!"

Veronica Hudson stood at the foot of the stairs, pitching her voice to cut through the noise — she refused to call it music — coming from her son Michael's bedroom. The drums sounded like pneumatic drills, the saxophone like a demented foghorn. Someone was obviously in the process of destroying a perfectly good piano, and she didn't know what on earth was making that other sound. Could that really be a guitar? She thought of guitars as being nice quiet civilised instruments, quite unlike these new electrified monstronsities. And on top of all this noise was some screaming Negro howling complete and utter gibberish. Honestly, it was just too, too much. That infernal racket was literally rocking the house.

No response. She tried again, louder.

"*DAR-ling!*" Pause. "It's TIME for DIN-ner!"

Still nothing. Sighing theatrically, she climbed the stairs and rapped sharply on the door. "MICHAEL! Turn that noise off IMMEDIATELY! It's time for your dinner and your father's waiting!" The music ceased abruptly and suddenly the house was basking in heavenly, heavenly peace and quiet. "*Kah*-ming!" announced an irritated little voice from behind the door. With a final "Hurry up then!," Mrs Hudson retraced her steps downstairs. Honestly, life had been an absolute *nightmare* since they'd foolishly agreed to buy Michael a little gramophone for his birthday, but at least it was an improvement on having to put up with that awful American muck he liked on the big Regentone radiogram in the living room. And he'd been *so* insistent that a gramophone of his own was what he wanted. He'd chosen it as his reward for entering his third year at grammar school in the A stream. It may not have been at the right school — Michael's father, Frederick Hudson, taught English, Latin and history to O level at Reading's most prestigious school; Michael's disappointing results in the eleven-plus exam had only entitled him to a place in the second-best school — but at least it was the top stream. Hudsons were *always* in the top stream. It was the family rule.

Michael half ran, half tumbled down the stairs. Such a graceless, clumsy boy: tall, skinny and so utterly uncoordinated that it was no surprise that he was useless at games. Which didn't mean, unfortunately, that he was an intellectual: his teachers undoubtedly relished telling a master at the town's top school how disappointing Michael's results generally were. Maybe his high placings in the previous year's exams had been some kind of fluke. Certainly all he seemed to care about was that bloody music. He always complained that he received less pocket-money than any of his classmates whose parents weren't actually poor, and most weeks he denied himself sweets and comics and trips to the cinema, sedulously hoarding his pennies to buy those dreadful records. And he played them so loud that half the time it was almost impossible to listen to the radio downstairs.

He was still wearing his school uniform, delighted by his first pair of the long trousers which announced to the world that, while he was not yet an adult, he was at least no longer a child. However, Mrs Hudson noted disapprovingly, his shirt collar was unbuttoned, his tie was loosened and pulled to one side, and his hair a complete mess.

Mr Hudson was waiting for him at the dining table. As ever, all Michael could see of his father was an unfolded copy of that morning's *Daily Telegraph* from behind which puffs of aromatic blue pipe smoke would periodically ascend languidly towards the ceiling. The three of them emitted a perfunctory unison mumble which a keen-eared listener might have deciphered as the family saying grace and then addressed themselves to their grey, flavourless roast lamb, mashed potatoes, and watery overcooked peas and carrots. Mr Hudson's laden forkfuls disappeared behind his newspaper. Conversation was brief and sporadic.

"Have you finished your homework?"

"Done English and geography. Haven't finished the Latin."

"Well, there'll be no more of that racket until it's all done. If you've finished before nine o'clock, you can listen until then, but only if you turn it down."

"Oh, *mum...*"

"Listen to your mother now, "from behind the *Telegraph*. "That decision is final."

There was a jaunty rat-a-tat-tat at the door. Sighing, Mrs Hudson went to answer. A few seconds later, she was back: a tall, cheerful-looking individual hovering behind her. "Michael, it's Mark come to see you." Mark Reynolds was the twenty-two-year-old son of their next-door neighbours: when he'd been fourteen to Michael's six, he'd spent the best part of a summer in a wholly unsuccessful attempt to turn Michael into a decent cricketer. Absolutely mustard for what he called 'modern jazz,' he had joined the Merchant Navy purely to take advantages of stopovers in New York, which allowed him two or three days on each voyage to scour the shops for obscure records and night-owl his way around the Village Vanguard, Birdland and other celebrated Manhattan jazz clubs, where he would worship at the feet of musicians with strange names like Thelonious Monk and Charlie Mingus and John Coltrane.

Before setting off on his most recent jaunt across the Atlantic, Mark had asked Michael what he wanted for his upcoming birthday. Michael couldn't believe his good fortune. "Get me some rock and roll records," he had begged Mark. The birthday had come and gone while Mark was still at sea. But now Mark was back, carolling "Hello youngster!," and he was holding a huge parcel behind his back.

"Please may I leave the table?" he pleaded, and after a seemingly eternal delay while his request was considered, Mrs Hudson allowed, a trifle grudgingly, that she supposed it would be all right. Mr Hudson issued a vaguely affirmative grunt from behind his paper. Michael scampered up the stairs, Mark following him at a more dignified pace. "Not too long now," Mrs Hudson called after them. "Remember you've still got homework to finish." Safe in his room, Michael cleared a space on his narrow bed for Mark and sat down, fingers itching. Smiling, Mark held the gift-wrapped parcel out to him. Michael tore away the wrapping and sat back, stunned. "Woowwwwwwwwww," was all he said. Then he remembered his manners and stammered incoherent thanks.

The parcel was a whole stack of LPs. Michael's pocket-money would only stretch to singles: he had never had any long-players of his own before, only the ones his parents had bought him. He had a couple of 78s, but mostly he collected the new seven-inch 45s. He had a few by Elvis and two by Little Richard. The only British artists represented in his sparsely populated record rack were Lonnie Donegan and a new bloke, Cliff Richard, whose first record, Move It, he'd bought two weeks ago. And now here he was with his bed practically covered in LPs: proper American ones with stiff matt cardboard covers, not the floppy shiny ones English LPs came in.

"I got you some stuff I thought you'd like," Mark said, smiling benignly. There was *The Chirping Crickets,* with Buddy Holly on the cover holding this really strange-looking guitar with horns and a blond-wood neck. There was the Everly Brothers' first LP — the brothers on a motor-scooter, the Everly riding pillion had a guitar slung across his back — and no less than two by Elvis: one had a picture of Elvis, mouth open, strumming his guitar while his name ran down the left-hand side of the cover and across the bottom in fluorescent pink and green; the other, *Elvis' Golden Records*, had just about every Elvis hit he'd ever heard.

"And I got you some that you won't like now, but you will when you grow up," Mark continued. Michael's heart sank as little: that was the sort of thing his parents would say when they bought him classical records, or boring sentimental songs for old people. These were more promising, though: one was called *Miles Ahead*, by a trumpeter called Miles Davis, and there was one with a really weird cover by the mysterious Thelonious Monk, who Mark said was a really great piano player.

"These ones here," Mark said, handing over the last three LPs, "are people you haven't heard of, but if you like that rock and roll stuff you'll probably like these. It's called blues." They were all by Negroes.

The first record was called *The Best Of Muddy Waters*. The second, *The Ray Charles Story*, had a bloke on the front in really big sunglasses. Michael immediately decided he wanted a pair like that for himself. "He wears those because he's blind," Mark said, evidently reading Michael's mind. The third had a man in a bright red suit on the cover, doing the splits with a guitar held behind his neck, against a rich blue circle. It was called *Once In A Blue Moon*.

"Which one do you want to play first?" Mark asked mischievously. The kid was obviously drowning in indecision: starved of music and then suddenly confronted with an epicurian feast in gourmand quantity. Michael's forefinger stabbed out at the Blue Moon LP. "This one," he announced decisively. He took it over to the Dansette gramophone in the corner, switched it on, proudly flipping the speed control to thirty-three, the first time he'd ever done so for a record he'd willingly chosen to listen to. He turned the volume down to what he hoped was a parent-acceptable level, reverently removing the record from its cardboard jacket and paper inner sleeve, placing it on the turntable, carefully lowering the needle onto the opening groove.

The first thing he heard was a slicing electric guitar playing an insolently teasing line, answered by a heavy *ba-whump* from bass, drums and brass. Then the same again. Then a voice, simultaneously deep and nasal, started to sing...

And then his mother was in the room carrying a tray with a plate of chocolate biscuits and two cups of tea. "You boys can listen for ten minutes," she conceded, "and then I'm afraid Michael has to finish his homework before his bedtime."

"Oh, *Mu-ummm...*"

"You can have lots of fun listening to your new records over the weekend, or you can play them... *quietly!*... tomorrow evening. Thank you very much, Mark," she added, "I'm sure he'll be delighted. Have you said thank you to Mark for your new records?" she asked Michael sternly.

"Yes he has, Mrs Hudson," Mark interposed quickly, "like a real little gentleman."

"That's all right then," Mrs Hudson said, not quite certain whether Mark was poking fun at her or not.

Mark and Michael listened to almost half of the first side of the LP before Mrs Hudson knocked at the door to demand that Michael return to his homework immediately. Latin translation was hard enough even when Michael was concentrating, but tonight it took more than twice as long as usual. All he could think about was the man in the red suit with the piercing guitar and that voice which seemed to be the absolute incarnation of worldly wisdom.

Later, tucked up in bed, he just wanted to be listening to that record. Then he wanted to pick up his own guitar and try to play along. He'd shown little aptitude for either piano or violin and, when he'd first asked for a guitar when he was eleven, his patents had compromised by buying him a ukelele, possibly envisioning him accompanying them at family sings of Tea For Two or If You Were The Only Girl In the World or even, yeuuchhh, How Much Is That Doggie In The Window.

Then they'd finally capitulated and bought him a guitar for his birthday. Mr Hudson had seen it advertised on a school notice-board and bought it, for £2 10/-, from a fifth-form pupil. It was next to impossible to get it to play in tune all the way up the neck, and the strings were so far off the fretboard that it was actively painful to try and press them down. Mr Hudson had hoped that the guitar's shoddiness and unapproachability would put young Michael off all this Negro foolishness

and bring him to his senses, but against all the odds Michael had perse-
vered with the instrument and could already play three or four chords.

Now Michael, drifting off to sleep, was imagining himself in a bright
red suit like James Blue Moon's and a pair of big sunglasses like Ray
Charles's, playing a ferociously loud electric guitar while girls — particularly that tall snooty blonde from the convent school who he sometimes saw at the bus stop but didn't have the nerve to talk to — swooned
before him and impossibly complex phrases fell elegantly from his fingertips.

And he wondered what James Blue Moon's life was like. A man like
that, who played so brilliantly and looked so — what would Mark call
it? Cool? — must have lots of money and loads of girlfriends. He must
know all the other stars, like Elvis and Little Richard and Buddy Holly
and that blind guy Ray Charles, really well. And he probably drove a really fabulous car, probably a Cadillac — Michael wasn't quite sure what
a Cadillac looked like, but all the articles he read about American stars
said they drove Cadillacs — with darkened windows and a radio and
leather seats that smelled of sex, whatever sex smelled like. Wherever
he went the tough guys all knew him and admired him for his talent. He
was probably a tough guy himself. Michael could imagine Moon in mid-
performance, swinging his guitar to one side, gracefully fast-drawing a
gleaming automatic from beneath his billowing red jacket in a single
smooth action, drilling a thief trying to rob the place he was playing
with one shot, then finishing the song to wild applause.

He couldn't think of anything he wanted more in the whole wide
world right now than to play the blues and be exactly like James Blue
Moon when he grew up. He'd never really wanted to grow up before, because his parents and all his parents' grown-up friends were so boring,
living in a grey world where thin grey daylight could barely force its way
through tightly-drawn net curtains, where all the colours and flavours
were bland and muted and the volume control was always turned right
down.

James Blue Moon was the first grown-up Michael Hudson had ever
wanted to be.

CHICAGO, ILLINOIS, 1958

These stairs sure as hell never get any easier, Blue thought as he hauled his guitar, amplifier and suitcase up to the apartment. Don't get any cleaner, neither, he added, narrowly avoiding a pool of piss on the landing. At his approach a rat skittered away into the darkness. Lights gone upstairs, too. He better get on to the super about it first thing tomorrow.

He was dog-tired. Been out on the road thirty-five days. Last show'd been in St Louis. He'd driven straight from the gig still wearing his red stage suit, now stained, crumpled and stinking, and he'd had to drop Levi the drummer off at his crib, drum set and all, before finally making it all the way home. The only consolation was the thick wad of cash in his wallet, over eight hundred bucks. All he wanted to do now was take a shower, wash off the road and the sticky residue of sweat and bodily fluids from that girl he'd had in the alley back of the club in St Louis, maybe catch a shave — he ran a thumb over the rasping stubble on his cheeks and jaw — and then sleep for about a week. It was late now, what with the storm damn near lashing the car off the road, a five-car collision blocking the highway and slowing him up for hours, and then taking Levi home and having one last drink with him. Or maybe it had been two. That damn Chevrolet was about to die on him after all that roadwork; he thanked his lucky stars it had still been able to crawl those last few miles. Damn roof was leaking, too, steady drip of water right down the back of his neck.

Idly, he wondered who owned the big black Lincoln parked outside on the corner, then dismissed it from his mind. With a little luck Mary and Venetia would be asleep and he wouldn't have to talk to them until he'd gotten clean and had himself a good few hours stacking up them zees.

Unlocking the door, he was faintly surprised to find the lights on. Mary normally switched everything off before going to bed, Blue thought as he dropped his suitcase next to the other suitcases.

Other suitcases? What in the...?

Mary was waiting up for him. She was wearing her church dress. Through the open door he could see Venetia, asleep on her bed but also fully dressed.

"James..." she said. She always called him James. Reminded him of his mom and dad. Everybody he knew in music just called him Blue, but Mary said Blue was his worldly name, that the folks called him that weren't nuthin' but sinful trash.

"James... me'n Venetia can't live this way no more."

WHOMP. Soaked, stinking and tired as he was, Blue felt like he'd been punched in the gut. Mechanically he put down his guitar and amplifier and sat down heavily in his armchair. "What you talkin' about?"

"James, six years now you been making records, supposed to be some big *star*..." she positively spat the word out "... and we got a little more money'n we had when you was drivin' a truck, but them Jews you workin' for don't be payin' you nuthin' like what you should be gettin', all them records they say you sellin' for them. We still living in this same crummy apartment with the heat go off half the time an' rats outside in the halls ..."

"Big mice," Blue interrupted, with a warning glance into the tiny room where Neesha lay sleeping.

" ... big mice and drunks'n junkies all around. And half the time you ain't even here. When you *are* here, you out playin' clubs when you ain't in the studio. When you ain't here, I get floozies on the phone for you all the time, callin' from Houston or New York or I don't know where. Most'a the time, Neesha don't even have a daddy.

"James, we tired'a livin' this way. I'm tryin' to raise my daughter to live a decent life. I ain't bringin' her up to hang out with lowlifes in bars. I'm raisin' her up to work hard, live clean, go to church..."

Moon found his voice at last. "I was wonderin' when we was gonna get to talkin' about the church," he said, his voice crackling with fatigue.

"James, I'm gonna say it as plain as I can. I want us to be a family again, like we was before you started makin' records and went to the road. I want you to stop travellin', get yourself a real job right here in Chicago..."

"You want me to go back to drivin' a truck? You want me to throw away everything I been workin' for since nineteen-and-fifty-one? You want...?"

"I ain't finished yet. There's one more thing I want. I know you spent your whole life runnin' from Jesus. I want you to stop runnin'. I want you to turn around and embrace Him. Me'n Neesha done took the Lord into our lives, and we need you to do the same if you want us all to stay together."

Her voice softened. "James, I know you love us. And you know we love you, too. I know that in your heart you're a good man. But you move in a world where the devil be callin' loud and clear even to a good man like you. You got to leave that world, honey. You got to follow us to a place where you can be that good man I know you are. The Reverend Holland say…"

The anger simmering below Blue's surface was bubbling now. He raised a bloodshot gaze to stare straight into Mary's eyes. "The Reverend Holland? *Oh* baby. Things is startin' to get *real* clear now. I suppose you done embraced the Reverend Holland right along with embracin' Jesus?"

Mary flushed. "Well, you know I spent some time comfortin' him after his wife passed…"

"Comfortin' him? *Com*-fortin' him? That what you call it now?"

"Now that the devil talkin' for sure. Reverend Holland is a man of God, and nuthin' like that done happened between us." She sighed and knelt down beside his chair, taking his hand in hers. "James, it's true me and the Reverend done a lotta talkin'. He willin' to take us on, me'n Neesha. I told him I needed one last talk with you, see if me'n Neesha can bring you back. I need a man gonna be there for me'n Neesha and help me raise her right. Nuthin' in this world make me happier than if that man was you. But if it ain't…"

She took a deep breath and clasped his hand tighter. "James… I want a divorce."

Now Blue felt like he'd been kicked in the head by his daddy's old mule. "I thought you'n your Reverend Holland didn't hold with divorce."

"Most'a the time that's true. But this is an emergency. If I got to get a divorce from you to protect my daughter, give her a daddy gonna be there to look after and help me raise her right, then I'll get a divorce."

Neesha appeared in the doorway. She was eleven now, solid and sturdy like her mother, and like her grandfather.

"Daddy," she ran into his arms. "You gonna stay with us, daddy? Don't leave us, please daddy."

There was such a tightness in his chest that he could hardly speak. He hugged her fiercely. "I don't wanna leave you, sugar. But your mom say she gonna take you away." He looked up at Mary. "You leave if you want to. But Neesha stays with me."

"Now you talkin' crazy. You know you away half the time, an' when you here you in studios'n bars. How you gonna look after a young girl?

You know you can't raise her by yourself. What you gonna do? Take her on the road, have her raised up by drunks'n gamblers'n floozies in bars? You know you just talkin' foolishness now. Neesha stays with me. The only question is whether you gonna stay with *us*."

"Daddy," Neesha snuffled. "You got to stay home with us. And if you ask the Lord Jesus for help, He gonna give you the strength to quit livin' like you been livin'."

God damn. Now my own daughter talkin' in my daddy's voice. Everything I been tryin' to get away from my whole life done followed me home. An' everything I spent my life workin' for gonna be taken away. If there's a God and I ever meet Him, Blue thought, I'm'a ask him one question: why me? I don't gamble, not for big money anyways. I don't steal. Don't lie. Don't cheat folks. Pay my musicians well. Don't drink but a little. Never raise my hand to my wife or my daughter. Work hard tryin' to make people forget they troubles, get happy in the evenin's and weekends. Work my ass off puttin' food on my family's table. Study music, read books. Be as good a man as I can be. Now I done reached a fork in the road and I don't know which way to go.

I could use me some serious help round about now.

And something loosened inside Blue. It was the strangest feeling he'd ever had. It was a little bit like what happened sometimes when he was playing, when he stopped thinking and planning and composing in his head and just went to a timeless place deep down inside himself, where he was no longer choosing what note or lick to hit next but almost sitting back and listening to what he was playing, surprising himself by the sounds his fingers were making come out his his amplifier. It was moments like that kept him going, moments when he felt warm, free and clear, wired direct to the mains power of the universe singing right through him.

And now he was still sitting in his chair, and words were coming out his mouth, and he was just listening to what something inside of him was making him say. "This music I play, this work that I do, it ain't no hobby. It ain't no game. It ain't no trick so I don't have to do a regular job. It's what I was put here on this earth to do. This music is a callin'. Yeah, a callin', just like what a priest get. And there ain't no evil in it. Every night I play, I look down at the peoples and I see they faces. I see 'em come in the place weighed down by they troubles, worryin' 'bout they jobs'n money an' The Man. And I see 'em smile'n laugh'n dance'n go home with a smile on they face an' a weight off they shoulders.

"The blues ain't no devil's music. The blues put on this earth to make folks feel better, an' I was put on this earth to play the blues. Anyone say any different, they the ones been listenin' to the devil, not me. If there's a God like you say, then I'm doin' His work, right here, with what I'm doin'. I love you both like crazy, an' I would never leave either one'a y'all. But I can't quit what I'm doin' an' still be a whole man."

Mary's face froze. "Then you gonna be a whole man by yourself. We goin' now. The Reverend be waitin' up."

Blue looked over at Neesha. Her head was bowed so he couldn't see her eyes. He took her in his arms and gently tried to lift her head so he could look at her, but she obstinately fought to keep her head lowered.

"Neesha... honey... just remember this. Never forget this. I love you and I ain't leavin' you. You bein' taken away. I didn't leave."

Her voice was small and tearful, but resolute and firm. "Daddy, you been leavin' us for a long time now. Now *you* remember *this*. We may be leavin', but you the one lettin' us go. *That's* what I'm gonna remember my whole life. *You* let *me* go."

She pulled away from him to stand with her mother.

"Goodbye, James," Mary said. "We gonna pray for you."

All of the accumulated fatigue of the road suddenly came back. It was like a huge weight pinning Blue to his chair. With a massive effort he hauled himself to his feet. The inner voice was no longer speaking for him. All he could do was mutter, "Neesha... Mary... please... don't," but it wasn't doing a damn bit of good. They picked up their cases and, without so much as a backward glance, walked out the door, slamming it behind them. He listened to their footsteps recede down the hall, realised whose limo it was downstairs and who it had been waiting for.

Absentmindedly, he unlatched his guitar case, took out the big Gibson he'd saved so long to buy and cradled it in his arms, waiting for a song to come to him, listening to the rain lash the building and the wind moan high and lonesome through that window that never would quite shut, desolation descending around his shoulders like a cold wet blanket. *If this ain't the blues*, he thought, *I surely don't know what is.*

TWELVE

LOS ANGELES, SUMMER 2004

By now, Hudson and Adrienne had reached the coffee stage. He'd ordered a large Armagnac to go with his, she was considering whether to join him. She wasn't used to drinking so much: a couple of glasses of wine with a meal being her usual limit. But tonight she'd had that martini before dinner and they'd somehow gotten through two bottles of wine, though she had to admit that he'd had more of it than she had.

"No thanks, I'm good," she informed the hovering Todd, who disappeared before returning moments later with Hudson's Armagnac. Hudson tipped half of it into his coffee and sipped at what was left.

"I had a real nice time tonight," Adrienne told him. "We talked about music and old times, we talked about my jewellery business and all the wonderful things I could make for you and your kids, we even talked about damn Dubya Bush and the election, which I normally do not do 'cause it makes me so mad. We have *not* talked about what's going on right now back at my house and..." she placed her hands palms-down flat on the tablecloth "... we ain't said word one about why Venetia hates you so much. Blue said you and her had a thing a long time back and it went wrong, but that doesn't tell me very much at all. So c'mon..." she fixed him with the penetrating gaze that generally worked when Donna was reluctant to tell her something she wanted to know "... 'fess up."

His face closed tight. "Yeah... what Blue told you's true, as far as it goes. She and I had a thing thirty-odd years ago, and it went wrong. Let's just leave it at that."

"Mi-ick..." Damn, but the wine was getting to her. Now she remembered why she hardly ever drank very much: it put her judgement out. Shut your mouth, girl, she told herself. Instead she said, "I want to know what it is you're not telling me."

Enunciating a little more deliberately than he usually did, Hudson said, "It's not my secret... it's not my story to tell."

"It *is* your story," she shot back. "You just don't want to tell it."

"You're right there," he said. "I don't. And while we're on the subject of who's not telling who what, you haven't told me why *you* hate *her* so much you won't be in the house if she's there."

"Blue say anything about that?"

"Yeah. He said she came by while you were pregnant with Donna and insulted you."

"That's one way of putting it," she said, the emotions of that moment fourteen years earlier washing back over her in a hot-blood flush. She could feel the veins swelling up like cables on her neck and arms. "Yeah, I was big with Donna and she came by. She's walkin' round my kitchen telling me that I didn't have things organised the way her daddy liked it... though how she could know how her daddy liked things when she ain't lived with him since she was eleven or something, I don't know. She said I was nuthin' but a gold-digging ho, only after him for his money, and that as soon as I had his kid I was gonna be taking him to the cleaners. She said there was no way a *fine young gal* like me could really want an old fool like him for himself, and that one day he was gonna regret he ever met me.

"She said the devil had sent me to steal what was left of her daddy's soul."

Hudson reached across the table and lightly rested his hand on her shoulder. Beneath the satiny skin it felt like a ball of hard rubber. "Hey," he murmured gently. "Easy up. Chill out a bit, Missis Blue." She looked down and saw that she was gripping the tablecloth in both pale-knuckled fists. With an effort, she released the bunched fabric and sat back in her chair, suddenly aware once again of where she was and who she was with, like the background murmur of the other diners and the muted clatter and clink of cutlery on crockery had suddenly been switched back on. She closed her eyes, breathed slow and deep, looked down and watched the veins in her arms gradually deflate. "Maybe I'll have that Armagnac after all," she said.

Hudson was looking at his watch as he waved Todd back over to their table. "We're supposed to wait for Blue to call us, right?" he asked. She nodded yes. "Well, it's getting late, and Blue and her've been at it for a fair old while now. Do you want to stay here 'til he calls or should we go and wait somewhere else?"

Maudie Lam had been watching TV in the living room. She heard the doorbell ring, put down her knitting, flipped on the hall light and went to answer it. She opened the door to the visitor she'd been told to expect.

All she knew was that this woman was her new employer's daughter, that she was a very famous singer, and that her name was Venetia.

"Good evening," Maudie said politely. "My name is Maudie Lam, and I am Mr Moon's nurse." She took a step back, partly to let Mr Moon's guest in, and partly because the force of the woman's spirit was pushing her back. Such strong *chi*, she thought, very strong and pure. There is a lot of love pent up in this one, but it is blocked. Sometime in her life something has bent her out of shape, but her chi is too powerful for that to have stopped her growing. No matter how rich and famous Venetia was, Maudie could not stop herself from feeling compassion towards her, burdened as she was with so much pain and sorrow and anger, all mixed up so completely that there was no longer any separation between them. Maudie wished she had this one on her massage table. There was so much she could do for her.

The woman in front of Maudie was small, stocky and strongly built, carrying rather more weight than Maudie would have thought good for her, but not soft. Maudie guessed Venetia was some years older than herself, somewhere in her fifties, wearing a richly coloured floor-length African print dress with a heavily-jewelled crucifix pendant and matching earrings, her hair in a glossy black Cleopatra bob. She barely acknowledged Maudie's greeting.

"I'm here to see my father," was all she said.

If that is how you want it, Maudie thought, that is how it will be. At least for now. She led Venetia down the hall to Blue's music room. "Mr Moon is in there," she said. "If there is anything you need, call me." She returned to the living room and settled back down on the sofa facing the TV.

Venetia waited in the hall for a few seconds, trying to place what she could hear through the door, couldn't. She knocked, and then entered without waiting for a response. She could see Blue sitting in his wheelchair in a sweatshirt and baseball cap, his back to the door, guitar in his hands. He was playing some old-time ragtimy riff and singing quietly to himself. He was singing, "*Down South the hog is man's best friend.*" Something tore inside her. She slapped a mental Band-Aid over it. She cleared her throat ostentatiously.

Blue returned his old Stella guitar to its stand and wheeled to face her. She was struck momentarily speechless by the change in him. The last time she'd seen him he'd gained weight, a far cry from the lanky figure she remembered from her childhood. Now he was thinner than he'd ever been, impossibly thin, white-bearded, shrunken. He looked up at her.

"How you been doin'," he said without inflection. It didn't sound like a question.

"I'm good. How're you." Likewise.

"Dyin'." Ornery old man wasn't budging an inch, she thought. He'd pulled all these stunts — or rather, he'd gotten Mick Hudson to pull them for him — in order to get her here, and now she was here and ready to talk he was pulling an Old Stone Face routine on her. He picked up the guitar and, almost under his breath, started back into the song about the hog.

"Stop that!" she snapped. It came out louder and fiercer than she'd intended. He stopped playing and singing, raised his eyebrows. "You always useta love that song," he said.

"Yeah, when I was six."

This wasn't going right. She took a breath, centred it in her gut. "Look... daddy," she said, calm as she could. "You got..." she couldn't bring herself to say the name "you got... *him*... to hunt me down, tell me you're dying and say you're gonna make one more record and you want me to sing. You want to talk, here I am. You want to play games, play 'em by yourself."

Blue considered that. "Okay, that's fair," he said. He indicated the armchair. "Put your bag down an' res' yourself. You want a drink? Somethin' to eat?" She dropped her bag and lowered herself into the armchair.

"Just some water." He wheeled over to the water cooler in the corner, drew some off into a glass from a nearby tray. He rolled to where she was sitting, held the glass out to her. Their fingers touched. She wanted to take his hand, warm those dry sticklike fingers between her palms. She didn't. She sipped at the water, put the glass down on the floor beside her chair.

"Where's your wife? Your daughter?" She'd kind of been hoping Adrienne would be here. Last time they'd met, she'd misjudged the girl and shot her mouth off. It'd've been good to have the chance to make that right, because she'd gotten Adrienne completely wrong. All these years later and she and Venetia's dad were still together and, by all accounts, happy. And there was a new half-sister she'd never set eyes on, in her teens by now, older than she'd been when her mother had left her daddy for Reverend Cleotis Holland. Late in life, Blue had finally found him someone with whom he could build himself a solid family. There had been comparatively few times in Venetia's life when she'd felt that she had some making-right to do. This was one of those times.

"Donna's stayin' with friends from school. Adrienne's out for dinner. I thought you'd want me'n you to have the house to ourselves tonight." She nodded grudgingly. "Okay. Like the man said: let us not speak falsely now, the hour's getting' late. I'm'a lay it out for you 'bout as straight as I can." He wheeled a little closer, angling his chair so he was looking straight at her.

"'Bout two months back, doc told me I had liver cancer. Gave me 'bout a year. Tops. Started talkin' about surgery an' chemotherapy an' whatall. Told him I druther die in one piece with my git-tar in my hand."

Reflexively, Venetia kept her face frozen and masklike. She'd learned to do that during her years as stepdaughter to the Reverend Holland, who frowned on just about every expression of youthful spontaneity. It was a knack which had stood her in good stead throughout her life. Whenever anything threatening or distressing manifested itself in her life, she'd always found that one of two basic responses were enough to resolve most situations in her favour. She could either unleash her formidable temper and blast all opposition through the back wall, or else harden her features into an impregnable, unreadable shield and remain remote and safe behind it, where nothing anybody threw at her could ever reach her.

And now here she was, trying to keep her feelings off her face when she didn't even know exactly what her feelings were. Inner selves jostled for dominance at the forefront of her mind. A little girl who loved the daddy who made up funny little songs to sing her at bedtime and called rats 'big mice' so as not to scare her was trying to fight her way past a teenager abandoned by a father who'd rather clown around with a guitar on stages all over town, then all over the US and finally all over the world, than stay home and face the responsibility of living a decent Christian life and raising a child who needed him desperately. Between them, a grown woman who had learned over the years that the relationship between the sacred and the secular was never as clearcut as it might seem, and that relationships between men and women, especially under the pressures of racism and poverty, were even more complex, tried fruitlessly to intercede.

Blue was still talking. "I'm'a make one more record 'fore I go. I want to cut that record with my family. That means I want to sing with you, and I want Calvin to come do what he does: rap, produce, mix, whatever."

Keeping her voice as calm and still as her face, Venetia said, "When you say family…"

Blue nodded. "Yeah. Mick is gonna play, he's gonna sing a little and he'd gonna produce the album with me."

Venetia said, "Why does *he* have to be there?" Blue raised his eyebrows and nodded to himself.

"Because him and me been knowin' each other forty years, ever since he was a young boy in England tryin' to figure out which end of a git-tar was up, backin' me up, learnin' my style. Never know anybody listen to me close as him. He studied me like for a college degree. Nobody understand my music the way he do. Because he done looked out for me over the years, gettin' me work when there wadn't none from my own peoples, makin' sure I got paid, sayin' my name to reporters all over the world, tellin' 'em I was his idol, tellin' all his fans to go see me an' buy my records."

"Yeah, right," Venetia said, "and he stole every lick you ever played and made millions off your music."

"Sure, he wouldn't be where he is without what he learned from me'n my music. He know that, an' he told me so. But I wouldn't be where *I* am…" he waved a hand to take in his room, his house, all the things he had "… without him helpin' make me famous. Now *I* know that and I done told *him* so." Blue pushed down on the wheels of his chair and raised himself to a straight-backed upright position. How weak he is, Venetia thought, how frail. The simplest movement, even straightening up in his chair, is an effort for him. Two months ago they said he had a year. If he's gotten so puny so quick, how's he gonna last out a whole year? With crushing finality she thought, he ain't gonna make it. Maybe they're telling him he got a year, but I bet he got a lot less than that.

And what makes him think he's gonna have the strength to sing and play again? His hands all wasted, don't even look strong enough to bend a guitar string.

Inside her, all her warring selves fell silent as it sank in that, whether or not her daddy had been there for her as a child, pretty soon he wasn't

Charles Shaar Murray

going to be there, PERIOD.

It had never been harder to keep her mask in place.

Blue was saying, "So Mick is gonna be there. He's part of my family." His features shifted slightly behind the close-trimmed white beard. He was looking at her the way he'd looked at her when she was just a little girl and she'd been bad and he wanted her to know that he knew she'd been bad but he wasn't mad at her.

"You oughtta know that better'n anybody."

He knows, Venetia thought, and a second later, like the sound of thunder immediately after a flash of lightning, another realisation hit. *He's always known.*

Her composure broke. "You old *bastard!* Go ahead and *die*, muth-a*fuck*a! You can't be gone soon enough to suit me!"

She picked up her bag and marched out of the room, slamming the door behind her. An instant later, the secondary slam of the front door. Blue slumped in his wheelchair, let out a rattling, gasping sigh. Then he rolled over to the counter and picked up his phone.

"No, just coffee."

Hudson got up and headed for the kitchen. "Make that a *lot* of coffee," Adrienne called after him. "No milk, no sugar."

"Like they say at BK, you got it," he shouted back over the music.

From the depths of the black leather sofa, Adrienne had a panoramic view of the living room of Hudson's rented Hollywood Hills bungalow. It didn't have a lot of personality, but few rented places did unless you were gonna be there long enough to make it worthwhile furnishing. Apart from a couple of framed photographs — one of his two daughters splashing coltishly in a swimming pool and another of her and Blue which he'd taken around five years ago — a stack of guitar cases next to a little old tweed amp like Blue's and a pile of DAT cassettes and reference CDs by the sound system, it could pretty much belong to anybody with the money to pay for it.

Old as Mick is, he still likes his music loud, she thought. Mick had almost finished work on his live album, and right now he was blasting a version of Blue's Smile When You Say That from a concert he'd played in Philadelphia. Sounded good, she thought. She thought of all the people who probably associated the song first and foremost with Mick Hudson, or that heavy metal band who'd cut it a while back, rath-

113

er than with Blue. Those metal guys had obviously learned the song off one of Hudson's versions. God knows he'd recorded it often enough: she'd seen Blue's publishing royalty statements. She wondered if the metallers had ever heard Blue play it himself. Or even knew he existed.

Hudson came back into the room with two steaming coffee mugs. "Here ya go," he said, putting one down beside her. "Hot, black and strong." She looked at him. "The coffee," he said. She sipped. It was delicious. She raised an interrogative eyebrow. "Ethiopian," he told her. "Best coffee in Africa."

"It's good." She sipped again. "How many times you gonna cut this damn song, anyway? You been playing it practically since you were a baby. Now you've done it on at least three live albums already that I know of."

"That's what my record company says, too," Hudson said. "It always goes down great at shows, and I always do some of my best playing on that one. So there's usually a version every time we do a live record. I've had a few different guys through the band over the years, though, so it never sounds quite the same. Mark of a good song, that."

The music crunched to a halt. An avalanche of applause filled the room. "Thank you Philadelphia and good night!" the recorded Hudson shouted, and then the room was silent again.

Despite the coffee, Adrienne was starting to feel sleepy, and a little bit drunk. She was also resentful at being barred, even temporarily, from her own home because the Princess of Soul wanted to visit. She was longing for her bed. Why hadn't Blue phoned? Was something wrong? If she didn't hear from him within the next ten minutes, she was going to call Maudie's mobile and find out what was going on.

"I'm just gonna close my eyes for ten minutes," she told Hudson. "I'm a respectable middle-aged housewife who generally goes to bed early and I'm not used to all this decadent rock and roll lifestyle y'all got."

"Go ahead, I'll stand guard. Want some cushions?" He tossed her a couple from the other sofa. With a small sigh, she stretched, yawned mightily and closed her eyes. Hudson went back to the kitchen, poured himself a healthy snifter of Armagnac, and settled into the armchair opposite the sofa to watch her sleep.

He'd always thought Adrienne was dead attractive, but she'd been part of Blue's world, and Hudson was quite old-fashioned about that kind of thing. He'd never been around Adrienne without Blue being there, either right there in the room or just next door or something. They'd just been out to dinner together without Blue's physical presence, and he'd seen her afresh, outside of her usual context. Now, just for a few seconds, she wasn't Missis Blue: she was simply a rather gorgeous woman having forty winks on his rented sofa. Her face was partly obscured by her tumbling braids, but he could still see her full lips and broad, slightly upturned nose. Great figure, too: like a fitness model except without the hideous, disfiguring breast implants which put him off so many California women. He caught himself wishing she wasn't Blue's wife, but someone lovely he'd only just met.

As soon as the thought surfaced, Hudson stifled it. Right, that's enough of that. Put it away, matey-boy. What was he thinking about? She was his friend and idol's wife. His friend and idol was dying. And he'd already caused enough chaos and misery by getting involved with a member of Blue's family. Plus there was absolutely no reason to believe she'd be interested in him even if she wasn't totally committed to someone else. The whole thing was just ridiculous. He was too old for crushes, and she was the worst possible choice to get a crush on. And yet his eyes kept returning to her gym-toned brown arms and sweet sensual face.

It came as a blessed relief when, at long last, the phone rang.

Adrienne felt like she'd only just dozed off when Hudson gently shook her awake.

"Officer of the watch reporting, Captain," he said. "Just got the call." Adrienne yawned, stretched and rubbed her eyes.

"What'd he say?"

"And other Ray Charles favourites. It wasn't Blue, it was that new nurse you've got. Said he and Neesha had a bit of a ruck, she stomped off and he's really upset. Barely said two words to her and went to bed with a bottle of Jack. You should probably get back there."

"Damn right," she said, shrugging into her jacket. "I'd'a been there, I'd'a punched that fat bitch into the middle of next week."

"You want me to drive you back?" She looked at him derisively.

"Are you kidding? Much as you've had to drink, you ain't driving anywhere. Don't worry, I've got a car service I can call. I'll be fine."

Adrienne scrabbled in her bag, pulled out her mobile, punched in a number, gave her name and Hudson's address. Within a couple of minutes the doorbell rang.

"That'll be the car," she said, hefting her bag. She embraced him lightly. He bent down so that her lips could brush his cheek. "Thanks for being my date," she said. "I enjoyed it. You coming by tomorrow?"

"If I should."

"Well, *I* think you should," she said. "I got a feeling Blue's going to want to talk to you about whatever it was happened tonight. Donna'll be home tomorrow, and you know she likes to see you. Around three work for you?"

"Sounds good."

He stayed leaning in his doorway to watch her climb into her ride. He was still there when the car turned the corner and was lost to view.

"Don't go anyway *near* there, pal," he said to himself, and headed for the bathroom to clean his teeth.

THIRTEEN

In dreams:

Clad in head-to-toe ninja black, Glock in hand, Calvin Holland drifts like smoke down the long stone corridor. At the far end he sees Screwdriver and Omega Man shouting into radio microphones and busting dance moves. The corridor is cloaked in a suffocating silence, but since this is, after all, a dream and dream logic embraces an infinity of contradictions, he knows they are performing Battyman 9/11. He moves closer and closer to them, but they are completely unaware of his presence.

He is within easy reach of them now. One slippered foot lances upwards and outwards in a kick which connects perfectly with Screwdriver's jaw and sends him crashing senseless into a wall. Omega Man turns towards Calvin, but he's moving far too slowly to make any difference. A palm strike crushes Omega Man's cheekbone to splinters and he slowly crumples to the stone floor next to his breddamon.

There is a metal door set into the wall. Next to it is a security-lock keypad. Calvin punches in a four-digit code and the door slides open with a hiss of compressed air. Behind the door is a vast, dimly-lit office. At its far end is a huge desk under a pool of warm golden light which is almost the office's sole illumination. Behind the desk is a window through which can be seen a panoramic view of the Manhattan night sky-line.

Between the desk and the window is a luxurious leather chair, its back towards Calvin. The occupant of the chair is contemplating the spectacular view from the window. Above the back of the chair, all that can be seen is the top of the occupant's head. He is a white man with spiky grey hair.

Without moving or turning, he speaks. "So, Mr Holland," he says. "We meet at last. I have been following your progress with some interest. However, there is absolutely nothing you can do now which could possibly have even the slightest impact on my project." A pause. "Immobilise him, but do not harm him. I have plans for Mr Holland."

Calvin feels impossibly strong hands grab his ankles and upper arms. The Glock is twisted from his grasp. His hands are pulled behind his back. He hears the snick of handcuffs, feels metal bite into the skin of his wrists. A fraction of a second later, another snick as his ankles are cuffed. A derisive whisper from behind him, "Lickle weak paleface batty-boy, y'wan play games wid we now?" He hears his mother's voice shouting, "Now what did I tell you? I *told* you not to go there..." The man behind the desk spins his chair around to face Calvin. Calvin recognises him...

And then he was back in his body, suddenly, vibrantly awake, every nerve tingling, his pillows and sheets soaked with sweat. Thanking Allah that he was alone, he concentrated on recalling his dream. Every detail came alive with CGI clarity, except the face of the man behind the desk.

In dreams:

Adrienne Moon walks steadily forward through dense rolling mist which comes halfway up her thighs. The mist seems to be everywhere. She can't see more than a few feet in any direction. She is terribly, terribly cold. She is wearing only a black-and-white zebra-print bikini, but her body is flabby and slack the way it was just after Donna was born, rather than the lithe, defined form she'd worked so hard to achieve, the source of so much real-life pride. In the distance, through the fog, she can just about see a faint blue glow. She heads towards it; after all, it is the only thing she can see anywhere.

As she moves closer to the blue glow, faint images flicker in and out of visibility. First she sees Donna and calls her name. Donna shouts something back to her, but the fog seems to muffle sound and the next moment she is gone.

Adrienne keeps moving forward. She feels thick and slow and weak, and she wishes she had a robe or a dress or something to cover herself up. What if he sees her like this? Would he still love her?

Another figure looms out of the mist. Guitar slung over his shoulder, eyes closed, Mick Hudson's fingers are racing over the frets as he plays a frantic solo she can't hear. She calls to him, too, but he is lost in his silent music, and he ignores her. Soon he, too, is lost to view.

One... foot... in front... of the other. One... foot... in front... of the other. The blue glow seems to be getting closer, but in this treacherous world of freezing fog and chilly mist terms like 'closer' have little meaning. She trudges towards the glow.

Someone is blocking her path. Venetia Moon glares at her through a break in the mist. "I'm his daughter," she says. "You just his ho." She walks straight at Adrienne and right through her. Adrienne turns and looks around, but once again she is alone in the mist.

When she faces forward again, the blue glow is almost directly in front of her. The clouds part. The glow resolves itself into a stylised outline of a human face, etched in blue neon. The face belongs to her husband. Its mouth opens. Hollow, deafening laughter is still ringing in her ears as she snaps into wakefulness, Blue snoring fretfully beside her.

In dreams:

Donna Moon is tucked up in her bed, a protective honour guard of stuffed animals all around her to shield her from harm. She is six years old again. Next to her bed sits a skeleton in a wheelchair, holding a guitar. Its bony fingers pluck at the strings, knucklebones clattering against the neck. Its jaw opens cavernously wide. In a dry skittering voice, it begins to sing,
Down South the hog is man's best friend...
Donna woke up shivering despite the warm night. It took a serious exercise of will power to stop her calling out for her mama.

In dreams:

Venetia Moon is naked, blindfolded and gagged. She lies spread-eagled on a bed, wrists and ankles secured to the four corner bedposts. She cannot see or speak, and she can move only slightly and with real discomfort. Two men are seated on chairs at the foot of the bed, with guitars on their laps. Because this is a dream, and dream logic embraces an infinity of contradictions, she recognises them, despite her blindfold, as Mick Hudson and her father. Hudson looks the way he does now. Her father is young and fit, a pencil moustache outlining his upper lip, his hair in a glossy black pompadour, wearing a bright red suit.

"Go 'head on, young man, take her," says her father. "She don't mean nuthin' to me. She even more of a bitch than her mama."

"Mmmmmm," says Hudson. "I dunno. Not my type. I like tall elegant blondes. This one's fat, she snores and she's got the worst temper in the world."

"What you care, young man?" Blue asks. "You just gonna be foolin' with her awhile. Ain't like you gonna stay with her or nuthin'. No-one stays with Neesha. She just naturally too mean for anyone to stick with her for long. Like I didn't. You more important to me than she ever was, so jus' use her'n throw her away."

She wants to cry out, to tell them that she isn't mean or a bitch, that all she wants is for someone to love her and hold her and stay with her and show her they care about her, that she's just frightened because she's been hurt and rejected too many times, that she has all this love and wants to give it to someone with whom she feels safe, that she never wanted to have to be tough. But she can't; the gag makes sure of that. All she can do is make frantic muffled wordless noises, try and get them understand what she wants to tell them.

"Listen to the way the pig grunt and squeal," says Blue.

"Cor dear," says Hudson. "Bloody 'ell. That's disgustin', that is."

"G'wan," says Blue. "Fuck the pig. Fuck the pig *good*."

Now Calvin is there with them in his white sportswear. "Reason I'm fucked up the way I am," he says, "is 'cause my mama was an English cracker's ho."

Hudson turns towards the bed, starts undoing his suit pants. His cock is just like the head and neck of a Fender guitar, six vicious little tuning pegs protruding from it. Blue is plucking his guitar and singing, *Down South the hog is man's best friend...*

Venetia awakes ready to tear someone limb from limb. Make that *two* someones.

In dreams:

Mick Hudson and Adrienne Moon are making noisy sweaty wreck-the-room junglefucking love. She's sat astride him, eyes rolled right back into her head until only the whites show, drops of sweat clinging to the stiffened tips of her dark puckered nipples, tendons and veins standing out quivering all over her body, the etched muscles of her stomach undulating like satin-covered cobblestones in a slow-motion earthquake.

Hudson's head whips from side to side on the pillow as her pelvis twists and grinds down on his again and again. Suddenly his eyes open and he sees Blue standing over the bed, his wheelchair beside him. "Young man," he says, "Ain't there nuthin'a mine you got too much shame to take?"

Venetia steps out beside him. "See? I told you," she says, "All any'a us ever been to him an' his kind is easy pickin's." She takes a gun from behind her back, hands it to Blue. He aims it square between Hudson's eyes and pulls the trigger.

Mick Hudson woke up shaking with terror, a long-unfamiliar stickiness on his thighs. He hadn't had a wet dream since he was an adolescent sleeping in that narrow bed in his little room at his parents' house. Until tonight.

In dreams:

Blue isn't dreaming.

When she heard Hudson's signature ring, Adrienne answered the door herself. She was wearing a short white towelling robe. "C'mon in," she said, leading the way into the kitchen and scooping him a beer from the fridge.

"Blue's sleeping right now," she told him. This was something of a euphemism. Blue was indeed sleeping. To be precise, he was sleeping off most of a bottle of Jack Daniel's he'd consumed the previous night and, since Maudie had taken the morning off and therefore hadn't been around to stop him, he'd had the remains of it this morning. "Me'n Donna are out back by the hot tub. Care to join us?"

"Affirmative, Number One," Hudson said in a fairly creditable Jean-Luc Picard voice. "Any more word on what happened last night?" he asked, as himself.

Adrienne shook her head. "He was asleep when I got in. This morning he was in full-on grumpo mode and barely said a word. I just got back from the store and now he's asleep again."

Hudson shrugged. "Oh well. More news on the hour as it happens." He popped the beer can.

"By the way," Adrienne said, "I brought you something from the store." From the pocket of her robe, she produced a small presentation box and handed it to Hudson.

"Well, thank'ee kindly," he said.

"Go on, open it." Inside, on a silver chain, was a silver pendant in the shape of a miniature National Resonator guitar, accurate in every exquisite detail.

"Wow," he said. "This is amazing. Thank you." She took it from his hand.

"Here," she said. "Let me put it on you." As she reached up to clasp the pendant's chain at the back of his neck, her robe fell open. Beneath it she was wearing a black and white zebra-print bikini.

"This is brilliant," he said. "How much do I owe you?"

"On the house. Compliments of the management." Dropping her robe on a chair by the back door, she ushered him towards the hot tub in the garden. Donna was sprawled on a lounger in a blue bikini. She was just beginning to shed her puppy fat; a navel ring peeping from between two remaining rolls of flesh.

"I hope you brought a swimsuit," Adrienne said. Hudson was wearing black Versace jeans and a white Levi's shirt. "Or at least some shorts."

"You've got to be joking," Hudson said, "Unlike too many of my distinguished contemporaries, I have chosen to conceal the ravaging effects of the passing decades on my once-enviable physique. Especially in the presence of two such dazzling beauties. Under conditions of genuine emergency, I may possibly remove my shoes and socks."

"Okay, I'm declaring an official emergency right now." Adrienne settled back on her lounger next to Donna and reached for the sun cream. Hudson sat down opposite them, unlaced his Old Skool Adidas trainers and peeled off his socks.

"Ahhh... free at last," he sighed, wiggling his toes. He raised his eyes to meet Donna's. "How you holding up, kid?"

"I'm still getting my head around everything that's happening," Donna said quietly. "It doesn't seem real, but I know it is." She looked up at Hudson. "People keep saying oh, it's amazing he's still with us, being eighty-three and all, but it still seems like he'd being taken away from us before his time.

"I know he's an old person and everything, but if he hadn't gotten sick he'd be with us for years and years. He was so strong, so full-on, so high-energy before he got sick, it was easy to forget how old he was. He wasn't like an old person before."

"He's not like an old person now," Hudson said. "He's like a guy who's ill. Someone half his age'd be like this if he was as sick as Blue is."

"Y'know," Adrienne said, "I get asked what it's like having a husband who's so much older, but I always say Blue never seems like an old man to me, just a man." Hudson glanced over at her, saw her languidly rubbing suncream into one taut thigh, was uncomfortably reminded of his dream. He hastily switched his gaze back to Donna, saw that she'd followed his eyes from her to Adrienne and back.

Adrienne gave absolutely no sign of having noticed any of this. She got unhurriedly to her feet. "Just going to see if Blue's awake yet. You want anything from the kitchen? Another beer?"

Hudson hefted his can. There was still some beer left in it, but now it was warm from the sun. "Wouldn't mind a cold one," he said. "Sure thing," she replied, picking up his discarded can and heading for the kitchen. Hudson deliberately kept his eyes on Donna, not watching Adrienne walk away.

"Everybody looks at mama," Donna said. The kid was practically reading his mind. Hudson felt himself blushing. Was he really that obvious? "Even the boys I know from school. They say she's the hottest mom of anyone in our class. I just keep telling myself I'm gonna look like that when I'm older."

"I reckon you will," he said.

"What were you like when you were a kid at school, Mick?"

"A complete mess," Hudson said, relieved at the change of subject. "Total geek. Skinny, tongue-tied, not really good at anything. Didn't really get on with my folks. They didn't mistreat me or anything, but it was like me and them were from different planets. Hardly spoke the same language. I was only really interested in music, and the music I liked they absolutely hated. Probably a blessing to all concerned when I left home."

Adrienne was back, handing him another beer. "He's still asleep. Sorry you had to come all the way out here and have him not be ready for you."

"Not to worry," Hudson said. "I mean, Jesus, Blue should do whatever he needs to do to feel better. He probably needs all the rest he can get." He took a swig of his beer. "Tell you what, if he's not up in the next half-hour I should probably head back.

"Listen, I've been thinking," he said after a moment. "I ought to go back to England, even if it's only for a week or two. Sort a few things out, spend a bit of time with the girls."

"Why don't you bring them out here?" Donna asked. "It'll be cool! You've got enough space at your house, haven't you? And they can hang with me and my friends."

"Oh, space ain't a problem," Hudson said. "That place has rooms I haven't even been in yet. And I bet they'd have a really good time with you and your mates. It's just that I don't want to bring the girls out and then leave 'em on their own all the time because I'm doing stuff with Blue." And, he added silently, I don't want them anywhere near all this stuff with Neesha. Even more than that, he suddenly realised, if he was so obviously getting hung up on Adrienne that Donna could spot it quick as she had, he didn't want them to see him mooning — the corner of his mouth twitched involuntarily at the unintended pun — over his mentor's soon-to-be-widow.

The whole situation was freaking him out. The better the chances were that some of this stuff might resolve itself in his absence, the more determined he felt to get the fuck out for a couple of weeks, touch base with all the normal day-to-day stuff in his life. Put in lots of time with his daughters, get a decent cup of tea — he didn't know why tea always tasted wrong in the States, maybe it was something to do with the water — take a few hikes in the grounds of his Thames-side mansion, get reacquainted with his dog Rusty, have a few meetings with Henry and the marketing guys from the label, get everything sorted out for the live album release. Then he could come back here, see where everybody was at and get down to some proper work on doing the thing with Blue.

"Well, think about it," Adrienne said. "We'd love to meet your daughters..."

Hudson heard the unmistakable sound of the slide of an automatic pistol being ratcheted back. It had been many years since he'd heard it anywhere other than on TV or in the movies, but no-one who'd ever heard it for real was likely to forget it, or mistake it for anything other than exactly what it was. He'd heard it often enough those crazed tours, back in the 1970s, when Henry had forbidden his road crews, on pain of dismissal, to score for him or allow dealers backstage, when he'd managed to slip his handlers and head out into the badlands of whatever city he was in to score for himself.

He turned around. Blue had wheeled himself out back to the hot tub. He was aiming an old Browning straight at Hudson's head. His eyes were bloodshot but his gun hand was remarkably steady.

"You done took my music," he rasped. "You done took my daughter. But damned if I'm'a let you take my wife."

Into the frozen silence, the doorbell rang.

FOURTEEN

The sound of the doorbell hung in the air like toxic smoke, Hudson, Adrienne and Donna still freeze-framed in place. The front door opened and closed. There was an indistinct mutter of voices from the hall. Blue's eyes refocussed. He worked the slide of his automatic again, uncocking it. Blue grinned, not altogether pleasantly.

"That's the first line, anyway," he said. "Y'all got a rhyme for it, young man?"

Adrienne let out a single, explosive breath. She moved forward and gingerly took the gun from Blue's unresisting hand. Then she gently nudged Donna towards the door. "C'mon, honey. Let's go to your room."

Donna felt like she was walking through quicksand. Each step was an effort. The air was so thick she could barely breathe. Her mother's hand at the small of her back kept pushing her forward. I don't understand any of this, she thought, her mind looping around a circuit of questions, going faster and faster until it spun itself into utter paralysis. What's Daddy talking about? Why is he so angry with Mick? Why's he drunk? Where's he been keeping that gun? When Dad said, 'you done took my daughter?,' what did he mean? Does he mean me?... I don't understand any of this. What... ?

Behind them, they heard Hudson saying to Blue, "The fuck was *that* all about, then?"

In the hallway they came face to face with Venetia. Maudie Lam was right behind her, eyes widening as she saw the gun in Adrienne's hand.

Venetia stopped dead in her tracks and blinked. Adrienne in her zebra-print bikini was like something out of a James Bond movie, clutching a pistol, ridged belly heaving like she'd just run a mile, face tight with stress. Beside her was a slightly plump fourteen-year-old girl with shocked staring seen-a-ghost eyes. Must be Donna. Her baby sister. She saw her own face in Donna's, saw Donna seeing the same in hers.

Donna was looking at a small squat woman in her fifties wearing a conservative cream pantsuit, her hair in a stiff Cleopatra bob, a crucifix at her throat. She was kind of fat, but not soft or round, more squarish, what people meant when they said 'built like a tank.' Her eyes, nose and mouth were uncannily similar to what Donna saw when she looked in the mirror. Will I look like that when I'm old?

Venetia said, "You must be Donna" at virtually the same moment Donna asked, "Are you my sister?" A beat, and then they both said yes. Venetia looked up at Adrienne and said steadily, "First time we met, I got you wrong. I'm here to say I'm sorry for that. I apologise." Then, eyes raking Adrienne from head to foot and back again, smiling as disarmingly as she could, she said, "But I still hate you 'cause'a that belly."

Adrienne left the baited olive branch exactly where it was. Drawing herself up to her full height and squaring her shoulders, she said, "Donna, this is Venetia, your big sister." The emphasis on 'big' was infinitesimal but unmistakable. "Now go to your room and put some clothes on, honey." Looking back at Venetia, she said, "Excuse me," and headed back to retrieve her robe. She shouldered into it and cinched the belt tightly around her waist. Blue's gun was still in her hand. She ejected the clip, dropped both into the pocket of her robe. Donna backed away towards her room, eyes still wide and confused. Adrienne hugged her daughter and kissed the top of her head. "I'll come in and talk to you in just a minute, sweetie," she whispered into Donna's ear. To Venetia, she said, "The folks you want to see are out that way," pointing the way out back. Then she marched away to the bedroom, hung her robe up in the closet. Without bothering to shower the sun cream off her body, she pulled jeans and a T-shirt over her bikini, started trying to figure out a safe place to stash that goddam gun, somewhere Blue wouldn't be able to find it again in a hurry. And somewhere different to hide the ammo.

What the hell was the matter with Blue? What had Venetia said to him last night?

And back by the hot tub, Hudson was saying to Blue, "Only rhymes I can think of right now are 'life,' 'knife' and 'strife.' There's always 'rife,' of course, but that's a bit over-literary." Attack padded over to sniff curiously at his feet. He started pulling on his socks, lacing his sneakers.

"Meanwhile, back at *my* question, what the fuck is going on here, man? You just pulled a fucking *gun* on me!"

Blue didn't reply, just kept staring at Hudson with his bloodshot eyes. His jaw was quivering and his hands shook a little in his lap. "You'n 'Neesha is what's goin' on," he said at length.

Hudson exhaled. "She told you, then," he said.

"No... he told *me*." They looked up, saw Venetia framed in the doorway. "He knows," she said, moving forward to loom over them until, small as she was, she seemed to block out the afternoon sun.

"He's always known."

"'Course I did," Blue said. "I may be black, I may be old, I may be sick an' I may be from Miss'ssippi... but I ain't stupid." He pointed at Hudson. "I know *you*..." His finger swung to Venetia. "I know *her*..." He dropped his hand back to his lap. "... An' I know the boy. Calvin. Soon's I set eyes on him, I knew who his daddy was."

Venetia and Hudson looked at each other.

"But you never said anything," Hudson muttered incredulously.

"Maybe I was waiting to hear it from you," Blue said. "Or from my daughter. An' maybe I just didn't want to deal, act like I didn't know nuthin' 'til somebody told me. But since I been sick I had a lotta time to think about a whole bunch'a different stuff. An' I ain't gonna go to my grave with no mess left behind."

"See," Venetia said, "how you talkin' direct to him, like I wasn't here. Neither'a you said nuthin' to the other 'bout this for more'n thirty years 'case it messed up your locker-room guitar-buddy guy thing. All I know is that you two are the biggest pair'a cowards I ever met in my whole damn life. You scared of each other an' you both scared'a me. My son don't know how lucky he is. Growin' up without a daddy sure beats havin' a piss-poor excuse for a man like you in his life. You left us by ourselves so you could stay with your blonde junkie model bitch, and then she didn't even stay with you.

"An' *you*," she swung on Blue, "all you ever cared about was your goddam old-time raggedy-ass music that ain't got but three lines in it anyway. You let me an' my mama walk away, and *you*..." swinging back to Hudson "... you let me and my son walk away. When I needed you, neither'a you was there for me. Both'a y'all had other stuff goin' on was more important than me'n anything I might need from you." She drew a deep, shuddery breath.

"And now you two sorry-ass cowards need *my* help."

She squared her shoulders, let the mask fall securely into place. She could almost hear it click.

"So here's the deal, an' it's the only deal you're getting. I'm'a sing three songs on your album, an' *only* three. *He*..." looking up at Hudson "... ain't gonna be in the studio while I'm workin'. Any song I sing gets put out as a single, it comes out on my label. Anything I sing, I get co-production credit, 'cause I'm'a mix it myself with producers of *my choice*. An' my mix be the final one. No sneakin' back and remixin' nuthin' while my back turned. None of this negotiable."

"We don't negotiate shit," Blue said. "We the artists. We here to make the music. Negotiatin's for managers. He got him a manager, name Henry, back in London. I got me a manager, Simon, right here in LA. You got yourself a whole office full'a managers back in Chicago. An' Calvin got a big company, manage a whole heap'a different artists, so I guess he be able to speak for himself."

"You talkin' Calvin this'n Calvin that," Venetia said. "Bet anything you like nobody talked to him. Bet Calvin don't know nuthin' 'bout any'a this."

"Well," Hudson said. "My son..." The phrase felt unutterably strange in his mouth, like in that Indiana Jones movie where they had to eat eyeballs and small living crustaceans "... doesn't know me from a hole in the ground. You're his mother and you're his grandad, so I guess that means one of you's elected."

"Yeah," Venetia sneered. "Let somebody else do it. That's your basic approach to everything, ain't it, *Mick*?" She spat his name so hard Hudson half-expected it to clatter onto the flagstones. "If *some*body else'd done *some*thin' else, my son might'a had himself a daddy. That's one thing me'n Calvin got in common. Neither'a us ever had a daddy worth a damn."

"I'll do it," said Blue. "I'll speak to the young man. Figure at the very least he oughtta know his grandad's sick." He turned to Hudson. "You still goin' back to England?"

"Run away home, why don't you?" snapped Venetia.

Hudson's throat was dry. His heart was slamming in his chest. All his energy went into keeping his face straight and his voice steady. "I've got to see my kids," he told her. "And I have to talk to Henry about our..." he bowed ironically to Venetia "... *negotiations* for the album. I'll be back in ten days or so. Maybe we should all meet then."

"Yeah, you got to see your kids," Venetia shot back. "Bet them kids you need to see got a white mother."

Blue started to cough, rocking back and forth in his wheelchair, phlegm rattling deep in his shrunken chest. Hudson and Venetia moved to him simultaneously, each slinging an arm around his shoulders, pulling back as if electric-shocked as their hands touched. Maudie Lam bustled into the garden. She looked furious.

"Mr Moon very ill man," she scolded. "He need rest and peace and quiet, not shouting and upset." She grasped the handles of Blue's wheel-chair. "Mr Moon, you very difficult patient! You take no medication last night or this morning. Now you need shower and massage and drink much water. No more whiskey!"

Shooting another contemptuous gaze at Hudson and Venetia, she wheeled the unresisting old man back into the house.

"Well," Hudson said dryly "See you in ten days." He took a reflexive swig on his beer, then wished he hadn't. The taste of it was foul in his mouth.

Venetia didn't reply, just swept out. On the way she passed Adrienne and Donna, now cuddled together with the dogs on the living-room sofa, talking quietly. She started to say goodbye, then thought better of it. Adrienne turned her head away as Venetia let herself out to where her limo sat waiting. As soon as he heard the front door slam, Hudson ambled through the house to join them.

"You hear any of that?" he asked flatly.

"Pretty much all of it," Adrienne replied. Her eyes were cold. "We both did. Just full of little secrets, aren't you?"

The warmth and mischief wiped from his face, Hudson suddenly looked his age. "Yeah, well..."

"It's every woman's nightmare," Adrienne said. "You meet someone you think cares about you. You have a child. And they turn you from their door, act like you don't exist, wipe you out of the world like you're something they just wanna scrape off their shoe. I used to wonder why she was the way she is. Now I know."

She stood up. "I think our family needs to be by ourselves now. Let us know when you're back in town."

Hudson's face was tireder than ever. "Bye, Donna." Donna didn't look at him, buried her face in her mother's shoulder. He trudged towards the door, the longest walk since the trek from the stage at Duke's. Outside, he fumbled in his bag for the emergency packet of cigarettes he'd carried since the last time he quit smoking, just before the start of his last tour. He sat down on the steps, scrabbled in his pockets until he found a matchbook from the Mirabelle, lit the cigarette and pulled out his phone so he could call for his ride. And while he was at it, to get someone from the office to book him a flight back to London,

Where everything was going to be different.

Yeah.

Right.

Like *fuck* it would.

Calvin woke up with his dream filling his head 'til it crowded everything else out. He didn't feel rested: matter of fact, he felt like he hadn't slept at all. He ran through his mental checklist of what he was supposed to be doing today, trying to figure out if he needed to go into the office today or whether BLT could take care of whatever needed to be done.

He threw back the bedclothes and padded across the snowy carpet, feeling its thick softness caressing his toes with every step. He looked at himself critically in the mirror, turning this way and that, flexing so his tats jumped and crawled, pumping his biceps 'til they reached critical mass. Lookin' good enough not to need a workout today, he decided, and wandered back to bed.

Calvin had what KanD, who was currently his personal trainer, called a 'jailhouse bod': undertrained legs and overtrained upper body, "like a brown paper parcel with a coupla matchsticks stickin' out." That, and the tats — a meticulously-rendered AK-47 across one shoulder matched by a stack of $1,000 bills on the other, a Lock N Load logo across his chest, the acronym D.A.M.N. (Don't Anger Me Now) inscribed across his back — gave him that street-warrior vibe he needed.

A few years back, after Calvin Holland's first couple of hits as Ice Blue, one of the music rags had run a Top Ten list of white rock stars who could conceivably — someone at the office must have been proud of the pun — have been his father.

Mick Hudson had actually been fourth on the list, after Mick Jagger, David Bowie and Jimmy Page. This was slightly unfair to Venetia Moon: after all, she'd never even met David Bowie or Jimmy Page. Calvin never talked about his anonymous white father if he could help it, and the more powerful he got in the music business, the more he could help it. Discussion of Calvin's father — who he might be, how growing up not knowing had affected him — was absolutely top of the list of questions which, if asked, would trigger instant termination of an interview, if not the interviewer.

Calvin had chosen to take the surname of his step-grandad rather than his mother and blood grandad because he didn't want to be seen as simply the latest in a three-generational dynasty. James Blue Moon was a legend of the blues; Venetia Moon had been the Princess of Soul since the late sixties. Calvin had no time for comparisons. His music had nothing to do with his mother's, or his grandfather's, though calling himself 'Ice Blue' had indeed been a nod to the old man, who'd encouraged him to take his first steps in the music business when his mama had wanted him to become a doctor or a lawyer. Everything about his career was his and his alone, free and clear. He'd ended up making it way, way bigger than either of them, and he didn't owe nobody nuthin'. He was never going to be Calvin Moon, Chapter Three in no TV-movie saga of the Moon dynasty. As Calvin Holland, he was Chapter One of his own story, his own man in every possible sense.

He'd never wanted to be President — "job don't pay shit," he liked to say — but he had his very own White House. Every home he'd ever lived in since he left his mama's house to strike out on his own had been decorated almost entirely in white, with a few touches of cream, beige or light pastels just for variation. Every car he rode or drove was also white, inside and out. And so, apart from the occasional dramatic splash of bright colour, were all his clothes. It was a memorable visual signature which he'd chosen long ago for one simple reason: surrounding himself with white made him look darker.

Calvin had started out in hip-hop in the early nineties with three strikes against him in public, and an extra one he kept to himself. The first had been purely geographical: Chicago wasn't much of a hip-hop town. It had a powerful dance music scene happening in the Eighties with House Music busting buck wild in the clubs and finding a huge audience first in England and then in the rest of Europe, but all that meant was that a Chi-town rapper had to work five times as hard if he was gonna get any place. The second was that with so much emphasis put on keepin'-it-real and word-from-the-streets and scary tales of drive-bys and O.D.'s and shoot-outs in the projects and all that gangsta shit, living lakeside with a rich famous mama whose main audience was a mix of white baby-boomers and conservative church-going Nee-grows was about as far away from being righteously Down as you could get.

The third strike was that Calvin was, as an earlier black generation used to put it, Light Bright And Damn Near White. There were straight-up white people, mainly Greeks, Italians, Spanish and what-all, who could haul their asses into the summer sun for three days and get darker than Calvin. His hair was curly but soft, what Uncle Tom Nee-grows used to call 'good hair'; his nose was long and narrow, and his lips were thinner than the guy outta Aerosmith. In fact, every time he saw the Rolling Stones logo it felt like someone white was laughing at him.

A lotta girls, and quite a few boys, thought he was crazy cute just the way he was, but back in the day when he'd been getting his start, African-continent pendants were everywhere and the Nation of Islam was making plenty sense to people, talking about how the white man was the devil. Calvin had no big love for white people and didn't need much persuading about the last part, but he wore his devil heritage right there on his face. In the end, he just got disgusted with having to take shit about it from some of his darker brothers, whose views on skin colour were an exact mirror-image of those sad-ass Nee-grows who fried their natural African hair and spent whatever money the beautician didn't take from them on skin-lightening creams and nose jobs. He'd flirted with the NoI and still called himself a Muslim, but he'd never felt at ease with them, either. Identity politics, he'd decided quite a while ago, only worked for folks whose identity had never been in doubt. The only safe place if you'd been born rich, half-white and bisexual was the place you made for yourself.

That dream was still fucking with him. Was the guy behind the desk his father? He'd knocked out Screwdriver and Omega Man, so how come they were back on him soon's his back was turned? He couldn't picture the face of the guy behind the desk or remember the precise tonality of his voice, but the taunt — "Lickle weak paleface batty-boy, y'wan play games wid we now?" — was playing on an endless loop in his head.

Fuck that shit. He'd changed his mind. He *was* going into the office, and if there wasn't any serious work for him to do he'd invent something. But first he was gonna take his work-out after all, an extra-tough one. Calvin wanted to be on top form today. He didn't know why, but his instincts told him he needed to be.

He'd been at his desk for less than twenty minutes when his secretary buzzed him.

"Your grandfather's on line one, boss."

"Okay, put him through."

"... and your moms is on line two."

FIFTEEN

LONDON, ENGLAND, 1964

Mick Hudson always used to say that the inspiration for the invention of Velcro must've been the floor of the Marquee Club. Take a bunch of cheap but heavy-duty industrial carpeting, marinate it for decades in a toxic blend of sweat, trodden-in cigarette ash and spilt drinks, and you had something which stuck to the soles of your boots like it loved you so much it didn't want to let you go, making this weird *schlup-schlup* sound with every step you took. And, strangely enough, this phenomenon seemed to remain constant no matter how many times The Marquee shifted location. The prosaic explanation was, of course, that an economy-minded management simply took the same old carpet with them whenever they moved.

Mind you, four decades and change as a professional muso, with all the attendant substance abuse involved, must've played absolute hell with Hudson's memory for minutiae. The first time he'd played the celebrated rock dive, where every big name from the Stones onwards had gotten their start, had actually been at the original premises in Oxford Street, and in those days the club hadn't had carpet at all, just a bare wooden floor.

That was when he was playing lead guitar for Bluebottle, his first professional band. 'Professional', in this particular context, simply meant that they didn't have day jobs: whatever meagre income they managed to scrape together derived more or less exclusively from playing gigs. And their so-called manager was about as much use as a chocolate teapot. Arthur Blunt wasn't even really a manager at all, just a friend of the drummer's dad who'd played piano in music halls a long time ago and fancied 'keeping his hand in with show business.' Under his 'expert guidance,' the band had released one single on EMI's HMV subsidiary, a Brill Building pop song wished on them by their producer, which they'd attempted to roughen up with the wailing harmonica and rustling maraccas standard for post-Rolling Stones R&B groups with pop ambitions, but it had been a disaster. Simultaneously too poppy for the band's small but growing live following and too raucously bluesy for mainstream pop fans, it had fallen between the two stools with a resounding thud, selling barely 500 copies.

The reason Bluebottle were hanging around the Marquee at half two in the afternoon was that they were there to play backup for a visiting American bluesman. The likes of The Yardbirds and The Animals had both backed up Sonny Boy Williamson a year or so ago, but now they were already too successful in their own right to do that kind of thing any more, and so the backup jobs were farmed out to any competent R&B group on the books of the various agencies who hadn't had any hits yet and therefore weren't currently overburdened with prestigious high-paying work. The Groundhogs, John Mayall's band and a couple of other outfits were already spoken for, backup-wise, so this particular job had fallen to Bluebottle. Most of the band — organist Paul, bass- ist Phil, drummer Tony and especially Clive the singer and harmonica player — found the idea of touring as someone else's backing group slightly demeaning, but their lead guitarist was thrilled. The most com- mitted blues fan of the bunch, he wanted to meet and play with as many of the great original Real Guys as he possibly could.

They'd set up their gear on the stage and had a desultory jam ses- sion, more to make sure that their tatty old gear was still working than anything else. Phil's home-made set-up, an old hi-fi amp which blew up every third gig and a massive speaker cabinet he and his dad had built in the garden shed which took at least three people to carry, was a per- petual source of hyper-anxiety. A couple of bass notes on the keyboard of Paul's fifth-hand Vox Continental organ had gone dead, so he had to remember to stay away from them even when in the deepest throes of improvisation. And Hudson's old Vox AC30 guitar amp had developed a nasty intermittent buzz.

Broke as ever, Bluebottle had pooled whatever change they had in their pockets to buy a round of halves from the bar. The band nursed their drinks as stingily as they could, but now their glasses were almost empty and they were down to one last cigarette each. Simon Wolfe, the agency tour manager who would be looking after the star of the show, could probably be induced to buy a round and a couple of packets of Senior Service when he arrived, but he and his distinguished charge were running late. So Bluebottle whiled away the time by reading: Paul flicking through last night's Evening News, Phil thumbing a battered old Saint paperback, Tony poring over some World War II bollocks with a big swastika on the front, Hudson and Clive arguing about comics. Clive was devoted to Superman, Batman and the DC Comics characters, Hudson enthusing about the new Marvel Comics heroes like Spider-Man and The Incredible Hulk.

When that got boring, they started speculating about exactly who it was they were supposed to be backing. John Lee Hooker? Little Walter? Memphis Slim? Phil was sure it wasn't going to be Memphis Slim because the piano on the stage was still locked up. Bollocks to that, said Tony, Simon'll have the key when he gets here, or else he'll just get the club manager to unlock it. Clive was hoping it wouldn't be Little Walter, because if they were playing with the greatest blues harp man in the world there'd be nothing for him to do except shake his bloody maraccas. "At least if it's Memphis Slim," he argued to Paul, "he'll be on piano, so you can still play organ."

Footsteps from the back of the club, muffled thumps and Simon muttering fierce scouse imprecations under his breath as he lugged in an AC30 with his briefcase clamped between his elbow and his thick torso. Behind him sauntered a tall dapper individual in his early forties sporting a snapbrim fedora and silver-grey mohair suit, a guitar case swinging lazily at the end of one long ropy arm.

"Afternoon, lads," Simon said, dropping the amp at the foot of the stage. "Sorry we're a bit late. Had a bit of trouble getting Mr Moon here settled in at his hotel. Seems there's still a little colour prejudice going on here..."

Mr Moon? Mr *Moon*? The new arrival put down his guitar case and took off his hat, revealing a gleaming black pompadour only slightly disarranged. Hudson took a closer look, clocking the lanky frame, the pencil moustache...

The group had all jumped to their feet, standing in line like troops about to be inspected by a visiting foreign dignitary. "Meet James Blue Moon," Simon said proudly. "He was here a couple of years back with the Folk Blues Festival, but this is gonna be his first solo headlining tour. I've told him that you fellas already know some of his stuff, so don't let us down now.

"Mr Moon..."

"Call me Blue, young man," the new arrival said pleasantly, hand held out to shake, "I'm sure these boys is gonna do just fine."

"Blue, meet Bluebottle."

"Bluebottle, huh? Okay..."

"This is Tony. He plays drums."

"How you doin', young man?"

"Phil on bass..."

"Pleased to meet'cha."

"Paul on organ..."

"All right."

"Clive, vocals and harp..."

Blue stopped to think, stroking his chin. "Hmmm... harp, huh? Reckon we can use a little harp round 'bout the end of the show, but..."

"It's okay, Mr Moon, I understand..."

"That's 'Blue,' young man. Anyway, that mean you a lucky so-an'-so 'cause you get to stand at the bar and chitchat to all the pretty ladies while these guys do the work."

"And this is Mike..."

"*Mick*," Hudson corrected him. It was almost as hard to get the guys in the group to call him 'Mick' as it was to persuade his parents to address him as anything other than '*Mi*-chael.' 'Mick' was much better than 'Mike.' 'Mick' sounded raffish and Celtic; 'Mike' was just boring and ordinary. After all, Mick Jagger had been responsible for an entire generation of Mikes suddenly becoming Micks. So to speak.

"*Mick*, right... Mick plays lead guitar, and he's a real big fan of yours. Got one of your records when he was just a kid, taught the band a few of your songs..."

"That right?" Blue seemed impressed. Well, maybe not *impressed*, but at least interested. "Which songs you know?"

Mick Hudson pushed his hair out of his eyes. "Well, Mr Moon..."

"Blue."

"Blue... we do Piece Of The Action, Ain't Nuthin' Wrong That Money Can't Cure, Telephone Bill, Smile When You Say That..."

"Mm-*hm*!" Now Blue *did* look impressed. He bent down, unlatched his guitar case. The musicians crowded round, eager to see what kind of instrument the legend had brought with him. Blue swung the sunburst Jazzmaster across his shoulder. "All right, fellas. Soon's this young man here..." he gestured towards Simon "... gets my amplifier all warmed up, we'll see what y'all done learned."

Simon lugged Blue's rented amp up onto the stage next to Hudson's, plugged it in and they got down to work. It rapidly became apparent that while Bluebottle might have learned Blue's repertoire to Hudson's satisfaction, there was considerable work to do before their versions of the songs met the originator's standards. Not only had Hudson gotten several important chord changes wrong, but they had learned just about every song in different keys to the ones Blue preferred. This was particularly difficult for Paul. Not only did the new keys land him right where he needed those bass notes his organ no longer had, but he just wasn't that good a keyboard player in the first place. It always took him longer than anybody else in the band to learn anything new and now, under the taskmasterly discipline of a veteran Real Guy, the poor sod was struggling.

Another problem was that Bluebottle were contracted to perform their regular set to open the show, and their regular set was so heavily dependent on cover versions of Blue's songs that they needed to drag out some old Muddy Waters and Howlin' Wolf and John Lee Hooker songs they'd stopped playing months ago because every other band in England was already doing them. Clive and Phil had written a few songs, but Hudson thought they were pretty pathetic, just feeble re-writes of Beatles songs and blues standards. Maybe he should start trying to write a few himself. Couldn't do much worse than the other lads, that was for certain.

What was really bugging him was his guitar, a Czech-made Stratocaster copy seemingly designed by someone who'd never actually seen, let alone played, an actual Strat. Considering that he was practically professional by now, it was an embarrassment to still be playing a piece of schoolboy shit like this. It was almost as crappy as the cheap acoustic his parents had bought him when he was just learning and, like that nameless abomination, it just wouldn't stay in tune all the way up the neck. Everything he played on it required an effort. By contrast, Blue only had to brush the fingers of his left hand casually against the neck of his Fender and rich, clean, twangy lines came leaping out of his amp, gamboling like frisky little lambs. It couldn't be his amp, because Hudson's was the same model, albeit older and more battered.

Part of it was undoubtedly his technique, honed for decades in the kind of Chicago blues bars of which Mick Hudson had dreamed ever since he first heard the *Once In A Blue Moon* album, which still had pride of place on the record rack in the Kilburn bedsit he shared with Phil. Part of it was simply that he was a Real Blues Guy who spoke the blues as his native language, whereas Hudson was still struggling with the second-year phrase book. Hudson had no illusions: he knew that if he was playing Blue's set-up and Blue was playing his, Blue would still sound a million times better than he did. But he also knew that Blue's guitar was working for him, whereas his was working against him. Here he was getting a masterclass from one of his idols, learning the right way to play songs he'd been listening to for almost a third of his life, and he was having to do it on a guitar so shit that using it for firewood would be an insult to fire. Whenever Blue had cued him for a solo, he'd wanted a neat trapdoor to open up in the stage so that he could sink smoothly into the lower depths of hell which, he was convinced, were reserved for presumptuous little white boys from Reading who dared to play lead guitar in front of Real Guys. Yet Blue had nodded approvingly when he played, even — especially! — when he fumbled through a phrase he'd learned off one of Blue's own records.

By seven o'clock, the Marquee staff were just about ready to open the club's doors, so Simon took Blue and the musicians across Oxford Street to a pub on a Soho street-corner. Bluebottle were due to play their opening set at eight, with Blue taking the stage around 9:15. That left just under an hour for a council of war.

"Y'all never heard'a cold beer in this country?" Blue asked, taking a sip from the pint of bitter Simon placed in front of him. "My lord. This may be warm, but it's strong! Too much'a this stuff, I be wantin' to sleep rather'n do a show."

They'd worked through seven songs at their makeshift rehearsal. Out of those seven, Hudson was confident that the group would be able to play five of them perfectly and bluff the other two more or less acceptably. Yet Blue had told them they'd be doing a dozen songs that night.

"So what do we do for the ones we don't know?" Tony had asked.

"See," Blue replied. "They all blues. Straight-up twelve-bar blues, nuthin' fancy, nuthin' tricky. Here's what we gonna do. Before each song I'm'a tell you the key we gonna be in. Then I'm'a count off the time, one-two-three-four. Y'all play the beat I give you in the key I give you, we gonna be just fine."

"Tell me again how that bit in Piece Of The Action goes again," Phil asked Blue.

"Okay. It go *da-da-dum-ba-bum-bum-bum...*"

Hudson's bladder was exploding. He excused himself to visit the gents', and when he emerged Blue was waiting for him.

"A word in your ear, young man," Blue said, taking him by the arm and leading him to the opposite end of the bar from the table where the others were gathered. "You play good. You play *very* good. You a very talented young man."

Hudson blushed to the roots of his hair. Here was James Blue Moon, *the* James Blue Moon, telling him — him, little Michael Hudson from Reading — that he played good. He started to stammer his thanks for the compliment, but the older man held up a regal hand to shush him. Blue hadn't finished talking yet.

"I know a lotta cats back in Chicago don't have the feel you got. There's sump'n special 'bout you, young man, an' I reckon one day you gonna be big. *But...*" Blue held up an admonishing forefinger "... you ain't goin' nowhere with that cheap no-brand git-tar you got right now, damn thing won't even let you play in tune."

"I know that, Mr Moon," Hudson said miserably, "but..."

"I told you, call me Blue."

"I've been saving up for a new one, but I don't have enough money yet to get what I want."

"Yeah? What you want?"

"Gibson 335. Or maybe a Strat."

"The Gibson a good guitar. The Fender too. Way you play, I reckon..."

There was a new customer standing beside them, surrounded by a selection of bags, rapping on the bar with a coin and calling for a large Scotch in a strong Glasgow accent. Over six feet tall, it was hard to ascertain his body shape through his layers of threadbare overcoats. His hair was greasy and long under his shapeless hat, not a hip Rolling Stones kind of long, but simply uncut. His face was rough and reddened, patched with dry skin like an ocean in the atlas is patched with land masses. Panting at his side was a large mongrel dog looking in as bad a condition as its master. Both smelt awful.

"... an' a bowl'a wattuh fer ma dug."

The odoriferous apparition focussed his eyes and registered Blue and Hudson beside him.

"Hey... are youse musicians?"

"Yeah," Blue said. "Matter of fact, we playin' a show here just tonight."

Their new friend thought for a second. "Ef youse boys is musicians," he said, "then ah might huv somethin' here fer youse." He opened up the largest of his bags. Hudson's eyes widened as the tramp pulled out a grimy, rusted once-white Fender Telecaster. "Wanna buy et then, do ya?"

"How much?" Hudson asked eagerly.

"Sixty poun'."

"Do the electrics work?"

"Everythin' works."

Sixty quid! That was a really good price for a Telecaster: used ones generally went for between £80 and £100. What was more, £60 was about as much as Hudson had saved up in the jam jar back in Kilburn. He hadn't considered getting a Tele, but they were good guitars and if he didn't like it he could always sell it for more than this guy was asking. An inner alarm went off in his head. This was almost too good to be true. What if it was stolen or something?

"Wait a minute," he said. "Where did you get this from?"

The tramp looked cunning. "Let me tell yu, wee boy," he answered. "Ef ah tell youse where ah goat et, the price goes up to a hundred poun'." His eyes gleamed beneath the shade of his hat-brim.

Blue held out his hand. "Lemme take a look at that." He sat down on a bar stool with the Telecaster in his lap. Lightly tapping first the neck and then the body, he listened critically to the instrument's resonance. He played a few figures on the low frets, then a couple of runs higher up and then finally an extended string-bending melody right at the top of the neck. Then he struck a series of harmonics on different strings, checking their interaction.

Then, very carefully, he tuned the guitar and repeated his sequence of runs, bends and harmonics. Finally, he held it out to Hudson. "This is real nice," he said. "Needs a little adjustment and some new strings, but this git-tar got a lot'a music in it. An' it'll sure beat that piece'a crap you got right now."

Hudson took the guitar, knelt on the floor with the instrument braced across one thigh. He fished a pick from his pocket, played a couple of chords and then one of the trickier riffs Blue had shown the band that afternoon. Even with the sticky, worn-out strings fitted to the Tele, the notes danced off the fretboard so smoothly and easily that Hudson nearly dropped the guitar. "Wow," he said.

"Listen up," Blue said. "You got the money for this thing?"

"Not here," Hudson gasped, "but I've got sixty quid at home..."

"All right then," Blue said. He slipped his wallet from inside his jacket and peeled off six crisp tenners from an impressive looking wad of notes. "Now you pay me back first thing tomorrow." He handed the notes to Hudson. Hudson passed them to the Scotsman, who tipped his hat and stashed the money somewhere inside his filthy coat. The dog growled once, very quietly.

"Pleasure doing business with you gentlemen," he said. If Hudson hadn't still been staring entranced at the guitar in his hands, he might've noticed that tramp didn't sound nearly as Scottish as he had a few moments earlier. And if he'd been watching the tramp and his dog slouching towards the exit, he could've seen the man's eyes flash beneath his hat as he turned back to look at them before disappearing back out onto the street.

Blue was looking at his watch. "I reckon when we get back to the club you got about four an' a half minutes to put some clean strings on that thing and then it be time to go to work." Simon and the band were finishing their drinks and coming over to get them. Simon stared at the guitar in Hudson's hands.

"Fookinell," he said. "Where'd that come from, then?"

Hudson looked innocently back at him. "It just walked in the door," he said. "Maybe it was a gift from God."

"Well," Simon said, "unless God's going to be playing lead guitar for the first set we better get moving."

As they recrossed Oxford Street towards the Marquee, Blue fell into step beside Hudson.

"Here's the thing," he said. "You see that guy sold you the git-tar? See his dog? Well, I betchoo he didn't choose that dog. I reckon the dog chose him. Raggedy-ass an' stinkin' drunk as he is, that dog figure here's a man gonna look after him. Now, git-tars be like dogs sometime. You didn't choose that git-tar. You wanted a Gibson or a Strat'caster. But this particular git-tar just walked right into the joint an' chose you. Guess it figures you gonna look after it, which for a git-tar means you gonna play some music on it that it want to play. That's your git-tar now. You take good care of it, that git-tar gonna take care of you."

There was a good crowd in the club. Hudson was so nervous and fumblefingered that it took him forever to change his new Telecaster's strings. "An' make sure you stretch 'em out *good*," Blue instructed him. "If'n you don't, they gonna go loose on you on the stage while you tryin' to play." Bluebottle ended up hitting the stage more than five minutes late, but as soon as they were up there nothing else seemed to matter. Everything Hudson could think of, the guitar delivered for him, and even when they took the stage for the second set to play behind Blue, he felt like twice the player he'd ever been before.

The pub in question was at the intersection of Dean Street and Carlisle Street. Not exactly the junction of Highway 61 and Highway 49 in terms of mythic resonance, but a crossroads is still a crossroads.

SIXTEEN

LOS ANGELES, AUTUMN 2004

"How you doin', young man?"

His grandfather's voice sounded a little strange: weaker, hoarser than Calvin remembered.

"Same shit, different day," he replied. "How *you* doin', gramps?"

"That's what I'm callin' about. I need you to get your rich Hollywood ass down to my crib."

"When?"

"How 'bout now?"

"We-e-e-lll…"

Ensconced behind his creamy maple desk in his snowblinding white office, Calvin was feeling antsy. Screwdriver and Omega Man were turning into a major pain in the ass. They'd just had three dates in England cancelled on them because of that damn Battyman 9/11 track, and their Lock N Load album wasn't even out yet. He could see all the time and money he'd invested in launching them about to go up in a cloud of ganja smoke unless he could lean on the muthafuckas to pull the single. Fuck that, they didn't just have to pull the single, they needed to issue a statement apologising for it and disowning all those kill-queers lyrics or else they'd never work England or most of the rest of Europe ever again. They'd backed down on including the single on the album, just as Calvin had known they would before the meeting at the Mondrian, but that was about as far as they were prepared to go.

He'd just gotten through drafting a terse statement of his own at the request of Lock N Load's international distributors, who could see a shitstorm coming and didn't want any of it splattering on them. Specifically, they didn't want any of it impeding their shareholders' chances of carrying home a nice fat dividend this year.

Thus far, he'd written: "Screwdriver and Omega Man's song Battyman 9/11 will not be included on their forthcoming Lock N Load album *Dance Pon The Ashes*, Lock N Load CEO Calvin Holland confirmed today. 'Battyman 9/11 was recorded and released independently in Jamaica after we signed Screwdriver and Omega Man,' he said. 'Domestic

143

Jamaican releases are not covered by the terms of our contract with them. Lock N Load was unaware of this song and its content until it was already available to the Jamaican public, and elsewhere via import and download. At no time was it ever considered for release by us. Lock N Load Productions unequivocally dissociates itself from this record and considers its content totally unacceptable. We will be giving very serious consideration to the future of our professional relationship with Screwdriver and Omega Man.'"

So Calvin had a situation on his hands. He'd worked his ass off on that album and despite what he'd told Jethro and Julian, the tracks he'd produced had been so absolutely tailor-made for the Jamaican duo's idiosyncratic dancehall chat that he'd have to work his ass off all over again to get the tracks sounding anywhere near as good with anyone else fronting them. Plus his street sense told him that dropping the act and pulling the album was gonna make him look like some pussy-ass sell-out. Problem was that now that Lock N Load had sucked the corporate white-devil dick, he was no longer just answerable to the street, but to a bunch of German guys in suits who simply wanted the biggest possible profit with the least possible hassle.

Calvin would much rather spend the day hanging with his gramps, whom he hadn't seen for over a year, than dealing with all this bullshit, but he had to get busy with some major damage-limitation or else he'd have a big muthafuckin' hole in his company's year-end accounts. And he was a businessman as well as an artist and producer, with shareholders of his own to worry about.

"Got work to do, gramps. How 'bout tonight?"

There was a moment's silence. Calvin could hear a faint rattly undercurrent to the sound of his grandfather's breathing. Then: "If that's the best you can do, young man. See you 'round eight."

"You got it. Eight o'clock. Peace out."

The old guy sounded in kind of a bad way, Calvin thought. Wonder why he's in such a hurry. No sooner had he hung up the phone than it rang again. "Muthafucka," he said under his breath, but he picked it up.

"Calvin?"

Damn, he'd forgotten his moms was still holding on line two. Normally, Calvin hardly heard from his moms and gramps from one year to the next, but now here were both of 'em calling him one after the other. The fuck was goin' on?

"Moms. How y'all doin'?"

"Calvin, it's about your grandad." Venetia sounded... *weird.*

"I just got through talkin' to him."

"What'd he say?"

"Said he needs to see me. Wanted me to drive out to Venice'n visit with him right now, but I'm'a be busy at the office so I said I'm'a see him tonight."

Another long humming silence. Calvin fancied he could see Venetia's face, brow wrinkled with concern.

"Calvin... son..."

Son? She never called him that.

"I want you to call me as soon as you've seen him. On my cellphone. Will you do that?"

Calvin was starting to get a little freaked.

"Where are you, moms?"

"I'm here in LA. At the Beverly Hills."

"Why don't I come see you? Have some lunch? You can tell me what this is all about."

Another silence. "I think you better talk to your grandad first."

Even though he knew she couldn't see him, Calvin shrugged. He had a major problem looking to boil over any second, and now he had gramps and moms trippin' out on his ass. Still, he'd find out tonight from his gramps what the fuck was up. Shoving the whole mess into a mental desk drawer, he said as soothingly as he could, "Okay, moms. I'll do that. Peace out."

Frowning, he dismissed his screen saver with a click of his mouse and brought back the text of his statement about that whole Screwdriver and Omega Man mess. When he had it just right, he'd have to email it to his distributors' Vice President of Creative Affairs, and they'd have to send it to the suits in Germany and then everybody could start arguing all over again. Pain in the muthafuckin' ass — literally, in his case, he thought acridly.

"No muthafuckin' calls for an hour," he told his secretary. He switched off his cellphone to be absolutely safe from interruption. Then he absentmindedly rasped a palm against his cropped scalp — should he get the Lock N Load logo recut into his hair or let it grow out? — before pulling his keyboard towards him and starting to type again.

Blue's gotten a lot stronger since Maudie Lam started looking after him, Adrienne thought. That acupuncture shit really works, though she had to admit she'd been a little freaked the first time she'd seen Blue prone on Maudie's massage table, his back bristling with needles like some elderly African-American porcupine. After the day he'd pulled the gun on Mick Hudson, she'd also kept him well away from that ol' Tennessee sippin' whiskey, and weaned him off the chilled water he was used to drinking from his cooler. Warm water, she insisted, would be less of a shock to his system.

And the massages were helping too. He was still weak, of course, but he had fewer aches and pains. He could stay lively longer, and he didn't reach for the painkillers quite so often. He was spending more time playing his guitars, as well, cutting little demos on his little DAT recorder. He had, he announced proudly, written two new tunes and rearranged three or four of his old ones. He was also talking about "gettin' Mick back here so we can get started on doin' some work."

Adrienne wanted the project started just as much as Blue did. She knew how important it was to him, and she didn't want his current rally to go to waste because his collaborator wasn't here. But at the same time, she wasn't sure how she currently felt about having Hudson back in their lives again. Learning that he'd concealed the fact that he was Calvin's father for over thirty years had shocked her. And his callous abandonment of Venetia and her unborn child had made certain that she could never look at that seamed, smiling face and beaky nose in quite the same way ever again.

And she also wasn't sure quite how she felt when Blue told her that Calvin Holland was coming round to visit with them tonight.

"Do I have to go out again?" she asked eventually.

Blue chuckled. "Naw, baby, not this time," he said. "You like my grandson, he likes you. I'm'a want to talk to him private tonight, but I want you in the house. Keep Donna from buggin' him to sign a buncha records, if nuthin' else."

Adrienne smiled. Uncle Calvin was a hero to Donna and her schoolmates in a way that old folks like Blue and Venetia could never be. Over thirty he might be, but records bearing the Lock N Load logo were in the collections of just about every one of Donna's posse except for a few white kids who listened to nothing but rock groups, and those of them who weren't already clad in Fully Loaded sportswear probably made their parents' lives miserable every time they went to a mall. Donna was always having to fend off requests to get a bunch of autographs the next time Calvin came by. Plus she'd be thrilled to bits seeing Calvin for the first time in over a year.

"Why don't I take her to the movies?" she suggested. "I know she's been wanting to see *Shrek 2*. Keep her out of everybody's hair for two-three hours, anyway."

"Yeah, okay," Blue conceded, "but get her home back here by ten. Calvin come by visit with us and she don't see him, she gonna put us both in a whole world'a hurt."

"You're gonna tell him," Adrienne said. It wasn't a question.

"I'm'a tell him I'm sick," Blue answered. "I'm'a tell him I'm'a make this record. I'm'a tell him who's gonna do it with me. An' I'm'a tell him I want him with us."

"That's not what I meant."

"I know it ain't."

"Did you really know about Mick and Venetia and Calvin for all those years and not tell nobody?"

Out of habit, Blue wheeled himself towards the water cooler, then remembered and wheeled himself back. He pumped himself a glass of hot water from the thermos flask on the counter. He sipped, made a face. "This shit warm like English beer," he said.

"If I wanted the subject changed," Adrienne said. "I'd'a changed it myself."

"You a feisty headstrong girl got no respect for your elders," Blue told her, mock-frowning. He put his empty glass back down on the counter. "Yeah, I knew," he said. "But I didn't know I knew."

Adrienne shook her head, as if to clear it after taking a punch. "Run that past me again," she said, "at half speed with subtitles." Blue grimaced.

"I know it sound weird," he said, "but I just kinda kept it at the back of my mind. Never put the pieces together. Matter of fact, I took all them pieces and hid 'em as far apart as I could get 'em to go. Didn't want to have to admit to myself that I knew what I knew, so I made like I didn't know it."

Adrienne thought about that one for a while. "I still can't believe you never said anything to Mick. Or to Venetia." A thought to occurred to her. "You spoken to Mick since he left? Or to Venetia?"

Blue looked a little shifty. "Yeah, I talked to him."

"Did you ask him why he cut Venetia loose when she was pregnant with his kid?"

"Yeah, I did."

"What'd he say?"

"He said when she called him and told him she was havin' a baby, he an' the girlfriend he had at the time — you know, Jocasta, she were married to Simon for a while — just lost one, had a kid born that same week, died after two hours. He said he couldn't jus' up'n leave her. She was havin' a breakdown."

"That's rough," Adrienne conceded.

"He told Neesha he couldn't leave Jocasta long as she needed him."

"Okay, I can see that... if I'd just lost a baby with a guy and he told me he was goin' away to be with some other woman havin' another baby'a his, I don't know what I'd do."

Blue grinned. "I know 'xactly what you'd do," he said.

"Yeah, and I'd walk out of that courtroom a free woman. But what about all those years after, when he had nuthin' to do with Neesha or Calvin? That was *cold blooded*."

"Says that's what Neesha told him she wanted. Told him never to come anywhere near either of 'em. Told him she was never gonna let Calvin know who his daddy is, an' she wanted him to keep his mouth shut about it."

"You believe that?"

"Yeah, I do. I know Mick. Mick don't lie to me. I won't say that he *never* lie, but it don't come natural to him. An' I know Neesha, I know how she can be. He said it damn near broke his heart. Said he lost two babies that week, an' one of 'em wasn't even born yet. It was right after he started gettin' heavy into drugs."

Whoo. That was a cold shot and no mistake. Adrienne sank back into the armchair, closed her eyes. How would she have coped with that? Lose one child because of a bad birth. Lose another because you have to stay with the mother of the first. Things didn't look quite so straightforward any more. She started out liking Mick because he was warm and funny and friendly to her and because he obviously cared so much about Blue. And she'd disliked Venetia because the woman was such a bitch and, back when she was pregnant and vulnerable, had treated her like shit, trying to stir Blue up against her. Then she'd been angry with

Mick because he was a white man who wouldn't claim his black woman and the child she was bearing him, and sympathetic towards Venetia because she'd gone from being a kid whose adored daddy had left her with her moms into a grown woman whose lover had left her with her child. Worse: her father had seemed to care less about his own daughter than he did about the rich white boy who wouldn't come to her when she needed him.

Now she didn't know any more. She thought about Mick and Venetia, and all she knew was that she felt desperately sorry for both of them. No, scratch that. She thought about Mick and Venetia and Calvin and Blue, and her eyes filled with tears for all four of them. Matter of fact, there was also Donna and — why the fuck not? — herself who weren't exactly top of the Shiny Happy People charts right now. This was a fucked-up situation for everybody in it. She couldn't see any good guys and bad guys any more, just people trying to deal the best they could with where they found themselves.

"You spoken to Venetia?" she asked Blue. She still couldn't bring herself to use the affectionate diminutive of her daughter-in-law's name. He shook his head. "So you don't know if she's told Calvin yet?" He shook his head again. "You gonna tell him?"

"Ain't my place. That's his moms's job."

"How about his daddy's?"

Blue threw up his hands. "Calvin's daddy's still keepin' a promise he made to Calvin's mama thirty-some years ago. He ain't gonna break that promise 'less she release him from it."

"Has it occurred to you that it's about time Mick started thinking for himself?"

Blue closed his eyes. "I'm startin' to feel tired. Think I might take me a nap 'til Calvin get here."

"Gonna 'ave a nice little kip, then, dear?" Adrienne said in a passable imitation of Hudson's accent. Blue's eyes remained closed.

"Yep. Gonna do me just that."

Adrienne was remembering what Venetia had said, calling Mick and Blue a pair of cowards. She knew that Venetia's accusation was only slightly more fair or balanced than an average night on Fox News, but there was still enough truth in it to sting. What was more, she was beginning to get seriously angry with Blue. She thought of what it must have been like over the past thirty years for Venetia, with loss and abandonment and rage all boiled up inside her like a soul full of sulphuric soup; for Calvin, growing up with a father-shaped gap in his life filled only by a shadowy white man whose identity wasn't so much unknown as deliberately kept secret from him for the emotional convenience of others, and even for Mick, living with a gutful of guilt and self-loathing, emotions so flammably unstable that he couldn't even write lyrics about them, emotions which could only find expression through his guitar.

Three thoroughly fucked-up people, Adrienne thought. Or maybe make that four. After all, if Blue had stepped up to his responsibilities as the patriarch of this fucked-up family which didn't even realise the extent to which it *was* a family, there might have been a conflagration — come to think of it, with Venetia involved, there was no 'might have' about it — but at least there wouldn't have been three decades of torment. Three decades of suffering for each of three people meant ninety pain-years. And Blue had waited until he was practically on his deathbed to sort this whole mess out. If he hadn't decided to make this final record, would he have said anything to anybody? Ever?

Adrienne didn't say any of this. She looked over at her husband, dozing more or less peacefully, the quiet whiffly snoring and slight rise and fall of his chest the only signs of life. For the first time in their marriage, she wasn't 100% certain whether she liked him or not. Mouth tight, she went off in search of Donna to tell her they were going to the movies.

Maybe *Shrek 2* would lighten her mood. Maybe. Right now, though, she wouldn't be putting any money on it.

SEVENTEEN

LONDON, ENGLAND, AUTUMN 2004

Ahhhh, you just couldn't beat autumn in London, Hudson thought. Bloody lovely. Just like when he was a kid, he enjoyed the satisfying crunch his feet made with every step through the dry leaves on the pavement. There was something just too brash and vulgar about the way the LA sun blazed and blared practically every single day: exhilarating for a week or two but deadly boring once you'd been there for awhile. Hudson considered himself fundamentally a Londoner even though he hadn't moved to the capital until he was almost nineteen. After all, his childhood and teens had been little more than a preparation for his move up to The Big Smoke, where everything relevant to his life as his real self had taken place.

Strolling through Soho enjoying the combination of warm sunshine and a pleasant breeze, his body rather than his mind registering the landmarks of his past, each one setting off a resonant cluster of physical sensations. *There* was where the second Marquee used to be, and for a moment his feet stuck to the pavement and he needed to *rrrrrrip* them loose to keep walking. *There* was the pub where the Scottish tramp with the mangy mutt had sold him the guitar he still played today, and suddenly he could smell the guy's piercing aroma of stale whiskey and even staler sweat and piss cutting through the usual pubby miasma of cigarettes and beer. *There* was where the London offices of Boulevard Records' European affiliate had been when he was still leading Cabal, and he could see the cluttered desks covered in albums and ashtrays and cartons of promo T-shirts and badges, the cupboards stuffed with vinyl albums, the walls plastered with posters and even the odd free-standing lifesize cardboard cut-out of his band or another of the company's acts.

And *here* was Soho Square, where his manager Henry MacShane's company Raintree maintained a comfortable office suite. There was just enough sunshine today to tempt the odd sunbather to sprawl amongst the office workers munching their sandwiches and drunks gulping their lunch. In LA, Hudson mused, weather like this would have people putting extra clothes on rather than running out in public to take them off.

Behind the reception desk was a sallow South Asian girl with sideburns like Elvis and one of those *faux*-pearl nose-studs that always reminded Hudson of plump whitehead zits. She greeted him with a dazzling smile. "Hi, Mick. Great tour! We're all looking forward to the live album!" Hudson had never met her before, but considering the huge Mick Hudson tour poster dominating the lobby, it was no surprise that she recognised him.

"I'm Amina, by the way. Henry will be with you in just a moment. Can I get you a drink?"

Hudson requested a sparkling mineral water and she bustled away to fetch it, but before she returned the man himself was sticking his head round the door.

"'Ello mate, good to see you!" They bearhugged, Henry easily lifting Hudson's skinny frame clear off the floor. "C'mon back to my room. Amina'll bring your drink." He led the way through his office to his inner sanctum sanctorum, Hudson feeling quite the visiting dignitary, like the Dalai Lama or the Pope or Bono or something, as staff rose from their desks to congratulate him and shake hands. It was a relief to sink into the guest armchair in Henry's cluttered office, a marked contrast to the rest of the premises. He'd spent his entire working life with everything all over the place and, in his late sixties, saw no reason to change. Plus the only designated exception to the strict non-smoking-office rule was Henry's own room.

Managers come from all sorts of backgrounds. Some start out as lawyers or accountants, some as college social secretaries, some as agents, some as publicists, and a very few as musicians. Henry MacShane had gotten into the business the old-fashioned way. A hulking, burly East Londoner, he always insisted on being called Henry because "I never felt like an 'Arry, 'Al's too posh and 'Hank MacShane' sounds like summink aht a fakkin' cowboy comic." He'd started out in the 1950s as an amateur boxer of little distinction who supplemented his meagre income by working as a club bouncer. He'd then been hired by one of the big agencies as a minder, bodyguarding visiting American artists and making sure they got paid. From there he'd graduated to tour management, then to booking gigs. Finally he'd taken over management of Bluebottle after the unfortunate Arthur Blunt had proven his hapless incompetence once too often. "That berk'd be out of his fakkin' depth in the bleedin' shallow end of a washing-up bowl," he'd expostulated to the band. The inevitable retort had been, "Why don't you have a go, then?" Henry took them at their word. Within six weeks he'd renegotiated their record contract, eliminating the more egregious rip-offs written into the small print of the boilerplate contract to which Blunt had signed them, and booked them on their first US tour. After Bluebottle broke up, he identified Hudson as 'the talent' in the group, helped him put Cabal together and got them signed to Boulevard on outrageously favourable terms, nurturing the band and building them up until their American popularity was exceeded only by Led Zep, the Stones and The Who. And when Cabal disintegrated in their turn, Henry had encouraged Mick to go solo and bulldozed right over Boulevard Records' misgivings concerning the risks of a massive investment in a songwriting guitarist who'd never sung lead before.

At sixty-eight, Henry MacShane was still a seriously imposing figure. Six foot four and weighing over 250lb even after a drastic medically-advised 100lb weight loss a few years ago, his ponytail was long gone, replaced by a meticulously shaved skull, and his bristling once-black beard clipped back to trim white stubble. These days Hudson — still 'the boy' after almost forty years — was just about Henry's only remaining personal client, but a eager stable of younger associates took care of the interests of an equally eager stable of younger acts, with Henry hovering in an advisory capacity, much to the occasional chagrin of Raintree's co-directors. They weren't quite sure which was more irritating: their chairman's continual backseat driving or the fact that, at least three-quarters of the time, he turned out to be right.

On innumerable American tours before he grew too old and sedentary for the travails of the road, Henry had bellowed and bulldozed his way around the USA, adamant in his determination that no-one was ever going to bully his acts except him, and woe betide anyone who tried, no matter how powerful and connected they may have thought they were. He was, everybody agreed, one of the grand archetypes of rock and roll management. He was also just about the only person on the entire planet whom Hudson trusted absolutely. How sad is that, Hudson thought. Sixty bloody years old, one of me best mates is dying and the other one's me manager.

They talked shop for a while, sparring over the sequencing of the live album and checking out roughs of various options for the cover design. Finally they stepped out for a bite of lunch, passers-by respectfully scattering from their path as Henry marched purposefully along Dean Street towards Quo Vadis, where they had a 1:30 reservation. Virtue having been satisfied by the mineral water he'd drunk at the Raintree office, Hudson opted for a proper grown-up Bloody Mary as an aperitif and a nice rough Chianti to go with the food. Henry, whose doctors had taken him off the drink a few years back after deciding that the only thing more amazing than the scale of Henry's booze intake over the decades was the fact that he was still alive, mock-tutted, lit a cigarette and gazed at him benignly.

"All right, young Michael," he said once they'd ordered, "what's *really* on your tiny mind?"

Hudson took a deep breath and a deeper glug on his Bloody Mary. "Got a cig?" he asked. Once Henry had lit him up, Hudson told him. All of it. Every last bit. Henry sat back and took it all in, eyes slowly widening, so gobsmacked that he barely noticed when his meal arrived.

"Blimey O'Reilly," he said eventually. "You really are in a bit of a pickle, old son. What you wanna do?" Henry always asked that. No matter how dire the situation, it was never 'what are we going to do?' but 'what do you *want* to do?' Everything Henry did was based around helping his clients to fulfil their wishes. He called his approach 'talent-driven.' His detractors claimed he indulged his boys — or, latterly, just 'the boy' — quite shamelessly. Henry didn't hold with the current management philosophy that it was the artists' job to do what their managers told them. He still believed in asking the talent what it wanted and then going out and getting it for them. He figured that if the talent was good enough, they'd hold up their end, and if they held up their end and he held up his, then there'd be platinum aplenty for everyone.

"I want to get this album with Blue done," Hudson told him. "Haven't really thought about much after that."

Henry spread his big callused hands. "Doing the album's no problem," he said, "provided you and poor old Blue can get La Diva and your homeboy kiddy in the studio long enough to finish it. And," he added, "providing the old feller doesn't croak before you're done."

"But we've got to sort out the business end," Hudson said, "Everybody's got different labels, different management..."

"No worries," Henry said. "If everybody wants the same thing, there's no way management or labels are gonna get in the way. Soon's you tell me what kind of deal you want, I'll 'ave a word with old Si about Blue's end of it."

"I don't really want much at all," Hudson said. "Blue's the featured artist, so the album should come out on his label. I'll take a co-production credit, but I don't want any money. I want half my royalties going into a trust fund for Blue's wife and kid, and the other half split between cancer research and setting up the James Blue Moon Foundation for blues education in schools..."

Henry patted him on the shoulder. "Don't you worry about any of that, young Michael. Me'n Si'll sort all that out. But when I asked you what you wanted, I didn't mean all this music business bollocks. I mean: what... do... *you*... want?" He pointed a forefinger into Hudson's face, giving him the stare with which he'd intimidated dodgy promoters from Glasgow to Guam. "What do you, Michael Hudson Esquire, in your heart of fakkin' hearts, actually want to get out of this situation?

"Here's how I understand it." Henry began ticking points off on his sausage-like fingers. "One. Thirty-whatever years ago you shagged La Diva. She got pregnant. She wanted you to come to the States chop-chop so's you'n her could make like the Three Bears and live happily ever after. You couldn't do that because Jocasta'd just miscarried and you didn't want to leave her in the lurch. When you tell her that, she throws the biggest hissy fit since 'Itler invaded Poland and tells you never to darken her towels again. Am I right?"

"Right."

"Okay. Two. The kid's one of the biggest producers in the business, and he doesn't know you're his dad. If he finds out, you've got absolutely no way'a knowing how he's gonna react, right?"

"Right. Though my guess is he's probably going to want me drive-byed."

"Okay. Three. Poor ol' Blue's on his last legs and he wants to bring his whole family — which includes you, old son — together to help him make his last record. La Diva hates your guts, and the kid *would* hate your guts if he knew who the fuck you were. Right?"

"Right."

"Okay. As your long-suffering manager *and* as your oldest mate, I know exactly what my personal *and* professional advice would be. I also know that there ain't a cat's chance in hell you're gonna take it."

"And your advice is...?"

Henry muttered, "Ahhhh, fuck it," and poured himself a small glass of Hudson's wine. "As your attorney, I advise you to just walk away from the whole fakkin' thing. Tell Blue — or, if you like, I'll tell Si — that you're sick, or that one of the girls is, and you're confined to barracks until furver notice. I know how deep it is between you'n Blue and how much you wanna do this thing for him, and if it was just you'n him I'd say go do it, old son, and godspeed.

"But bringin' in La Diva and the kid, with all the fakkin' weirdness that goes along with that, makes the whole thing really bloody iffy. I'd be lying if I didn't tell you I've got a really bad feeling about all of this. Remember the old saying: let sleeping dogs lie. You, me old mucker, are about to wake the Hound of the soddin' Baskervilles from a sound an' refreshin' slumber.

"But you ain't gonna take my advice, are you?"

"Wish I could. But I promised."

"Yeah, like you promised La Diva to stay clear of her an' the kid. Don't take this the wrong way, young Michael, but how come you've managed to reach your current advanced age without ever learning anything about women?"

"Pardon?" Hudson spluttered into his wine.

"Oh sure, I know you've shagged fakkin' 'undreds'a birds and lived with a few. You even got married once, which still provides loads'a fun for our accountants every time your ex phones up to tell 'em about all the excitin' things the girls need an' 'ow much they cost. You still don't know the first bleedin' thing about women."

"Which is, O Wise One?"

"That sometimes when a bird tells you to fuck off, what she really means is *don't go*."

Hudson raised his hands. "'Ang on, mate. What is this, the Marx Brothers?" He did his Groucho voice. "'Just when I tell you to go you leave me'? That sounds dangerously close to all that old crap about how when a woman says no she really means yes. I've met too many women who've been raped by drunken bastards who wouldn't take no for an answer to give that one any house-room, and I've believed that since I was a kid, before I ever heard of feminism."

"Yeah, but those geezers you're talkin' about were stupid as well as fakkin' evil. If a bird tells you to fuck off, a bloke with his eyes open an' 'is wits about him ought to be able to figure out if that means he really *should* fuck off or whether it's 'is cue to move in an' give 'er a great... big... *hug*."

"Okay, Master, what should I have done, then?" Maybe it was the wine, but Henry was starting to look positively buddha-like.

"Let me ask you this. What is it I do for a living?"

"You yell at people and intimidate 'em into doing what you want 'em to do before you break their legs. It's what's made you a legend."

"Okay, apart from that... what I do is I negotiate with people. I put a little pressure on an' then I read 'ow they react. If I can push 'em a little bit furver then I push. If I can't, I pull back before I make 'em move to a position where they won't move any more. Now, I don't know La Diva. Never met the woman in my life. But what I would've done was to wait a few months until it was all over with Jocasta..."

"Yeah, we broke up when she tried to stab me. I was lucky it was only a breadknife so I managed to take it away before she sliced me to death..."

"... and then I'd'a called her up and said, 'I'm free now, you still want to be together?' If you 'adn't 'ad Jocasta to worry about, would you 'ave wanted to be with 'er?"

Hudson looked troubled. "I really don't know. I mean, she's a brilliant artist and we had some amazing sex, but... look, she's got the worst temper in the world. Even a trivial argument could end up with broken glass everywhere and blood on the walls. Dunno if I could've handled that on a long-term relationship basis."

Henry looked grimly amused. "Well, I can tell you straight out: you couldn't've 'andled it. Not unless you 'ad me on twenty-four-hour call-out to smooth things over, and that's not part of the Raintree service, not even for you. One reason you'n ol' Blue've got on so well all these years is that you got summink in common: yer both fakkin' rubbish at facin' up to stuff. You just want to make your music, 'ave a bevvy or two and get yer leg over once in a while. That's why he needs Si and you need me. Neither me nor Si play guitar or sing worth a shit, but we're good at facin' up to stuff. Not always our own stuff, but definitely uvver peoples'. It's what we do. That's why Si'n me are managers and you'n Blue are talent.

"Look. I'm not gonna tell you just how much you're currently worth 'cause you'd only go out an' spend it all on lollipops, but I will say this.

If you decided, right now, that you never ever wanted to play another bloody note of music for money as long as you lived, you could still live the rest'a yer life exactly how you like anywhere in the world you fancy. I don't care. I've made me pile many times over, not just from you, either, and now I'm an old-age pensioner I've even got me bus pass. Any time you want to quit, I can stop getting up at eight every bleedin' morning to get the train into work. The kids in the office'd probably be delighted if they only saw me once or twice a week. An' frankly, I'd be delighted if I only saw *them* once or twice a week.

"Listen... Michael, bizwise I'll do whatever you need me to to make this thing happen. La Diva and the kid got their own management and record deals, and I don't mind hosting the conference call, or even flying out to LA to chair the meeting in person. But if it was up to me I'd be movin' heaven an' fakkin' earth to get your arse out of this situation as fast as I can. I know you just wanna do the right thing by your mate, and I'm all for that. I know just how much you like the old fucker, and how much you owe him.

"But I don't feel good about it. If everything was the way it was supposed to be, I'd be the number one fakkin' cheerleader for this project. You know that.

"Listen, me old son." Henry reached across the table and took Hudson's hands in his. "I've been looking after you since you were old enough to vote, and the one thing I've always dreaded is you gettin' yourself into summink I can't get you out of. Every instinct I got says this is one of those."

"I'm sorry, mate." Hudson was moved. He hadn't seen the old pirate this upset since Jocasta lost the baby. "Frankly, I'm scared shitless and I'm really not looking forward to it at all, but I have to do this. It's a debt of honour." Henry released Hudson's hands and signalled for their bill.

"Debt of honour my fat hairy old arse. Suppose a man's gotta do what a man's gotta do and all that old bollocks." He flipped the waiter his platinum Amex card and drained his water glass. "So what are you doing for the foreseeable?"

"Picking the girls up from their mother's tomorrow and takin' 'em for a week in Barcelona."A villa on the outskirts of his favourite town was Hudson's primary residence for tax purposes, mainly because he was a sucker for Gaudi's architecture. "Then I'm going back to LA to get started on the record. I was originally gonna take 'em to LA with me, but what with all the weirdness..."

"Well, at least you're bein' sensible about something." Out on the pavement, Henry hugged Hudson again, even tighter. "Keep me up to date, all right?"

"Fer shur, dude." As he walked away, he heard Henry roaring behind him. "Don't forget now, Holmes... the footprints of a gigantic hound!"

EIGHTEEN

VENICE, CALIFORNIA

At two minutes to eight, Maudie Lam answered Calvin's brisk, assertive ring on the doorbell. She saw a muscular light-skinned mixed-race guy in dazzling white sportswear. He saw a plump, middle-aged East Asian woman in a cheap velour tracksuit with a stopwatch pinned to it, smiling warmly like she knew him. The fuck was up? Long as he was sure up front who it was, Blue always liked to answer the door himself.

"You come this way," she said, leading the way to the music room. She knocked twice on the door and then ushered him in.

For a second or two, Calvin literally didn't see Blue. He was checking for a big boisterous figure with an energy belying its age and wearing, even indoors on a no-count ordinary evening, a slick suit. It took him a heartbeat or two to register the wheelchair and its occupant, a child's stick-figure drawing in jeans, baseball cap and sweatshirt — not even, he noted, one of his, and he'd certainly sent them enough samples. The stick figure raised its head towards him. Behind a trimmed white beard was the face of his grandfather, but his grandfather reduced to the barest essentials. It was like half his grandfather had gone away, and this was what was left.

"How you doin', young man," the apparition said in what sounded like maybe half his grandfather's voice. "Y'all forgive me if I don't get up. My ass been welded to this chair for quite a while now."

Calvin dropped to his knees beside the wheelchair. "Shit, grampop, what done happened to you?"

"I got old," Blue said, "but that ain't the all of it. I got cancer. Liver cancer. Doc says I got maybe a year, tops. Most likely a lot less'n that."

Calvin shook his head to clear it. He just kept muttering, "Shit... shit... shit" under his breath.

"It ain't that big of a deal," Blue said. "Hell, I'm eighty-three years old. Lotsa guys don't need to get no cancer to be dyin' at eighty-three. Lotsa guys don't even make it this far down the line in the first place." He looked at his grandson. "What'ch'all expect? I was gonna live forever or somethin'? You ain't been to see me in more'n a year. I could always not be here." He chuckled. "Havin' cancer just the cherry on the god-dam cake."

Calvin found his voice. "So what'ch'all doin' about it? Operation, chemotherapy?"

"None'a that." Blue said. "I may be old, I may be black'n I may be from Miss'ssippi, but I ain't no fool. I know when it's my time, and whatever months I got left I ain't gonna spend pukin' what's left'a my guts out or gettin' my ass cut up. I got a nurse here, Maudie. You met her when you come in. She keep me comfortable, give me acupuncture, massage, all kinds'a stuff. I got my pills..." he held up a small brown-tinted plastic bottle and shook it gently "... for the pain, an' that's about it."

Calvin just keep shaking his head, muttering, "Damn." He reached out, put his hand on his grampop's knee. All he could feel beneath his fingers was bone. "Gramps, I got money. I got crazy fuckin' money. Anything you need..." Blue put his hand over his grandson's.

"I know you got money, young man. You got ten times more money'n me an' your mama put together, maybe a hundred times, I don't know. But I don't need your money. What I need from you right now is your talent an' your skill." Calvin looked puzzled.

"See, here's the thing. I'm'a gonna make one more album while I still got the strength to hold my git-tar and sing a few songs. This album gonna be a family affair. Your moms's gonna sing with me, an' a young man from England I been knowin' since he was a baby, name'a Mick Hudson..."

Calvin frowned. "Mick Hudson? The old rock guy?"

"Guess you might call him that. But I been knowin' him forty years now, and he know my music back to front'n back again. He gonna run the band, help produce, help me get what I want. But I want you to come in too. This gonna be my last record, I want my whole family makin' music together. Chance ain't never gonna come again."

"Grampop, I don't know how I can help you make a record. You been making records since way before I was born. An' I don't know nuthin' 'bout no blues. Way before my time. Stevie'n James'n Marvin'n P-Funk is where I came in."

"You pretty much the top producer around right now, they tell me. Got records on the radio and the MTV all day long an' all night, too. I don't want to make no record just for the old folks. Been doin' that for years. Mick, he sixty years old. Your mama, she fifty-seven or so. We all old folks 'part from you. I want you to help me make a record young folks can listen to also. My daughter Donna, she fourteen. She love your records." Blue chuckled. "Don't listen to none'a mine. I need a record sound like me, but somethin' more folks gonna like than just another Blue Moon record. Some'a them kids you cut records on can't sing or play nuthin' at all but you still make 'em sound good. I need you to make me sound good.

"Else I'm'a haveta ask Donna to produce my record."

Calvin got up from the floor next to Blue, sank into the armchair. Blue had always been good to him, encouraged him to stay with music even when his moms was chewing his ass out about going to law school. He'd always felt more secure and comfortable with his grandfather's relaxed, streetwise, been-round-the-block take on life than he ever had with his mother's frenetic oscillations between Baptist piety and regal showbiz hauteur. The first time he ever heard the term 'non-judgemental', he thought immediately of his Grampop, who told him one time when he was getting started that blues singers were just the rappers of their day. That had stayed with him: when he was first getting into writing rhymes and rapping he called himself Ice Blue as a tribute to the old man. It'd be cool to work with real voices like his moms and gramps, even a rock guitar player like this Hudson. Make a change from fucked-up yardies and kids off the block couldn't see no further into the future than their first gold chain. Hell, he might learn something new from doing this. And it'd be a break from all the bullshit up at Lock N Load, give some of the youngbloods a chance to test out their own shit in the studio. Fuck it, why not?

"Okay, gramps," he said. "I'm'a do it. Don't know how it's gonna work, but colour me in." He paused a beat. "But you got to do somethin' for me. I need you to answer me some questions, tell me what fuckin' time it is.

"Do you know who my father is?"

Blue sat very still in his wheelchair. Calvin felt like his mind was in bullet time, zooming across the room while Blue sat there like a digitally-frozen still image.

"Yes, I do."

There was an iron band around Calvin's chest, remorselessly tightening. "How long you known?"

"Ever since your mama first brought you to see me. First time I set eyes on you, I knew."

The iron band got tighter still.

"You gonna give me his name?"

"I can't do that. Only two people got the right to answer that question. One'a them's your mama. The other one's your daddy." Blue sat up fractionally straighter in his chair. "Now, I got one for you. Back in the day, when you first made yourself some money, you could'a hired yourself a private eye, do some investigatin', got you the information, your moms wanted you to know or not. How come you never did that?"

Calvin grinned mirthlessly. "Don't think I didn't think'a that. An' my moms thought of it too. Before I did. She made me promise never to try to find out."

Blue was chuckling now, a rusty rustling noise deep in his chest.

"What's so funny?" Calvin asked.

Blue coughed lightly into a kleenex, crumpling the tissue too quick for Calvin to be able to tell if there was blood on it. "So why'd you keep that promise?"

Calvin said, "Huh?"

"You heard me. You gave your moms your word. But if you wanted to know so bad, how come you didn't go 'head on an' do it anyway?"

Calvin spread his hands. "'Cause I'm a man always keep his word, gramps. Once I make me a promise I stick to it. An' I got no respect for any muthafucka that don't."

Blue was laughing again, but this time he didn't cough. "Young man, you just like your daddy."

Calvin said, "Huh?"

"Now, like I told you, I can't give you his name. But I can tell you this one thing. The reason you ain't heard from your daddy all these years ain't 'cause he don't care about you or your mama. It's 'cause *he* made a promise to her, too. She made him swear never to try'n see her again, or you. An' he jus' like you: a man always keep his word even when he wish he never given it."

Commotion in the hall, a knock at the door and in burst Donna. She ran straight to Calvin. "Yo, Pint Size!" he cried, hugging her. "How's my favourite li'l auntie?" He hefted his bag, pulled out a fistful of CDs and a couple of the latest limited edition Fully Loaded T-shirts. "Got my Auntie Tax right here." Adrienne walked into the room and Calvin hugged her too. "Yo, whassup, Grandma?" She clenched a mock-threat-

163

ening fist. "When Josh or Donna start havin' babies, that's when you allowed to call me grandma. Not before!" She stood on tiptoe to kiss him on the cheek. "I'm really glad you're here, Calvin. Blue's been looking forward to talking with you for the longest time.

"You gonna help him make the record?"

"Yes," Calvin said. "Yes, I am."

"Is it gonna be strange working with your grandad?"

"Yeah," Calvin said. "But not nearly as strange as it's gonna be working with my moms."

Donna was pulling at Calvin's arm. It was a ritual whenever he visited that he would spend half an hour or so with Donna in her room, checking out her latest clothes and CDs and computer games, letting her pump him for tidbits of gossip about the Lock N Load artists and anybody else famous he'd bumped into since the last time he saw her.

As soon as the pair of them had disappeared into Donna's room, Adrienne turned to Blue.

"You tell him?"

"Yeah."

"What'd you tell him?"

"Everything 'cept his daddy's name."

"How long you gonna let that boy hang by his thumbs while everybody waits around to tell him the one thing he needs to know?"

"I'm'a wait 'til Mick gets back. Wouldn't be fair to nobody to say nuthin' while he ain't here. When we all together in one room, if his moms ain't told him I will."

"You better," Adrienne told him, "'cause if she don't tell him and you don't tell him, then *I* will."

Maudie knocked at the door. Now that Adrienne was back in the house, Maudie was free to go home just as soon as she'd supervised Blue's ingestion of the day's final tranche of medication. Blue kept teasing her by requesting a cigarette and three fingers of Jack on the rocks. "Mr Moon, you very difficult patient," she told him, laughing. "It will be very bad sign when I bring you cigarettes and whiskey. It mean you enjoy yourself tonight because you not going to be here tomorrow. Long as I not bring, you know you safe."

She said her goodnights and let herself out just as Calvin and Donna emerged from their summit. "Can Calvin stay for dinner?" Donna implored. Adrienne and Blue said 'course he could, but Calvin, taking a completely unnecessary peek at his watch — a Fully Loaded digital to-night, rather than his usual Rolex — told 'em he was outta here like he stole sump'n 'cause he was running late, and he'd be on the set when-ever they were ready to go to work.

Back in his white Hummer, he drove round the block, then pulled over, grabbed his cellphone and called his mother. She answered on the first ring.

"Calvin? Hi, baby."

"Hi, moms. Yeah, I just come from grampop."

"What'd he say?"

"Said he was dyin'. He looked real bad, moms. *Real* bad."

"Yes." She was whispering, so low he could barely hear her. "Yes, I know."

"Said he was makin' one last album, that you were gonna sing. Said he wanted me to work on it too, with you'n him'n this limey guitar guy been his friend a long time."

Silence. Then: "Yeah, that's right. That's what he wants." Another silence.

"Moms? You still there?"

A sigh. "Yes, baby, I'm still here."

The fuck was up with her? He'd never heard his moms sound like this. Whether she was happy or sad, up or down, angry or chilled-out, she always seemed to know exactly who she was, what she felt, what she wanted and who was to blame for anything that might be going differ-ent from the way she'd decided it ought to be. Now her voice was small, uncertain, hardly like her voice at all. She didn't seem her usual self any more than grampops did, but he was that way because he was sick.

"He tell you anything else?"

Calvin felt like he'd been living in a world of bullshit his whole muth-afuckin' life, and he couldn't stand the stink of it in his nostrils any more. "Yeah, moms, he did. He told me the reason my daddy never had nuthin' to do with me was 'cause you told him not to. That right?"

This time her silence told him all he needed to know. He didn't wait for it to end, just jabbed the red button with his thumb and tossed the phone into the back seat. Almost before it had time to bounce it started to ring again. He ignored it, gunned the Hummer with a screech of rub-ber on asphalt. He was going to go home, change out of his trademark whites and go visit a small and very discreet club where he only went when things were going either seriously right or seriously wrong.

So those two Jamaican fools had themselves a problem with batty-men, did they? Well, he was one battyman they did *not* want to fuck with. One battyman they should've killed *last* year. One battyman who was going to seriously fuck them, one way or another.

One battyman who was on his way to have himself some hot tight batty right now.

LOS ANGELES/LONDON

"Si?"

"Yeah."

"It's old Henry here."

"How are you, you old bastard?"

"Not so bad, not so bad... listen, I just had a spot of brunch with young Michael, and he told me about Blue. Just wanted to send him me best and say how sorry I am. I liked him a lot..."

"Hey, let's keep it in the present tense, Henry. Blue's still with us, y'know."

"Yeah, well, y'know what I mean. If there's anything we can help with, just let us know."

"Mick tell you about this record he and Blue want to do together?"

"'Course he did."

"So what d'you reckon?"

"Well, you ent gonna have any problems from our end. Mick just wants to make the record. He don't mind whose label puts it out, and he don't want any money. Says he wants half his end to go into a trust fund for Blue's wife an' kiddy, and the other half split between cancer research and some memorial foundation in Blue's name to teach blues 'istory in schools. All he wants is a co-production credit."

"That's nice. We appreciate that. Our thinking is that it should go out as a James Blue Moon record with Mick and the others as guest stars."

"That'll be fine with us. Dunno about the diva and the hip-hop laddie, though. You talk to their people yet?"

"No, mate. That pleasure still awaits."

"D'you wanna start sorting that out, then? Get a conference call to-gether? Or if you wanna do it face to face I could fly out and..."

"No thanks, Henry, I don't think it'll come to that. Phone'll be fine. Wouldn't want to drag an elderly gentleman away from gracious living in the lovely English countryside."

"You fakkin' cheeky scouse cunt."

"Oh, so it *is* you, Henry. All this no-problem-whatever-you-want'll-be-fine stuff, I thought it was Mike Yarwood doing your voice."

"Mike Yarwood? Cor dear, you *have* been away a long time. It's so long since he was on the telly I can't even remember who was Prime Minister then. It's Rory Bremner does all the voices now."

"Who?"

"Exactly. Proves my point, dunnit? Now if you stayed a little longer next time you come to Blighty, you could watch some proper telly 'stead of all that rubbish you have in the States."

"What, you mean rubbish like *Deadwood, Curb Your Enthusiasm, The Sopranos, Six Feet Under*...?"

"Yeah, that's what I mean. Crap like that."

"You're a hopeless case, Henry. Meanwhile, back at the subject of our conversation, d'you think the suits at the label are gonna get arsy about giving Mick a release to appear on Blue's album?"

"Not a chance, me old son, not a chance. I absofakkinlutely guaran-fakkintee you will not hear a single peep out of 'em."

"Now I *definitely* know it's really you, Henry, and not Rory Whati-sname. Take care'a yourself."

"Cheery-bye, me old mucker. Speak to you as and when."

NINETEEN

Lately Blue had gotten into the habit of getting himself wheeled down to the beachfront two or three evenings a week just before sunset, when the tourists and the skaters and weightlifters had all gone home and he could have the Pacific Ocean all to himself. He said he hadn't been further from the house than his back yard for almost two months, and what was the point of living right by the sea if you never went out and looked at it any? It rapidly became a ritual, Adrienne or Maudie wheeling him out and across the footpath and down onto the sandy beach. They'd take the dogs out, too, but after a few visits Blue decided that he wanted to be on his own to look out at the sea and let his mind wander where it would, so they worked up a routine where whoever was chaperoning him would head up to the cafe up on the far corner where they could still see him, have a cappuccino or a glass of wine or something, keep an eye on him while he sat.

Originally they'd left the dogs with him to keep him company, but after awhile he started saying, no, take dogs with. After all, if they took it into their doggy heads to go running off after something that smelled interesting, he couldn't hardly go chasing after them, now could he? "No-one's gonna fuck with an old man in a wheelchair," he said.

"... who happens to be a legend..."

"... an' who ain't had his picture took in quite a while, so I ain't exactly gonna be mobbed by autograph hunters. 'Sides, I got my phone 'case I need somethin' and you'll be right up there in the coffee shop, all you got to do is look up, see I'm okay."

So he'd sit and relax in his chair while Maudie caught up on her knitting and had herself a cup of green tea just up the way. Let his eyes go slightly unfocussed, the ripples in the darkening sea dancing like choreographed fireflies as they caught the rays of the setting sun, the reassuring sussuration and plash of the ocean lulling him into more and more vivid reveries of earlier times. This time he was back in the troughs of the late seventies and early eighties, when Bobby Bland and Albert King and BB were just about the only bluesmen with serious record contracts and everybody else scuffling for the crumbs, living in what was then Watts but is now South Central LA with Rita, both of them drinking whiskey like it was an Olympic event and they were representing America, gigs getting fewer and further between and money drying up, baby Charlene sitting there wide-eyed and scared as her parents shouted and fought.

Rita and Charlene had come to visit just the other day, and even on a warm evening the memory sent a rippling wave of shivers through Blue's body. Looking into Rita's stony eyes, it had taken a massive effort to recall that there'd ever been any love there. She'd taken his hand for an instant, then dropped it like he was infectious. All she seemed to have on her mind was whether she was taken care of in his will. Hell, he'd bought her the damn house even though they'd been long since divorced because the guy she'd left him for was long gone like a turkey through the straw, she got money every month so she didn't have to work, and when Adrienne had come in to say hey, Rita'd stared at her like she wished she had heat vision like goddam Superman and could fry her to a crisp, she might as well had a thought balloon over her head saying that skinny bitch got what's mine. As soon as Blue'd told her yeah sure, there'll be money, she'd looked at her watch and gathered up her topcoat and bag.

And Charlene... at least she'd hugged his frail frame and kissed him and called him Poppa, just like she always did. But she was looking ashy and she had the shakes and her clothes smelled like she'd slept in 'em three-four nights. At least she didn't have one of those damn gangsta-ass boyfriends with her you had to watch all the time make sure they didn't steal nothing, and he thought, my little baby girl need so much help and protection, still can't hardly fend for herself and there ain't no-one gonna look after her when I'm gone.

When they'd left, he'd cried for an hour. There's always so much more to lose than you ever thought you had.

And now he was twenty years old again, back at the railroad station in Clarksdale the night the Klan burned down his father's church, his guitar across his back and the few clothes he hadn't outgrown stuffed into a cardboard suitcase, waiting for the train to take him to Memphis so he could change onto the Illinois Central train folks called the Chicago Nine for the sixteen-hour ride to the Windy City, nothing in his pocket but a scrap of paper scrawled with the names of a couple of cousins he'd never met and fourteen bucks more than the twelve he needed for his fare.

It had been damn cold, he remembered, but picking on his guitar at least kept his fingers warm. There'd been some guy there he'd talked to for awhile, had a dog with him, told Blue he was gonna be successful and have a long and interesting life, but Blue couldn't recall much more than that. He remembered the dog licking his fingers, helping keep him warm. Matter of fact, he could feel the warm rasp of the dog's tongue on his fingers right now...

Blue opened his eyes, looked down. Damn if there wasn't a dog right there next to him licking his fingers now, big brown sonovabitch wagging a stumpy tail. And there was a guy with the dog, hunkered down on his haunches beside Blue's wheelchair, one hand resting lightly on the dog's back, black guy around forty-something in a windcheater and baseball cap.

"Don't I know you, brother?" he asked Blue.

"Maybe. I'm..."

"Yeah! You're Reverend Moon's boy!"

Blue sat bolt upright in his wheelchair. The fuck was going on?

"You remember when you got your first git-tar? At Sam's Barber Shop back in Clarksdale? You'd'a been sixteen years old, needed ten bucks but you only had five..."

Blue swallowed hard. He felt like the breath was being pumped out of his body. "I ain't never told nobody that."

"You sure 'bout that? You sure you didn't tell that story to some white boy from *Living Blues* magazine back around 1987?"

Blue's mouth was suddenly dry. "Yeah, I'm sure."

The guy patted him on the knee. "Relax, brotherman. Just fuckin' wit'cha." He grinned at Blue, a gold front tooth catching the fading light. "You know, you a hard man to get to see these days. You know you ain't been dreamin' once since they put you on them pain pills? Make me haul my ass all the way out here just so's you'n me could have us a little talk."

The dog let out a single quiet whine and settled down on the sand next to Blue, curling up around his feet.

"First off, I'm'a interview you just like the white boys do," the guy said, one fist at Blue's mouth, holding an imaginary microphone. "Tell me, Mr Moon, why'd you decide you were gonna devote your life to playin' the blues?"

Blue said, "You know so much about me, how come you got to ask?"

"Oh, *I* know the answer to that one. I just wondered if *you* do."

Blue said, "Okay, brother, let's play it your way. When I saw Little

Robert playin' on the corner by old man Birnbaum's store, I thought, one day I'm'a do that. Be dressed up slick. Gonna play git-tar. And when I sing and play, my music gonna make folks *feel* stuff deep down inside, make 'em feel *good*.

"An' I think I done that over the years. Put what I know 'bout life into music, let folks know they not alone in they troubles..."

"So savin' the world was your top priority, an' gettin' rich'n famous'n bein' chased by lots'a ladies didn't have nuthin' to do with it."

"I got to say," Blue told him, "that not spendin' six days a week workin' on a farm an' every Sunday in church was pretty high on my list."

"So that's why you started playin' the devil's music."

"Never played no devil's music in my life," Blue said firmly. "Not one note, not one word."

"But that ain't how your family saw it, now was it?" And the guy's face suddenly changed. Same physical shapes and forms, sure, but it was like there was a different spirit behind those features now. His eyebrows drew together, came forward and down. His mouth clamped into a hard angry line. His neck seemed to get thicker, his shoulders broader. And when he spoke again, his light mellifluous voice had became deeper, harsh and grating.

"I'd rather see you in a hearse," he growled in a voice Blue never thought he would ever hear again. "I'd rather follow your coffin to the graveyard than hear that you had become a musician." Right there in his wheelchair on Venice Beach, in his eighty-third and final year, Blue was face to face with the Reverend Solomon Moon.

And then, just as suddenly, the Reverend Moon was gone. Now the guy's features were heavy and sorrowful, lower lip pooched out in a pout Blue recognised: once he'd found it so sexy it damn near drove him crazy. "I know you spent your whole life runnin' from Jesus," the guy said in his ex-wife Mary's soft low tones. "I want you to stop runnin'. I want you to turn around and embrace Him. Me'n Neesha done took the Lord into our lives, and we need you to do the same if you want us all to stay together." Now a shrill edge was creeping into his voice. "You move in a world where the devil be callin' loud and clear even to a good man like you. You got to leave that world, honey. You got to follow us to a place where you can be that good man I know you are."

Blue opened his mouth to speak, but the guy wasn't finished yet. Now his face was smooth and soft and plump and unlined and his eyes were big and round and a tear snaked its way down his cheek. His voice was high and childish. "Daddy, you been leavin' us for a long time now. Now *you* remember *this*. We may be leavin', but you the one lettin' us go. *That's* what I'm gonna remember my whole life. *You* let *me* go."

Blue drew in a deep rattling breath, started to cough. The guy pressed a tissue into his hand as he was wracked with a long spluttering coughing fit. By the time he could speak again, there were traces of blood marbling the phlegm on the tissue.

"Just 'cause they thought it was the devil's music," he said at length, "don't make it so."

The guy applauded softly. "Yeah, you right," he said, once again in his own voice. "You know who said it best? You did." Now his cheeks drew in, and his face was longer and leaner, with a quizzical gleam in his eyes. Blue was looking at himself.

"This music I play, this work that I do, it ain't no hobby. It ain't no game. It ain't no trick so I don't have to do a regular job. It's what I was put here on this earth to do." Blue's own voice, too, to the life. "This music is a callin'. Yeah, a callin', just like what a priest get. And there ain't no evil in it. Every night I play, I look down at the peoples and I see they faces. I see 'em come in the place weighed down by they troubles, worryin' 'bout they jobs'n money an' The Man. And I see 'em smile'n laugh'n dance'n go home with a smile on they face an' a weight off they shoulders.

"The blues ain't no devil's music. The blues put on this earth to make folks feel better, an' I was put on this earth to play the blues. Anyone say any different, they the ones been listenin' to the devil, not me. If there's a God like you say, then I'm doin' His work, right here, with what I'm doin'."

Once again, he applauded softly. "Here's the thing, Mr Blue," he said in his own voice. "I know you ain't a religious man. But you right. The blues is God's work. The blues is part of God's plan. God's plan is huge an' complicated. It's so complicated you practic'ly got to *be* God to understand it. *I* don't understand it. *You* sure as hell..." he grinned "... don't understand it. But I understand my own little bitty part of it, and my guess is you understand yours."

"I don't know what you think it is I understand," Blue said. "But you right about one thing. I ain't a religious man. Most'a the religious folks I ever met just so eaten up with hate'n fear, never wanted to be like them.

I don't mess with no God or devil. I deal strictly with people."

"Don't matter if you religious or not. I just said 'God' and 'the dev-il' 'cause those are terms you familiar with. If you was into *Star Wars* I'd'a talked about the 'the dark side'a the force.' If you was Muslim, I'd say Allah and Iblis. If you was Hindu or Buddhist I'd'a said it different still, 'cause they don't think in quite the same dualistic terms which the Semitic desert religions inherited from Zoroastrianism." For a second there he reminded Blue of some Harvard professor teaching a comparative religion class, rather than a Southern-sounding brother in a windcheater.

"But it works like this. When I say 'God,' I mean all the good'n positive energy in the universe, and when I say 'the devil,' I mean the bad negative shit. Don't worry, brother, I ain't tryin' to drag your tired old ass to no church at this stage in your life. The devil wants folks either so beaten down with sufferin' that they can't think about nuthin' but their own pain, or else so hooked on pleasure that all they lookin' after be they own nose or they own peepee. Either way, they can't pay no 'count to nobody else's situation. Blues works against both those things, makes folks see that they pain and they pleasure same as everybody else's, an' that we all in this world together. Like your good friend who done passed said it, 'Blues is the healer.' Ol' Johnny Lee Hooker was one'a ours, though he never knew it for sure."

"Wait a second," Blue said, "One'a ours? Who's ours? Who's us?"

The guy smiled, and gently scratched his dog's ears. The dog stirred slightly, let out a muted whine, went right back to sleep. "Well, I could tell you that 'us' is the good guys, but it ain't that simple, 'cause we're the bad guys too. Let's just say that 'us' is the part of us that's the good guys. Just like regular folks, you might say." He stroked the dog more roughly until it awoke with a louder whine of complaint. He stood up.

"I got to be goin', Mr Blue. Pleasure talkin' to you." He pulled a leather lead from his windcheater pocket, bent down to attach it to the dog's collar.

"Just one more thing. Right now, you under some powerful protection, but the folks closest to you ain't, so they at risk. An' if you ever lose that protection, you be in the worst danger of all, 'less you find someone prepared to go your bail.

"But then you already took out some insurance. Back in England, weren't it?

"Okay. See you in your dreams, brother." He raised one fist in salutation, gently tapped it against Blue's, tugged on the dog's lead until it got to its feet, and ambled off along the shoreline.

"Mr Moon! Mr Moon!" What?... oh, Maudie was back, Attack and Wu Li at her side, gently shaking his shoulder. "You been asleep! If you tired, why you no phone me to take you home?"

His thoughts seemed fuzzy. "Hi, Maudie," he said, suppressing a yawn. "Damndest thing just happened. I got talking to this guy..."

"But Mr Moon," Maudie interrupted him, "I was watch you the whole time you were sitting there and there was no man here with you."

"Sure there was," Blue insisted. "Had a dog with him, too."

"Oh, I see the dog," Maudie told him, "Dog sit with you long time. But no man. Look, Mr Moon," she said, pointing at the sand around Blue's chair. "Here are wheelchair tracks. Here are my footprints. Here are prints of dog. No man's footprints here."

Blue shook his head, took a closer look. She was absolutely right. "Well, *damn*," he said, half to himself. Maybe old age, sickness and heavy-duty pain pills were finally getting to him. And maybe not.

Someone had talked. Someone always does. It started with a blind item on the London-based DirrtyDawg pop gossip website. "Which swaggering hip-hop mogul isn't quite the all-conquering hetty stud his frequent appearances with hot-babe arm-candy might suggest? According to our spies, there's nothing he likes better as an occasional special treat than hanging out at an extremely exclusive private club in LA, picking up skinny white boys and giving them one up the arse so energetically that a couple of them have required medical attention and considerable hush money. He's recently been picking up plaudits from gay activists for ostentatiously dissociating his label from homophobic lyrics and performers, but there may be something a little more personal involved than simple humanitarian concern. Is his his motivation for taking this potentially unpopular stand really whiter-than-white?"

The DirrtyDawg item then migrated, almost verbatim bar slightly coyer language, to the pop goss page of a notorious English tabloid. From there it was all over the internet. No-one directly confronted Calvin Holland with the item or challenged him to confirm or deny that it referred to him, but copies of it were emailed to him anonymously from seven different sources. And someone who withheld their number kept calling him on his cellphone and playing him Battyman 9/11, over and over again.

Most disturbing of all, someone in his own muthafuckin' office was leaving highly explicit gay porn mags on his desk. No matter how early he came in in the mornings, or how late he left, they'd still be there the next time he arrived. He'd stomped into BLT's office, threw the magazines across his main man's desk, said, "Somebody leaving their shit on my desk. I like to find my desk just the way I left it. I wanna know who treating my office like a goddam dumpster." BLT got straight onto Big Ray, who headed up Lock N Load's internal security. Big Ray was both an ex-cop and an ex-con, which meant that there were two types of people didn't trust him an inch. Calvin had hired him anyway, and Big Ray had rewarded him with heavy-duty loyalty. This was a brother who'd take, or hand out, a serious beatdown for Calvin, but he'd been a detective as well as a thug, and his investigative skills hadn't atrophied significantly even while he was doing the best part of a dime in San Quentin. He'd even come out of the pen without too many more scars than he'd had when he went in.

Big Ray delivered. Two days later, he manhandled a fat kid called Feets who'd been interning in publicity into Calvin's office and slammed him down in the chair facing Calvin's desk. He tossed a handful of the magazines into Feets' lap, said, "You want me to have a little talk with this fool, boss?"

Calvin said, "Good job, Ray. I'm'a deal with the sucka myself, holler if I need you." Ray walked out. Calvin stared at Feets, didn't say anything, just stared. Feets was shaking, his eyes goggling. He let out a small, whimpering fart.

Calvin picked up a sheaf of paperwork from his desk, ostentatiously fanned the air in front of him.

"What was that?" he asked. Sweat was pouring down Feets's round face. He shook his head helplessly. "Fart," he said eventually.

"You know what a fart is?" Calvin asked him. "It's air escaping from your bowels. Air that's been in contact with your shit. When you fart, tiny molecules of your shit float out into the air of this room, and anyone who can smell your fart..." he fanned the air with the papers again "... is breathing your shit in. In this room, right now, that means me. I'm breathing your shit right now. You're making me eat your shit." He dropped the papers, bent over Feets 'til he could smell the fat kid's sour breath.

"And you know what I do to people who try to make me eat shit?" Now he had Feets by the front of his sweatshirt, pulling the butterball halfway out of the chair.

"Do ya?" Mutely Feets shook his head again. "If you don't wanna find out the worst way, you better start flappin' those liver lips'a yours. You got thirty seconds to tell me what's up with this bullshit or else a lotta folks be wondering whatever happened to that fat fool used to work in publicity."

"I got this homey," Feets muttered. His voice was high and squeaky, didn't sound like it ought to be coming out of that bulbous frame. "He's down with these niggaz from Jamaica. They wanted to fuck with you cuz'a y'all keepin' Screwdriver an' Omega Man from puttin' the 9/11 song on the album. Them niggaz really got mad hate for faggots."

Calvin kept his game face on. "What's your homey's name?" Feets's face scrunched up like he was going to cry, but he didn't say a word. Calvin stepped up to him, bitch-slapped the fat boy hard, backhand to his left cheek, an open palm to his right. A bead of blood blossomed on Feets's lower lip and started to trickle down his chins.

Now Feets was looking so scared Calvin got worried he was gonna piss himself, and then he'd have to get the chair cleaned, maybe even toss it out. He'd paid over a grand for that chair, too.

"Now you may be thinkin' that what they gonna do to you if you tell me gonna be worse that what I'm'a do if you don't," Calvin said. "What you need to bear in mind, dawg, is that right now you here with me. So whatever I'm'a do gonna happen to you first. You give me the name else I open this door'n call in Big Ray. Now Big Ray use'ta be a cop, did more'n five hard for brutality, an' he remembers everything he use'ta do in the back room'a the precinct. So you turn over the name or I'm'a turn you over to Ray.

"An' you best believe you'll turn it over to him. So whassup *now*, sucka?"

The fat boy gave it up. "They call him Ghostbuster. Eight-trey Blood."

Mobbed up, Calvin thought. He'd managed to keep Lock N Load out of the LA gang wars which had wasted so many artists as well as ordinary brothers and sisters off the block. With everything else going down, did he want to take it to the streets with the Eight-trey Bloods? He walked to the door opened it.

"Ray? In here, brother." Big Ray followed him back into the office. "Ray-Ray, get this fool out of here. Make sure he understands the health benefits of keepin' his fat mouth shut. And get me anything you can on a nigga name Ghostbuster, run with Eight-trey Bloods."

"I'm on it," Ray told him.

"Low-key, y'understand? Keep them gangstas outta the game. I wanna know who this Ghostbuster be runnin' with. 'Specially any Jamaicans."

"You want me to pick him up?" Ray asked.

"Not yet, dawg. Check him out first."

Ray dragged Feets out. The fat boy was gonna get himself a beatdown, but nothing that wouldn't heal in a few weeks' time.

Calvin didn't find any porno on his desk the next day, nor the day after that. But when he found his desktop Macintosh running a little slow, some instinct prompted him to run a quick check on his hard drive. He soon found an eighty-megabyte folder called Goodies, which he didn't recognise. He opened it up: it was stuffed with JPEG images of boys fucking and sucking and whipping each other, some of them very young indeed and all of them white. Calvin trashed the folder, then ran an optimiser program to defragment the hard drive and — more important — erase all of the newly freed-up space. He knew that simply dumping files in the trash only removed their names from the disk's directory; the now-invisible files themselves remained in place until they were overwritten or erased. When he had the time, he'd move his legitimate files onto a brand-new drive and reinitialise this one so no file-recovery program would be able to detect even the faintest traces, but right now this would have to do.

Maybe Feets had installed these images so that they could be 'discovered' later on by someone else. The question still troubling Calvin was how Feets had been able to get into Calvin's locked office despite Ray's security night shift. Ray said Feets had told him that Ghostbuster had given him a key, but so far Ray hadn't been able to explain how Ghostbuster had gotten his hands on that key when the only copies belonged to Calvin, BLT and Ray himself.

If Calvin thought that busting Feets had put a stop to all this crap, he was wrong. Two days later, when he walked into his office just before eight in the morning, sitting right smack in the centre of his desk was an impressively large and extravagantly veined snow-white rubber dildo.

TWENTY

Adrienne fresh from the shower and frowning at herself in the mirror, deciding she's been exercising too much and eating too little. Working out was her patented stressbuster. Whenever she felt worried or uptight she'd drive herself through more and more laps when she ran, more and more reps when she lifted, just to tire herself out so she could sleep soundly without a pill or a drink. When Blue was first diagnosed she'd intensified her fitness regime, and then just kept cranking it further and further. Now the mirror was telling her she'd worked off so much body-fat that she could see veins on her lower belly, climbing her abdominal wall like vines.

Sure, that'd make her the envy of her gym buddies. In her mind's ear, she could hear Sonja yelling, "You're too thin? You're too defined? Why can't you just stay fat like the rest of us, BITCH!" but then Sonja was a transplanted Brooklynite and yelling was her native language. Problem was that while Adrienne might be looking fitter in a pared-down marathon-runner kind of way, she sure as hell didn't look or feel any healthier or happier. Her breasts were beginning to shrink and sag, and her face was drawn and baggy-eyed and haggard. Migod, she thought, I look ten years older than I did two months ago. It was the most graphic proof imaginable of how badly all this shit was getting to her.

Adrienne resolved to take a week or so's break from her workout regime. She began to fantasise about ordering in a pizza, eating the whole thing, following it up with a Sara Lee cheesecake straight from the freezer, maybe even washing it all down with a couple of beers. Then doing the same tomorrow night, and the night after that. And what about all the things she could do by freeing up the seven or eight hours she devoted to her workouts each week? It was about time she started designing next spring's new range. She'd been thinking about an Arabic motif this time, and bought herself a whole stack of reference material, including a large and very expensive book of photographs of the Alhambra in Granada. She'd seen a TV documentary about it once, been fascinated by the elegant curlicues of Arabic script in all the places where European architects would have put carvings of people or animals. She wanted to try and bring the same sublime sense of line and proportion to her confections of gemstones, silver, beads and bone. Her fingers itched for her sketchpad, get some roughs down, then scan 'em in and fire up the graphics program on her Mac.

The doorbell drilled into her reverie. Damn, she'd forgotten Simon Wolfe was due round to see Blue. Donna was in school and Maudie had the day off, so there was no-one else to let him in. She scrambled into jeans and a T-shirt, answered the door still towelling her hair.

Blue had known Simon Wolfe for as long as he'd known Mick Hudson. In fact, technically he'd known Simon for longer, albeit only by a day or so. Simon had been the road manager assigned to Blue for his first British tour, when Hudson's old band Bluebottle had been the backing group, and he'd stuck with Hudson for years, first with Bluebottle, then Cabal and then finally into the solo career. Then he'd decided to go into management, trying and failing to persuade Mick to quit his management deal with Henry MacShane. Adrienne suspected that Mick's decision to stay with Henry had been only partially based on his loyalty to the old bully. The fact that Simon was living with Mick's ex-girlfriend Jocasta Meadowes might also have had something to do with it.

In the late seventies, Simon had relocated to LA with Jocasta, opened up for business as Macro Management, gradually built up a roster mingling old blues and soul singers whose careers he wanted to resuscitate with a few up-and-coming punk and hard rock indie bands whose careers he wanted to kick-start. Now, twenty-odd years later, he didn't manage any superstars, but he didn't handle any losers or time-wasters, either. Macro Management's roster was solid, respectable and reasonably profitable. Simon Wolfe himself enjoyed a reputation for quiet tenacity and absolute financial scrupulousness. Blue trusted him completely. Adrienne found him cold and boring, and saw as little of him as was diplomatically possible. She wasn't surprised that Jocasta hadn't stayed with him more than the few years she needed to recover from the trauma of her miscarriage and the collapse of her relationship with Mick Hudson. These days, she was living in Bel Air with a septuagenarian movie star.

Simon and Adrienne greeted each other warily. Almost despite his best intentions, Simon had acquired a slight tan over the years he'd been living in LA, but otherwise he was still an archetypal expat rock Brit: stocky, roundfaced, denim-clad, thinning grey-blond hair in a stubbornly retained mullet, cold grey-blue eyes, irregular teeth.

"You're looking very fit," he said at length.

"Thanks," she replied. "You're looking good yourself." Relieved that a bolt of god-sent lightning hadn't struck her down for lying so blatantly, she led the way to Blue's music room, knocking on the door, showing Simon in. She offered them drinks, but both of them said they were fine. Suit yourselves, boys, she thought, heading off to the kitchen to get herself a beer. Sitting on the sofa in the middle of the day with a cold brewski felt as deliciously, guiltily illicit as cutting school had back when she was a kid.

Adrienne felt better already.

In the music room, Blue and Simon were checking each other out, Simon looking at Blue, Blue watching Simon looking at him. Simon hadn't seen Blue in over a month, and his shock at Blue's inexorably increasing frailty was leaking around the edges of his professional deadpan.

"Well," Simon said.

"Well," Blue replied. Simon shifted uncomfortably in his chair.

"Looking good, ain't I." Blue said. It wasn't a question.

"Like a frolicking young lamb." He still had a trace of the Liverpool accent which had originally led Adrienne to nickname him Ringo. "So what's the word from the quacks?"

Blue shrugged. "Still got cancer."

"Okay." Simon unlatched his briefcase, pulled out some paperwork and a notebook. "We probably need to talk about this album. First thing to report is that I talked to Mick's manager..."

Blue chuckled. "Old Henry. Oh, he was a bad one once upon a time. Remember when he held that jive promoter in Frankfurt out the window by his ankles, wouldn't pull him up 'til he paid...?"

Blue was rambling, Simon thought. He cut short Blue's flow of reminiscence. "... and we're not going to have any problems there. He wants a co-production credit, but since he'll be working with you on choosing the material and the musicians and doing the arrangements I reckon that's fair."

"Yeah, it is."

"Henry says Mick doesn't want any money. Wants half his royalties to go into the trust fund for Donna and Adrienne, with the other half split between cancer research and this foundation he wants to set up in your name for blues education in schools."

Blue laughed. "Old Henry say whether he takin' his percentage off the top?" Simon said, "Good point," and jotted something down in his notebook.

"I had a good talk with a bloke named BLT at your grandson's company. Says Calvin still ain't too certain what you want him to do on this record, but he'll help out any way he can." Blue's eyes were half-closed. This guy ain't going anywhere anytime soon, Simon thought. Thank fuck Calvin and his techies had come in like the cavalry. "He says he can help set up a remote studio right here in this room, use a private web page with a webcam and a broadband connection so you can sit here, see and hear everything going down in the studio, even sing down the line. Calvin's guys can handle all that for us, which is great. Plus he'll do it on the same financial terms as Mick: half to the trust fund, twenty-five per cent to cancer research, twenty-five per cent to the foundation."

"That's great," Blue said. "That's beautiful." Simon wasn't sure he was concentrating.

"Now things may not be so easy with your daughter. I just got all this emailed over from Chicago." He held up a hefty wodge of printouts. "She wants a co-production credit for each track she sings on, with final mixes to be done by her and/or producers of her choice. She also wants a suite at the Beverly Hills, plus accomodation for..." he whipped out a pair of gold-rimmed glasses, perched them on his nose, and consulted the printout again "... her PA, personal trainer, hairdresser, make-up artist, publicist, musical director and two bodyguards, all of 'em to be flown in from Chicago by private jet. Plus twenty-four-hour limousine service — and apparently Lincoln Town Cars don't count as limos — and $5,000 pocket-money *per diem*."

"Hm." Blue refocussed for a moment. "That all?"

"No. Young Michael and her can't be in the studio at the same time. If he's there when she comes in, either he leaves or she's turning right round again and goin' back to Chicago."

Blue slapped his palm lightly on his thigh. His mouth set firmly. "That's all bullshit. My daughter gonna work with Mick. The whole reason we doin' this is to work together. I'll talk to her on that, or Calvin gonna talk to her. 'Bout all this personal trainer an' hairdresser an' private jet an' Beverly Hills Hotel... just who she think be payin' for all'a this?"

"Sure as hell won't be Bronzeville, that's for sure," Simon said. The small label to which Blue was signed had profited beyond its wildest dreams from Blue's last few albums, but its budgets were still stranglehold-tight compared with the major companies. Bronzeville's CEO, Paul Malone, would be thrilled to be releasing an album guest-starring major names like Mick Hudson and Venetia Moon — Malone paid so little attention to the hip-hop world that he wasn't even sure exactly who Calvin was — but demands on this scale would probably trigger his fourth and final heart attack. "And it ain't gonna be us." He shook his head wonderingly. "I don't understand it. She's got pots of fucking money. How come she wants to bleed you dry like this when Calvin and young Michael aren't taking a penny?"

"One thing you got to understand about Venetia," Blue told him. "It's about the money, but the *money* ain't about the money. You understand what I'm sayin'? Rich as she is, what the money mean to her is that whoever's payin' puts a high value on her. Venetia don't feel valued 'less she gettin' paid a *whole* lotta money. She don't feel like she important to nobody, an' so money done took the place'a love. If she can't get no love, then she gonna get money instead.

"An' it's my fault she this way. Her mama left me'n took Neesha with her, but the way she feel is that I left the both of 'em 'cause I wanted to keep playin' my music. An' when she got pregnant with Calvin an' Mick wouldn't leave Jocasta..."

He broke off. Simon was staring at him, open-mouthed.

"Fookinell. You seriously telling me... young Michael is Calvin's dad?"

Blue thought, awwwww, *shit*. Sit on something more'n thirty years and then just blurt it out, why doncha. These pills doing me worse'n I thought. "My ol' damn-fool mouth runnin' away with me," he said heavily. "Yeah, Mick is Calvin's daddy. He found out Neesha pregnant just days after he'n Jocasta lost they baby. She wanted him to come to the States, be with her. He tell her he can't just up'n leave Jocasta there and then, shape she was in. Neesha told him stay away from her'n her kid as long as he live."

Simon was still staring at Blue. "And Calvin still doesn't know?"

"No, he don't know," Blue told him.

"Who *does* know?"

"Me. Adrienne. Donna. Now you. 'Part from Neesha'n Mick theyselves, that's it. Far as I know."

"Wow. Fuck. Poor little sod. Ain't it about time somebody told him?"

"That's for damn sure," Blue agreed. "Next week, Mick comin' back from Spain. Neesha flyin' in from Chicago. We got us a record to make." He looked Simon straight in the eye.

"But before we gonna be able to make the record we got to take care'a business. Family business. When we all together, we gonna clean this mess *up*. Once'n for all."

Simon was ready to leave. Blue called for Adrienne, but got no response. He wheeled himself towards the door to show Simon out. As they passed the living room he put his head round the door. Adrienne was dozing on the sofa, a can of beer loosely grasped in her hand. Another can, empty, was perched before her on the coffee table. She was smiling.

In dreams:

Simon is wheeling Blue into the Marquee Club. Blue's beard is white and grizzled, his clawlike hands so shaky he can barely hold his guitar. Young Michael and the guys from Bluebottle are waiting for them. "Meet James Blue Moon," Simon tells the lads in the band, but they all give him funny looks and start backing away.

"You're taking the piss, man," Hudson tells him.

"Yeah, c'mon, Si," the others are saying. "Stop fuckin' about. Where is he?"

"No, this is him, honestly," Simon protests, but the band are already starting to pack up their gear.

"Nah, bollocks, you're winding us up," Hudson says. "We know what he looks like. I want to play with the real James Blue Moon, not this old fraud. Look at him, he's gonna peg out any second."

"Look," Simon tells the old man in the wheelchair, "you'd better play these boys something so they know who you are." Blue nods, his lower jaw quivering. He starts to sing and play the guitar. His voice is a rusty tuneless croak. He's hitting wrong notes all over the place, picking the wrong strings, muffling the notes because his fingers no longer command the strength necessary to press the strings firmly onto the frets. He sounds like shit.

Shaking their heads, Mick and the rest of the band carry their gear out of the club, leaving Simon and Blue there alone.

"What the fuck are we going to do?" Simon asks the old man, but he doesn't say anything, just sits in his wheelchair lost in thought or memory. Suddenly Henry MacShane is standing beside them like he'd been there all along. "Bleedin' typical," he says. "No respect for the older artist these days, is there?"

Simon awakes to his wife's gentle snores. The bedside clock reads 4:30. For the first time in many years, Simon feels a faint surprise that it is someone other than Jocasta curled up beside him.

In dreams:

Donna Moon is the belle of the ball at her high school prom. Boys are queueing up to dance with her, even the really cute ones. Suddenly her mother sashays in wearing her leopard-print bikini, spike-heeled pink fuck-me shoes, a huge fruit-basket hat like Carmen Somebody she once saw on TV and half a ton of her most elaborate jewellery. Adrienne is lean, oiled and fabulous, Wu Li's explosion of platinum hair trotting behind at the end of gilded-leather lead. All the boys turn away from Donna and flock around Adrienne.

Then her father is there, slumped in his wheelchair. She runs towards him for consolation, puts her arms around him, slides onto his lap. He crumbles into dust. Her dress is ruined. Everybody is pointing at her and laughing. Adrienne is laughing loudest of all.

She's just lost her daddy and everybody is just laughing at her.

She awakes to find herself sobbing helplessly into her pillow.

In dreams:

Clad in head-to-toe ninja black, Glock in hand, Calvin Holland drifts like smoke down the long stone corridor. At the far end he sees a metal door set into the wall. Next to it is a security-lock keypad. Calvin punches in a four-digit code and the door slides open with a hiss of compressed air. Behind the door is a vast, dimly-lit office. At its far end is a huge desk under a pool of warm golden light which is almost the office's sole illumination. Behind the desk is a window through which can be seen a panoramic view of the Manhattan night sky-line.

Between the desk and the window is a luxurious leather chair, its back towards Calvin. The occupant of the chair is contemplating the spectacular view from the window. Above the back of the chair, all that can be seen is the top of the occupant's head. He is a white man with spiky grey hair.

Calvin feels impossibly strong hands grab his ankles and upper arms. The Glock is twisted from his grasp. He is spread-eagled face-down across the desk. A raucous jeering voice from behind him, "Lickle weak paleface batty-boy, y'wan play games wid we now?"

Without moving or turning, the man behind the desk speaks. "You know what he wants. Give it to him." Calvin feels his trousers being roughly pulled down around his ankles. There is a blinding flash, then another. He sees a couple of photographers he recognises. They work for *The Source* and *Vibe* magazines. "Fuckin' faggot," says the *Source* guy. "Cocksucka," the man from *Vibe* chimes in. A twisted handkerchief is forced into his mouth before he can protest that hey, dawg, he doesn't take it up the ass, he gives it.

A beringed hand tauntingly holds the white dildo that had been left in his office where he can see it for a second. Then it vanishes again, and suddenly his asshole is split with the most unbelievable pain as voices behind him chant, "Battyman, battyman, 911" over and over again...

... and he awakes wishing he had a gun in his hand right now and those goddam Jamaicans up against a wall in front of him.

In dreams:

Mick Hudson is halfway through the long, gruelling climb up to the spire of the Gaudi cathedral in Barcelona. He tries not to look out of the windows as he ascends the narrow staircase, but he can't help himself, and every time he catches sight of the distance between himself and the ground he suffers such intense vertigo he almost passes out.

Henry McShane is climbing beside him (how? It's such a narrow staircase even skinny young Michael feels claustrophobic. Yet there's room for big fat Henry...) and he's saying, "You should have let me get you out of this while I still could, young Michael. It's too late now. You have to keep going."

And Hudson looks behind him and sees that the stairs he's just climbed have disappeared. There's nothing but thin air between him and the earth far below. Even the step he's currently on is starting to soften. He looks up the remaining stairs to the summit of the spire. Waiting at the top are Blue and Adrienne with their dogs, and Venetia.

She is naked and suckling a baby at one heavy brown breast. None of them look welcoming. Their faces are frozen in a collective rictus of contempt and disdain.

And he has to keep climbing towards them if he's not going to fall hundreds of feet to the hard ground below. He increases his pace, but the steps are disappearing faster than he can climb.

He falls... straight into his bed in his room in the Barcelona villa. His daughters, exhausted by a night's clubbing, are sound asleep in their rooms down the hall. He shudders, switches on his bedside lamp. Propped on his nightstand is his plane ticket to Heathrow and thence to LAX.

In dreams:

Henry MacShane and Mick Hudson are waiting in the wings of a giant stadium stage. Hudson's wearing his stage gear, his guitar in his hand. The audience are whooping and hollering. It's thirty seconds to showtime.

On the darkened stage, the band are already in place. The amps are warmed up, all the red and green lights glowing present and correct. The MC strides to stage centre, grabs the mic. "All right!" he says. "This is the moment we've all been waiting for. Please welcome... Mister! Mick ! HUDSON!!"

Bedlam. Pandemonium. A lighting tech hits a button and the stage is ablaze with light. Hudson gives Henry a thumbs-up, hefts his guitar, walks out on stage... and keeps walking. Right across the stage and into the wings at the other side. He turns around, throws Henry a farewell wave...

... and disappears.

Henry is back in his four-poster bed in his house in Worthing. He gets out of bed very quietly so as not to wake his wife, pads bearlike into the living room downstairs, pours himself a very large single malt. He has a bad feeling about all this. He's wondering whether he should head out to LA while young Michael is recording with Blue and the others. Just to keep an eye on things.

In dreams:

Venetia Moon is topping the bill at a black-tie charity show at Carnegie Hall. It's a cancer research benefit and she's storming the place with a bravura canter through thirty-some years' worth of her greatest hits. Then she sends her musicians offstage and sits down at the piano. She pulls the mic towards her and says, "It's a real honour to be here tonight, and I'm very grateful to the organisers for inviting me to perform for you. There's a particular reason why this event is very special for me, and that is because my father..."

She pauses dramatically. "... the great blues singer James Blue Moon, is himself suffering from cancer. That's why I am flying to Los Angeles next week to record with him for an album to benefit this very charity." Applause, a buzz of conversation as those members of the audience who've actually heard of James Blue Moon digest the news. Some of the people in the press seats pull out cellphones to inform their newsdesks.

"So right now I'd like to dedicate this song to my father," Venetia says, and launches into a song she hasn't played in public for years, Blues For Now. She thought the applause was never going to end.

She awakes in her Manhattan hotel realising that she was dreaming about what had actually happened earlier that same night. Except that on the real show, she hadn't been headlining.

In dreams:

Adrienne awakes, reaches out, pats the bed beside her. Blue is not there. Where the hell is he? She gets up, switches on the light, pulls a robe around her. She looks in the music room: no-one there. Then she hears weeping and looks into Donna's room, but Donna isn't in her bed. She wanders through the kitchen, checks her study, the living room, the guest room, both bathrooms. She heads out the back by the tub. Still no-one around.

Then she looks in the garage. All the cars are there, cold and locked. Then she tries the basement (wait a second: they don't have a basement...), but that's empty as well. (At some point she realises that she is holding Blue's gun.) A door at the far end of the basement opens on to a succession of different rooms she's never seen before. There's what looks like a shabby deserted nightclub, a tenement apartment, a rural railroad station, a barbershop. All are heavy with dust, like not only is no-one there right now, but no-one's been there for years.

She retraces her steps, back through the basement and up into the house. She's still all alone there: no Donna, no Blue, no dogs. Even the wheelchair is gone. She grabs the phone, dials a succession of numbers. No-one answers, not even a machine. Maybe she should throw on some clothes, head out into Venice, see if there's anyone around at all.

Because if there isn't, Adrienne will be utterly and completely alone.

Instead, she gets back into bed, pulls the covers over her head. Maybe when she wakes up, everybody will be back where they ought to be. And they are.

In dreams:

Blue's sitting in his wheelchair, parked right where the barber's chair used to be in Sam's Barber Shop. In his lap is a big Stella guitar. Standing by the door is a small slender man in an immaculate grey suit and snap-brim hat. He has long spidery fingers and a slight cast in one eye. He is shouting at Blue.

"Willie didn't have no right to sell you that git-tar!" he yells. "He didn't buy that in no pawnshop! He stole it right outta the room I was stayin' in! That don't belong to you! It belong to me!"

Shit. Little Robert.

Blue stammers, "Mr Johnson, sir..." but Little Robert just storms right up to him and starts to pull the guitar out of his hands.

"Just hold on a moment, now." The customer who'd been in there a few moments before, who'd given Blue the five bucks to help buy the guitar, was back in the shop. He prises Little Robert's hands off the guitar and pulls him back a couple of feet.

"Robert," he says. "That git-tar was yours in the old days, but it belong to this young man now. It's his turn and it gonna be his time soon. You done your part, and you done good. But right now it's time to rest yourself."

The tension goes out of Little Robert's body. His shoulders slump. He takes off his hat and wipes his face with a handkerchief. "My man's right," he says. He comes back up to Blue, holds out his hand for a shake. "You go 'head on now, young man. You look after that git-tar, it gon' look after you. I didn't look after it, and now I can't get me no rest nowhere the Greyhound bus can take me. You just make sure you do better'n I done."

He tips his hat to Blue, and walks back out onto the sunlit street outside. The customer turns to Blue.

"There you go, young man," he says. "Ain't this easier?" He's dressed the way he was on the beach. "By the way... you know this is a dream, don'cha?" He gestures at the wheelchair. "You don't have to be like this in no dream. You can be any way you want."

Blue puts the guitar down very carefully. He rises to his feet, smoothly and easily. His body feels loose and lithe, charged with enough energy to run a few miles or play a two-hour show. He looks down towards the floor. He is barefoot. His left foot has all its toes.

"All right," says the man from the beach. He gestures towards the door. "C'mon out an' walk with me awhile. We need to have us a little talk."

TWENTY-ONE

It was barely dawn when the phones started going crazy, messages stacking up at Simon's office, at Lock N Load, with Venetia's people in Chicago, at the Raintree office in London, even at Blue's house. Luckily no-one except their own people had cellphone numbers for Blue, Adrienne or Donna, but in the end Adrienne had to pull the plug on the landline just so's they could get some peace.

When Blue heard about what Venetia had said last night at Carnegie Hall, his mouth clamped into a tight thin line. He grabbed his cellphone, punched in a number.

"Neesha? The hell you playin' at? Why you tell ever'body?" There was a silence at the end of the line. Then:

"Dad, I needed to speak. I needed to say what was on my mind. I was there at the cancer benefit and the whole time I was on stage I could hardly get my words out 'cause I was thinkin' about you..."

"Yeah, honey, an' I bet you got yourself a real big round of applause. I wanted us all to be able to work on the record in peace'n quiet, now we gonna have reporters'n TV an' God knows what-all else on our backs."

"Daddy..."

"Neesha, wasn't your secret to tell. You been big on who you 'llow to say what to who when it come down to your own self, but y'all throw other people's lives around like they nuthin'..."

"Daddy, listen to me..."

"We gonna hafta see what we can do straighten out this mess you done made."

"DADDY!"

"What."

"Daddy, the whole time I was growin' up, nobody let me speak... 'cept you, when I was real little. Mama didn't. The Reverend Holland didn't. First few years I was at Boulevard, they didn't. Now I'm big an' I been runnin' my own life a long time, and ain't nobody gonna tell me what I can or can't say. Ever again!"

Blue thought about that a moment. "Guess what I'm sayin', Neesha, is that it don't haveta be about what someone else be tellin' you to say or not say. Sometimes you want to say somethin', and then you think about it, and then you decide your own self not to say it, 'cause sayin' it ain't the right thing to do. I spent thirty-some years not sayin' nuthin' to nobody 'bout you'n Mick'n Calvin. You hardly spent thirty days not sayin' nuthin' 'bout me bein' sick. That's what I'm talkin' 'bout.

"An' one more thing. Simon show me all that bullshit your office done sent 'bout hairdressers'n publicists'n twenty-four-hour limos'n five grand *per diem* an' such. Mick be payin' his own way on this thing. Calvin too. Matter of fact, Calvin gettin' his people to help us record, an' he payin' for that, too. Now when you come out here to work, you live how you want to live. If you wanna bring all them people with you, you bring 'em.

"But you ain't gonna be takin' no money from me to pay for it, from my little label neither. If you do, you be takin' money from my wife an' my daughter, an' from that cancer research charity y'all told the people you care so much about.

"You say you big. Well, act like it."

Silence again. Then: "I'll see you next week, daddy."

"Okay, honey... yeah, all you need to bring's your voice."

At noon, Simon's office issued a brief statement on behalf of Macro Management and Bronzeville Records. It ran as follows:

"Macro Management and Bronzeville Records regret to confirm that eighty-three-year-old blues legend James Blue Moon was diagnosed with liver cancer two months ago. However, he is receiving the very best treatment, and he is at work on a new album, for which he will be joined by his daughter Venetia Moon, the legendary Princess of Soul; his grandson Calvin Holland aka Ice Blue, platinum-selling rapper and one of the most successful hip-hop/R&B producers of modern times, and his long-term friend and admirer, British rock legend Mick Hudson.

"Mr Moon thanks his many friends and fans for their interest and concern, but requests that the media allow him and his family to concentrate on making this recording in peace and quiet.

"Bronzeville Records CEO Paul Malone and Mr Moon's manager Simon Wolfe said, 'We offer our best wishes to Mr Moon and emphasise that we hope his request for privacy will be honoured by our many friends in the media.'"

Back in LA, Calvin was already lying low because of all that Screwdriver and Omega Man mess. Unusually, he wasn't available for interview. His people told the media that he was chillin' so that he could focus on recording with his grandfather. "Blues was the hip-hop of its time," they quoted him as saying, "and my gramps is one of the all-time don of dons. I'm also looking forward to working with my mother for the first time."

It was noted that Calvin didn't mention or acknowledge Mick Hudson's involvement in the project.

The next call Blue took on his cellphone was from Mick Hudson, stopping off to repack at his English country retreat before catching his flight to LA.

"I thought no-one was supposed to say anything about you being sick until you gave the all-clear," he said.

"Yeah, that's what I thought, too," Blue told him, "but you know Neesha..."

"I'm not sure I do, these days. Listen, Adrienne and Donna must think I'm a right shit. Are they still pissed off with me?"

"Not like they were," Blue told him. "Once they knew Neesha made you promise not to say nuthin' an' that you wasn't just coverin' your own ass, they been easin' up on you some."

"So it'll be safe to show up at your place? No-one's going to try and kill me? Remember, it was you pointed a fuckin' gun at me last time."

"Well, they don't 'llow me near no more whiskey, so I guess ain't nobody gonna try'n kill you, young man. But we all gonna haveta get together sometime. An' Calvin got to know who his daddy is." Silence. Then:

"So we're gonna tell him?"

"We gonna tell him."

"How's Neesha with that?"

"I told her: if she don't tell Calvin, I will. An' Adrienne done told *me* if *I* don't tell him then *she* will. So I reckon one way or 'nother Calvin gonna know who his daddy is."

"And after that?"

"After that we gonna be in a whole 'nother world. All kinds'a things gonna be different after that." Silence.

"And then we're gonna make the record?"

"Then we gonna make the record. You been thinkin' 'bout songs?"

"Got a few ideas. You?"

"Yeah, me too."

"Okay. See you day after tomorrow. I'll call you when I'm settled in."

"Yeah? Where you stayin'? Same place?"

"Same place. It was either that or the Chateau Marmont, and all the noise from the Belushi bungalow keeps me awake at night."

"All right, young man. See y'all in a couple'a days."

Calvin at home, sitting on his bed in shorts and a T-shirt, slowly pumping the 20lb dumbbell in his left hand, listening to the Robert Johnson CD he'd sent an office gopher out to buy earlier that day. It sounded flat-out weird to him. He wasn't used to listening to one man singing against one guitar. He also wasn't used to music which sounded so thin and distorted, but then there was only so much digital cleaning-up you could do with records that old.

It didn't even sound much like his grampop's music to him. Oh sure, he'd heard Blue playing by himself around the house sometimes, and this wasn't that far away from what he played when he was on his own. But the records he'd heard by his gramps had bands and grooves on them: sometimes he had horn sections that sounded like old-time jazz or swing or jump, and sometimes clanking piano and wailing harps behind the old man's voice and guitar.

But this shit was different again. He shifted the dumbbell to his right hand, listened more carefully. This was some spooky shit, dawg. How'd that last one go? *Me and the devil walkin' side by side/Got to beat my woman 'fore I get satisfied.* That was some hardass gangsta shit right there. If he found him a young rapper writin' rhymes like that, he'd sign the muthafucka right there on the spot, rename him Robbery, have himself a hit by next Tuesday.

When'd the guy cut these jams? Dropping the dumbbell on the white deep-pile carpet by his bed, he picked up the CD box and fumbled out the booklet. Said so right there, 1937 and 1938, back when his grampop was still a kid.

More and more lines started jumping out at him. Two songs in particular, Cross Road Blues and Stones In My Passway, had these stop-time lines at the end of each verse, starting with a single vibratoed guitar note. He started jotting down CD timings for the lines he liked on a notepad. *Help poor Bob if you please. I been shamed by my rider. I believe I'm sinkin' down.* Cool. He wanted to sample those. He made another note: call BLT or one of the kids at the office to get in touch with whoever controlled the rights to these cuts. Start getting legal clearance to use some samples. They might not allow it for some regular commercial record, but he thought they'd probably make an exception for Blue. Fuck 'em if they didn't.

Oh yeah. Get someone to pick him up the Johnson records on vinyl as well as CD. He hadn't DJed for quite a while, but he still had enough turntable chops to get some mad scratching down.

He still didn't know exactly what his grampop wanted him to do on these records they were gonna make. But he knew one thing, whatever his gramps needed him to do, he was gonna be ready. And he was gonna give his grampop a sound like nothing he'd ever had before.

The storm had been raging for a couple of hours now. First Venetia had arrived, brows drawn down, rolling into Blue's music room like a Russian tank heading for Berlin. Maudie had heard all three voices raised, and a couple of times she'd almost had to go into the room, pull Mr Moon out, make him go rest in the bedroom.

Then twice Venetia had stormed out towards the front door, and Adrienne had gone out after her, pulling her back, Venetia shaking the younger woman off each time until Adrienne had almost worn a groove in the hallway floor holding onto her, whispering fiercely into her ear and dragging her back in.

Then, at last, it had quieted down, the voices subsiding to a murmur. Finally Maudie had gone in to check on Mr Moon. He looked tired and worn, but insisted that she leave the three of them together.

Then the English guy arrived. The level of the voices rose again, and fell. Then the Englishman emerged, went into the kitchen, helped himself to a tumbler of whiskey, patted his pockets for cigarettes, and wandered off out back. She saw him sitting out by the hot tub, smoking a cigarette, staring at nothing, fingertips tapping out a fast, complex rhythm on one skinny knee.

Everything was quiet, but Maudie felt her own breathing tighten.

Then Calvin rang the doorbell. When Maudie opened Blue's front door to him, his grampop, his mama and Adrienne were in the music room, waiting for him.

Blue and Adrienne were both looking expectantly at Neesha. She had her mask on, but it was cracking round the edges. She was working hard to hold it together, trying not to cry. She walked to him, took him in her arms for a long moment.

Neesha said, "Sit down, son," led him to an armchair.

Calvin took a deep breath, trying to slow down what was revving inside him.

She said, "There's someone here for you to meet."

His breath whooshed from his body like it couldn't wait to get away. The room was going dark. Tiny silver fish flipped across his vision.

"Someone you should'a met a long, long time ago."

Adrienne slipped to the door, came back in a second later, someone walking behind her. Tall, skinny white guy in a black suit....

Calvin saw the spiky grey hair, like the man behind the desk in his dream, the man whose face he could either never see or never remember. He saw the beaky nose, not too much different from the one he saw in his own mirror. Something was rising within him, something locked down but about to bust out...

And then Venetia said, "Calvin... son... this is Mick Hudson."

Calvin knew. Even as Venetia started to say, "He's your father," Calvin was already moving, up out of the chair. It was like there was a magnet in Hudson's face, pulling on his fist so's he couldn't have held it back even if he'd wanted to. It wasn't a slick martial arts move like the stuff he'd studied so hard a few years back: more like the kind of wild clumsy swing you saw in fifties Westerns, with fat middle-aged actors pretending to have a saloon brawl, or some kid's sloppy schoolyard punch.

Whatever. He managed to land two hard ones, a left and a right, before Adrienne dug her calloused jeweller's fingers into his biceps with painful, wiry strength and dragged him back. Hudson went down, right into Blue's parade-ground line of guitars. The sickening crunch from the back of his head sounded simultaneously with the splintery crash of the shattering body of an acoustic guitar

Blue sucked in a long shuddery breath. He said, "Oh, you a big man all right. Tough guy. You just sucker-punched a skinny guy twice your age."

Hudson was shakily hauling himself to his feet. His face was a mask of blood. On his left cheek, just under his eye, the Lock N Load logo from Calvin's signet ring was neatly imprinted in red for a second before the blood started to well. Calvin's other punch had caught him flush on the point of his nose, which was now bent and swelling, and on his upper lip. One of his upper front teeth was askew, hanging precariously halfway out of its socket. And the shards of wood from the acoustic guitar into which he'd fallen had lacerated his scalp, his grey hair already matting with blood.

"Pleathed to meet you too, thon," he lisped. "You'll be hearing from my dentitht." Then a wave of dizziness overcame him, his eyes rolled up in his head, and he started to slump again. Adrienne caught him, slowed his fall just enough so she could lower him gently to the floor. Looking around, she saw a quick flash of satisfaction on Venetia's face before it was replaced by an expression of concern.

Guitars and their stands were scattered across the music room floor. The solid-bodies appeared relatively unscathed, but the old acoustic guitar couldn't have been in worse shape if someone had gone for it with a bad attitude and a sledgehammer. The neck had broken at the headstock joint and the lower half of the front was all stove in from soundhole to rim.

Blue's face had gone ashy. "Awwwwwwww, no," he breathed. "Awwwwwww, *no*."

Maudie had heard the crash from the kitchen, where she'd been making herself a cup of tea. She came barrelling into the room. Her eyes went wide with shock when she saw Hudson on the floor, sprawled all bloody in a pile of guitars and bits of guitars. Then her professionalism kicked in. She pointed at Calvin.

"You," she said. "You help me get him to bathroom." Calvin stood paralysed. The others were all staring at him like he'd turned into a werewolf or something. Maudie raised her voice. "You help us NOW." As if in a trance, Calvin knelt so that he could get his hands beneath Hudson's shoulders and half-raise him to a sitting-up position. Hudson's eyes were flickering open now. He was groaning, very quietly. Maudie bustled out, came back a few seconds later with a damp cloth, started to wipe Hudson's head and face so she could gauge the extent of his injuries.

"Can you hear me?"

"Yuh."

"Can you stand?" No answer: he was out again. "Get my bag and something to put under his head," Maudie ordered. Adrienne ran to the living room, came back with Maudie's medical bag and a pair of cushions from the sofa. Maudie carefully raised Hudson's head, slipped the cushions beneath him. "You go in other room. I look after him here.

And somebody call for doctor and ambulance." She stared at Calvin. "Who hit him? You?" Her gaze panning to Blue and Adrienne, she added, "Maybe call police too."

"I think we need to talk, don't you? Let's go out the front," Adrienne told Calvin and Venetia. She moved to wheel Blue's chair along with them, but he was bent downwards, half out of his chair, fooling with the bloodstained fragments of the trashed acoustic guitar. "Blue, let's go," she said chidingly. "We can pick all that stuff up later." He gave no sign that he'd heard her, just kept trying to gather up the pieces of the old guitar and fit them together like he thought it would just heal back into one piece if he could fit it all together tightly enough. Tears were trickling down his face.

"Blue!"

"You don't understand, sugar," he said in a dry distant voice. "I done had this old Stella guitar since I was sixteen. I learned my first music on this guitar. I done kept it safe all my life. And now won't you look at it."

"Blue," Adrienne said. "Some of the best guitar-builders in the whole world work right here in LA. Call any one of 'em, get this guitar fixed up just like new. 'Sides, you forgotten something? Your grandson just damn near half-killed one'a your best friends while your daughter stood there grinnin'. And you cryin' over a *guitar*? Mick come all the way over here so's he could help you, and this happens to him in our home? That may be the guitar you had when you were a boy, but it's still just a guitar."

The dogs crept from the corner of the room where they'd crept when Calvin had punched Hudson. Now they nuzzled Blue's shaking fingers as he fooled with the fragments of the guitar. Adrienne saw, with a cold flash of cold shock, that they were lapping at the drying splatters of Hudson's blood. "Gyaaaaaaa!" she shouted, and Wu Li yipped in fear, bolted out of the room. Attack retreated back to the far corner of the room.

"It's still just a guitar," she repeated.

"No," Blue said. "No, it ain't. An' I don't care who you call, this git-tar can't never be fixed like it was." But he put the pieces of the guitar down, very carefully, on the floor, and allowed Adrienne to take him out into the living room to join the others.

"I'm calling Simon," she told Blue. "Someone needs to take charge'a this mess, keep it all out of the papers. We already got too much publicity we don't need." Simon said he'd be there in half an hour and he was better than his word, arriving in twenty-three minutes, just in time to ride the ambulance to hospital with Hudson, take care of business at the other end.

"Fuck knows what old Henry's gonna have to say about all this," he muttered to Adrienne. "He's already wants to come out here and keep an eye on things. You say it was Calvin hit him?" Adrienne nodded yes. "Well, keep the little cunt well away from me or I'll fookin' 'ave 'im. I've often wanted to thump young Michael, but fooked if I'll let anyone else do it."

The ambulance doors slammed. Adrienne watched it recede into the distance, then stomped back into the house. Maybe the Moon family were finally ready to sit down and talk.

TWENTY-TWO

Adrienne headed for the living room, walking into a silence which throbbed like a bruise. The fucking Moon family, she thought, go through just about anything to avoid talking to each other. Venetia and Calvin were sitting on the sofa, each staring straight ahead. Blue in his wheelchair, head lowered, hands clasped in his lap, adrift on a sea of grief. Probably thinking about that damn guitar, Adrienne thought.

She went and faced them, standing up, her ass braced against the dining table.

"Y'all satisfied now?" she demanded. "Y'all happy?" She rounded on Venetia. "Well, you must be pretty pleased, seeing Mick get his butt kicked by a son you never let him see'n get to know." She turned to Calvin, narrowing her eyes into a gangsta stare, throwing gang signs with her fingers like an MTV rapper. "So now you know who your father is, big man, the first thing you do is put him in the hospital."

Now she looked straight at Blue. "And the reason we're all still dealing with this screwed-up mess is that *you*, the big daddy of this family, just sat on your hands for thirty years and let everybody suffer because you were scared to do the right thing by this boy here..." she pointed at Calvin "... and the limey in the hospital, in case you upset Ms Diva here." She threw up her hands. "And even now I can't tell whether you're all freaked out because of Gangsta Boy here damn near killing Mick, or because your precious fucking guitar got trashed."

Silence. They all just sat there like chastened children, half in shock, half unsure of where they could go next. "What kind of fucked-up family have I married into, anyway?" Adrienne asked. Rolling her eyes skyward, she stalked out of the room. A few seconds later, they heard the front door slam; a few seconds after that, it was echoed by her car door.

Adrienne headed for the gym. She had some serious weights to lift. It was either that or punch the crap out of Venetia before starting on Calvin.

She scooped a surprised Donna up from the school gates and whisked her off for a movie and a snack. Halfway through the drive back home, she pulled over to the side of the road.

"A few things happened today," she said. "We told Calvin that Mick

199

is his father."

Donna's eyes bugged. "Oh... my.... God," she said softly, then again louder: "OH... MY... GOD! What did Calvin say?"

"He didn't say nuthin'," Adrienne told her. "He just punched Mick out. Broke your daddy's oldest guitar, too."

"Oh... my... God," Donna repeated. "Is Mick all right?"

"He's in the hospital right now. We're still waiting to hear how he's doing."

On cue, her cellphone rang. "Adrienne, hi. Si here. I'm still at the hospital."

"Is Mick all right?"

"They've just finished with him now. Fractured cheekbone, broken nose, scalp torn open, mild concussion and he's gonna need some dental work. Otherwise he's fine. They want to keep him overnight for observation, and if he seems okay in the morning they're gonna let him out around lunchtime tomorrow."

"Should we come and see him?"

"Not a lot of point to that, really. He's probably gonna sleep right through 'til morning. Look, I'm gonna come round the house in a little while. I need to talk to Blue."

"I think I need to talk to him myself. See you there in about a half hour." She closed the phone, returned it to her bag, started the car up again. "Mick's gonna be okay," she told Donna. "With a bit of luck he'll be out tomorrow."

"Mama..." Donna was looking thoughtful. "When we get home, are you gonna send me to my room so I can't hear what's going on?" Adrienne opened her mouth to answer, but Donna held up one hand to let her know that she wasn't finished yet. "Mama, I'm not a baby any more. I'm almost fifteen years old. I'm gonna be losing my daddy soon. I'm just as much part of this family as anybody else, and what's happening now is stuff I'm gonna remember all my life. Stuff I'm gonna be telling my own kids when they ask me about our family, about who we are and where we come from. What am I gonna tell 'em? Oh yeah, this happened and that happened but I didn't see or hear any of it because my mom and dad were always sending me to my room.

"This stuff is a very important part of my life, and my life is part of what's happening. I don't want to be treated like the baby and kept out of things any more."

Adrienne put her arms around Donna, hugged her tight. "You got it, sweetie," she said. "Fifteen ain't that old, but we gonna let you into the grownup world on a visitor's visa, at least. You're not just part of this family; right now I think you're the *only* member of this family who isn't totally nuts." She kissed Donna on the top of her head, and drove back onto the road that led to home.

When they pulled up outside the house, Simon was pacing about outside smoking a cigarette. Adrienne reflected, irrelevantly, that she had seriously misunderestimated Simon all those years, that he wasn't just an adding machine with a Ringo accent. He cared deeply about both Mick and Blue, and the money was merely an incidental. He came over to the car as he saw them arrive.

"That nurse of yours won't let me see Blue," he told them. "Says he's so freaked out by what happened that she's put him to bed with a sedative." He did a quick impression of Maudie's accent. "'You come back tomorrow! Call first!'"

"Ms Diva and Gangsta Boy still here?"

"No, they left. Separately, Maudie says."

"Did they say anything?"

"Not to her, they didn't. But then I don't figure either of them as the type to chitchat to the help. One thing was weird, though. Maudie said the dogs are acting up. Neither of 'em seem to want to go anywhere near Blue." He checked his watch. "Look, if I can't see Blue tonight there's no point me hanging around. I'll talk to the hospital first thing in the morning, let you know what's going on. If they're ready to let Mick out I'll pick him up, take him back to his house." A thought struck him. "He could do with a nurse for a day or two, I bet. Hey, Maudie doesn't have a twin sister, does she?"

Adrienne laughed. "Not that I know of, but we can lend her to you for the afternoon just to make sure Mick's comfortable." She embraced him, kissed him on the cheek. All those years he'd managed Blue, and she'd never done that before.

She let herself and Donna into the house. The dogs were on the sofa. Maudie was reading in the kitchen, cup of green tea at her elbow. "He will sleep soundly until tomorrow, Mrs Moon," she told Adrienne. "I will be back first thing in the morning."

"Thank you very much, Maudie. For everything."

"How Mr Hudson?"

"Pretty beat up, but they should be letting him out tomorrow. Would you mind going up to his house tomorrow afternoon and making sure he's comfortable?"

"No problem, Mrs Moon."

"And if he needs a nurse for longer than that, can you recommend someone?"

"Of course. I have a sister. She very good. Take good care of Mr Hudson."

Adrienne grinned. Looks like something was finally going right. She turned to Donna. "Looks like no show tonight, sweetie. Anything you feel like doing?"

"You want to come into my room and listen to some records with me?"

"Right now, sugar," she told Donna, "there's absolutely nothing in the whole world I'd like better. How about some ice cream to go with that?"

In dreams:

Sam's Barber Shop was dark. One window was boarded up, the other smashed. The door was hanging open. The big mirror had been broken and fragments of glass crunched beneath the wheels of Blue's chair. The place stank of stale moonshine and staler piss. Blue fumbled around for a light switch, but even when he found it the power was off. So he decided to sit and wait.

He didn't have to wait long. A lighter flared, and the customer sitting in Sam's barber chair lit himself a cigarette, the flame glinting momentarily off his gold tooth.

"Lord, what a mess," he said wearily. He pulled a bottle of Sam's moonshine from inside his windcheater, took a long pull on it and handed it to Blue. "Man, we in trouble now."

Blue said, "What you talkin' 'bout?" He swallowed a mouthful of moonshine and nearly choked. Man, when you been used to good mellow storebought whiskey all these long years, that old-time corn liquor tastes just like gasoline.

"What I'm talkin' about," the customer told him, "is that you ain't protected no more."

Blue shook his head: huh?

"Little Robert's git-tar done got broke," the man said. "That git-tar had power in it. Robert done played that git-tar, and he put himself into it, but it was made for you."

"Felt like that first time I ever picked it up," Blue said. "Just felt right for me. Still do... or it did before today."

"No point in gettin' it fixed up by any'a them fancy guitar makers down in LA, either," the man said. "Might's well throw it in the trash right now. They could fix it up so it look just the same an' even sound pretty good, but now it been broken it ain't never gonna be nuthin' but an old cheap git-tar someone bought outta the Sears, Roebuck catalogue a long time ago. What was in that git-tar made it *really* special be gone for good.

"There was a whole lot more to that git-tar'n just soundin' good or even havin' that extra somethin' made you wanna play an'learn all the time. Lotta good git-tars like that. This one special 'cause it had the *power* in it."

"The power?" Blue asked.

"Yeah, man, the *power*. The power to protect you from ever havin' to find out the hard way whether your daddy was right after all. That was your shield. Now it gone. Your ass ain't safe no more. All those years you kept that git-tar. Even when you was broke an' your wife in Chicago told you sell it, you kept it. Before you got your Gibson, you put a pickup on the Stella so's you could use it electric. No matter how rough the bars you was playin' got, you kept the git-tar safe. It kept you safe. That was the deal."

"Hey, brother, I never cut no deal. I never went down to no crossroads at midnight, never signed nuthin' in blood with no devil."

"Man, you gettin' stupid as well as old'n sick? You never went down to no crossroad 'cause the crossroad done come to you. Ain't you learned nuthin' in this life? The crossroad always come to you. Crossroad be wherever *you* are."

"Still never signed no deal."

"You didn't need to sign nuthin' to make a deal. An' the small print don't need to be written down. You made the deal, all right."

"When'd I do that? Where'd I do it?"

"Right here. Why d'you think we keep draggin' our sorry asses back to this place?"

He snapped his fingers. Sam's was suddenly lit with blazing sunshine. The windows and the mirror were whole. Even the stench was gone: it was like the floors had been freshly swabbed down just minutes ago. Blue could even smell the antiseptic tang of the soap Sam had used. He blinked against the strong light.

The man in the barber's chair was holding out a five-dollar bill. "I think you got yourself a talent, boy," he said. "A *gift*. And I believe talent should be encouraged."

Blue stared. "That was the deal? Way back then? When you gave me the five bucks so's I could buy the git-tar from Willie?"

"That was the deal, right there."

"Who'd I make this deal with?" The man began to laugh.

"Why," he said, "you made it with me."

"Well, if I made it with you, what's the problem? You my friend, right? We on the same side, ain't we? You know: 'us', 'ours', all that stuff you was sayin' first time we talked. You cut a deal on me then. Let's you'n me cut another one now. We good guys together, right?" A pause. "Right?"

The man shook his head. "It don't work like that, brother." His voice took on a plummy Royal Shakespeare Company tonality. "'Each man in his time plays many parts'," he said. "Like I told you before when we was down on the beach, we the good guys *and* the bad guys both, just like all y'all on this planet.

"Remember what your daddy, the Reverend, told you?"

"My daddy told me a lot'a things. Didn't believe *none* of 'em."

The man's face and neck began to swell. "Do you know what that man was doing?" he rumbled in the cavernous tones of Solomon Moon. "He was doin' the devil's work. He was tryin' to drag your soul down to hell."

"The ol' man was full'a shit."

"The *devil* live in the git-tar," growled the voice of Solomon Moon. "And the worst music you can play on the git-tar is the *blues*. The devil's own music. Every blues singer work for the devil."

"I told you. I never worked for no devil."

From his own face this time, the man began to chuckle quietly. "The part he wrong about is that it won't be what he calls God send you down there. It ain't God you got to fear. Never was. Matter of fact, you spent most'a your life under God's protection. But since that grandson'a yours smashed Little Robert's ol' git-tar, you ain't protected no more. An' there ain't nuthin' I can do 'bout that."

He climbed out of the barber's chair, drained the last of the moonshine and put the bottle down carefully on the counter.

"I gotta go. Be a shame, 'cause I done enjoyed these little chitchats we been havin'. But all good things must come to an end."

"Hold on. Wait up. You still ain't told me why that git-tar was so all-fired important."

The customer shrugged. "Man, I *know* you done figured this out. The power had to be in somethin' you was gonna take good care of. An' it worked, too. Worked good. For a long time. You looked after the git-tar, an' it looked after you.

"Up 'til now, that is." He clasped Blue's hand, briefly, waved goodbye, strolled to the door. Then he turned and looked back.

"An' I know there's somethin' else you done figured out, too. I seen you grabbin' at it. Find yourself someone to pay your bill. Someone to go your bail. Someone to carry the weight." He grinned, pulled down the brim of his baseball cap.

His eyes flashed briefly in the shadow of the cap brim as he walked into the blazing sunshine pouring through the barber shop door. Then he turned back once more.

"You took yourself out a little insurance policy 'bout forty-some years back. Over in England, wasn't it?"

He touched the brim of his cap with two fingers, and was gone. Then the shop, and the street outside, was dark again, the darkness heavy once more with the stench of neglect and decay.

Blue sat there, not moving, until he awoke the next morning in his own bed. In the music room, the undamaged guitars had been neatly returned to their stands. The space in the line where the Stella always used to sit leered at him, mocking his loss, like a missing tooth in the smile of a beautiful woman.

"Can't wait for old Blue to see me in this," Hudson said. "We can have wheelchair races."

His spiky grey hair was gone. They'd had to shave his head to stitch the lacerations in his scalp, a woolen beanie pulled over the dressings on his newly bald skull. His broken nose had been straightened and set and was now heavily bandaged. A stratospherically expensive Beverly Hills dentist was going to be seeing him the day after tomorrow. A plaster covered the Lock N Load signet ring mark high on his left cheek.

"They only want you in it for today," Simon told him, wheeling him through the Cedars-Sinai hospital's parking lot. "Tomorrow you can walk just like everybody else, you lazy old sod." They reached the car, a people carrier driven by one of Simon's assistants. "Blue and Adrienne are lending you Maudie for the afternoon to make sure you're comfortable. She's waiting for you up at the house."

"Florence Nightingale reincarnated, bless her," Hudson said. "The woman's a bloody saint."

"Yeah well, she was certainly bloody by the time she got you cleaned up." Hudson got groggily to his feet. Simon helped him into the back of the people carrier, then folded up the wheelchair and chucked it into the back. Then he climbed in beside Hudson and they took off for the Hollywood Hills.

"So, Daddy," Simon asked, "what d'you make of your offspring, then?"

"Well, he's a very naughty boy and I'm going to have to stop his pocket money for at least a month."

"And other than that?"

"Other than that... shit, I don't know, man. Venetia brought him up to hate me. He's spent his whole life convinced that his father's a total bastard who despised him and rejected him and never wanted anything to do with him. Probably have done the exact same thing under the circs if I'd been him.

"Listen, Si... very important, this. I don't want even a squeak of this getting back to Henry. The last thing I need is him showing up here with a couple of tasty geezers from Walthamstow going 'You wot? You wot?' all over the place.

"Did the docs ask what happened to you?"

"'Course they did. I told 'em I tripped over the carpet and fell into the guitars. They thought it was quite funny, actually."

"Funny?"

"Yeah. Guitars made me rich and famous and now guitars put me in casualty. Cosmic irony, man. Weird fluky manifestations of karma. They understand that sort of thing in California."

"Glad someone does. Look, we probably shouldn't be talking about this until you've rested up, but if this album's still going to happen we need to start booking studio time, getting some musicians in... how much have you and Blue actually worked out?"

Hudson sighed. "As far as musicians are concerned, I wanted to use some of my guys, but it's probably more important to have players Blue's comfy with. I don't want him to have to make any more adjustments than he has to, so I guess we'll use some of his band. Guitars him and me'll do, so I guess it's just bass and drums. Maybe a piano player."

He snapped his fingers. "You know what? How about getting JP in for a song or two? Blue likes him and he'd eat this off a stick."

"Little Johnny Kinkaid? Way ahead of you there, pal. Already checked with his people. Blacklight aren't working at the minute, but apparently he's not well."

"Oh, well... shame. Still, that just leaves more guitar for me and Daddy Blue. Send him a card, willya?"

"Already done. So what are La Diva and Mike Tyson gonna do?"

"Fuck knows. All that's Blue's big idea, so I guess he'll tell me when he feels like it."

"What about songs?"

"We've got about half a dozen so far. We're gonna redo a few of Blue's old ones..."

"Oh fuck. Not Smile When You Say That again..."

Hudson laughed. "No, not this time. We'll do Piece Of The Action, Nuthin' Wrong That Money Can't Cure and maybe County Jail and Telephone Bill. I've written one called Sign Language On The Radio that he likes, and he wants to do John Lee Hooker's Burnin' Hell. Oh yeah... I had this arrangement of a Robert Johnson song called Hellhound On My Trail..."

Simon nodded. "Yeah, I know that one."

"I played it to him and he was dead insistent that he didn't want to do it, but now he seems to have changed his mind."

The people carrier was pulling into Hudson's driveway. An immaculate white Hummer was already parked there. Leaning on it was Calvin Holland.

TWENTY-THREE

Looking up at Calvin from his wheelchair, Hudson said, "You know that thing they do all the time on American TV shows, where they hug and go, 'I love you, dad,' 'I love you too, son'? I fuckin' hate that. Sentimental bollocks. So can we skip it?"

Simon and his bulky Chicano assistant Luis moving up behind Hudson, protectively flanking him. The front door opened and Maudie Lam was standing there, a cellphone in her hand. "You take one more step to Mr Hudson," she shrilled, "and I call police!"

Calvin took off his baseball cap and scratched his scalp. "I just want to talk, dawg," he said quietly. "What do I call you, anyway?"

"Call him Mister Hudson," Simon snapped.

"Mick will do just fine for now," Hudson said. "Look... Calvin... I don't want to turn you away and traumatise you all over again, but I've been under anaesthetic for the best part of a day and right now I've got a splitting headache. I want a father-son heart-to-heart as much as you do, but let me get some rest first. Okay?"

Calvin said, reluctantly, "Okay."

"Why'n'cha come back in the morning, say about ten? I'll answer every question you've got, and hopefully you can answer a few of mine." Hudson aimed a gap-toothed grin up at Calvin, winced as the movement strained his stitches. "If we manage not to kill each other, we can go on up to Blue's afterwards."

"You got it. See you at ten, daw... Mick." Calvin extended a fist to Hudson, who knuckled up and tapped Calvin's fist with his own. Calvin tugged his cap back onto his head and walked back to his Hummer, climbed in and drove away.

Hudson exhaled violently. "Wheeeeeewwwww... for a moment there I thought he was gonna start trying to bash me up again."

Luis chuckled. "Never happen," he said confidently.

Immediate peril having receded with Calvin's departure, Maudie stashed her phone and bustled them inside. She had her massage table set up ready and waiting in Hudson's bedroom and was soon methodically kneading the knots out of his weary frame. "Fuck's sake roll us a joint, Si," Hudson muttered as soon as she was out of earshot, but Simon — who hadn't heard *that* one since he left Hudson's employ to

208

set up Macro all those years ago — simply smirked and replied, "Sorry, la, doctor's orders." Soon Hudson had been put to bed, albeit without the tumbler of bourbon which had been his second request, and was sleeping soundly.

In dreams:

Hudson and Blue are sitting in their wheelchairs at a table in a pub on the corner of Dean Street and Carlisle Street in Soho. It's a lovely warm summer evening. Blue is wearing his old red stage suit, Hudson his slick black Paul Smith. He catches sight of himself in a wall mirror: his hair is black-dyed, spiked, perfect. In front of them on the table are doubles of Jack Daniel's and pints of cold crisp refreshing lager. Hudson's sticker-covered Telecaster is propped against the wall next to their table. Somewhere in London tonight, they have a show to do.

They're sitting there shooting the shit about this and that, Blue telling Hudson about the time some woman came up to Albert King — he done passed now, rest his soul — to ask him for a photo of himself and Albert snapped back, "Buy my album, there's a picture of me on that." They're suddenly aware that something or someone in the pub really stinks, a majorly unlovely miasma of sweat and piss and booze and un-washed dog.

Wrinkling his nose against the olfactory incursion, Hudson looks around for the source of the stench, spots a hulking old tramp over by the bar. Catching Hudson's eye, the tramp drags his mutt and his bags and his large Scotch and pint over to their table.

"Excuse me, sir," Blue says. "Me'n my friend havin' a private conver-sation here."

"Aw, doan mind me," the tramp says in a heavy Glasgow accent. "Yu boys got nae secrets frae me." He reaches inside his layers of stained, reeking coats and shirts and pulls out six old-style £10 notes, the ones which were currency in the sixties. "Ah've come fae ma guitar." He reaches past the startled Hudson and grabs the Telecaster, examining it carefully front and back. With a filthy fingernail, he picks at one of the stickers — long since laminated under a protective coating of poly-urethane varnish — and tuts disapprovingly. "Yeh've made a terrible mess outta this puir thing," he says resentfully. "Et's gonny tek me for-ever tae get this all cleaned up."

Hudson says, "The fuck you talkin' about?"

"Ah'll tell yeh whit the fuck ah'm tawkin' aboot," the tramp says. "Whin ah sold yu this guitar, ah said win day ah wis gonny be back fae it. That day es now. Here's yir sixty poun', so gimme ma guitar an' ah'll be on ma way."

"No, you didn't," Hudson says. "You never said anything about coming to take it back." He pushed the ancient notes back towards the tramp. "You sold it, you got your money, end of story."

"Et's niver the end o' the story," the tramp tells him. "An' jus' because nuthin' wis said disny mean et wisny understood."

"Not by me it wasn't," Hudson says. "This has been my main guitar for forty years, and as long as I got fingers I'm holding on to it."

"A deal's a deal," the tramp says.

"Fuckin' right a deal's a deal," Hudson shoots back, "and as far as I know the deal didn't have any time limit."

"Whit dae yeh know aboot time?" the tramp asks. Jimi Hendrix's voice emerged from his mouth. "Is this tomorrow, or just the end of time?" He grins, smugly. "Remaimber: the daevil's in the details. This is whit yeh get fae nae readin' the small print."

"The small print in what?"

Blue stirs in his wheelchair, puts his pint glass down on the table. "The small print in the papers you didn't sign," he tells Hudson. "This is the way it works, young man. You do somethin' and years down the line you find out there was more goin' on than you thought, and then you got to deal with whatever that means. I know this man, or whatever he is, an' I know you got no choice."

"Listen tae the old geezer," the tramp says. "He knows the rules. He knows whit's whit. Yeh wanted somethin' an' yeh goat et. Or rather, yeh got the use uv et all these years. Yu goat rich, yu goat femmus, yu found oot whit et's laike tae fly oan the wings uv music wi' thoosands a'people cheerin' fae yeh. But nae fucker ever said et wis gonny last forever. An' ef ah didny say et wis gonny last forever, then et woan't. Yeh're finished."

He leans over the table, getting up right in Hudson's face, his foul breath scorching Hudson's nostrils like a blast furnace from hell.

"Et's over, wee boy. Yeh've had yir chips." His voice is now a subsonic rumble which shakes the pub until the glasses rattle on the tabletop. His dog stares hungrily at Hudson. "Now give... me... ma ... *guitar*!"

"Fuck that," Hudson says. He snatches the guitar back from the tramp and clasps it to his narrow chest. "You're full of shit, you old fucker. At least you smell like you are. I paid for this, and I'm keeping it."

The tramp stands up and gathers his belongings. Pointedly, he leaves the wad of tenners on the table.

"Ah wis hopin wi cud dae this laike civilised men," he says. "But ah'm warnin' yeh ah'm gonny hev et back. An' ah proamess yeh willny laike whit's gonny happen ef ah hafty take et back the hard way." He stares at Hudson. His eyes are small pools of fire. Hudson feels like he's being inexorably dragged down into the blaze. Then Blue plucks at his sleeve, and the spell is broken. The dog growls, a low rumbling which seems to reverberate even more than its master's voice had done, and bares its yellow teeth.

"The next time wi meet," the tramp says, "et wilny be as plaisant as this." He grips the string attached to the dog's frayed, greasy collar, and shambles out into the Soho night.

Blue is shaking his head. "This ain't good, young man," he murmurs. "This ain't good at... *all.*"

Hudson awoke with a dry mouth and the muted throb of his residual headache. He gulped thirstily at the glass of water on his nightstand, switched on the bedside lamp to reassure himself that his trusty old Telecaster was still exactly where he'd left it, propped up in a corner of the room. Then he went back to sleep. This time he did not dream, and by morning nothing remained in his waking mind other than a vague but irrepressible sense of foreboding.

Driving away from the house in the Hills, Calvin was still getting his head around the idea that after all this time he finally knew who his father was, and that it was Mick Hudson. The man and his music had always existed in a sort of limbo somewhere on the peripheries of Calvin's awareness: one of those old British rock guys who played some blues, gutsier and ballsier than Eric Clapton, but not prancing around dressed all wack like the Rolling Stones.

Apart from all the stuff he'd heard from his mom when he was coming up, what else did Calvin know about Mick Hudson? Well, he had a sense of humour in that dry limey kind of way, and he didn't seem to bear grudges. Which was just as well, considering how much shit Calvin would've been in if that Chinese nurse had called the cops on him like she'd threatened.

Right now, he didn't quite know what he felt. He'd fulfilled two life-time ambitions: the first was to learn his father's identity, and the other was to put the muthafucka in the hospital. Now he had to deal with the fact that he was going to have to work with his father on his grampop's record, and not just work with him: he had to do the whole thing with his moms there as well.

And the worst part was that he was actually beginning to like the guy.

Back in his workroom at the White House, he started riffling through the stack of Mick Hudson CDs he'd had KanD go out and buy for him. Homeboy's a musician, after all, he thought. Best way to understand a musician is to listen to his music. Specially if you gonna be working with him. He wasn't looking forward to it, though. Riffy guitar-heavy whiteboy rock and roll had never been his favourite music, though he'd sampled enough of it in his time, mainly because they had them some badass drum sounds in there. Wandering up to his CD shelves, he cleared some space next to Venetia's records and slid the Hudson CDs in there next to them. Selecting a live album called *Road Fever*, he dropped it into the tray of his CD player and pressed PLAY.

Maudie Lam had been as good as her word. Her sister Cindy showed up at eight the next morning, letting herself in with the spare key Maudie had passed on to her. Cindy was ten or so years younger than her sister, considerably thinner and, despite a trace of accent, spoke fluent Cali-fornian. Hudson felt considerably stronger after a night's sleep. He was good to go in terms of walking, he decided, but he wasn't going to be planning any extended hikes for awhile. The wheelchair was folded up in the hallway, whence someone would be assigned to return it to the hospital.

"Oh, wow," she exclaimed to Hudson when she'd unwrapped his bandages, "you've been in a fight fer shur."

"That wasn't a fight," Hudson said. "That was an ambush. I haven't had a proper fight since I was thirteen, and I lost that one."

"I guess you guys don't get on too well,"

"Matter of fact, he's coming round here later." Hudson told her, winc-ing as she cleaned the caked blood away from his scalp. "So in about half an hour we'll be finding out... OWWWW!"

"Sorry, sorry, sorry!"

Hudson was sitting, freshly re-bandaged, in the living room of his bungalow, a pot of strong coffee at his elbow, when the doorbell rang. He went to answer it, found Calvin waiting on the doorstep. Hudson didn't say anything, just stood aside and gestured Calvin to follow him, led him into the living room, indicated two facing armchairs.

"Coffee?" Calvin wordlessly hefted the bottle of Evian he was holding. Hudson shrugged. "Cool." He poured himself a mug of coffee, sat down.

"Well."

"Well." Silence.

"Are we just going to stare at each other all day or what?"

"Can't get over how much alike we look," Calvin said. "I ever took a serious look at your picture, reckon I'd'a figured it out for myself." He rummaged in his bag. "Mick, I... uhhh... I brought some stuff for you." He pulled out a white Fully Loaded sweatshirt and a matching white woollen cap. "This is some'a the stuff we make. Been doin' pretty good with it, too."

"Thanks," Hudson said. He pulled the cap over his bandaged skull, held up the sweatshirt to examine the logo, and draped it carefully over the arm of his chair. "I'll put this on later when we go out."

"An' I got you these as well," Calvin said, handing Hudson a stack of CDs. "This is some'a the *other* stuff we make, a few new things from the label."

Hudson fanned through them. "Already got 'em," he said, pointing one of the CD stacks by the sound system. "I've got all your records. Most of 'em are back in England, but I've got another set in my house in Spain."

Calvin said, "*All* my records?"

"Yep. Started with the ones you made when you were rapping, Ice Blue, then the ones you produced. Even the ones that just say your name in small print as executive producer."

"Wow." So his father hadn't ignored him his whole life. It was like Mick had been watching over him from afar even though he'd been forbidden to approach him.

"Look... Mick... there ain't no easy place to start, so I'm'a just jump in here. What went down with you and moms?"

Hudson looked at him keenly. "You want it straight?"

"Only way."

"Okay... what happened was that I played on one of your mother's records back in the late sixties. Nothing organised. It was just that they needed a blues guitar player and I happened to be in the building working on something else next door. I played the tune, they said thank you very much, I went back to work with my own band. Then a few years later we were on the same show and one of your mother's musicians asked me to get up and jam on the tune I'd cut with her. We did that, it went great and we sort of got together the same night.

"That was it, really. Both of us were working all over the place. You're in the business, you know how it is. We were hardly ever in the same city at the same time. We managed to get together a couple more times in different places, but it wasn't really happening between us like it had that first time."

"Moms said you had a girlfriend in England and you were gonna leave her..."

Hudson nodded. "That's pretty much right. Things hadn't been going great with me and Jocasta even before my scene with your mother, and I'd probably have ended up leaving her anyway. But then she got pregnant..."

Calvin's eyes widened. "Your girlfriend in England? She got pregnant?"

Hudson sighed. "Yeah. Then we lost the baby."

"That's rough, man," Calvin said sympathetically.

"Yeah," Hudson said again. "It was. It was a really difficult birth and the poor little sod barely lived two hours. We were shattered. Just sat around the house getting fucked up and staring at each other. Hardly said anything. Couldn't find the words. We had nothing in common any more except the pain, and the stuff we were taking to try and get through it.

"But..." he raised his eyes to stare steadily into Calvin's "... I couldn't leave her. Not then. Not with the shape she was in. I had to stay with her until she was strong enough to leave me. Which she did, in the end. Married my mate Simon, used to be my tour manager. You know, Blue's manager. You met him outside yesterday."

"That who that was? Okay..."

"What I'm getting to," Hudson said, "is that *that* was when your mother called me to tell me you were on the way."

Calvin wondered how he'd'a played that hand if it had ever been dealt to him. Probably have done the exact same thing. He was watching Hudson's face. Shorn of his rock and roll hair, every minute of his sixty years was showing on his seamed, beaky face. Absently, he sighed and massaged the bridge of his nose, the only part of his hooter not covered in bandages.

"It was less than a week after we lost little Laurence. She wanted me to fly out to the States there and then, just drop everything and go. I tried to tell her that I couldn't do that, not so soon after what had happened to me and Jo."

Calvin said, "Moms told me you said she had to have an abortion. Told her to get rid of me."

Hudson sighed again. "As I remember it — and I was pretty out of it at the time — I didn't tell her to have an abortion. All I did was ask if she was absolutely sure she wanted to have this baby. Then she told me to stay away from her, and you, for as long as I lived. I felt like I'd just lost two babies, and one of 'em hadn't even been born yet.

"That was when I really went off the deep end. Drink, smack, the works. Stayed out of it for most of the seventies. Made two or three really crap albums, as well. Some of my biggest hits, as it happened." He laughed, humourlessly. "Oh, I was a proper little handful for the poor bastards in my road crew. Got to the point where I was either trying to sneak dealers in past security so I could score, or sneak myself out so I could go to some extremely dodgy parts of whatever town I was in and cop some horse. Even started carrying a fucking gun. Almost had to use it a couple of times when the guys I'd just scored off would be trying to rob me on the way out."

Calvin said, "You reckon if it all hadn't come down the way it did, you and my moms might'a stayed together?"

Hudson shook his head. "I really don't think so. We're very different characters, Venetia'n me, and we didn't really have very much in common other than one tune we played really well together. As far as I was concerned, the relationship had pretty much burned out by the time you came along.

"But I'll tell you this much for nothing. Even if me'n Venetia couldn't've lived together and had a Three Bears kind of happy family, I'd've always been in your life. If she'd've let me, that is. I'd've been around as much as I could. I'd've still tried to be your dad."

A weight was lifting off Calvin, the kind of weight you hardly know you've been carrying until the day you finally get to put it down. He stood up and spread his arms. "I... uhhh... I... awwww, shit!...I..."

Hudson rolled his eyes skyward. "Oh, *fuck*," he said, "I just *knew* this was going to happen." But he moved forward into Calvin's embrace. In a solemn TV-actor voice, he said, "I love you too, son." For a long moment, they clasped each other tight.

Then Calvin said, "Yo, dawg, let's go. We got us a record to make."

TWENTY-FOUR

Adrienne, opening the front door, couldn't believe her eyes. There was Calvin, and he had someone with him, a tall skinny old guy in a big baggy white Fully Loaded sweatshirt and a woollen hat pulled down over his shaved and bandaged head... Mick?

"Thought I'd bring my pops along," Calvin said, grinning broadly. "After all, he ain't exactly the worst guitar player in the world."

"This Christmas Day and nobody told me?" Adrienne asked. "C'mon in." Wait'll Blue sees this, she thought as she led the way to the music room.

Blue stood up when he saw them. Shaky as he was, he took a couple of faltering steps towards them, arms outstretched. The three of them hugged. Hudson cast a warning glance at Calvin.

"Don't fucking say it," he said. "Once was bad enough." Adrienne came up and put her arms around the three of them. "Group hug?" Hudson asked. "What *is* it with you California types?" But he didn't make even the slightest effort to pull away.

"My moms comin'?" Calvin asked.

"Due any minute," Adrienne told him. Calvin had him a lightbulb moment, snapped his fingers.

"I got me an idea," he said.

When Venetia arrived, Maudie took her to the living room rather than the music room. The three men were waiting for her on the sofa, Hudson in the middle.

Venetia knew when it was time to throw in her hand. She dropped her bag, walked towards the sofa. "Move your asses and let me sit down," she said. It was a tight squeeze and Blue winced at the jolt to his aching limbs as Venetia plopped her butt down heavily between him and Hudson, but they managed it. Adrienne produced a tiny digital camera from her pocket, snapped off three quick shots. "I'm gonna be submitting this for the album cover," she told them.

Calvin shook his head. "No way, grandma. Maybe somewhere in the booklet, real real small. What'choo reckon, pops?"

"Did I tell you my contract specifies full photo approval?" Hudson asked. "And since my hairdresser and my wardrobe and make-up people don't seem to have arrived yet, I have to tell you I don't fancy your chances much."

"People," Blue said, slapping his thighs lightly with his palms, "let's go to work. Sun's high in the sky and we got us a lotta cotton to pick 'fore the bossman come checkin' on us." Adrienne wheeled his chair up to the sofa and he gratefully settled down in it. She rolled him into the music room, the others following. The line of guitars had been rearranged to close the gap where the old Stella used to be. At Calvin's insistence, Adrienne had dispatched the wreckage to a top acoustic guitar-builder for repair, but she was fairly certain that no matter how beautifully and meticulously it was restored, Blue would probably never play it again.

Blue picked up his Martin D-45 acoustic, tentatively struck a few chords and runs, a delicacy and lingering care for the intonation of each note replacing his customary force and authority.

"All right," he said. "What we gonna sing first?"

They'd been tossing songs around for a couple of hours when Maudie Lam called a halt and took Blue away for his nap. Mostly, Blue let Hudson call the tunes and teach Venetia the arrangements. He felt a swell of pride in both his protégé's intimate knowledge of his music and in the speed with which Venetia absorbed the idiosyncratic feel of his music. Either she was a damn quick study, he thought, or else she been keeping in touch with my music all these years. For a girl raised by a hellfire preacher she can play her some good blues on the piano; that much run in the family, at least.

Meat and potatoes blues tunes like County Jail and Telephone Bill were going down so smooth Blue kind of wished they were in the studio right there and then. He said as much to Calvin, who rummaged in his bag and wrestled out a big gleaming white — of course! — notebook computer.

"Got me a studio right here," he said with a wink.

Blue said, "Huh?" Calvin brandished his computer.

"I told you. I got a studio right here. This is the top-of-the-line Apple prototype MacBook Pro running ProTools off of a one-point-five megahertz Intel chip. Got two gigs of RAM, 200-gig hard drive. Got me a couple of tame Apple geeks make sure I get the latest prototypes, do a little moonlighting, customise this baby right up the ass, give me some stuff no-one else has. This here..." he rummaged in his bag again "... is what we call a breakout box. Run a few mics into this, plug the breakout box into the MacBook, and we can record right here." As he spoke he was suiting the action to the word, setting up microphones on stands to pick up the three singers, Blue's acoustic guitar and the small amp into which Hudson has plugged his Telecaster, direct-injecting the little digital keyboard Venetia was playing and from which she'd managed, against all the odds, to extract a reasonable faux-acoustic piano sound

"I don't understand me none'a that," Blue told him. "Least if you was speakin' Chinee, I could get Maudie in here, tell me what you said."

"All you need to know," Calvin told him, "is that if I say I can do it with this, that mean I can do it. Y'all carry on just like you been doing. I know we goin' into the studio to record y'all with the band, but we might get some stuff we can use here, too." He booted the computer and fired up his music software, ran them through a quick mic check and flashed an A-OK high sign.

Blue grinned, started to sing The Hog Is Man's Best Friend. Venetia looked embarrassed and then joined in. They sang a couple of verses together before the take broke up in laughter.

Then they got back to business, running through Blue's old chestnuts Piece Of The Action and Nuthin' Wrong That Money Can't Cure. A basic format was beginning to emerge: Blue would sing the first and last verses of each song and Venetia and Hudson the middle verses, with solos up for grabs between the two guitarists and Venetia's piano. On John Lee Hooker's Burnin' Hell, Blue sang the lead and added a few pithy electric fills to Hudson's driving, stomping acoustic guitar and Venetia's remorselessly riffing piano.

When they started checking out Sign Language On The Radio, the new song Hudson had written for the sessions, things got a little more complicated. The song was what Hudson described as a sort-of-blues, adding a few extra changes to the standard twelve-bar pattern. Venetia sank her musical teeth into the progression like a dog with a particularly tasty bone, and it was rapidly decided that they should go with a piano-led arrangement. Problem was that Blue wanted Hudson to sing it instead of him.

"Too many changes, too many words," he grumbled. "I'm an old man, memory ain't what it was. You sing the song, young man, and I'll take the solo."

Calvin looked up from his monitor. "Everything y'all played so far is old time shuffles and slow blues."

Blue stiffened. "Yeah? Well, I *am* old time, young man."

Calvin was undeterred. "You got to have you some variety in an album, different flava now'n again. If he..." indicating Hudson " . . . sing it, gonna sound like it should be on his album, not yours."

"I'm gonna record it myself," Hudson interposed, "but only after Blue's had his version out. I want Daddy Blue's version to be the original."

"I ain't got me the energy to learn no new tunes," Blue protested.

"Trust me on this," Calvin insisted. "This gonna be great. We gonna write the words out on cards, nice'n big. Hold 'em up where you can see 'em. All you got to do is remember the tune an' read the words right off the cards."

Hudson found a Magic Marker and started scrawling the lyrics in large letters onto a legal pad, one verse per sheet, while Maudie was dispatched to fetch Adrienne from out by the hot tub where she was quietly sunning herself and reading Elmore Leonard's *Tishomingo Blues*. She pouted some but agreed to act as Cue Card Girl for the runthrough of Hudson's song. Blue laid his guitar aside and whispered the words to himself while Hudson strummed through the chords. His voice was weak but he mastered the phrasing immediately. By the second runthrough his singing was stronger, and Venetia was playing along like she'd known the song all her life. Calvin was human-beat-boxing a drum part. It wasn't what Hudson would've demanded from a drummer, but it worked. Sounded modern.

"Let me stop y'all right there," Calvin said. "I got a groove here. Let me take this one and do it like I'd do it with one of my kids, and I'm'a get you senior citizens a hit."

"Fine by me," Hudson said. He started playing the funk-blues groove he'd created for his revamp of Hellhound On My Trail. Blue picked up his resonator and added an orthodox Delta slide riff, faltering but still funky. Hudson shifted the rhythmic emphasis of his part to accommodate what Blue was playing and suddenly the two interlocked in a rhythmic dialogue just crying out for bass and drums. Calvin was human-beat-boxing again. They were just getting into it seriously when Maudie bustled in to shoo them out so Blue could have a massage before his afternoon nap.

Calvin unplugged the mics, packed his PowerBook and split. "I got me some homework to do here," he said, grinning. Hudson wandered up to Venetia, gestured towards the back yard. "Got a few minutes for a little chat?" he asked.

Adrienne was off on a run by now so, apart from the two dozing dogs, they had the space around the hot tub to themselves. They sat down opposite each other.

"Seems a shame to bring this up now that everything's all sweetness and light," Hudson said, "but I still need to know why you shut me out all those years, kept me away from Calvin. You know as well as I do that we'd never have made much of a couple, but at least I could still have been his dad."

Venetia sat up straight, looked him in the eye. "You wouldn't come to me when I needed you," she said. "An' if you can't be there when I need you, then you ain't gonna be there at all." Hudson opened his mouth to answer, but she held up a hand to shush him. "I know about you and Blonde Princess losin' your baby," she said, "but after that was over you could still have come to us. An' you didn't."

"'Ang on a minute!" Hudson exploded. "You *told* me to stay away from you both!"

"That was 'cause I was mad at you!" she shot back. "An' if you'd been any kind of a man 'stead of a slobbering goddam jelly-boned junkie you'd'a come for us anyway whatever I said!"

Henry, you old bastard, Hudson thought to himself, don't you ever get sick of being right all the time? He exhaled, pulled off the woolen cap, twisted it in his hands. Venetia flinched at the sight of his shaved, bandaged skull.

"You said no to me," she continued, her tone softening slightly. "Ever since I left the Reverend Holland's house to go my own way, I decided no-one was ever gonna say no to me and get away with it. I figured you were the same way, but I guess I was wrong. First time anyone says no to you, you just leave."

"Told you we were different," Hudson answered.

"Never thought you'd walk away from a woman and a child so easy."

"It wasn't easy," he told her. "I was royally fucked up for years."

"I know that," she said. "I saw all them pictures of you makin' that guy from the Stones look like an ad for a health club. Thing of it is... Mick... you ran away from your pain. You ran into drink'n drugs'n girls you forgot by the next night. You'd'a run into your pain 'stead'a runnin' away, you'd'a come out the other side, 'stead'a havin' it stay with you your whole life. And we could'a raised a son even without bein' together."

Hudson sat and thought. "Yeah, well," he said finally. "I'm a lover, not a fighter."

Venetia smiled. She patted his knee.

"Pretty good lover back in the day, as I recall," she said. "But if you gonna make it through this world, there's times when you got to be both."

The dogs were awake now. Wu Li jumped into Venetia's lap, Attack nuzzling and sniffing at Hudson's left hand.

"We okay?" he asked.

"Yeah," she said. "We okay."

She put one hand on his knee, kissed him lightly on the cheek.

Maudie got so mad she damn near quit on the spot. She got as far as starting to pack up her massage table before Adrienne managed to talk her down. She thought Blue's decision to go to the studio on Sunset Boulevard in person was just plain foolishness. "I wash my hands of this," Maudie kept repeating, progressively louder. "I wash my hands!"

Calvin's techie guys had been in the previous day to set up the remote link to the studio. On the face of it, the hookup was foolproof. A closed web page with a webcam at each end linked by a broadband connection so that Blue could sit right there in his music room, microphone poised a few inches from his lips, guitar in his lap, and watch the band and the control room on a twenty-eight inch monitor while he sang and played. It'd be just like being there, they assured him.

Except that it wasn't. Every so often the connection would glitch, and even if it was only for a tenth of a second, that was still enough to throw Blue's timing off. The first song they tried should have been a doddle, an easy canter through Blue's oldie County Jail, with Hudson taking the middle verse and second guitar solo, as well as joining Venetia and Blue for the harmonised choruses. Blue's rhythm section were more than familiar with the song, since they played it at just about every show Blue did, but Blue kept stopping the take, complaining that the feel was wrong. Needless to say, he blamed the technology. "I wouldn't mind doing overdubs like this," he grumbled. "Close my eyes, I could be anywhere. I can sit on a groove that's already there, but if I'm gonna make the groove happen with the drummer'n all, I got to be there myself. Simon, send someone over right now, pack my shit and get me in there. We gonna do this, we do it *right*."

So Simon dispatched Luis in the people carrier to bring Blue, his little Fender Deluxe amp and a couple of guitars to the studio. Once Maudie had reluctantly accepted that Blue was going no matter what, she insisted on coming too. The musicians were all set up, balanced and ready. Blue had rounded up his usual bass player and drummer, but since Venetia had been formally installed behind the ivories, it didn't matter that his piano player was currently out on tour with Big Slim Reynolds. The previous week, they had actually discussed possible substitutes for almost three minutes before Hudson did a Homer Simpson "D'oh!," slapped his forehead, hissed with pain from his tender scalp and pointed out that they actually had a pretty good piano player right there.

After an uncomfortable session in the dentist's chair, Mick Hudson had emerged with temporary bridgework which at least enabled him to sing without lisping. His bulky bandaging had been replaced by lighter, less cumbersome dressings, but he still kept his brand-new Fully Loaded woollen hat pulled firmly down over his ears. Hudson's role in the production collective had involved supervising the basic arrangements and balance: he wanted to record as live as possible. "After all," he told them, "we did the first Bluebottle album in a day and a half, just got everything set up and then played what we did on stage. Last time I was in the studio it took that long just to get a fucking bass drum sound. Most of Blue's old records were done like that: four songs in three hours, no overdubs."

Calvin was around, but mostly he just sat in the control room watching and listening. "I wanna see how y'all do it," he told them. Frank, the veteran engineer Blue always demanded when he used this particular studio, was something of an industry legend because he knew just about everything there was to know about the ancient science of microphone choice and placement. He looked like he was just casually dumping microphones in front of drums and amps any old how, but almost invariably everything sounded great almost immediately. Calvin, who very rarely used live drums or acoustic instruments of any description on any of his own sessions, was watching Frank like a hawk.

When Maudie wheeled Blue in, closely followed by Luis lugging his instruments, he received a spontaneous standing ovation. Within moments Frank had determined the optimum location for Blue's little Fender amp, mic'ed it up, put baffles around it to prevent leakage into the other microphones, twisted a couple of dials and had Blue's archetypal guitar sound happening. Furball the drummer — his legal name was Freddie Gonzalez, but he'd earned his nickname by being so hairy that even when, as now, he was stripped to the waist, he looked like he was wearing a black T-shirt — counted off the groove. Four minutes later, they had a perfect version of County Jail in the can. Ten minutes after that, an equally flawless rendition of Telephone Bill had joined it. Then they started in on Piece Of The Action, once again nailing it within three takes. If they could get Ain't Nuthin' Wrong That Money Can't Cure before Blue's stamina failed, they'd've done a superb day's work.

Blue, Hudson thought as he doubled the bass line and punctuated it with sliding ninth and seventh chords, was giving the performance of a lifetime. He could teach the world's environmental agencies a few things about energy conservation. He wasn't wasting a single breath, or playing any notes he didn't need to. Blue was paring each song down to its barest essentials, distilling his art and style into its purest fundamentals, and relying on Hudson to supply the additional lines he was no longer playing, cueing him with a flicker of eye contact whenever he needed Hudson to fill in a gap.

Four tracks down in less than two hours, and much euphoric high-fiving as they sat in the control room listening to the playbacks. Blue wasn't joining in. He just sat there, eyes closed, nodding approvingly, one finger tapping the beat on his knee.

"Very good music," Maudie said. "*Very* good music! Tomorrow you make even more good music, but now it is time to take Mr Moon home."

"Just one second," Venetia interrupted. "I just want to try something here." She hauled herself off the control room's plush sofa and marched back out into the studio to seat herself at the piano. She began to play the opening chords of Blues For Now. Hudson nodded to the rhythm section. Furball and Kenny the bass player followed him out to join Venetia. Blue whispered to Maudie. She frowned. He whispered some more. Then she wheeled him back into the studio.

"From the top," Hudson told them. "You know the words to this one?" he asked Blue.

"'Course I do," the old man retorted indignantly.

"Okay... if you wanna take first and third verses..."

Blue stared at him with real anger. "Young man," he said, "I don't need nobody tell me how to sing with my daughter."

Hudson stared back, thought of a couple of dozen different retorts, didn't utter any of them. Metallica had the right idea bringing a therapist into the studio, he thought. Pity it was the wrong therapist. Instead, he caught Frank's eye through the glass. "Roll it," he said.

"Wait a second," Venetia said. "Mick, you gonna sing?" Hudson shook his head — *nuh*-uh — and hefted his guitar. "This'll do my singing for me," he said. Furball clicked his sticks and, like a diver filmed in slo-mo, they plunged into the deepest, most turbulent waters of the blues.

Blue took the first verse. Leaning right into the mic, he seemed to be floating the words out on the shallowest of breaths. It was blues singing at its most intimate, when even the singer sounds like he's not quite sure whether he's talking to himself or to someone else. Hudson gave him plenty of space, a two-note lick here and a trill there, making sure he was building the mood rather than cutting into it.

Venetia took the second verse, intensifying the piano chording and lighting a gospel fire under the lyric. "You tell 'em, girl," Blue murmured into his mic as she finished the first line, and Hudson added a thumbed-off bass-string commentary, answered in turn by a sharp rim-shot from Furball's snare drum. Blue'd been dead right, of course — how the hell could people make music like this unless they were together in the same room at the same time, united in space and time and feeling?

Solo coming up, Hudson thought as he built the final fill of the second verse into the launchpad for his guitar break. Then he stopped thinking altogether. Within the warm blue bubble of the music, he felt like he could see auras glowing around both Blue and Venetia, two completely different kinds of fire, both expanding until they encompassed him also. Blue's focussed blue flame was cool but nevertheless still paradoxically warming, Venetia's a roaring blaze of scarlet and gold. He reached out to them both with his guitar, spinning out lines which could contain both their different energies, meld them into one seamless unified whole...

And he'd played right through the first stoptime verse, just as he had in Miami, but here it was coming up again, Venetia and Blue trading lines like duellists in love. He reached down into the lowest frets of his guitar, leaving them space to work the high wire at the top of the sound. By the time they hit the final verse, he was feeling like what they were doing ought to be swallowing up the whole of LA, people stopping on the sidewalks even miles away, wondering what the hell was that?

"*I don't know what's happenin,*" Venetia sang, "*but I'm'a figure it out somehow,*"

"Yes you are," Blue told her. "Make me know it, baby."

"*I said I don't know what's happenin' people, but I'm'a figure it out somehow,*" Venetia repeated. "I hear you," Blue interposed.

"*I don't know what's buggin' me,*" Venetia sang, hitting one almighty chord on the piano, Hudson, Furball and Kenny slamming the down-beat right along with her, holding one chord as a carpet of sustain upon which she could send her voice dancing.

"*But you can call it the blues...*"

And Blue was there with her. "*Ye-ahhh, you can ca-all it the blues,*" he sang.

"*Well, well, well....*"

"*Well, well, well, well...*"

"*I said...*"

"*Ye-ahh, I-I-I-I said...*"

It was like Blue and Venetia were alone in the room. And as long as he and Kenny and Furball didn't fuck up and shatter the vibe, they'd have the blues equivalent of Holy Communion here. He kept one eye on the rhythm section, the other on the two singers.

Venetia brought one hand down sharply, Hudson and Furball and Kenny meeting her with a single slam. Into the silence, she and Blue harmonised the last line like they'd practiced it for a week. Hudson, about to cue the ending, simply held his hand up for silence, then slashed it quickly across his throat. For several seconds, nobody moved.

Then: a collective exhalation. "That was great," Frank crackled over the talkback. "You wanna come in and hear it?"

Blue was panting. Sweat stood out on his forehead as he pulled off his baseball cap. Maudie was already at his side, mopping his brow. "Don't need to," he said. "Need to go home."

Maudie cast a venomous glance at Hudson. "You make him work too hard," she scolded. "Mr Moon get tired so quick. You should not make him sing two hours." Hudson shrugged helplessly.

"It's what he needs to do, Maudie," he said at length. "He wants to make this record."

Simon looked up from his notepad. "Today we got five tunes," he told Maudie. "Almost twenty-five minutes of music. That's nearly half the album right there."

"And how you think he make other half?" she retorted. "Tomorrow he rest. No recording tomorrow!" Blue sat slumped in his chair, eyes closed, chest rapidly rising and falling in shallow breaths. She wheeled him out into the parking lot. Simon replaced Blue's guitars in their cases and followed them to where Luis waited with the people carrier.

In the control room, Hudson turned to Calvin and Venetia. "You reckon it's worth coming back in tomorrow?" he asked.

"Got to see how he's feeling," Venetia said. "He might come in if he's strong enough."

"We could try the hookup again," Calvin suggested. "Or maybe cut some backing tracks and record grampop at the house."

Venetia was gathering up her stuff. "You boys want some dinner?" she asked Calvin and Hudson. "I'm buyin'."

Hudson shook his head, feeling a touch on the woozy side. His scalp ached beneath his bandages. "I'll take a raincheck, if you don't mind," he said. "I'm feeling pretty knackered myself."

"An' I got to catch up with some bidness," Calvin told them. "I'll check both y'all out in the morning."

Back in the parking lot, leaning on his Hummer, Calvin pulled out his cellphone. He had an uneasy feeling and decided to act on it, called Big Ray at the office.

"Ray-Ray," he said. "Gonna need some security round at my gram-pop's house for a few days... naw, nuthin' obvious, dawg. Coupla brothers outside just'a keep an eye on things. Don't want my gramps even knowin' they're there."

"No problem, boss," Big Ray told him. "Consider it done." When Calvin disconnected, Ray punched a number into his phone. "Need a coupla brothers for the job," he said. He reeled off Blue's address. "You know the deal."

"Yahmon," said the voice at the other end of the line. "Mi know the deal ta raas."

Ray listened to the click-brrrr for a few seconds after the man he'd spoken to had hung up, breaking the connection to Kingston, Jamaica.

TWENTY-FIVE

Maudie was on her way down the hall towards the music room to bring Blue his medication when she heard the dogs: Wu Li's trademark high-pitched yip was familiar enough, but Attack's deep-throated rumbling growl was something she hadn't heard before, and it was loud enough to be clearly audible even above the music. Maudie covered the last few yards in a loping run, shoved the door open.

The dogs had Blue's wheelchair boxed in. The old man was backed up against the counter, cowering in his chair with his old rubbed-raw Jazzmaster in his lap as they inched closer to him. "Easy up. Easy up," he kept saying in a quiet cajoling tone, but they were ignoring him. Attack kept right on growling, Wu Li yipping.

Maudie yelled, "Gyaaaaa!" at the top of her lungs, shooing the dogs out of the room and also bringing Adrienne rushing in from out back. She helped Maudie push the dogs into the corridor, then slammed the door behind her, leaving Attack and Wu Li impotently barking and growling in the hall.

"The hell's going on?" she demanded.

Slumped in his chair, Blue was gasping and grey-faced. His right hand was massaging his left arm, which hung limply at his side. "They just like to went crazy," he told her, still breathing heavily, his speech suddenly slurred. "We's all just sittin' here, I'm listenin' to the music from the other day, an' suddenly they movin' in on me like they ain't been fed in a week an' I'm a big juicy T-bone steak. I don't know whas-sup with them, I really don't."

Adrienne made a rapid decision. "This is some really weird shit," she said, "and until I can figure out what's goin' on, I'm gonna put 'em in kennels." Maudie was already setting up her massage table as Blue gulped thirstily from the water glass she'd just brought him. Adrienne slipped out into the corridor, keeping her body between the music room and the dogs until she'd closed the door. She shepherded the dogs out to the back, closed the back door firmly and scooted to the bedroom to riffle through her address book for the kennel's number.

Blue's spare frame felt frailer than ever beneath Maudie's strong probing fingers. She frankly didn't know what was still holding him up. At least he seemed to be dozing off comfortably...

In dreams:

"Well, young man, this *is* a surprise," the man with the gold tooth said. "Didn't think you was still here."

Blue looked around him. Everything except the two men and the chairs in which they were seated was in darkness, nothing visible above or below or anywhere around them but deep, thick impenetrable clouds of purple and blue smoke.

"Where's 'here'?" Blue asked.

"Why, this is nowhere," the man from the beach told him. "And no-where is pretty much where you at now. You very close to the end of your road, young man."

"I know it," Blue said. "An' t'be honest with you, I'm about ready to close my eyes. Tired all the time, achin' every which where, can't hardly play no more, only just about able to sing. Just need a few more days, finish this record.

"But I done one thing I'm proud of," he said, raising his head and staring straight into the eyes of the occupant of the chair opposite. "I brought my family back together. Neesha, Calvin an' Mick all workin' together now, they talkin' to each other. I reckon they started to ap-preciate each other, appreciate themselves. An' whatever happen now, no-one can say I ain't done that much at least. I ain't gonna hafta go out with my family in pieces."

The man with the gold tooth applauded ironically. "Yep, you surely did, young man. Took you thirty years longer'n it should have, but you done it. An' don't think we ain't impressed.

"So why," he leaned forward in his chair, "you need to finish this record? You cut five tunes, right? Them others can finish it off they-selves, cut 'em some tribute tracks or whatever you music-business peo-ples call 'em. You already done what you set out to do. Why not..." he stood up, extended his hand "... leave all that pain behind an' just come with me right now?"

"'Cause I ain't ready," Blue said steadily. "Be ready soon, but I ain't ready right now. I'm'a go when I done what I need to do."

"Gonna be a whole lot easier if you come now," Sam's customer said. He was still standing over Blue, hand still reaching down. "You carry on with this foolishness, it ain't gonna end well. Not for you, not for the others. Not to mention your wife'n your kid. Trust me, young man, I ain't lyin' to you. If you take my hand right now, you be savin' yourself an' all them peoples you love a whole bunch'a pain an' grief."

"You could be right," Blue said. "Hell, you most likely *are* right. But what's left'a my gut tells me that even if you right, you still wrong."

He looked up at the man who'd helped him buy his first guitar, now shattered beyond meaningful restoration in some upscale repair guy's workshop, who'd gotten him out of the low lands when the deputies and the dogs were running him down, who'd sat with him in the Clarksdale railroad station waiting for the Memphis train. "Whatever goes down is gonna be whatever *needs* to go down. An' I ain't runnin' out no back door. I'm'a ride this highway *all* the way. All the way to the end'a the line.

"Neesha feels like I copped out on her'n her ma way back in the day when I let the Reverend take 'em away from me. An' I feel like I copped out on her'n Calvin an' Mick by keepin' my mouth shut all them years about who was who to who. Maybe they right. But this time, this *one* time, this last time... I ain't coppin' out. Not on my family, not on the folks love my music, not on myself... an' not on you.

"'Cause I know there a part of you want me to win. Whatever you s'pose to tell me, I know what you *really* want. An' one way or 'nother I'm'a give it to you."

Blue took another look around him. There was still nothing he could see but clouds of dark, rolling smoke. Slowly he revolved the chair, waiting for any sign, no matter how tiny, that might guide him in deciding which way to go. His instincts told him nothing, remained unresponsive, silent.

In the end he simply spun the chair at random and started rolling in the direction he found himself facing. He didn't look back to see if the man with the gold tooth was still there. Whether he was or he wasn't didn't make a damn bit of difference any more. Head held high, humming an old song called You Got To Move under his breath, James Blue Moon set forth into the darkness.

Somewhere in the distance, one dog growled, and another whined in frustration.

Calvin on the phone to BLT, staring in disbelief at the PDF file which had just unfolded from the email on his screen.

"The fuck is this bullshit?"

He was looking at a letter from a London lawyer, one Jack Chaizey of the firm of M&J Twist, stating that Screwdriver & Omega Man would be taking out a breach of contract action against Lock N Load Productions in the British courts.

"The fuck are they suing in Britain?" he asked BLT heatedly. "They ain't British, we ain't British, the company ain't British, deal wasn't cut in Britain. If they wanna drag this mess into court — an' I can't believe they that dumb — how come they ain't suing here or in LA?"

"They just fuckin' with us, boss," BLT told him. "I checked our London lawyer an' he says the court'll toss 'em out, tell 'em to sue in the US if they got a beef."

"*They* got a beef?" Calvin asked. "*I* got a beef. Taken about as much crap off of those two clowns as I can handle. I'm done playin' kid games with these prejudiced no-talent muthafuckas. Plenty'a young talent comin' up in Jamaica doin' positive music, won't be draggin' all this hassle to our door. Throw their asses out. They off the label."

"Could be a problem, boss."

"Problem?"

"Lotta the kids in the office really like 'em, boss. You ain't gonna be too popular."

"I'm the boss, dawg. I own all this shit. I don't need to be popular."

"One more thing... you remember those two we had the meeting with at the Mondrian? They out of the picture now. Screwdriver and Omega Man got themselves some new management."

"Yeah? Who?"

"Company called Raintree. Based in London. You heard'a them?"

Calvin's eyes narrowed. "Lemme get back to ya, B. Need to make a couple of calls."

Calvin called Mick Hudson. Mick took a while to return the call, because he'd been in the studio all day with Venetia and Kenny and Furball cutting rhythm tracks. But when he got home and picked up Calvin's message, he called Henry MacShane's home number and left an urgent message.

Dr Strong had been and gone. No-one was feeling any better or more optimistic because of his visit. Matter of days, he said. Could go any time. Can't imagine what's still holding him up. Apparently Blue had had what would have been, for a fit man, a minor stroke. For a guy

Blue's age already in a seriously weakened condition, it was a hammer blow.

Now he looked more than ever like a bundle of dry sticks wrapped in old clothes. A transparent pouch of saline solution hung suspended from a rod attached to the back of his wheelchair, dripfeeding him the nutrition his exhausted body could no longer derive from food. His right arm was curled protectively around the guitar he could no longer play, his left hanging uselessly at his side until Adrienne cradles his unresponsive hand in both of hers and gently places it in his lap.

He hadn't reacted to Doc Strong the way she'd been expecting. No sardonic wisecracks, no anger, not even the jut-jawed determination to survive as long as he could that he'd shown in the past. He just whispered lines from classic blues songs. "I hear my train a-comin'," he croaked. "I believe my time ain't long."

But mostly he just dozed. It was only when he heard music that he'd open his eyes.

In dreams:

Blindfolded in his cage at Guantanamo Bay, Mick Hudson is rudely awakened by heavy boots thudding into his ribs and strong calloused hands hauling him to his feet, dragging his enfeebled, half-starved body away, sun-heated sand scorching his soles. His blindfold is abruptly torn away.

He finds himself on an anonymous English high street on a drizzly grey afternoon, still wearing his day-glo orange prisoner jumpsuit, the pavement wetly chill beneath his sore feet. His card has just been inserted into a cashpoint machine. The screen is informing him that he can only withdraw up to a daily maximum of £500. He is surrounded by a bunch of masked guys all wearing some kind of hi-tech Kevlar commando bodysuits.

"We need one million pounds, Mr Hudson," one of them says to him. (What's that accent? Middle Eastern? Eastern European? He cannot recognise it. All he knows is that it isn't his, that it is in some way 'other'.)

"I've *got* a million pounds," Hudson tells his captors. "I've got a damn sight *more* than a million pounds. I've got *loads* of fucking money. I just can't get a million pounds in cash out of this machine with this card."

"That is unfortunate, Mr Hudson," says his interlocutor. "All your bills are due, and there are very specific penalties for late payment."

"I can pay," Hudson says, as steadily as he can, "just not with this card."

"That's a pity," the guy replies — what *is* that accent? Israeli? Ukranian? — "because it's the only card you've got."

Helpless, Hudson feels his captors raise him up from the cold damp pavement, tugging his blindfold back onto his head in the process. His bare feet leave the ground. He is thrown through the air. He lands hard and painfully. A flare of pain explodes through his ribs as his back crunches into sun-heated steel bars. Once again, he is in his cage in Guantanamo Bay, blind, battered and baking. Fumbling around him, his hand encounters what feels like another human body. A cellmate? "Whoa, whoa. Take it easy, young man," a voice says. Somewhere an alarm bell is ringing. A tape loop in his head keeps unreeling the phrase, "Kill me.... kill me... kill me..." over and over again.

Hudson's consciousness claws its way to the surface. Desperately, he reaches out. The alarm bell stops ringing. He has a telephone receiver in his hand. A tinny voice is saying, "Michael? You awake, son?"

Calvin had been sitting at his desk for almost an hour now, head in his hands. He'd told his secretary not to put through any calls.

On his monitor was the latest update from the DirrtyDawg website. He looked up again to see if one specific item hadn't said quite what he thought it had, but it was exactly the same as it had been the last time he'd looked at it, a minute and a half earlier.

"The LA-based hip-hop/R&B supremo with the highly secret gay life has been neglecting his business in order to spend more time with his family, including his dying grandfather, his diva mom and maybe even his mysterious long-lost father. We wouldn't normally intrude on private grief by mentioning this, but some of his employees are starting to talk."

He reached out, clicked back to the DirrtyDawg home page, moved around the site, looking to see if there was anything else new about him. There wasn't. He started to shut down his browser, then clicked back to the page he'd been staring at before. The page blanked and reloaded, but now there was an underlined blue weblink below the kryptonite paragraph. He closed his eyes for a second, inhaled deeply three times.

Then he exhaled with a whoosh, reopened his eyes and clicked on the link.

A new window opened up on his screen. Inside it was a Photoshopped image of himself, his face, snarling and distorted, taken from his last video. In the video he'd been shown beating a cop, but here he was putting the hurt on a young white surfer type in a French maid outfit. His hand moving almost of its own volition, he clicked on the image and it sprang into jerky animated life. Now he was fucking the kid to the sound of a tinny ringtone version of his last rap hit. Thirty seconds later it froze, reset itself back to the start.

Sweat was running down his face. He pulled off his baseball cap. The inside of it was soaked. A couple of drops rolled off his chin, dripped onto the desk. He wiped his forehead on his sleeve. How many muthafuckas were lamping that page right now? How many were clicking the animation link? How many were laughing?

Shit, only one thing to do. And he didn't want to do it. Absently he clicked the video link again, watched the animation run its half-minute course. Then he killed the page. Stood up. Sat down again.

He looked at his office door, protectively closed, imagined it yawning invitingly, a world of possibilities beckoning just beyond the threshold. I could just get up, walk right out, he thought. Go straight home. I got enough money last a normal man ten lifetimes. I could just sell this business, buy myself an island somewhere. Live however I want, never have to think about any of this shit again.

And if I do that, be nuthin' but a joke the rest of my life, leave my grampops without his last record. I could run out on me, Calvin thought, wouldn't be the first time. But running out on Blue?

Naw.

Let's go to work, he thought. Let's get in character. He slapped his palms down onto his thighs and reached out to buzz his secretary. Then withdrew his hand. Then reached out again. Then withdrew again. Finally, he mumbled, "Shit," and pressed the buzzer.

"Yo, boss."

"Staff meeting," he started to say, but his voice had cracked. Sounded weak and squeaky.

"Boss? You okay?"

"Staff meeting," he said again, his voice crisp, back under control once more. "Ten minutes. In the conference room," he told her. "That mean *everybody*. No exceptions. We're closing the offce for an hour. No visitors, no calls."

Precisely ten minutes later, Calvin strode into the conference room. He'd never realised the corridor from his office to the conference room was so muthafuckin' long, but when he reached the end of it he had his game face on. This wasn't Calvin Holland any longer. This was Ice Blue.

Everybody was there. The room was crowded, but they'd left him a clear space at the head of the table. Everyone stopped talking as he moved to take his place. BLT and Ray moved protectively to his side, flanking him.

"You cool, boss?" Ray whispered.

"Yeah, I'm cool," he whispered back. Then he raised his voice and put the hard Ice Blue eye on them.

"There's been a lotta rumours flyin' around," he said without preamble, "and I figure it's about time to get everything out into the open. First thing: I finally found out who my father is."

Buzz of conversation, quickly hushed as Calvin raised his hands for silence. He caught the tail-end of one excited whisper. "No, it ain't David Bowie," he grinned. "My father is Mick Hudson... yeah, the English rock guy. Him and me and my moms are all workin' together now, helpin' my grampops make his last record. Anyway, this gonna be all over the media soon, so I wanted y'all to be the first to know."

He raised his hands again. "Okay, there's one more thing. Been a lotta speculation an' gossip'n bullshit, so I figured it's time to straighten some shit out."

They were all looking at him now. He took a deep breath.

"I'm gay."

Under other circumstances the look on all their faces would actually have been funny.

"Not all the way gay," he continued, "but not all the way straight, either. I got two lives goin' on. Straight most'a the time, gay once in a while. I make it with women, but sometimes I make it with men too. That's the way I am, and I figure that's the way I'm always gonna be. I ain't gonna change, but I *am* gonna stop hidin' it."

He looked up at his crew, staring them in the eyes one by one. Nobody dropped their eyes.

"Anyone'a y'all here got a problem with that?"

No-one spoke.

"KanD?"

She shrugged. "Not a problem for me, boss. My brother's gay and I love him."

"BLT?"

"Don't make no nevermind for me. You still who you are, an' that's all that counts."

"Ray-Ray?"

Big Ray shrugged in his turn. "Ain't a damn thing changed. You still the boss, an' you still my brother."

Calvin didn't realise he'd been holding his breath until he exhaled. "All right. Now y'all know why I got so teed off at them Jamaicans an' their..." he spat the words out "... Battyman 9/11. No way shit like that was ever gonna be on a Lock N Load production."

He clapped his hands together. "I got to say I'm proud'a all y'all. I got me the best team in the world here, and I got to say it feels good to be..." he laughed..." straight with y'all after all this time. It's gonna be weird for a few weeks, then everybody gonna forget about it and we can get back to what we do: makin' the best muthafuckin' records in the whole goddam world."

He raised a clenched fist. "Peace." He clapped his hands again. "Okay. Back to work, y'all."

BLT started applauding. KanD joined in. Then everybody else. Calvin walked back to his office to the sound of an standing ovation.

Half of Mick Hudson is still in Guantanamo Bay, the other half in his room at the rented house in the Hollywood Hills. The sound of Henry MacShane's voice pulls his scattered sensibility together: he is safe in bed. Nothing really bad can possibly happen to him while he's talking to Henry. The icy fist clenched around his heart fractionally relaxed.

"'Ang on a sec," Hudson muttered into the phone. He took a swig of water from the glass at his bedside, washing away the parching residue of Guantanamo Bay. "Right... what's going on with this Screwdriver and Whatsisname? Is Raintree managing them now or what?"

"Well, sort of," Henry told him. He sounded a little embarrassed, which was unusual. "You know I don't handle everything myself these days, yeah? Well, apparently one of the kids in the office is helping out on a temporary basis because they're in dispute with their label. Something like that, anyway. The whole thing's a bit iffy 'cause the shirtlifters are all up in arms about something they recorded..."

"Now now, Henry," Hudson interrupted. "You can't say stuff like 'shirtlifters' any more."

"Fair enough... don't mind it being legal as long as it's not compulsory."

"You're hopeless, you are."

"Comes with old age. Anyway, young Tommy in the office says it's a free speech civil liberties kind of thing, but those geezers hate poofs and love guns a little too much for my liking."

"Yeah, they fit right into George Bush's America... problem is, the label they're in dispute with is Lock N Load... yeah, that's right. Calvin's lot. Now he's got a letter from some lawyer threatening to sue him in the British courts."

Now Henry *really* sounded embarassed. "Oh, that's all complete bollocks, that is," he told Hudson. "Total bluff. Kiddy was just flying a kite. I've had a word with him about that, and you can tell Calvin he won't be hearing any more about it. Now, what else is going on your end? Sorted out your family problems yet?"

Hudson took another gulp of water. "Yeah, reckon," he said.

"How'd it go?"

"Bit rough to start with."

"But it's okay now?"

"Yeah, just about."

"Well, that's good... how's old Blue holding up?"

Hudson sighed. "Not too clever. Poor old sod had a stroke yesterday."

"Oh fuck."

"'Oh fuck' is right. Left arm paralysed, left leg none too good. Doc says he could go any time. Doesn't know what's still holding him up. Sleeps most of the time. Adrienne says he only really perks up when he hears the music, and then he's almost his old self. It's like the music keeps pulling him back."

"How much stuff have you lot recorded, then?"

"One good studio day with Blue. Five songs, vocals and all. Another day's worth of backing tracks. Four more, gonna need vocals and a few overdubs. And Calvin recorded some jamming we did at the house, says we might be able to use some of it."

"You reckon you got an album?"

"If Blue can hang on long enough to put down a few more vocals, we might have something. No way he's ever going back to the studio, though, so it'll be down to cutting him at the house."

"Yeah, well, good luck with that, mate. Look, I'd like to see the old sod one more time, and I'm not too busy these days, so how about if I came out...?"

Oh, fuck, *no*, Hudson thought. Henry bulldozing his way around LA was the last thing he wanted. He was due to have the stitches in his scalp out that afternoon and his face was almost back to normal, but his regrowing hair had barely reached the Number One Crop stubble stage and it was coming back in stone white. Basically, he still looked like shit, and he didn't want to face an interrogation from Henry about it.

"Blue's got enough on his plate coping with the people already around him," Hudson said. "And it's all been dead stressful for everyone. He and Adrienne even sent Donna away for a few days with her son Josh. Don't know if he can handle anybody else, even an old pal like your good self."

Pause at the other end of the line. Then: "Are you sure you're okay, young Michael? Your voice sounds a bit funny." Hudson involuntarily ran the tip of his tongue over his still-fresh bridgework.

"Early in the morning, innit?" he said.

"S'pose it is," Henry said. "Anyway, you take care of yourself. Give Blue my very best, and if there's anything he needs, just ask."

"I think we got it covered, matey-boy," Hudson said, "but if we think of something we'll give you a shout. Take care'a yourself, you old fart."

"Fack orf, ya cunt." Henry's idea of an affectionate goodbye. Hudson hung up the phone and wandered off to the shower.

Calvin back in his office, decompressing, the phone jolting him out of his reverie. "Yo."

"'Allo, son. Mick Daddy here."

"Hi."

"Blimey, you sound cheerful."

"Yeah, rough morning."

" Still, I got a bit of good news for you."

"I could use some. Whassup?"

"You know the lawsuit those two Jamaican clowns were supposed to be bringing against you in England? You won't be hearing any more about that. I had a word with Henry, and he had a word with this kid in his office who's supposed to be looking after them. That's all sorted."

"Thanks for that, man. 'Preciate it. How's grampops?"

Hudson sighed gustily. "Not good at all. That stroke pretty much laid him out. Could be a matter of days now. Or less. Listen, I've got a hospital appointment at two, and I'll be heading on over to Blue's as soon as they're through with me there. Want me to swing by and pick you up?"

"Naw, s'cool, blood. Got a few things to take care of here 'fore I can head out. I'll see y'all up there."

Miami airport was always a raasclaat pain for anyone coming in from the islands, so they'd decided to fly direct from Kingston to LAX. Now they stood in the immigration line, two big Jamaicans wearing Hilfiger and Timberland, one with dreadlocks hanging almost to his waist, the other with a clean-shaven skull.

Finally it was their turn, and the dreadlocked guy stepped up to the immigration officer's cubicle. The guy behind the glass wore a name tag identifying him as Jesus Garcia. He stared over his glasses at the big dread.

"How long are you planning to spend in the United States?"

The dread shrugged expansively. "Jus' a few days. Mebbe a week."

"Purpose of visit?"

"Me an' mi partner here for a business meeting. Talk wid we record company."

"You will not be performing or seeking employment, then."

"Nawmon. Simply reason a lickle wid a producer an' see de sights."

Jesus Garcia had an irrational feeling that he wasn't hearing the whole story. Still, he stamped the dread's passport and sent him through. If he or his partner were carrying drugs or weapons, Garcia thought, customs could deal with that. He motioned the bald guy forward and they went through the same routine again, virtually word for word.

Emerging onto the concourse with their bags, they scanned the throng for their welcoming committee. It didn't take long to spot him. They tapped fists.

"Irie," Omega Man said.

"Gentlemen," Big Ray replied, "Welcome to Los Angeles."

TWENTY-SIX

Got to hand it to Moms, Calvin thought. She lives large even when she payin' for it herself.

Venetia had come to LA without her army of flunkeys and retainers: no hairdresser, publicist, bodyguard, personal trainer, chauffeur, make-up artist or wardrobe person; no chief cook or bottlewasher. Even Ramon, the personal assistant who normally accompanied her everywhere except the bathroom and, when she fancied a confidential chat, sometimes even there, was still back in Chicago. Nevertheless, her suite at the Beverly Hills Hotel would have been spacious enough to accommodate all of them in relative comfort. It wasn't actually called The Presidential Suite, but it could have been. Calvin approved: you got it, flaunt it. He had special mad love for the white grand piano by the window. If he could do more with a keyboard than simply pick out a bass line with one finger, he'd have himself one just like it. Maybe two.

Room service had just delivered their brunch: steak, eggs and coffee for him — semi-lapsed Muslim he might be, but he still never touched pork — and fruit salad, cereal and mint tea for her. They ate in amicable silence, him chowing down big time, she picking delicately at her fruit salad.

Finally Venetia raised her teacup to her lips, took a sip. "Okay, son," she said, "what's on your mind?"

Calvin exhaled. It had been easier to tell his staff than it was gonna be to tell his moms. Back in the office, once he'd gotten himself together, he'd still felt like the boss: in charge, in control, telling everyone what time it was, ready to kick ass on anyone give him any shit. He'd even been ready to weather a media storm, look the whole world square in the face, staring it down. But his moms was different. Now, looking into Venetia's eyes, he felt like a kid again, fessing up to something that would change the whole way she felt about him. The speech he'd mentally rehearsed on the drive over fell apart in his mind.

"There's something about me gonna come out," he said at length, "an' you need to hear it from me rather'n see on TV or in the paper."

Venetia put her head on one side, raised an interrogative eyebrow. Just like she'd done when he was a kid. He pressed on.

"Moms... I'm kind of... I'm gay."

Venetia didn't drop her teacup, but she lowered it awful hard. Drops of tea spattered the glass tabletop.

She said, "Oh, *no*. Son..."

Calvin said, "Yeah."

She said again, "Oh, *no*... what about all those women you s'posed to have? That all bullshit?"

"No, it ain't," Calvin told her. "That's for real. It's just that there's guys too."

She shook her head like she'd just taken a punch.

"Oh... my... God," she said. "Oh... my... God. Can't believe I'm hearing this. I'm in shock. My own son..."

"Moms, I don't get it," Calvin said. "Since when you had a problem with gay people? Half the people work for you gay. Ramon just about the closest person to you in the world, includin' me, an' he gay. Why's this different?"

She stared at him, eyebrows lowered, mouth compressed into a thin hard line. "Wasn't me that raised 'em." She took a deep breath, gulped at her tea. Her hand was shaking slightly.

Calvin said, "So that's what this is about. You figure that 'cause I got a gay life goin' on it's 'cause you did something wrong as a mother." He emptied the coffeepot into his cup, slugged a mouthful down. "Well, maybe you did. You raised me my whole life to hate white guys, and one white guy in particular. An' somewhere along the line I found out that I wanted to fuck white guys, and make it hurt." He shrugged. "Didn't change how I was with women. That was a different thing. This was when I couldn't keep the anger down no other way."

Venetia shuddered. She turned away from him, plucked a kleenex from a box on the table, wiped her eyes, blew her nose. "You sayin' you actually... take...it..."

Calvin said, "How much detail you want, moms?" He stood up, grabbed his bag, headed towards the door. On the threshhold, his hand on the doorknob, he turned back. "Let's just say this. I pitch. I don't catch."

"You jailhouse gay, then," she said through gritted teeth.

Calvin paused for a second. "Yeah," he said. "Jailhouse gay." He wrenched the door open like he wanted to tear it off its hinges..

Behind him, he heard her say, "Stay." He turned in the doorway. She walked towards him, nudged the door shut, took him in her arms. She rested her head on his shoulder, strong fingers kneading his back, just like she used to do when he'd needed comforting back when he was a kid.

"I'm sorry," she said. "I'm sorry. You just got me by surprise. I never thought..." She gazed up at him. "Please don't go," she said. "Let's talk." She led him back into the room, not to the table but to a plush white leather sofa. She sat down, patted the space beside her. When he sat down she took him in her arms again.

"What about AIDS? The HIV?" she asked him. "Ain't you scared you gonna get sick?"

"'Course I worry. Condoms every time, man or woman. I get a test every three months, an' everyone I go with got to have a test too." She got up from the sofa, turned her back to him, paced to the window, stood looking out.

"Since Daddy Blue got sick," she said, "I've had to think about a lotta things. 'Bout Mick an' the way I was with him, 'bout you, 'bout my mama, an' 'bout the time I spent with my own stepdaddy.

"Now the Reverend Holland died 'fore you was born an' you know what?" She looked up at him, eyes blazing. "I was glad. I wouldn't've wanted him anywhere near any child'a mine."

"What you mean?" Calvin asked. "He didn't mess with you none, did he?"

"No," she told him. "Nuthin' like that. Messed with my head plenty, though. Had me all turned round.

"The night the Reverend Holland sent his Lincoln Town Car for me and my mama, I became part of his household, but I wasn't like his daughter. He prayed with me, but he never played with me. He sang to me, but only hymns. Never told me no stories 'cept outta the Bible. It was mama he wanted and he only took me on because I was part of the package. The Reverend never paid me no nevermind 'til he found out I could sing. Then it was like I was a trophy, like some kind of prize pony. A performing flea.

"Oh, I was daddy's little star! When we was in church, the Reverend would preach and I would sing and we'd have 'em in the aisles praisin' the Lord and speakin' in tongues. But when we was home, it was different. 'Til I got big, I got my ass whupped any time I moved the radio off the gospel station. I couldn't do a thing right." She deepened her voice, turned it rasping and gravelly. "'Why you so fat? Why you got all them zits? You got time to read, why you reading them sinful books when you oughtta be readin' the Lord's holy word?'"

"What kind'a sinful books?" Calvin asked.

"Dickens. Shakespeare. *Photoplay* magazine. Margaret god-damn Mitchell," she told him. "Any school science book with evolution in it. Anything wasn't the Bible."

"What your mama have to say about all this?"

She stared back at him, jaw jutting. "She didn't have nuthin' to say about it. She didn't have nuthin' to say about nuthin'. She'd gotten what she wanted. Had herself a man with *status* in the *community*. Not some no-'count raggedy-ass blues singer with nuthin' to his name but two guitars and three suits. This was before Daddy Blue got big in Europe and started makin' himself some money, gettin' written up in *Downbeat* magazine and *Rolling Stone*, all the white boys singin' his songs. This was back when we was livin' strictly ghetto style in that little apartment crawlin' with rats, savin' quarters an' havin' to hide when the rent man come round." She laughed suddenly. "You know what Daddy Blue used to call 'em?"

"Call who? The rent men?"

"Naw, the rats. He'n mama didn't want to scare me so they called 'em 'big mice'. But I knew they was rats."

"You were sayin' about grandma..." Calvin prompted her. Venetia's face clouded over, the smile disappearing like a feeble winter sun behind a thunderhead.

"Your grandma just wanted to do like a preacher's wife should. Whatever the Reverend said, that was what she said too. Talkin' to her just like talkin' to him, 'cept he the one made all the decisions. If she didn't know what he wanted, she just said, 'Ask your daddy.' It was like I didn't matter no more. She was a preacher's wife, I was a preacher's daughter. Nuthin' more than that. Like I wasn't my own person no more.

"An' if I was mean to Adrienne, it was 'cause I thought she was like my own mama, just lookin' to latch onto some man was rich and famous people looked up to. I did girlfriend wrong there. She better to him than she been to herself." Venetia poured herself another cup of tea.

"Now the Reverend Holland got cold to my mama when she got pregnant and lost the baby. She couldn't have no more kids after that, couldn't give him no child of his own. All he had from her was me, and I wasn't even his. Oh, he was *mad*. Talkin' about how if he was a king in old England he could put a barren woman away, get someone else who could breed. Two wives and no kid of his own.

"The Reverend," she said, "was not a nice man. Wasn't a good man, either. Cheated on mama from the day she lost the baby right up to the day she died. And when I first started wanting to sing worldly music, he beat me so's I couldn't go out for a week. Then he told me that if I was going to do the devil's work, I wasn't gonna do it under his name. Said if I was gonna be a sinner like my no-good daddy, I had to do it under *his* name. So I went out an' I did it. I got what was mine, and I made *damn* sure no-one was ever gonna tell me no again.

"And you know what? I never have rode in a Lincoln Town Car ever since."

She looked straight at Calvin. "I always wondered why you took his name 'stead'a mine when you went out on your own."

He shrugged. "Didn't want to look like I was trading on your rep or Daddy Blue's. 'Holland' was just another name was there, so I took it." Calvin grinned. "Figure what I do, an' who I am, gonna be burning the old bastard's ass in whatever place he's ended up in."

Venetia chuckled, patted his knee. "Amen to that!" She leaned over, kissed his cheek, got serious again.

"But the reason I'm tellin' you all this is that much as I hated the Reverend, a lotta that church stuff stuck. Just 'cause he was a mean nasty hypocrite didn't mean the Lord's word was all wrong. Leviticus an' all'a that, you know? After everything I went through with the Reverend, I still call myself a Christian. I learned to accept Ramon an' my other people for who they are, an' I learned to love 'em dearly, but some things still come as a shock. 'Specially when it's your own kid.

"But you still my son. I love you, an' I'm proud'a you, an' I got your back no matter *what*.

"Now — " she sat back on the sofa, squared her shoulders. "Why you goin' public with all this now?"

Calvin gave her the short version of the beef with Screwdriver and Omega Man. "If I beat 'em to the punch'n put all this shit out there first," he concluded, "ain't nuthin' they can do to me." She kissed him again.

"You know what? They mess with you, they messin' with *me*. An' my name still count for somethin' in this bidness."

"Now I got to tell Daddy Blue. An' I got to tell Mick."

"Mick ain't gonna be a problem. Not with all the shit he's gotten up

244

to in his time. An' he's been around gay guys long as he been in the bidness. All he gonna say is, 'Yeah? So?'"

"How 'bout Blue?" She frowned.

"Don't be tellin' Blue *nuthin'*," she said, her voice hard and even, stone cold. "You know how frail he is. He just hardly holdin' on." She stared at him, hard. "All this time you been in the god-damn closet, now you got to start layin' this shit on an old man just about barely hangin' onto his life? Straight or gay or whatever the hell you are, you still a fool, an' a selfish fool at that."

He got up, stared back down at her. "Moms, the whole reason this family's fucked up as it is is 'cause we all been lyin' to each other my whole life. You lied to me about why I had to grow up without a father. Blue lied to both of us 'bout what he knew about who my daddy was. Mick an' Blue been lyin' to each other about what went down between you'n Mick. Thirty-plus years'a lies.

"What this whole thing's about is that all this lyin's finally got to stop. I can't come true 'bout who I am an' not tell Blue. Even sick as he is, he's still strong enough to hear the muthafuckin' truth... for a god-damn change. Y'all can keep lyin' if you want. I ain't havin' no more of it."

Calvin slammed out of the room. He heard her call out to him as he stormed down the hall, but whatever she was saying was swallowed by the thick soundproofing.

As he waited for the valet to bring his ride around to the front, his mobile rang. "You sure you want to tell Daddy Blue, right?" Venetia asked. "Well, you got a couple hours before it's time for us-all to go to work. You wanna talk to him first, you better get your ass movin' else Adrienne gonna be mad at you.

"An' trust me. You don't want that."

Adrienne answered the door in sweated-up workout gear, looking a little surprised.

"Someone changed the clocks without telling me?" she asked. "I thought no-one was due 'til one. Then Mick and Simon show up and twenty minutes later you arrive..."

Shit, Calvin thought, I wanted the old man to myself and now it's like Grand Central Station in here. "How's Grampop?"

Adrienne made a face. "No better, no worse. He's had his meds and he's just having his breakfast. When he's through Maudie's gonna give him his physio, then he got to rest some more to get his strength up for this afternoon."

Calvin said, "I need to talk to him. "

Adrienne frowned. "Lemme just check with Maudie. Hell, most'a the time I practically need to make an appointment to talk to him myself."

"Few minutes is all I need."

She shrugged. "Few minutes is about as much as you'll get. Let me refer this to a higher authority. There's some coffee in the kitchen fresh brewed." She sauntered off to the bedroom. Calvin ambled into the kitchen, helped himself to a cup, didn't do more than sip at it, standing up at the counter. If the old man cool as moms was, he thought, I ain't got nuthin' to fear in this world. Bring them yardies on, let 'em do their worst. Another voice inside him sneered: and what if he ain't? What if he gonna treat you like you really deserve? What if he have another stroke or a heart attack?

What if you kill him with this? Whatchoo gon' do then, lickle weak paleface batty-boy?

Adrienne was back. From the hall Calvin heard Maudie's footsteps, the bathroom door opening and closing. "Okay, Maudie says you got ten. And you're not to upset him."

Calvin forced a grimace. "Like I would."

"Yeah, like you would," Adrienne shot back. She wasn't smiling. Calvin shrugged apologetically, but she turned on her heel, led him to the bedroom, shoved the door open, stalked away to finish her interrupted workout. Then she turned back to face him.

"You set him back any," she said, "and you and me are gonna have ourselves a talk." She was even more not smiling than she'd been before.

Blue was prone on Maudie's massage table, head resting on folded arms, a towel draped over his butt, a forest of acupuncture needles sticking out of his back. He was so skinny that Calvin couldn't figure out how he had enough flesh left to hold the needles in place. He looked up as Calvin came in, cracked a smile.

"Hey, young man," he said. "How you doin'?"

"Doin' good, grampop," Calvin told him.

Blue raised an eyebrow. "But...?" He registered Calvin's surprise. "I can tell by your face that you got youself some kind'a 'but'. What's on your mind, young man?"

Calvin exhaled.

"Go 'head on, son," Blue said. "Nuthin' you can tell me I ain't ready to hear."

"Okay," Calvin said. "Okay." Even after coming out to the team at the office and his moms, it seemed to be getting harder rather than easier. He chest tightened. For a second he thought he was actually going to pass out. He rested one hand on the counter to steady himself. His mouth was suddenly dry.

"This is somethin' everybody gonna know soon, but I wanted you to hear it direct from me." Blue was listening intently. "For a good few years now I've had me a gay life goin' on. I deal with women, but sometimes there's men, too..."

Calvin broke off. Blue was laughing. The acupuncture needles in his back quivered like leaves in a breeze.

"Grampop?"

He thinks this is *funny*?

"You know I always wondered about that," Blue told him. "An' I wondered if you was ever gonna tell me."

"Why'd you think that?" Calvin asked.

"Don't know. Just a feelin', I guess. I been around a long time, seen a lot of things. Learned some stuff along the way. An' I don't pay that shit no nevermind. Never did, never will. All I care about is if someone's a good person or not. You got yourself a few problems, but then everybody does. There's nuthin' wrong with you a little more living ain't gonna cure.

"I guess you know my daddy was a preacher. Mean ol' man. *Oh*, he was mean. Raised me up to be afraid'a faggots. Hated 'em. Called 'em 'abominations unto the Lord.' Said they was even worse sinners'n blues singers! But so much of what he tried to teach me was wrong, or just didn't sit right with me an' my own feelin's, that I had to turn my back on those teachings and go find my own way in the world. Everywhere I went, I would test those teachin's against what I could see around me. An' everywhere I went those teachin's come up short. All them different kinds'a people he said I had to hate!

"I always liked me love better'n hate. Oh sure, there was specific peoples I didn't like, but they come from all over. And out of every class of people, there was good ones and bad. Hell, I even liked me a record company boss once! And he was gay, too!

"'Course, we didn't say 'gay' back then. We said 'queer' or 'faggot' or 'sissy.' You wanted to rank someone out, you said 'god-damn faggot cocksuckin' sonofabitch'. That was just about the worst thing you could call a man, call him a cocksucker. You could get yourself shot callin' someone that."

"Still can," Calvin said. "But I don't suck no cock. I *get* my cock sucked. I don't give it up, I give it out." Blue laughed again. Behind him, Maudie silently re-entered the room, clocked the situation, glided back out on slippered feet.

"You think that makes a difference?" Blue asked. "You talkin' like them cats in the penitentiary now. 'Oh, I don't do that. I'm still a man.' Whether you pitchin' or catchin', it's all gay stuff, it's all the same... but it ain't wrong, an' you still a man. And the men you go with, they still men, too." A thought struck him. "You don't go with no little kids, do you?"

"No, grampop. I don't take no children. Young men, yeah, but..."

"Long as you don't mess with no children, you ain't doin' nuthin' wrong," Blue told him. "Shit, this ain't nuthin' new. You be surprised how many fellas from the old days was gay. There was even an old song from back then, Sissy Man Blues, went somethin' like, 'If you can't send me a woman, Lord, send me a sissy man.' Sang it myself a few times.

"I used to know this cat name Baby Boy Clark. Played harp. Little bit'a git-tar, but mainly harp. You ever hear'a him?" Calvin shook his head. "Yeah, ol' Baby Boy Clark. That really was his name. His mama just a kid when she had him, died givin' birth, papa long gone, nobody to name him. That was all it said on his birth certificate: Baby Boy Clark. Grew up in an orphanage down in Jackson, Miss'ssippi. Kept that name his whole life. He was gay. Some'a the time, anyway.

"Sang about nuthin' but women, though. Sang about women *all* the time. Those was different times."

Not that different, Calvin thought. Not that muthafuckin' different at all.

TWENTY-SEVEN

"Like my old mum used to say," Mick Hudson was telling Simon Wolfe out back at Blue's by the hot tub, basking in the morning sun, "it never pains but it roars."

"Bollocks, man!" Simon retorted. "You told me your mum never said anything except 'another cucumber sandwich, vicar?' or 'isn't that awfully loud, Michael?' Sounds more like Henry's mum. Or Henry, come to that."

Hudson shrugged. "Same difference. I always thought of Henry as a surrogate mum."

Simon looked at him keenly. "So if Henry's your mum and Blue's your dad, it's no wonder you turned out all peculiar."

"Yeah, well... Blue taught me my music and Henry looked after me. If it hadn't been for Blue I'd've ended up a librarian or a civil servant, and without Henry I'd probably be..."

"Broke, dead or behind bars?"

"Or all of the above."

"Forget it, la. The only way middle-class Home Counties boys like you end up in nick is if you get pissed and kill someone with a car, or forget to pay your taxes for about ten years."

"You're flexing your scally roots again, son," Hudson said, grinning.

Hudson's hair was growing back in nicely, stone white but almost thick enough now to hide the scars on his scalp.

"Barnet's looking good," Simon told him. "Reminds me of this mate I used to have back home. Aussie geezer, worked at EMI in the seventies. Had a little freak-out once and shaved his head. Told me that while it was growing back there was one week when it was the best haircut he'd ever had."

From inside the house they heard Calvin shout, "Yo! Get the old white guys in here!" before Adrienne popped her head around the back door to say, "Sounds like class is back in session." As she led the way to the music room, they could hear Venetia quietly singing to Blue in the bedroom. He had seemed a little stronger today, still sleeping a lot of the time but more focussed and lucid when he was awake. He also seemed to have perked up since he'd had his little chat with Calvin.

While Blue dozed or rested, Venetia would sit by his side holding his

249

hand, singing him just about every song she knew: his old hits, hers, Broadway standards, old blues and soul ballads, gospel songs, anything. When something she sang caught his fancy, he would squeeze her hand back and sing along, his voice still tuneful even when he was hard-pressed to pump up the volume above a whisper. Maudie Lam sat in the corner, one eye watchfully monitoring her patient, the other on her knitting, needles busily clicking away. Adrienne didn't have the faintest idea what Maudie was knitting, or whom it could conceivably fit, except that it was bright red with an intricate pattern picked out in gold thread.

As she passed the bedroom, she called in through the open door. "You ready to do a little work?"

"May not be ready, but I'm willin'," Blue said, and Venetia wheeled him into the music room. He was wearing pyjamas and a robe. A tube attached to a catheter snaked from one leg of his pyjama trousers. Simon and Hudson fell into line behind him.

"Y'arright, boss?" Simon asked.

"As I'll ever be," Blue said.

They assembled in the music room. Calvin was looking pleased with himself. "Sorry 'bout the delay, y'all," he said, "but me and Frank were havin' some trouble with the broadband link. Got it goin' on now, though." On the monitor Frank the engineer gave them an A-OK sign from behind the mixing desk at the studio.

"First off," Calvin said, "we got all the stuff y'all cut in the studio." They listened to the playbacks, Hudson and Blue with eyes closed, Venetia scribbling notes. When the music ended, she straightened her reading glasses, said, "Dunno 'bout y'all, but I reckon Telephone Bill and Smile When You Say That could use some horns. I got some good brass players in my band, and me an' my tenor man can write some charts."

A moment's silence, then Hudson said, "Sounds fine to me the way it is."

"That's 'cause you just a rock and roll guy," Venetia flared. "All you know is guitars. If the guitar is cool, you happy. I know what I'm talkin' 'bout. Those cuts need horns!"

"Whoa! Whoa! Easy up!" Calvin intervened. "Let's consider this. Grampop, what you think?"

"I like horns," Blue said. "Always have. Neesha, go 'head with that."

Venetia licked the tip of her forefinger, drew an imaginary mark in the air, smirked at Hudson. He mock-scowled, shook his fist at her.

"Okay," Calvin said. "Now we got that new song my pops wrote, Sign Language On The Radio. I'm'a play you the studio track with the vocal grampop did here." He launched the playback. They listened in silence.

"Gentlemen! Suggestions!" Hudson said in his Jean-Luc Picard voice.

"Most'a that's pretty good," Blue said, "but I'm'a do the last verse again." They listened to it again.

"I reckon the mid-eight could be better," Neesha said.

"You right," Blue told her, "But I'm'a do the last verse first and then try the mid-eight." But even listening to the music had tired him, and his voice was crackling with fatigue. Maudie Lam had entered the room during the playback, and now she said, "You not sing until you have rested a little more. Sing in an hour." And she wheeled him back to the bedroom. As they disappeared into the corridor, Blue was saying, "There was one time Howlin' Wolf was cuttin' in London and they had a kidney dialysis machine right there in the studio..."

True to her word, Maudie brought Blue back just over an hour later. He nailed the final verse in two takes and the mid-eight in one, but by then he was exhausted again. This time half an hour's rest was sufficient, and they started checking out the remaining tracks.

The version of Burnin' Hell they'd cut at the house with just Blue, Hudson and Venetia playing together received a universal thumbs-up just as it was, all five and a half minutes of it. There were a few other jams Calvin had recorded at odd moments: Blue and Hudson on acoustic guitars playing Key To The Highway, Stagolee and a hair-raisingly eerie version of Skip James's Devil Got My Woman, plus Venetia's storming, show-stopping take on Ray Charles's Drown In My Own Tears, cut with the band on the second studio day, topped off with an incendiary Hudson guitar solo and needing only brass and a lead vocal contribution from Blue to qualify it for inclusion on the album.

"You cool, grampop?" Calvin asked.

"Sound beautiful," Blue responded.

"Okay," Calvin said. "Now we need you to sing." They listened as Venetia sang the first two verses. Hudson was worried that the contrast between her bravura performance and Blue's flagging energies would drop the song in its tracks, but when Blue hit the mid-eight — the part that begins, "*I know it's true/that into each life/some rain must fall*" before taking the final verse and riding it all the way out over Venetia and Hudson's backing vocals— there wasn't a dry eye in the house. But he was utterly drained by the effort, and by the time the playback ended he had passed out in his chair. Casting a venomous glance at Calvin, Maudie wheeled him back to the bedroom.

No-one had noticed Adrienne enter the room. Now she approached Calvin.

"I need to talk to you out back." She led him outside, sat him down by the tub. Her eyes were aflame. Her brows had drawn together and down. Veins were standing out thick and pulsing on her neck and arms. She looked down to kill.

"Calvin, what the fuck you doin'? Don't you see you killin' my husband right before my eyes?"

"He dyin' already, an' I'm doin' just 'xactly what he wants me to do," Calvin said. "He want to make this record. He want it more than I do, more than you do, more than my moms and my pops do." A part of Calvin noted that he was getting used to referring to Mick Hudson that way. "Now my moms and my pops both done produced records, but they singers'n songwriters first, much as they play piano'n guitar. I'm the on-liest one here who a producer by trade. I ain't a blues man. I don't sing. I don't play no guitar or no piano. What I do is I make records. That's what I'm doin' right now. I'm workin' for my grampop, an' what he want me to do is to make this record for him while he still able to do his thing. An' if that mean workin' him hard, then I'm'a do it."

"Blue ain't one'a them no-talent teenagers you got rich off of, so don't treat him like..."

"That ain't what I..."

"I'M STILL TALKIN'!" Adrienne snarled. Calvin flinched. Even the vines climbing the back of the house seemed to tremble. Calvin thought, *damn, my grampop must be some kind of a man, old as he is, to keep a woman this strong so sweet all the time.*

Adrienne seemed as startled by her own outburst as Calvin was. She took a deep breath, leaned forward and patted his knee. "Look... I know what you're doing, and I know why you're doing it. My momma didn't have no stupid daughters. But you're still pushing him too hard. How much more d'you need him to do?"

Calvin shrugged. "Not too much now. Bits'n pieces. A line here, a line there. We got the major stuff. Far as singin's concerned, we just cleanin' up a little. But we got a real problem with one of his guitar parts."

"Then you *really* got a problem," Adrienne told him. "Since he had that stroke, he ain't playin' no more guitar. Not now, not *ever*."

"We'll burn that bridge," Calvin said, "when we come to it."

They broke for a couple of hours before Maudie would consent to bring Blue back in. "No more singing today," she scolded. "Listen a little, but *no sing!*"

"Now we got us a treat," Calvin said, grinning his face off and spreading his hands like a conjuror. "For my next trick, we proudly present, ladeez'n'gemmun..." He hit another key, and suddenly the room was filled with the strains of Down South The Hog Is Man's Best Friend. It sounded very different from the snippet he'd recorded Blue and Venetia performing in the house a few days earlier. What they'd done originally was little more than a minute long: two verses with a collapse into laughter at the end of the second verse. Calvin and Hudson had cut a couple of overdubs during some downtime, and now the original performance — Blue playing guitar, he and Venetia singing — had been embellished with Hudson playing a boomy, striding Leadbelly-style twelve-string guitar and a keening wacky almost-sloppy-but-not-quite slide line on the resonator. Calvin had also extended the tune by doubling up the original performance and separating the repetitions with a slide-guitar solo. For the finishing touch, Calvin had bled out the extremes of the original digital recording's frequency range so it became thin and tinny, and then added clicks, pops and crackles so that the whole thing ended up sounding like a beat-up 78 of some ancient field recording from the Twenties or Thirties. He'd even left in the laughter at the end.

It was a small miracle. Everyone applauded, even Blue, beating the armrest of his wheelchair with his still-functioning right hand.

"'Fraid that's all the good news," Calvin said when the applause and high-fiving subsided. "Here come the bad news." Laying hands to keyboard, he pulled up a menu, made a selection and double-clicked it. When the new screen appeared on his monitor, he hit a few keys and kicked off the playback.

It was Hellhound On My Trail, Blue's original vocal and guitar performance from the jam session at the house set to a backing track Hudson and Venetia had cut with Furball and Kenny in the studio. Furball playing the exact drum part Calvin had human-beat-boxed to him, Kenny dropping a deep slow pulse into the churning groove, Venetia adding sparse, ominous piano chords, Hudson playing a funkier, more clipped version of his original riff and overdubbing molten-lava fills and a solo like a distant scream. The vocals were working, too: the combination of urgency and fatigue in Blue's voice almost unbearably poignant against Venetia and Hudson's spooky faraway harmonies.

The problem was Blue's resonator slide guitar part. Cut during the jam session at the house, with Hudson constantly adjusting his own pitch and tempo to fit in with what Blue was doing, it had sounded superb. But heard against the steady, constant pitch and pulse of the studio band, it was clear that Blue's frailty was seriously affecting his ability to execute on his instrument what he was hearing in his head. Of course Blue knew exactly what to play. He always had, and he always would.

But Mississippi Delta slide guitar is weird, mystical shit. It's all down to nuances. Nuance of pitch, because when you play with a slide you're no longer dealing with precise fretted semitones, like on a regular guitar, but all the quarter-tones and microtones in between. Only the sensitivity of your ear and your precise control of where your hand is at can put you in the right place at the right time. And nuance of time, and an exquisite awareness of the exact degree of pressure and vibrato you apply to the metal or glass tube on your finger.

Then Calvin drove the blade home. He cued the track back to the top, hit the 'solo' button on the track dedicated to Blue's guitar. This time, Blue's guitar came in and played by itself, without the band or any of the vocals. It was clunky: out of tune, out of time, every happening lick followed by two that weren't. It came down to this: one of the world's greatest living bluesmen was sounding like a clumsy amateur. A clumsy, *white* amateur who couldn't hear where the note was at or feel where the beat should fall. It was stone pitiful.

Blue didn't say anything, just closed his eyes. None of the others said anything, either. They didn't need to. They were all musicians. They knew exactly what they were hearing.

With his right hand clenched into a fist, Blue started punching his paralysed left arm, harder and harder, like he was trying to punish it for letting him down, humiliating him like this, or maybe to wake it up so it could do what it was supposed to. Tears were coursing down his seamed old cheeks. Maudie caught his arm, stopped him punching himself.

"We done for today," he said eventually, and motioned for her to take him back to the bedroom. Venetia, Hudson and Calvin sat in silence for a moment.

"I could replace the part," Hudson suggested. "Use Blue's guitar, play

it in his style. It won't be *exactly* the way he'd do it, but it'll be close...
and we can credit him."

Calvin shook his head. "Nuh-uh," he said. "We ain't givin' up on this
one yet. Why don't y'all take a break, call it a night? I got me some work
to do here." He clamped on a pair of headphones, leaned over his laptop,
started tapping keys.

Ray was saying, "Still don't feel too great about this, man."

An upstairs room in a nondescript motel on Santa Monica Boulevard.
Drab yellow walls, faded burgundy furnishings and bedspread, big old
TV set with missing control knobs and a picture like a neon migraine.
Screwdriver, Omega Man and Big Ray were holding a council of war,
surrounded by bottles of rum and wraps of primo ganja provided by two
of the Jamaicans' LA bredrin: no fuckin' way was Ray using any of his
own people for this. Funkenstein was a big hulking muthafucka with a
messed-up face, Cash Money was small and dapper with a smile lots of
girls found really sweet. They'd pulled out a crack pipe when they arrived, as well, but Ray had nixed that: said it was gonna stink the place
out and he didn't want anybody in the hall passing by the room noticing
the smell. Screwdriver had his iPod hooked up to a charging dock with
built-in speakers, and they were playing their album, the one that was
supposed to have been their Lock N Load debut.

Omega Man sighed, exhaling a cloud of smoke.

"Mi bredda," he said, "Remember where you come from. You was
born backayard, in Nine Mile, where Bob from. Your fada, mi fada, dem
was bredrin. I and I is your blood. You mus' do dis ting nuh. No one can
do dis ting but you."

Ray was silent a moment, letting his face settle into the impassive
mask he always threw up when he hadn't made up his mind.

Omega Man's voice was more urgent now. "Wi started, wi mus' finish. Seen? Wha'ever you owe dis man, you owe the I more. Blood, mi
bredrin. Blood."

Ray dropped his gaze, whispered, "Shit."

A beat. Then:

"Okay. Sucker can't keep no secrets from me, I know every damn
thing about him... Bossman don't suspect a thing," Ray said. "Feets said
his piece just fine. Boss got me chasin' all round South Central, trackin'
down this gangbanger don't exist, name'a Ghostbuster, the one Feets

said give him the key. 'No boss, he ain't been around. They said he stayin' at his grandmas's, but she ain't seen him in a week.' 'Yo, stay on it, dawg.'

"Here's how it's gonna go. I got two'a my boys on security, watchin' the house Calvin gonna be at. Tomorrow mornin', nine o'clock, I'm'a go up there pull 'em out, say I got two new guys can take a few shifts, let 'em book for the day. That'll be your two buddies. Okay? Then I'm'a tell Calvin an' them that there's different guys on today. Then I'm'a split. After that, it's up to you to do whatever you wanna do."

"Battyman battyman nine-one-one," the Jamaicans chanted along with their recorded voices. Ray shook his head.

"I been LAPD, an' I done time. I know how it go. If a faggot disrespect you, he get himself a beatdown. That's the way it is, been that way for years, ain't a damn thing changed. But I got to say one thing. The man was good to me, gave me a break when I was down flat on my ass, trusted me when no-one else would. You wanna give him an ass-whuppin', go 'head. He earned it. But cousin or no, I got me some conditions.

"You don't use no weapons, an' you don't go inside the house. Pick him up outside, goin' in or comin' out, but you do *not* go in. That's his gramps' place. His gramps an old man, an' he dyin'. He's a great man of the blues, and you ain't gonna fuck with him or his family. His wife an' kid's in there, an' a Chink nurse an' Calvin's dad. Old white guy, rock musician. You ain't gonna fuck with them, neither. *None* a'them. You bust a cap, you go into the house, I'm'a hunt your yardie asses down myself. An' I'm a nigga you do *not* wanna fuck with. Y'all cool with that?"

Omega Man chuckled. "Seen I." They touched fists. Ray got to his feet.

"Okay, y'all. Enjoy your party. Check you out tomorrow. An' don't forget what I said."

"Arright boss," said Screwdriver. Ray touched fists with the four once more and let himself out. As soon as the door closed behind him, Screwdriver turned to Cash Money. "Y'ave wha' wi need?"

Cash smiled. "I got it." He reached into his bag, pulled out a Smith & Wesson nine-mil ten-shot automatic in a leather holster. He handed it to Screwdriver. Screwdriver racked the slide, squinted down the sight. Cash Money busted out the crack pipe, dropped in a rock, fired it up, took a draw, passed it to Omega Man. The music ended. Another song took over: not one of theirs, but a Jamaican hit from a few years back, one of their favourites. Once again, they chanted softly along with the music.

"*Boom boom bye in a batty-boy head...*"

In dreams:

Hudson can hear Blue singing as he walks through the dusty small-town streets and approaches the prison. He is playing an acoustic twelve-string guitar. It was one of his old songs, County Jail, and Hudson had first heard it when he was still living at his parents' house. He remembers struggling to master the tricky riff on his crappy old guitar, singing the words over and over until his mother called up the stairs to make him stop.

"I'm sittin' here, locked down in the county jail,
Oohh yes, sittin' here, locked down in the county jail,
I'm cryin' please please, won't somebody go my bail.

"I'm in the county jail, but I ain't committed no crime,
I'm in the county jail, but I swear I ain't committed no crime,
Judge believe lies they told about me, so I'm'a have to do some time..."

Even though his air-conditioned Lincoln Town Car is parked only a couple of streets away, the Delta heat is merciless. Hudson's suit is already soaked with sweat by the time he enters the jailhouse.

"I'm here for Mr Moon," he says to the fat guard sitting with his feet up behind a cluttered desk, peering through his mirrorshades at a tattered old skin mag he's probably slavered over a hundred times or more. A big black dog snoozes on the floor beside him.

"Ain't no Mr Moon here," the guard tells him in a deep grating voice. "We got us a nigger Moon, though." He jerks a grimy thumb over his shoulder in the direction of the cells. "That's him right now, squealin' like a stuck pig."

Hudson reaches into his inside pocket, pulls out his wallet, extracts a credit card, slaps it down on the desk. The card is intricately worked in patterns of gold, platinum and silver, studded with exquisitely cut diamonds and rubies. Lit by its glow, the guard's office seems even dingier by comparison.

"I'm ready to make Mr Moon's bail," Hudson says. He emphasises the honorific 'Mister.'

The guard looks him up and down. "Oh you are, are you?" He closes

THE HELLHOUND SAMPLE

his skin mag and carefully places it on one side of the desk. "And what's a fine English gentleman such as yourself got to do with a nasty ol' no-'count nigger like him?"

"He's my father," Hudson says steadily. "I'm here to make his bail. This..." he taps the card "... should cover it, whatever it is."

Now Blue has stopped singing and playing. Other than Hudson's voice and the guard's, there is no sound in the jailhouse. The silence is so deep it practically hums.

The guard picks up the card and examines it closely. He opens a desk drawer, produces a scanning device and inserts the card. For a moment, the room fills with red light.

"Oh yeah," says the guard. "*Oh* yeah. This'll cover it all right. This card's valid for every damn thing you got."

"That's right," Hudson tells him. "Everything I've got."

"And that's exactly what this is gonna cost," the guard says. "Everything you got. Sign here." Hudson taps a PIN into the scanner's keypad, puts the card back in his wallet. The guard hauls his potbellied self to his feet, grabs a ring of keys from a hook behind him, and waddles out the back.

"Hey, nigger!" Hudson hears him shout as the key clicks in the lock on Blue's cell. "There's some limey asshole here made your bail. Pack your shit. You're leavin'."

The guard leads Blue out into the office. Blue walks with small, shuffling steps, as if he were still in leg-irons. He carries his twelve-string as if it's almost too heavy for him to lift comfortably. He turns to Hudson.

"I thank you, young man," Blue says. "I knew you'd be here for me in the end." Gently, Hudson embraces the old man's frail frame, pats him twice on the back.

"There's a car just over the road," Hudson tells Blue. "We can go anywhere you want."

"Nuh-uh," says the guard. He takes off his mirrorshades. His eyes flash in the darkness. "Ain't no 'we' goin' no-place. Nigger's free to leave, but you stayin' right here."

Hudson says, "What?"

The guard says, "You heard what I said. You signed off on the payment. His bail was for everything you got. And part of what you got's your freedom." The dog awakens, growls deep in its throat.

Hudson swallows, takes a step back. The wallet is still in his hand. He pulls out the card. It is nothing but dull plastic now. Something sharp has viciously scored through the magnetic strip on the back.

The guard says, "Payment's already gone through. That card ain't valid no more."

Hudson looks at Blue, doesn't say anything.

Blue looks down towards his feet.

Hudson says, "You knew, didn't you?"

Blue says, "Young man..." but Hudson waves him silent, tells him, "Go." The guard grabs Hudson by the suit collar at the scruff of his neck, bumrushes him into the cell Blue has just left, locks him down with a twist of the key. Hudson hits the floor in a heap, hears the outer door slam as Blue walks out to freedom. The guard leans against the wall, stares at him though the bars. The dog pads in from the office, settles down, whines once. It doesn't take its eyes off Hudson, either.

"Aw right, wee boy," says the guard. Hudson blinks. He knows that voice. "Yir gonny be here an awfy lang time. Ah bet yir gonny be missin' yir wee guitar pretty soon now." He is holding Hudson's old Telecaster. He strokes it affectionately. "Ah ded tell yu the aul' darkie's bail wuz for everything yeh goat, ded ah no'?" He reaches into his back pocket, pulls out a wad of ancient £10 notes, riffles through it to count them, tosses it through the bars into the cell, waddles back out towards his office, still holding the guitar. "Paid en full," he says. The dog stays where it is.

At the door the guard turns back for a moment. "Nuthan laik a guitar tae help a musician such as yirself pass the taime away. Yir sairvin' laife, an' yir taime gonny seem even longer wi'oot a guitar tae play yir wee tunes. Ah bin waitin' fae this a loang, loang taime." His footsteps trail back into the office. The dog stretches to its feet, stalks forward. It puts its snout between the bars, staring hungrily at Hudson. It starts to growl again.

And it doesn't stop, not even when Hudson's mother walks in, her sensible flatties tapping irritably on the filthy floor. She's wearing a pink blouse with a beige skirt, and her hair is permed and baked into a dull brown helmet. She looks at him pityingly. "Oh, *dar*-ling," she says. "Your father and I always *said* your obsession with this awful music would end in tears." She wrinkles her nose. "By the way, dear, that dog smells *dread*-ful. Is there anyone here we can ask to have it washed? And why is it growling like that?"

TWENTY-EIGHT

Josh brought Donna back to the house bright and early in the morning. He waved to Junior and Fat Stuff, Ray's security guys, but they didn't wave back. Probably asleep, Josh thought. Security my ass.

Adrienne was making coffee, robe over bikini, when they bounced in. "Hi, stranger!" she said to Josh, sweeping him and Donna into a three-way hug. Maudie looked up from her knitting long enough to give them a quick smile, then resumed her labours.

"Where is everybody?" Donna asked.

"Your dad's asleep," Adrienne told her, "and so's Calvin. He's been up all night working."

Donna tiptoed into the music room. Calvin was indeed fast asleep in his chair by the long counter, still wearing his headphones, head resting on folded arms, snoring lightly. Adrienne led Josh into the bedroom where Blue lay in the converted bed. It had been a couple of weeks since he'd last seen the old man, and he gasped at the sight of the tubes and bags festooning Blue's wasted frame.

"Jesus, mom... how long has he been like this?"

Adrienne squeezed her son's arm. "About a week now." Her voice was almost steady.

"Anyone heard from Charlene?"

"Nope. She ain't called us, her phone's cut off so we can't call her, her mama doesn't know where she is and since she never reads the papers, she probably doesn't even know he's sick."

"You want me to go down to South Central, see if I can find her?"

Adrienne laughed. "They'll eat you alive down there, college boy."

Josh looked at his watch. "Listen, mom, I've got class in half an hour so I better take off. But I'm gonna come back tonight and stay for a few days."

"That," Adrienne said, "would be very nice. You and Donna have a good time?"

"Sure we did. She's a great kid. I missed her a lot after I moved out."

"She missed you, too."

"Did *not*," Donna said. "He's old and boring just like you are." Adrienne took a pretend swing at Donna, who dodged nimbly out of range and headed giggling for her room.

Outside the house, Fat Stuff's phone was ringing, waking him up. He nudged Junior awake, looked at his watch. Eight-thirty. Shit, they'd been asleep for a couple of hours now. Ray would kill them if he'd seen them stacking up Z's in the car. He found his phone, tried to sound competent, alert and on the case.

"Yo."

"Fats, this is Ray. I got a couple of new guys to work the rest'a your shift. We'll be there in a half hour. Let 'em know in the house so they won't trip out if they see some brothers they don't know."

"Got it."

"Boss there yet?" Fats didn't know. Shit, he could've left while he and Junior were out for the count. He took a quick glance out the window, lamped the white Hummer, still parked exactly where it had been a few hours earlier, exhaled with a whoosh of relief.

"He never left, Ray-Ray. Been there all night."

"Arright. Later, blood."

Hudson and Venetia arrived together about twenty minutes later, Venetia driving rather than using her customary chauffeur. When Donna let them in, they were swapping drummer jokes.

"What do you call a psychopath who hangs around with musicians?" Hudson was asking.

"A rapper?"

"C'mon, rappers never hang around with musicians. They just sample 'em."

"Oh...kay, how many drummers does it take to change a lightbulb?"

"Eyyyyy, you can't-a fool-a me, eh boss," Hudson said in his Chico Marx voice. "One! Two! Three! Four!"

"Ain't surprised y'all know that joke, it's even older'n you are..."

Inside the house, Adrienne was gently shaking Calvin awake, wafting a steaming cup of coffee under his nose.

"'Sup?" he asked groggily.

"Nothing much. Your man Ray's gonna have a couple'a different guys outside today, so don't flip if you don't see Fat Stuff and what's-his-name. Blue's still asleep. Mick'n Neesha just arrived... and Donna's here."

Calvin slurped noisily at the coffee. "Whoa! What you put in this stuff?"

"Just coffee," she told him. "Colombian."

"Co-*lomb*-ian? Might'a known. Tastes like rocket fuel."

"You finish what you stayed up to do?"

"Believe it, grandma. Can't wait for everyone to hear it."

"That's good," she said seriously. "Soon as Blue's up we'll have a show-and-tell. Meantime, you could probably use a shower. In fact... *snf snf*... you could *definitely* use a shower. You got a change of clothes?"

"Yeah, out in the ride. I'll go get 'em."

"No, you ain't. You're going straight to the shower. Gimme your keys, I'll get Donna to go fetch. DONNA!"

"I'm in the bathroom!" came the faint reply.

"Okay, soon as she's out, you go in. Right now, I'll fix you some eggs. You want another coffee?"

"Not many, Benny," Hudson said from the doorway. "Your coffee's almost as good as drugs."

Outside, Ray was pulling up alongside Fat Stuff and Junior's ride. Screwdriver, Omega Man, Cash Money and Funkenstein were close behind in rented wheels. He got out, slammed the door, walked over to Fat Stuff's car.

"Okay, troopers, you're relieved," he told them. "Back here tonight at ten. 'Kay?"

"You got it, chief," Junior said. They pulled away. Funkenstein moved forward to park in the space they'd just vacated, rolled down his window. Ray leaned into the car.

"It's all yours," he said. "Just remember what the deal is. I still wanna have my job when this is done. You don't go in, an' you don't touch the family. Do anything different, an' you got me to deal with. An' trust me... you don't want no part'a that." They touched fists, and Ray walked back to his car, unlocked it, opened the door. Just as he was about to climb in, Screwdriver called him.

"Yo... Ray. Wan mo' t'ing."

Ray turned. "What?" Screwdriver was walking towards him.

"Jus' dis."

Screwdriver was holding the silenced Smith & Wesson. He shot Ray twice — *blap! blap!* — in the throat. Then Funkenstein was out of the car, too. He ran over to Ray's ride, reached in, popped the trunk. He helped Cash Money drag Ray's body to the back of his ride and stuffed him in the trunk. Funkenstein tossed the keys to Cash Money.

"Cash, lose the ride. Then call me." Cash Money nodded, climbed into Ray's car and screeched away. "Now we wait," Funkenstein said, climbing back into the front seat of his own wheels. "If he ain't come out by noon, we go in."

"Yahmon," Omega Man said. "We go in, an' we tek de bitch dung."

Screwdriver pulled out the crack pipe. "Seen I, star," he said softly. "I an' I tek de bitch *all* de way dung."

Suddenly Funkenstein nudged him, hissed, "Check it out." The front door of the house was opening. "Showtime," Screwdriver whispered and started to open his door, but Omega Man held him back.

It wasn't Calvin Holland coming out, but a pretty fourteen-year-old in shorts and a Fully Loaded tanktop, tossing and catching a set of car keys in one hand. "She lickle but she fit," Omega Man murmured. Funkenstein wasn't looking at the girl. He was staring at the splatter of blood in the driveway where Ray had fallen. She was walking right up to it...

... and she kept walking. She was humming to herself, completely unaware of her surroundings. She strolled up to Calvin's Hummer, unlocked it, climbed inside. She opened the glove compartment, pulled out a stack of CDs and started riffling through them. She selected a couple, then reached into the back seat, grabbed a white leather gym bag with a Fully Loaded logo, climbed out of the Hummer, slammed the door, relocked it and disappeared back into the house.

The men in the car exhaled, and settled in for what looked like it might be quite a wait. The dashboard clock read 9:57.

A few minutes after ten, Maudie wheeled Blue into the music room where Calvin, Venetia and Hudson were waiting for him. Calvin's fingers were hovering over his keyboard. On the big monitor, Frank was standing by in the studio.

"Mornin', grampop," Calvin said. "I think you're gonna like..."

"I got a few things I want to say," Blue cut right across him. These days, he was generally at his best in the mornings, and today, frail as he was, he seemed more focused than at any time since his stroke.

"First off, we gonna call the album *Paid In Full*." He looked around the faces in the room. No-one raised any objection. "Okay, cool. The credit is gonna read 'James "Blue" Moon And Family.'" Another scan of the room.

"Yeah, fine," Hudson said.

"No problem," Venetia chimed in.

"Yep." Calvin.

"An' it gonna say 'Produced by Calvin Holland, The Family an' Frank...' Hey, Frank, what's your last name?"

"Ingenio," Frank's voice crackled over the talkback. "Frank Ingenio."

"You're an engineer and your last name's Ingenio?" Hudson asked incredulously. On the monitor, they saw Frank turn his palms outwards and shrug.

"So sue my parents," he said.

"Yeah," Blue said. "That's how I want it."

"Then that," Venetia said, "is how it's gonna be."

Blue made as if to clap his hands, but only the right one moved. He let it drop to his knee. "One more thing," he said.

"I done travelled a lot. A *lot*. I ain't been *all* over the world, but I played in a lotta different places. I played Russia, Japan, Israel, Scandinavia, just about everywhere in Europe and you *know* I played everywhere in the United States got a place hold more'n twelve people. Every place I go, I listen to the music the folks live where I'm at make.

"An' all the places I ain't been, I listen to their music too. I heard Irish music, Chinese music, Arab music, Spanish music, Jamaican music, African music, a'course... an' everywhere I been or listen to, I hear the blues. I hear a little bit of the blues in every music of every peoples.

"Everybody get the blues. Everybody *need* the blues. An' everybody love the blues, though a lot of 'em don't know it. But not everybody *play* the blues. We do. This our special thing. This our gift to the world, somethin' we made outta our own troubles.

"I hear some folks say the blues is an African music, but a lotta African music don't sound nothin' like the blues. Other folks say the blues is American music, but a lotta American music don't sound like the blues.

"Hear me now. The blues is a music that could only have been made in America, but it took African peoples comin' here to create it. We African peoples been through some shit here in America, but that shit done been like fertiliser, and the blues is the beautiful flower the shit made grow. An' it grow for a *reason*.

"Now all y'all know I ain't a religious man." He grinned. "I done had trouble with the religious folk all of my life, startin' with my daddy..." he looked at Venetia... "with your mama, res' her soul, an' back in the day with you. But I always believed, an' I *still* believe, that the work I do, an' the work we been doin' together, is part of the fight for a better world. I watch the news once in a while, and everything I see says the world be getting' darker an' colder an' uglier all the time.

"But I believe in a better world. I might..." he grinned again "... find myself in a better world any minute now. I'm talkin' about a better world right here, on this Earth we all on together. Right here, right now, we fightin' the good fight, an' don't none'a you kids ever forget that." He raised his right hand, let it fall onto the armrest of his wheelchair.

"Awright, y'all, here endeth the god-damn sermon. I done talked myself out now," he said. He looked at Calvin. "Okay, young man. What you got for me?"

Calvin reached out, hit a key on his laptop. The sound of Blue's resonator track from Hellhound On My Trail filled the room, but it was longer clunky and clumsy and fucked-up. The intonation and pitch were clean and crisp, the rhythmic feel authoritative and driving. It sounded exactly like it should, exactly what Blue had been hearing in his head when he was playing it and trying to make his hands obey him. It sounded like James Blue Moon in his prime, hammering out the full-on Mississippi Delta blues.

"*Wow.*"

"Jeez..."

"Young man... what the hell you do?"

Calvin tapped another key. "Took some work, I tell ya."

"Bet it did," Hudson said. "Fuck, man, you're good."

"Okay," Calvin said. "Here's what I did. I went through what you did bar by bar, note by note. You didn't play *all* of it wrong, grampop. I found the parts you did right an' I copied 'em an' printed 'em over the parts that weren't so good. Moved things around a little. Used a little pitch correction, beat synchronisation, SMPTE code..."

"Sumpty-*what*?" Blue asked.

"Society of Motion Picture Technicians and Engineers... or somethin' like that, anyway. Use it a lot with MIDI stuff to keep everything in synch."

"Young man," Blue said, "get your ass over here." Calvin walked over to Blue's wheelchair, dropped down on one knee. Blue reached over with his good arm and, with surprising strength, pulled the younger man to him. "You saved my ass," he whispered. "You lettin' me go out on my feet, go out soundin' *strong*. You done give me back my dignity. Young man... I can't thank you enough."

Calvin kissed his grandfather on the cheek. "I got your back, grampop. Always will." He straightened up, moved back to his laptop. Venetia hugged him.

"Let's hear that again with the whole track," Hudson said.

"I can do a little better than that," Calvin told him. He clicked a few onscreen buttons, pulled down a menu, made a selection and double-clicked it. "Frank... I'm uploading to you now. You ready?"

"Whenever you are," Frank said. He pressed a button on his mixing desk, raised a thumb. "Go." With a flourish, Calvin hit 'enter' and the music started to play.

The first thing they heard was a single urgent, tremulous slide-guitar note and a thin, haunting voice. It wasn't Blue, or Mick Hudson. It was Robert Johnson.

"*I been shamed by my rider,*" the voice sang. Beat. Pause. Then again: the single note, and the voice: "*I been shamed by my rider...*" Then in came Furball's funky drums as the Robert Johnson sample repeated yet again, and again. Finally, Blue's resonator, playing the song's introduction. Then Blue's voice, singing the lines he'd first heard outside old man Birnbaum's store in Clarksdale three-quarters of a century before.

"*Got to keep moving, got to keep moving, blues falling down like hail. Got to keep moving, got to keep moving, hellhound on my trail.*"

With the second verse, Hudson's funk-blues riff came in behind Blue's voice and resonator, joined by Kenny's bassline and Venetia's piano chords. Then the instruments dropped out, except for Furball's drums, now compressed and distorted, and another Johnson sample. "*Help poor Bob if you please,*" now joined by Hudson and Venetia, singing a keening, astringent harmony.

"*If today was Christmas Eve, if today was Christmas Eve, and tomorrow was Christmas Day,*" they sang, and then Blue's voice, langorous, drawling, intimate, as if he was murmuring right in your ear: "*Awwwww... wouldn't we have a time, baby.*"

Then the band crashed back in, Hudson's guitar riding high and lonesome over the groove, wrenching screams and sighs from his strings as the compressed drums and pulsebeat bass crunched along and Robert Johnson's voice called out in pain and fear from the depths of the mix, reverberating down across the decades to fuse with Blue and Hudson's guitars. Somewhere a key turned in a lock, but it was impossible to say whether the door was opening or closing, whether something was going out or coming in.

The psychic storm kept building, Blue's weary drawl backed by Hudson and Venetia's spooky harmonies and the dark, menacing undertow of the band until a final, slamming downbeat cut the music off, leaving only Robert Johnson's single vibrating note quivering in the silence. Calvin hit a key to stop the playback.

"You got that?" he asked Frank.

"All of it," Frank told him. "Man, that was something."

"Certainly fucking is," Hudson said. "Play it again." Calvin played it again. Blue was silent, but smiling. Venetia was moving to the music in her chair. Hudson paced the room, eyes closed, stroking his chin. When the playback ended, he picked up his guitar, plugged it into Blue's little Fender amp.

"I just had this idea," he said. "A little extra bonus riff for the end." He struck a few notes, frowned, then played the lick again, slightly altering the rhythmic emphasis. "Play it back again from the last verse," he told Calvin.

Calvin cued up the final section, kicked the track. Hudson started to play along with the music. Blue listened critically.

"That sound good," he said. "One more time, same place."

Calvin hit 'record.'

The time was 11:57.

Cash Money had been back for around half an hour now. He'd ditched Ray's ride, with Ray still in the trunk, and gotten one of his homies to drop him back off outside Blue's house. Now they sat in the car, watching the clock tick down to high noon.

12:00.

"Tek de bitch dung," Omega Man said.

"Tek de bitch dung," Screwdriver repeated. He checked the Smith & Wesson one more time.

They touched fists, got out of the car.

Cash Money ambled up to the front door and rang the bell.

TWENTY-NINE

Adrienne in the hallway, listening to the music through the closed door and about to go in and join the others, hears the doorbell ring. She goes to answer it.

"Who is it?" she calls.

"Miz Moon?"

"That's me."

"I'm Cash," she hears. "I work with Ray. We think you got an intruder. Could you open the door?"

And Adrienne, distracted, her head still full of the music, opens the door. On the doorstep, she sees a small man in a Fully Loaded sweatshirt with a sweetly ingratiating smile on his face. Behind him is a big guy with a whole bunch of scars and pockmarks... who suddenly shoulders the door all the way open and lands a looping roundhouse punch on Adrienne's right cheek, sending her careering back down the hall. The back of her head crunches into the wall and she flops like a rag doll.

Just before she passes out, Adrienne sends out a desperate mental message, *Donna, honey, stay in your room, don't make a sound, please...*

"Cash, you're on lookout," Funkenstein says. He motions Screwdriver and Omega Man forward into the house, Screwdriver taking the lead with the Smith & Wesson. Omega Man looks down at Adrienne, sprawled unconscious in the hallway, face beginning to swell, blood seeping from the back of her head, her robe fallen open. "She old but she fit, yunno star," he murmurs admiringly.

"Leave it, dawg!" Screwdriver snaps at him. They move through Blue's house, throwing open each door as they come to it. In the living room they find a plump middle-aged Chinese woman peacefully knitting on the sofa. Screwdriver snarls, "Move, coolie bitch!" He jams the gun to Maudie's head, shoves her out of the room ahead of them, still clutching her knitting.

Omega Man opens up the next door. Looks like a teenage girl's bedroom, posters of Aaliyah and Kanye West on the walls, stuffed animals, Barbie dolls. That's empty, too...

Cowering behind the door, shivering, Donna hears her own breathing and heartbeat so much louder than the music that she can't believe they don't hear her... but they move on.

Blue and Adrienne's bedroom... empty. Kitchen and bathrooms... empty. Guest bedroom... empty. Everybody in the house got to be in the end room where the music's coming from.

Funkenstein kicks the door open, shoves Maudie into the room ahead of him. Screwdriver moves up front with the gun. Omega Man follows.

There was the bitch! Nobody else in the room looked like they were any threat. An old man in a wheelchair, looking practically dead, all drips and tubes. A fat old woman. Another old guy, white, pipecleaner skinny, short white hair. No problem.

"Cut de music!" Screwdriver shouts. Calvin taps the spacebar on his MacBook, and the room falls silent.

In the studio on Sunset Boulevard, Frank Ingenio hears the music stop, looks up at the monitor carrying the webcam feed from Blue's music room, sees a stranger with a gun. "Jesus *fuck*," he mutters, remembering just in time to press the mute button on his talkback mic so he won't be heard at the other end. He reaches for the phone, punches in 911, hopes to God he gets a human operator rather than on-hold music or an answering machine.

Screwdriver aims the Smith & Wesson straight at Calvin.

"Lickle weak paleface batty-boy, y'wan play games wid we now?"

Calvin slowly pushes his chair back, climbs to his feet. The old man in the wheelchair rolls forward to flank him. He looks up at Screwdriver.

"Young man, you in my house," he says. "An' the onliest one allowed to run around gettin' crazy with a gun in my house is me. So why don't you get your yardie asses outta here 'fore there's trouble?"

Screwdriver laughs. "Old man," he says. "Wha' kind'a trouble you give we?"

Sprawled in the chair into which Funkenstein had shoved her, Maudie Lam carefully draws one needle free of her knitting.

Venetia Moon has one hand reaching down into her bag, on the floor beside her chair. She often carries a vial of pepper spray, and she's hoping that this is one of the days she remembered to pack it.

Turning slightly so that his guitar and the left side of his body mask the movement of his right hand, Mick Hudson rolls the volume control of his guitar all the way down. He pulls the jack plug of his guitar cord out of its socket, praying that the old amp won't crackle as he does so.

He drops the cord, coughing to cover the sound of the metal plug hitting the hardwood floor. Then he unclips the strap from the butt end of the guitar. *Thank fuck I went to the loo twenty minutes ago*, he thinks, *because it feels like me bum's gone.*

Hearing the cough, Omega Man looks over at him, but sees nothing amiss. He looks back at Screwdriver.

"Mi bredda," he says. "Tek de bitch dung."

Screwdriver raises the Smith & Wesson, draws a bead on Calvin. "Boom boom bye," he says, "Chi-chi man fe bu'n." He pulls the trigger three times.

But Blue is standing now, the tubes of his catheter and drip trailing. He's between Screwdriver and Calvin, shielding his grandson with his body. He takes the bullets square in the chest. The impact sends him back into the wheelchair, which rolls backwards to crash into the wall. Maudie moves to go tend to him, but Funkenstein waves her back into her chair.

In the studio, Frank Ingenio is still hanging on the phone waiting for the fucking LAPD to pick up. But now he's recording the video feed from the webcam onto another hard drive.

Then there's a new voice from the doorway. A small, shaky, young voice.

"Nobody fucking move!"

Semi-crouched in the doorway, arms extended, both hands clutching her father's old Browning automatic, is Donna Moon. Her mouth is clamped in a hard tight line, her eyes are blazing. The muzzle of the gun points straight at Screwdriver. It is wavering, but not very much.

Omega Man starts to laugh. "Baby!" he says. "Lickle wan faastie!" He advances towards her, one hand out, palm up. "This big people's business here. Give I the pistol. Give it up nuh!"

Donna racks back the Browning's slide. "Shut the fuck up!" she snaps at Omega Man. She sees him moving up on her, but her aim doesn't shift away from Screwdriver.

Screwdriver sees something in Donna's eyes that Omega Man doesn't. He motions his partner back.

Adrienne crawls into view from the hallway. Her braids are matted with blood, and one eye is swollen shut.

"Blow his ass away!" she hisses at Donna.

Then several things happen at once.

Frank Ingenio finally gets through to an LAPD operator. He starts talking urgently into the phone.

Calvin puts everything he can remember from his years of martial arts training and every ounce of emotion bottled up in his soul into a high front kick which catches Screwdriver square in the mouth. He goes down hard, the Smith & Wesson flying from his grasp.

Venetia rolls forward, scoops up the gun, finishes Screwdriver off with a blast of pepper spray, clamps a fist around a clump of his dreadlocks and channels all the strength in her squat, thick-shouldered frame into smashing the back of his head down onto the hardwood floor, over and over again. "*Fuck* with my *dad* and my *son*?" she repeats through clenched teeth, perfectly in sync with the soggy impact of skull against floor.

Maudie Lam rises up from her chair, firmly grasping a knitting needle. With unerring aim, she jabs its point into the nerve-centre meridian in Omega Man's forehead, paralysing him instantly.

And Mick Hudson, who hadn't had a fight since he was thirteen and lost that one, moves forward swinging his unplugged, unstrapped old Telecaster like some axe-wielding CGI warrior from a Peter Jackson battle scene, crashing the butt of the guitar straight into Funkenstein's face, splintering his teeth and sending him to the floor. Leaving Screwdriver sprawled in his blood, Venetia gives the big man a supersize portion of pepper spray and then smashes his head against the floor a few times for good measure. Then she stands over Omega Man, aiming Screwdriver's gun right between his eyes.

"Just move once," she says. "*Please.*"

Hudson drops his guitar with a crash. The neck cracks, a hairline fracture just below the headstock, but he doesn't look back. He walks over to Omega Man and kicks him twice in the head.

Donna's collapsed in the doorway now, eyes staring, breathing like she'd just run a three-minute mile. Adrienne crawls to her, kisses her, gently extracts the gun from her daughter's nerveless fingers. She moves to eject the clip... and there isn't one.

"The gun was empty?" she says disbelievingly.

Donna nods, eyes still wide. She's even paler than Hudson.

"I knew where the gun was," she stutters, "but I couldn't find the bullets."

In the studio on Sunset, Frank reactivates the talkback mic.

"Cops and paramedics on their way," he says. "Everybody okay in there?"

Calvin seems like the only one who's heard him.

"Yeah," he says. He's in cold shock. "But those muthafuckas killed my grampops."

Frank says, "Jesus, man, the fuck was all that about?"

Calvin thinks for a second. Then his brows draw down low over his eyes. "Fuckin' Ray," he says. "Fuckin' Ray sold me to those assholes, and they killed my gramps. I'm'a find him, and I'm'a kill him *slow*."

Maudie over by Blue's body, checking his pulses.

"Don't know how," she says, "but Mr Moon still alive."

In the distance, they heard sirens. Suddenly, the house was swarming with cops and paramedics. Blue was eased onto a stretcher and carried out to a waiting ambulance. Adrienne shook off a para trying to tend to her injuries, grabbed Donna by the hand and ran for the ambulance, still barefoot in her bikini and bloodstained robe.

"C'mon," Calvin said to Hudson and Venetia, and sprinted for his Hummer. Outside they saw more cops dragging Cash Money away. For the first and only time in his life, Calvin was grateful for the LAPD's penchant for grabbing any brother they saw he looked like he was somewhere he shouldn't be and beating the crap out of him.

Sirens screaming, a convoy took off for Cedars-Sinai Hospital, the ambulance in the lead, Calvin following in the Hummer with Venetia and Hudson, a cop car bringing up the rear.

In the ambulance, the paras were still frantically working on Blue, Donna and Adrienne clinging onto each other, Adrienne holding Blue's cooling hand. She could see his eyes fluttering beneath his closed lids. His lips seemed to be moving, but she couldn't hear him over the hysterical scream of the siren, the rattle and rumble of the ambulance over the roads, the paramedics' urgent colloquy as they worked, the irregular beep of the heartrate monitor, the hiss of air from Blue's shattered chest.

Shouldering the lead para out of the way, she clasped Blue's hand tighter, put her ear close to his pallid lips.

"I'm here, honey," she whispered. "This is Adrienne. Me'n Donna are here with you."

She strained harder to hear. His lips moved again.

"Awwwww...."

"Yes, honey, yes..."

"Awwwwww.... Didn't we have a time, baby..."

Then the para was pulling her out of the way.

"We're losing him!" he shouted. "We're losing him...."

Adrienne saw Blue's lips move. She couldn't hear him, but it looked like he was asking, "Am I home?"

"Yes, honey," she tells him, "you're all the way home."

And the pulse of the monitor became a continuous whine...

In dreams:

James Moon, aged five, walks into Sam's Barber Shop. His daddy is leading him by the hand. Reverend Moon motions him towards the big chair where Sam is waiting with his clippers. Sam gives him a big smile.

"Welcome home, young man," he says. "Step right up and sit right down. You about to get the best haircut you ever had in your life."

His daddy helps him up into the chair. With a flourish, Sam ties the sheet around his neck and tucks it into his collar.

"You ready?" he asks.

James replies, "Yes sir, I'm ready." Grinning broad enough to split his face, he closes his eyes in anticipation.

... Flatline.

THIRTY

None of them were Jewish, but they sat shiva for Blue anyway. None of them were Irish, but nevertheless they held a wake.

The SOCOs — Scene Of Crime Officers — had been there, done their stuff and gone. Calvin had dialled up a clean-up crew who'd scrubbed most of the blood off the music room's floor and taken away the damaged furniture and computer equipment, but the room still reverberated with the aftershock of noonday nightmare, and so they'd ended up congregating in the living room. The guitars still stood in line, an abandoned honour guard for their departed master, behind the locked door.

Screwdriver, Omega Man and Funkenstein had been charged with murder one; Cash Money as an accessory to murder. Frank Ingenio had burned his webcam footage onto a DVD and handed it over to detectives, but only after deleting the footage of Venetia doing her basketball-bounce routine with Screwdriver and Funkenstein's heads.

Big Ray's car had been retrieved from the West Hollywood parking lot where Cash Money had ditched it, the security honcho's body still in the trunk. They'd be holding an autopsy tomorrow, and if the forensics and ballistics posse matched up the two bullets in Ray's body and the three in Blue's with Screwdriver's Smith & Wesson, then Ray would be added to Screwdriver and his bredrins' tab.

They were all there: Adrienne, Donna, Venetia, Calvin, Hudson and Simon Wolfe. Josh was there, too, and Frank Ingenio. Maudie Lam had packed up her massage table for the final time. Now it was leaned up against the wall in the hall by the front door, next to her medical bag and Hudson's cased guitars. Hudson had attempted to play a few songs on his acoustic guitar, but his heart wasn't in it, and neither was anybody else's.

Adrienne had formally and ceremoniously presented Donna with what she fondly but erroneously believed to be her daughter's first beer. Just about everybody else was drinking beer as well, apart from Maudie, who would be driving, and Calvin, who rarely touched alcohol. Hudson was using his as a chaser for his brimming glass of Jack, which he kept steadily replenished from the bottle by his side. Every so often there was a brief flurry of conversation, soon dying out to be replaced by the simmering in-shock silence which was their collective default mode.

Adrienne had put some music on the stereo, a few of Blue's greatest hits, but when the CD ended no-one moved to replace it.

"What a way for my daddy to go," Venetia said into the numbed silence. "Shot down like a dog in his own home by lowlifes like that."

"He died on his feet protecting someone he loved," Hudson said. "Got to be worse ways to go out than that. Could've just let his life drip away with the cancer."

"I should've been here," Josh said. It was the first time he'd spoken all night. "If I'd'a been here..."

"... they'd probably've done you first," Hudson finished his sentence for him. "They'd've seen you as a threat, big strong b..." He caught himself just in time. Hudson knew better than to apply the b-word to any African-American male above the age of ten, though, at his advanced age, just about anybody under thirty-five with the appropriate chromosomes qualified as a boy. "... young fella like yourself. Only thing would've been different if you'd been here is we'd've lost you as well."

"An' they were only here 'cause of me," Calvin said sombrely. "I was the one brought this shitstorm down, an' it took my grampop to save my ass." He raised his water glass. "Here's to a hero."

"Here's to a hero," they murmured, and drank. Adrienne put her arm around Donna.

"There was more than one hero in the family today," she said.

"Damn right," Calvin said. "Goin' in there with an empty gun, I would'n'ta had the balls to do that."

"Where'd you learn all that?" Adrienne asked Donna. She smiled wanly.

"Staying up all night with Josh watching *Terminator* movies and Tarantino stuff," Donna said. Adrienne mock-frowned at Josh.

"You let her watch those? I'll kill you."

"No, you won't," Donna said.

"No, I won't," Adrienne agreed.

"Ms Moon very brave," Maudie Lam said. "Fearless warrior. Much honour to her family."

"I saw you with that knittin' needle," Calvin said. "You were pretty good yourself,"

Maudie bowed her head. "I was looking after my patient," she said, "as I always do." Adrienne clasped her hand.

Hudson caught Simon's eye. "Executive conference?" he asked. Simon nodded yes. They gathered their glasses and wandered out back to the hot tub. Simon produced a toothpick joint from his jacket pocket. He lit it, took a deep drag, passed it to Hudson. "Y'orroight, Mister Frodo?" he asked in an exaggerated yokel accent.

Hudson took a pull on the joint, held the smoke down for a long moment, passed it back. "Freakiest fucking day of my life," he said at length. "Still can't believe what happened. Not sure I ever will."

"I called Henry," Simon said. "He said it'd already been all over the news."

"Bet I know what he said," Hudson told him. He mimicked Henry's East End bullroar. "Told you I should'a fakkin' come aht and looked after everybody. If I'd been there I'd'a torn those little cunts limb from fakkin' limb like fakkin' overcooked chickens."

"Something like that," Simon said. "Only more profane. He'll be here day after tomorrow."

"Bloody 'ell. That's all we need."

"Know what you mean, la. Sometimes the only way to recognise a china shop is when there's a bull in it."

"You guys doin' what I think you're doin'?" Adrienne asked from the darkness.

"Guilty, yer honour."

"Gimme that for a second." She took a quick draw and handed it back to Simon. "And if you let Donna see you I'll kill the both'a y'all."

"See what?" Donna asked from the doorway.

"Donna..."

"Mama, Maudie's ready to go."

When they got back indoors, Maudie was all packed up to leave. She formally shook hands with all of them except Adrienne and Donna, who got pecks on the cheek. "I will never forget you, I think," Maudie said. Then the door closed behind her and a moment later they heard her drive away.

Frank Ingenio was the next to split. By the time Calvin had driven himself and Venetia off, promising to be back in the morning, Hudson had put himself outside an entire bottle of fine Tennessee sippin' whiskey and had started on a second. It wasn't much longer before he was asleep in his chair.

"We can put him in my room," Josh suggested. "I can sleep out here tonight..."

"He'll be fine on the sofa," Simon told them. "You keep your room, son. I guarantee he won't know the difference." He looked over at Hudson, head tilted to one side, mouth agape, snoring in the chair. "Wow. Haven't seen him this caned since the seventies. Back then, I had to do this practically every night." He slipped Hudson's boots off and wrestled him out of his jacket. He took Hudson by the shoulders. Josh took his feet, and together they manhandled him onto the sofa. Hudson grunted, mumbled something which sounded like, "thank you and goodnight," but he didn't wake up.

"You want to take his pants off?" Adrienne asked, dumping an armful of bedding onto the floor.

"Even the demands of a long and honourable friendship only go so far," Simon replied. He shoved a couple of pillows under Hudson's head, draped the duvet over him, tucked him in almost paternally. "I think it's cabby time," he told Adrienne, pulling out his phone.

To the oblivious Hudson, he said softly, "G'night, Mister Frodo."

In dreams:

Mick Hudson was having maybe the best sex of his entire life. Lying spreadeagled on the bed in the darkened room, unable to move his arms or legs (were his wrists and ankles tied up?) he was gazing up at the woman whose hips were grinding down on his, his gaze travelling gradually up her body, from her rolling stomach, separating with her every inner convulsion into a deep-etched grid ridged even below the navel, to her heaving sweat-slick breasts, nipples so tautly puckered with passion that their aureolae have virtually disappeared...

Adrienne.

... to her face.

Venetia?

... and then he was somewhere else entirely. Someone had built what looked like an old-fashioned barbershop into the interior of the old original Marquee Club in Oxford Street. Blue was sitting in the barber's chair in his iconic red stage suit, old rubbed-raw Jazzmaster in his lap. His hair was perfect.

"Well, young man," he said. Then, in Henry's voice: "Fancy meeting you here, me old son." As himself again: "Life sure be strange, don't it."

"Not many, Benny," Hudson said. "Christ, all this is so weird..."

"We ain't got much time," Blue said, "an' we got us some serious shit to talk about. First thing: I want you to take care of my wife."

"'Course I will. You know that. Anything she or Donna need..."

Blue put his head on one side, looked quizzically at Hudson. "You ain't getting' my meanin', young man." He repeated, with careful emphasis: "I want *you*...to take *care*... of my *wife*."

Recognition dawned. Hudson laughed. "What, you mean 'take my wife, please'? I get the impression Adrienne makes her own decisions."

Blue nodded solemnly. "You got *that* right. Always did, always will. All I'm sayin' is, if she choose you, I want you to let yourself be chosen."

"Look... Blue. They need you, and I'm not you. I can't be you. In my fucked-up whiteboy way, I've been trying to be you since I was fourteen years old. Now I may be white, but I ain't stupid, so I've finally got to admit that it ain't working, and it ain't *going* to work."

Blue nodded gravely. "Young man, when I was ten years old I wanted to be Robert Johnson, an' I never made it. But by tryin' to be him I found myself, just like you started out tryin' to be me, and you found *your*self. I ended up carryin' some of his burden, but I had me a mess'a help to do it. Includin' yours. But right now you got to carry mine, an' ain't nobody gonna be able to help you.

"Lord, I remember when we first met. Never met a young man so desperate to get *right inside* the blues. You didn't just want to *play* the blues. You wanted to know the blues all the way from the inside.

"And that was the biggest difference between you'n me, young man. You wanted to get into the blues, an' I wanted to get out. You wanted to find the blues. I wanted to lose 'em. I was *born* with the blues, an' I been tryin' to sing an' play my way out ever since.

"For what it's worth... I done made it now. I finally lost these blues a'mine. An' you made it, too. Right now, you as far into the heart of the blues as a man can get. An' I hope it's what you wanted.

"Long as we been knowin' each other, I been callin' you 'young man,' but we can't do that no more."

The barber's chair began to swivel on its base. Now it was slowly moving towards the club's exit.

"Everything I had is now yours. An' everything you had, you gonna lose. You paid my tab, and I thank you. You went my bail, and I thank you for that, too. But whatever happens from here on in you gonna have to handle by yourself." He plucked a brief, stinging riff on the un-

278

plugged guitar in his lap. Unplugged, but Hudson still heard it like it was coming out of an amp. "Time I was outta here."

By now, the chair had reached the door. Blue looked back over his shoulder.

"Y'all take care now... Mick."

Hudson was alone in the darkened club.

Adrienne awoke shortly after eight, much earlier than she'd expected, feeling surprisingly clearheaded despite the joint she'd smoked and the beers she'd drunk the night before. Blue's absence, the emptiness of their bed, struck her like a steamhammer in the guts, clenched icy iron fingers around her heart. She sobbed herself dry, forced herself to get up, shower, dress and brew herself some coffee.

She made a quick patrol of the house. Everybody else was still asleep, Donna and Josh in their rooms, Hudson on the sofa. She placed a glass of water from the cooler within easy reach on the floor beside him, and decided it was time to head over to the kennels and bring the dogs back. She hoped that they'd gotten over whatever the fuck it was had made them turn on Blue... how long ago was that? A few days, a lifetime.

An hour later she was back. Hudson, dehydrated and muzzily surfacing, reached out automatically for the glass of water on his bedside cabinet, realised it wasn't there, started to remember where he was. He heard the front door slam, the quiet jingling as Adrienne let the dogs off their leashes, the muted clack of their claws on the hardwood flooring as they padded round the house, refamiliiarising themselves with their surroundings.

Let the dogs wake him up gently, Adrienne thought. Then I'll bring him some coffee. Then I'll get Josh and Donna up and we'll all have a nice breakfast. She went into the kitchen and tipped several heaping spoonfuls of the Colombian blend into the cafetiere, fired up the kettle to boil water.

Hudson fumbled for water, finally found the glass, almost spilt it, gulped thirstily, emptying it. His head was still aching. Fuck me, he thought, I'm still pissed. Through the haze of residual bourbon fumes, he thought he heard the dogs enter the room. He forced one velcro eyelid open. Yep. there they were. He whispered, "Attack!"

... and the giant German Shepherd leapt at him, seized his left hand in his powerful jaws and crunched down hard. Hudson's first three fingers were inside the dog's mouth. He kept biting down with all his force. Hudson heard a thin, shrill screaming as if from an immense distance, realised it was him. Then Wu Li, the tiny crested Chinese... what the hell breed was Wu Li? He'd never found out... was at his throat, a new centre of white-hot pain, and the screaming abruptly ceased, replaced by a hoarse wheezing like leaky bellows as the dog's fangs cut deep into his throat, his vocal cords, his windpipe.

Adrienne, finishing off the coffee in the kitchen, dropped the cafetiere, heard it smash on the floor, didn't even look back as she sprinted for the living room. She saw Hudson half on, half off the sofa, his torso on the floor, his legs still tangled in the duvet, his hand disappearing inside Attack's jaws, his throat open and gouting, a great flap of flesh and muscle torn loose revealing tubes and tendons, blood pooling behind his head and shoulders.

"Christ, fuck, no!" she screamed. She heard Donna's door open.

"Mama?"

"Donna, don't come in!" Adrienne shouted. "Call an ambulance!" She hauled the dogs off Hudson, prising Attack's jaws from the unrecognisable mess of his left hand and throwing Wu Li bodily across the room. Then she dragged them out to the back, slamming and locking the back door as Donna dived for the phone, stabbing out 911...

At Cedars-Sinai, the surgeons worked on Hudson all day and most of the night. In addition to the mutilation of his hand and throat, he'd lost an awful lot of blood. In the end they had to admit defeat. The second and third fingers on his left hand had to be amputated, though they managed to let him keep the first joint of his forefinger. The doctors working on his throat said he'd probably speak again after extensive therapy, but he'd no longer be able to sing. And he'd certainly never be able to play the guitar — or any other musical instrument requiring a full complement of fingers — ever again.

James Blue Moon was buried with his original old Jazzmaster, wearing a bright red suit tailored specifically for the occasion. Against all expectations, Mick Hudson attended the funeral. He neither spoke nor performed. He was seated in a wheelchair. His manager, Henry MacShane, wheeled him around, flanked by Hudson's twin daughters, his round face a white-stubbled thundercloud. Approached for comments on his departed mentor, Hudson simply pointed to his throat, heavily band-aged under his high-collared black turtleneck, with his right hand, the one that wasn't bandaged and in a sling, and shook his head. Raintree Management, MacShane told reporters, would be issuing a statement on Mick Hudson's behalf, which would also be available from the Mac-ro Management website.

Hudson's wheelchair was parked in the aisle alongside the family: Blue's widow, their daughter, the widow's son from a previous mar-riage, Blue's middle daughter Charlene and her mother, Blue's manager Simon Wolfe and his wife. Venetia Moon, Blue's eldest daughter, sang an electrifying gospel medley and paid a moving tribute to her father, culminating in a brief performance of Down South The Hog Is Man's Best Friend. Her son Calvin also gave his testament to the grandfather who'd saved his life at the cost of his own. Many other noted blues, jazz and rock musicians spoke, sang and played. TV and film crews from all over the world were in attendance to document the event.

After the ceremony, Hudson, his daughters and McShane were driv-en straight to LAX. From there, a chartered jet flew them directly to Barcelona.

On Easter Monday of 2005, Mick Hudson walked into the music room of his villa in Barcelona. Long white hair hung to his narrow shoulders. A thick white beard grew low on his throat. He wore a black glove on his left hand.

Propped in the corner of the room was a gleaming National steel-bodied resonator guitar. Next to it was a small table and a folding chair. On the table was a brass tube approximately the length and diameter of his little finger.

Hudson sat down on the chair. With his right hand, he reached over to the guitar and carefully positioned it on his lap.

Then he drew the black glove off his left hand and placed it on the table. His left hand was a ravaged red pincer-like claw, only thumb and pinky intact, a mere nub of first finger remaining, the two middle fin-gers missing all the way to the knuckles.

Hudson slid the brass tube onto the little finger of his left hand. It hurt, the tender freshly-healed skin screaming in protest. He ignored the pain. With his right hand, he strummed the guitar's open strings, tuned to a chord of A. With his left hand, he applied the slide to the upper strings at the tenth fret, gradually moving it up to the octave.

Adrienne, silently padding barefoot into the room, rested one hand on his shoulder, gently kissed the top of his head.

Quietly, he grated to himself, in the painful voice of grunts and squeaks he still had trouble recognising as his own and suspected he always would, "*I got to keep moving, got to keep moving, blues fallin' down like hail. Got to keep moving, got to keep moving, hellhound on my trail.*"

It sounded like shit.

EPILOGUE

After **JAMES BLUE MOON**'s funeral, **MICK HUDSON** vanished off the rock and roll radar. He gave no interviews despite worldwide interest in the events which ended his career, and undertook no promotional activities for his final album, the live recording *Roadkill,* which documented what had turned out to be his last tour. His various homes, with the exception of the villa in Barcelona, were sold off, including the Berkshire mansion which he had owned for over thirty years. The bulk of his instruments and memorabilia were auctioned for charity, mostly benefiting the James Blue Moon Foundation and the Moon Family Trust. Following the 2005 release of a career-spanning four-CD boxed set, he repaid his record company the outstanding balance of his advance. His insurance company refused to pay compensation for his disabling injuries unless he sued the Moon Family Trust and Adrienne Moon, owner of the dogs which had mutilated him, for contributory negligence. This he refused to do, and a legal action against the insurance company, mounted on his behalf by Raintree Management, is currently pending. The posthumously released album *Paid In Full,* by James Blue Moon And Family, received a Grammy Award for Best Traditional Blues Recording as well as a WC Handy Award for best blues album of 2005. Hudson attended neither ceremony.

HENRY MACSHANE stepped down as head of Raintree Management, though the company continued to retain him as a consultant. He sold off the bulk of his Raintree shares and retired to his home in Worthing. He died of a heart attack on Christmas Eve 2005.

SIMON WOLFE continues to run Macro Management in Los Angeles. With Calvin Holland, he also serves as trustee and joint business manager for the James Blue Moon Foundation and the Moon Family Trust.

ADRIENNE MOON continued to live in the family home in Venice Beach with her daughter **DONNA**. However, she has recently put the house on the market, and her future plans remain unknown. Her son **JOSH** continues his studies at UCLA.

THE HELLHOUND SAMPLE

CALVIN HOLLAND still runs his Lock N Load empire. Using the backing track from the *Paid In Full* version of Hellhound On My Trail, albeit stripped of its Robert Johnson samples, he recorded the autobiographical Save Me, his first single as Ice Blue for several years. It was a minor hit, and was also included as a hidden bonus track on the European and Japanese versions of the *Paid In Full* album. The backing tracks he produced for the aborted Screwdriver & Omega Man album were subsequently used for a younger Jamaican act called Stem Sell, currently enjoying his fourth Top Ten hit. Calvin now shares his Bel Air mansion with his new girlfriend... and boyfriend.

VENETIA MOON retreated to her Chicago penthouse following the murder of her father and did not perform or record for over a year. However, it is rumoured that she plans to resume her career in the very near future.

SCREWDRIVER, OMEGA MAN and **FUNKENSTEIN** were convicted of the murders of Blue and Big Ray, and sentenced to life in San Quentin. After serving two years and four months, Omega Man was murdered in the showers in an altercation over the sexual favours of a fellow inmate. **CASH MONEY** was given a reduced sentence following his testimony establishing the premeditated nature of the other three's crime.

MAUDIE LAM enjoyed a brief flurry of celebrity on the talk-show circuit. She currently runs her own very successful practice as acupuncturist and herbalist to the stars.

FRANK INGENIO's webcam footage of James Blue Moon's murder has become a reality-TV classic.

HELLHOUND LINER NOTES
(an afterword)

The first draft of *The Hellhound Sample* was written in around three months, under odd and unpleasant circumstances, during 2004, the year in which it is set. It was then put aside to ferment until the spring of 2005 before undergoing approximately six weeks of revision. My first and most heartfelt thanks therefore go to my beloved comrade Anna Chen, who kept me alive and more or less functioning at a time when the latter seemed impossible and the former unattractive.

And major thankage also goes to Roz Kaveney, without whom *Hellhound* would have simply have sat around and festered on my hard drive. Roz not only took a major shine to the novel and offered up a forensic critique which led to the plugging of a few plot holes and the illumination of a couple of unlit corners of more than one character's inner worlds, but also informally acted *in loco agentis* while I was — ahem — *between representatives*, labouring long and hard (albeit unsuccessfully) to find this book a home in the publishing mainstream. Appreciation also goes out to a couple of editors at major houses who were indeed interested in buying it, but were forestalled by their marketing departments on the grounds that they couldn't figure out to which generic category it should be assigned.

Eventually, through a chain of acquaintance and circumstance involving Gary Lammin and John Sinclair, *Hellhound* found its way to Headpress, where the formidable trio of Caleb Selah, David Kerekes and Thomas Campbell decided to take a chance on it. My indefatigable agent, Julian Alexander of the LAW agency, ironed out the details with his inimitable combination of urbanity, thoroughness and enthusiasm. Mr Campbell also applied a final much-appreciated editorial polish, and guided me through the process of sealing the last few leaks in both the plot and character departments.

Speaking of character, Mick Hudson has been around for quite a while: since the early 1980s, in fact. He was originally named 'Joe Hunter' until a personage of that name appeared, wholly coincidentally, in a novel by my friend Mick Farren. He first appeared in a never-completed short story called 'Revived 45,' and a very different version of him later featured in an unsold screenplay treatment written during the late 1980s in collaboration with Lloyd Bradley. The relationship between Mick, Blue and Calvin was first explored in yet another uncompleted short story dating back to the mid-1990s, but it wasn't until 2004 that I figured out exactly what I wanted to do with the three of them... or rather, how the three of them already fitted together.

A fistful of caveats: I'd like to emphasise that this is not — repeat: *not*, repeat NOT — a *roman a clef*. Nothing in here should be construed as constituting reliable information about any actual individuals, be they living, dead or just feeling a bit ill. The characters in this book are all Grand Archetypes, stitched together on a slab in my lab from bits of various real people, fragments of legend and rumour and plain ol' ordinary making-stuff-up. I've never met a bluesman exactly like Blue, a soul-diva exactly like Venetia, an elderly Brit rock god exactly like Mick or a rapper exactly like Calvin (I have, though, met a manager not too unlike 'Enry). On the other hand, I did borrow a few locations. Though he's a few years older than I am, I gave Mick my own childhood home in Caversham just outside Reading, albeit with parents very different to my own. Blue's home is, in all structural essentials, John Lee Hooker's old house in Redwood City, CA, though I moved it a few hundred miles south to Venice Beach and built in a couple of extra rooms. I also took the liberty of hijacking a couple of guitars: Blue's Fender Jazzmaster was nicked, with utmost respect, from the late and legendary Roebuck 'Pop' Staples (founder of The Staple Singers), whilst Mick's old Fender Telecaster is, in all essentials, the same 1959 model which Jeff Beck gave to Jimmy Page in 1965 as a thankyou for recommending him for the lead guitar job in The Yardbirds. Page decorated his, too, but with rather different motifs than the ones I chose for Mick.

Furthermore, I don't believe, in any rational or literal sense, that there was anything supernatural about the life or death of Robert Johnson. The myth of the crossroads is just that: a myth... but it still provides a metaphor which won't go. Even now, a full century after his birth, he still remains a figure so mysterious that if you visit the state of Mississippi — and, if you have any interest whatsoever in the various worlds of the blues, you certainly should — you can find three different memorials, on three different sites, all purporting to represent his final resting place. And which crossroads was it, anyway? Highways 61 and 49 intersect in more than one place.

I don't believe — not *really* — that Robert Johnson sold his soul to the devil at the crossroads in order to gain his uncanny musical powers, except in the sense that we all, in our various ways, make deals, knowingly or unknowingly, with our own personal devils at our own personal crossroads to facilitate the journey towards our own personal goals... or maybe to ensure that we never actually achieve them. I did, however, fancy speculating as to how that spectral event *might* have gone down... if it *had* happened.

And — to extend that particular what-if — what if Mr Johnson's mysterious may-or-may-not-have-actually-happened occult transaction had also extended to his guitar, and if ownership of that guitar also carried with it certain... shall we say... responsibilities? What if there were others to whom the same had happened? And what consequences would arise if someone actually sampled Robert Johnson's voice or guitar from his recordings, and incorporated those samples into a piece of new music? Could that serve as some kind of invocation of... something? Would the perpetrator somehow inherit the burden... and the debt?

And those British rockers of the 1960s — the babies of the 1940s sort-of-grown-up and in search of a music which somehow suited their own inner landscapes, who were inspired by the blues, built their own Frankensteinian musical monster from its constituent parts and ended up richer, if not happier, than their mentors and masters? What was their deal? What transactions did they unwittingly make as part of their assumption of a cultural legacy created so far away under such painful circumstances?

All this stuff, and more, bubbled and fermented and was eventually distilled into what you've just read and — I hope — enjoyed.

This is as good a place as any for a shout-out to Deborah Grabien. Her long-running series character, JP Kinkaid, whose saga I discovered only after this book was written, is so similar to Mick and yet so different that we've compared notes and discovered that Mick and JP not only know each other, but share some history which we've already started exploring together. In the meantime, her Kinkaid novels are heartily recommended to anyone who's enjoyed this book... and also to anyone who hasn't!

All of which means that... Mick Hudson's story is *not* over. I'm not finished with him, and neither is the Hellhound. His true torment has only just begun. Stay logged in...

CSM
Somewhere in London, March 2011

A HEADPRESS BOOK
First published by Headpress in 2011. Revised September 2011.

Headpress, Suite 306, The Colourworks
2a Abbot Street, London, E8 3DP, UK
[tel] 0845 330 1844
[email] headoffice@headpress.com
[web] www.WorldHeadpress.com

THE HELLHOUND SAMPLE

Text copyright © Charles Shaar Murray
This volume copyright © Headpress 2011
Cover: Rachel Dreyer (design), Charlotte Parkin (concept), Rik Rawling (background art); Rachel Dreyer, Caleb Selah & Charlotte Parkin (photo selection).
Back cover photo: Charles Shaar Murray, by Allison McGourty
Layout & design: David Kerekes
Headpress diaspora: Thomas Campbell, Giuseppe, Dave, Lucy B.

A CIP catalogue record for this book is available from the British Library

ISBN 9781900486781

WWW.WORLDHEADPRESS.COM
the gospel according to unpopular culture

Lightning Source UK Ltd.
Milton Keynes UK
UKOW021825111011

180114UK00004B/1/P